THE
AWOKEN

THE
AWOKEN

A NOVEL

KATELYN MONROE HOWES

DUTTON

DUTTON

An imprint of Penguin Random House LLC
penguinrandomhouse.com

Copyright © 2022 by Katelyn Monroe Howes
Penguin Random House supports copyright. Copyright fuels creativity,
encourages diverse voices, promotes free speech, and creates a vibrant culture.
Thank you for buying an authorized edition of this book and for complying with
copyright laws by not reproducing, scanning, or distributing any part of it
in any form without permission. You are supporting writers and allowing
Penguin Random House to continue to publish books for every reader.

DUTTON and the D colophon are registered trademarks of
Penguin Random House LLC.

LIBRARY OF CONGRESS CATALOGING-IN-PUBLICATION DATA
has been applied for.

ISBN 9780593185285 (hardcover)
ISBN 9780593185308 (ebook)

Printed in the United States of America
1st Printing

BOOK DESIGN BY ALISON CNOCKAERT

Dedicated to:

Madin Lopez

and

Harper's future world

THE
AWOKEN

Not like the brazen giant of Greek fame,

With conquering limbs astride from land to land;

Here at our sea-washed, sunset gates shall stand

A mighty woman with a torch, whose flame

Is the imprisoned lightning, and her name

Mother of Exiles. From her beacon-hand

Glows world-wide welcome; her mild eyes command

The air-bridged harbor that twin cities frame.

"Keep, ancient lands, your storied pomp!" cries she

With silent lips. "Give me your tired, your poor,

Your huddled masses yearning to breathe free,

The wretched refuse of your teeming shore.

Send these, the homeless, tempest-tost to me,

I lift my lamp beside the golden door!"

—EMMA LAZARUS

PROLOGUE

I WAS TWENTY-THREE YEARS old when I died.

It wasn't at all what I was told dying would be like. There was no white light or harp music or warm peaceful serenity. It was cold and dark. The worst part of dying was that darkness. In the split second before I stopped existing, I saw a dark nothingness that still haunts me to this day. How horrible it is to live our whole lives with hope, curiosity, belief, and then, in one final instant, it's all ripped away. You are forced to see, without a doubt, that there is only emptiness on the other side.

The process of dying was no picnic either. I felt every healthy cell in me wither as the cancer reveled among the ruins of a once young and functioning immune system that fought hard, but not hard enough.

Dying hurt. They did tell me that, that it would hurt, and it did. Cancer's a real bitch.

I was young and otherwise healthy. Everyone swore that I would beat this disease. Having cancer was just going to be a road bump in my long and fulfilling life that I hadn't yet truly started. People were going to proudly exclaim how I was strong and survived.

But I didn't beat cancer. I lost.

In my life, I did everything else mostly right. I studied. I got scholarships. I volunteered. By no means was I perfect. I got detention once. I cheated on my first boyfriend by kissing my best friend's boyfriend. I never told my parents I loved them. I am not someone who should be idolized in death as a perfect human, but I tried.

It's just that I never had enough time.

I really did not want to die. Loved ones of those who've passed into the darkness comfort themselves by saying, *He found peace in the end.* Fuck that. I wanted life. I wanted to be twenty-four and fifty-four. I wanted kids someday, and to do something—anything—to make a difference in the world. At twenty-three, my whole life stretched out in front of me. In my mind, everything thus far had been a dress rehearsal for some real life that was yet to come. Then I was told it was over. I had lived all the life I was going to have. I wasn't ready to die because I hadn't yet lived.

Before my diagnosis, I had time. Time to be an unpaid intern because I was going to run for office someday. Time to live in a crap apartment because I'd buy a penthouse when I was older. Time to drop out of college because I promised to go back. Time to break up with people I loved because I was certain I could find someone better. Time was not a concern until I had none of it left.

And then I didn't even have time to grieve my own death.

It's a lonely process, dying. Those I trusted to help me couldn't—the doctors, the nurses, my friends, hell, even the priests who were there in my most desperate moments. It didn't affect them. Not really. I was the one rotting away in the hospital with cancer. I'm sure they all forgot about me after I was gone.

Well, all but one.

Max. My Max. He was my last sight. My last smell. The last good thing I felt. He loved me, and I loved him. More than anything. It was the most powerful thing I ever felt and yet the easiest. I'm not so narcissistic to think that we're the only people to have this kind of love, but I know for a fact that it's rare, especially at our age, and that we were lucky. I was lucky. Even dying of cancer at twenty-three, I was lucky to know the kind of love I had for Max.

If you are to take anything away from this story, know that, above all, this is a story about love. Everything else is a distraction.

I used to put my hand against Max's and watch the boundary between his olive brown skin and my pale fragile skin melt away as we fused together. Sure, maybe that was the cancer drugs, but the hallucination materialized what I'd felt for the entire sixteen months we were together: we were the same whole. He was me, and I was him, and we needed each other. Of course I needed him. I was terminal and my parents weren't in my life and I didn't have many friends, so I pretty much would've died on the street in the gutter without him. But he needed me too, and made sure I knew that. He didn't need anything *from* me. Just me. Like he needed his soul, he needed me.

The second worst part of dying was watching him watch me die. Nothing can break unbreakable love like cancer. In my lowest moments, I tried pushing him away. Still he refused to leave, which made me love him even more. Horribly, like some weird cult leader with a bowl of Kool-Aid, I found myself fantasizing about Max dying with me. Death is lonely—I get why you'd want the people who love you to come along.

In the end, Max did not Romeo to my Juliet and tragically take his own life on my deathbed. He did something much harder. He lived. Max held my hand when I lost the strength to hold his. As I took my last breath, he refused to look away. I was scared and conscious until the dark overtook his light. I was alone, but we were together. And for one last moment, we were parts of the same whole.

That's how I, Alabine Rivers, died. I was scared. Cold. And loved. Then there was darkness.

Looking back on it, I know now that I lived and died entirely unaware that I wasn't the person I thought I was. The person I hoped to be. The person who actually could make a difference in the world.

In fact, if I hadn't died, I don't think I ever would've become that person.

So that's why I've come here all these years later. Not to tell you the story of my death. I'm here to tell you the story of what happened next.

PART
ONE

1

I WAS 124 YEARS old when I came back to life.

First there was warmth. Not sit-by-the-fire-with-a-cup-of-hot-cocoa warmth that fills your bones. This was an uncomfortable dry heat that my soul wanted nothing to do with. It spread like poison through my parched veins. There was an incompatible opposition between this unnatural warmth and a primal cold I felt deeply imbedded in the pit of my stomach. A godforsaken cold I'd never be rid of and can feel to this day. This cold is only known to other people like me—though we rarely talk about it. It's a reminder of our first lives. Of our death. A scar of the darkness that can never entirely leave us.

My body demanded breath, but when I opened my mouth, a fluid that tasted like batteries flooded inside me. I gagged and choked, not even having the air to cough. A thick plastic surrounded me, suctioned against my skin, holding my body oppressively tight. I pushed and writhed as hard as I could, desperate to get away. Everything felt wrong. The heartbeat in my chest, the vibrations of sound in my ears—I wanted none of it.

Then the synthetic womb that had been my home for 101 years suddenly opened like an upside-down Ziploc bag.

I fell.

But the ground came quickly. The shock of colliding with the earth forced me, like a newborn foal, to take my first breath. Back arched. Neck rigid. A hoarse inhale filled my dusty lungs. Devouring the newly found oxygen, my heart quickened, painfully beating like a sledgehammer against my ribs. Blood pushed its way, uninvited, through my arteries. Inching up my chest, then my neck, until it pooled behind my eyes with so much pressure I feared they would pop out of my skull.

Something wasn't right. This wasn't right. I wasn't all right.

I had no idea where I was or even why I was. In that moment, I couldn't remember anything, not my name, not Max, not my death. All I could think about was the darkness calling me back to it, begging for me to allow it to consume my body.

It was angry, and so was I.

I wanted to sleep. Being dead is exhausting. It's like those nights you fall asleep and then feel as if you wake up only a moment later. You know a long time has passed, and you don't know what your body was doing, but it definitely was not resting.

My eyes fluttered closed and I found myself slowly drifting back to sleep. Back to the sinister and welcoming darkness. Before it wrapped itself around me yet again, I heard—

"Wake up, Al." The voice was comforting and loving. "It's time to get up." Finally I opened my eyes, and there he was.

Max. My Max.

In his soft gaze was a lifetime of love—a love that I didn't yet remember but instantly recognized as ours. He reached out his hand. Magnetically, I was compelled to take it. To accept the warmth. The darkness pulling me down was no competition anymore. Not to those eyes.

The sensation of blood rushing through my body began to feel less odd. My cells vibrated with hope. I took the hand of this man I knew but couldn't quite place. When we touched, my fingers tingled as they fused into his as we each became whole.

It only lasted a moment. As quickly as he appeared, he was gone.

The truth was, I was alone. Alone and naked. Like Eve, I became embarrassingly aware of my bare body and attempted to cover myself. After a century of death, not even knowing my own name, twenty-three years of sexual repression and bodily shame were still ingrained in me.

"Hello, Alabine Rivers." It was that voice again. Except this time, it wasn't Max. This was real. The unfamiliar voice crackled through the speakers in the room.

"Hello?" I responded in a daze. I pushed my heavy atrophied body to a stand, wobbling around on weak and unsteady legs. The cold inside me, while still very much there, faded into the distance as life took me in its clutches.

My eyes still struggled to find focus. Through the blurry patches of darkness and faded colors, I saw in front of me the soft outline of a woman's face. She was familiar, but I didn't know why. The embodiment of déjà vu. Her intense gaze met mine as her features poured out of the contours of her face like she was a mirage—a ghost unable to firmly root themselves to this world or the next. Utterly transfixed, and pushing through the haze of my reconstituting vision, I reached my hand out toward her. Immediately, my fingers stubbed into a glass barrier between us. Pressing my hand against the clammy translucent wall, I came to the gut-wrenching realization that this woman was no ghost: she was me. My reflection. Except the girl in the glass looked wrong. She had no hair, sunken cheeks, chapped lips, and a rigid pain in her eyes.

Panicking, and wanting to get as far away as I could from the haunted girl in my reflection, I reached behind me only to find yet another solid glass wall. I was trapped, having fallen from the plastic bag into a glass box. One coffin to another. The walls towered high beyond the reach of my fingertips. Claustrophobia overwhelmed me as I started to hyperventilate and pound the glass cage with my fists.

"Please stay calm," the voice over the speakers said reassuringly.

I didn't. I couldn't. Instead, no longer feeling breath fill my lungs, I collapsed back to the metal ground. The darkness crept in closer, excited that I was returning to it, where I belonged.

"You're going into shock. Breathe!" The disembodied voice kept me tethered to the real world as a high-pitched medical alarm blared.

Then a man jumped down into my cage with a loud thud. In my tunneled vision, I could barely see the blurred outline of his body. With an intensity that conveyed my life hung in the balance, he pulled my rag-doll body into his.

I forced my eyes on him, but all I saw was Max, and the chaos in the room faded to nothing but us. He radiated with a warm light. I sighed, ready for him to take me. It was the closest I ever came, in all the times I would die, to feeling like I was going home. But then—

"*Rosebud.*" The word was clear. Crisp.

.
.
.

And suddenly, I am not in the glass box sitting on the metal floor. The ghostly girl is no longer staring back at me. I can't see anything, but I know I'm somewhere else, far away. The coldness inside me is gone, and I hear Max.

"Rosebud. Remember Rosebud, Al."

.
.
.

Then, just as quickly, I was back on that metal floor, inside that glass box. As if I had been flung through time and space.

"Rosebud?" I muttered in half-dazed remembrance. This simple word gave me something to grasp in the fog. An anchor. *Rosebud*.

"Good." The voice over the speakers had materialized into a man crouched in front of me. The blurs of color and shadow collected themselves into coherent structures. I could see, finally. This man leaned close to me, so close that he filled my entire vision, studying my face for signs of recovery with a worried look that I would come to know well.

"Who are you?" The question slurred over my tongue as my consciousness settled more firmly. The high-pitched alarm stopped. Worry melted from his face, and then he laughed. He had curly black hair and a week's worth of stubble that read more of a lack of time for shaving and less of a fashion statement. He looked a few years older than me—in actuality, he was ninety-six years younger—and there was a youthful vibrancy about him, an unsettled energy that was all too alluring.

Stunned, I watched as he poked and prodded, checking my pulse and temperature. Searching for any markers of life. Before I could protest his intrusion, my attention was pulled to the world beyond the ghost girl's reflection. Outside of the glass wall was a dark medical lab. The large room was sparsely inhabited by strange machines that sat covered in cobwebs and disuse. The disarray of broken glass and trash littering the floor painted a clear picture that the lab had long been abandoned. Only a few of the lights worked, and the ones that did flickered in and out. Shadows cloaked the details. There was just enough light for me to see a blue logo on the wall: "CRYOLABS."

Something then tugged at me from above—a feeling, a fear, the darkness maybe. Reluctantly, my eyes turned upward, and a gasp plunged through me. It was a harrowing sight: a terrible crane-like machine with arms and a metal hook that still clutched the opened body bag. My death reverberated through its robotic limbs.

A long skinny needle stretched out from one of its arms. As I stared at it, the memory of a sharp pain prickled behind my ear. I instinctively reached up toward the sensation, and my fingers touched something metallic embedded in my skin. Before I could question it, the man started wiping my face roughly with a towel.

"Stop!" I shouted and pushed him off, trying to cover my body. I once again became very aware of how naked I was. It seemed, at the exact same time, he did as well. He quickly looked away.

"Who are you?" I demanded again, feigning a sense of authority.

"Sorry. My name is Damien. I didn't mean to . . . uh—" The words he was looking for were *rub my hands all over your naked body*, but instead he jumped right to "We don't have time to do this right."

A barrage of questions stampeded through my head: *Who is "we"? Time to do what?* But there was no time to ask them as Damien rustled through his bag and pulled out a simple white dress. He offered it to me, still averting his eyes. Eager to regain some dignity, I snatched the dress and slipped it on.

Then I froze.

I felt no hair on my head. It was just as my reflection showed. There wasn't much that I remembered about myself, but I knew that a shaved head was out of the ordinary for me. Yet here I was, almost entirely bald. My trembling hand gingerly grazed across the rough stubble until it eventually found its way behind my ear. My fingers traced a small metal device implanted into the skin.

"You're okay. It's normal." Damien nodded, a slight blush still on his cheeks. He appeared nervous and unsure, beads of sweat trickled down his forehead. Whatever we were doing in this abandoned lab, whatever he was doing with me, it seemed to be the first time he'd done it. Or something had gone wrong. Or both.

"What's happening? Where are we?" I asked, with less anger this time.

It was clear Damien had a million things to say, but he restrained himself. "It'll come back. Just remember your trigger word."

"What the hell is a trigger word?"

He responded as matter-of-factly as if I had asked him what color the sky was:

"Rosebud."

.
.
.
.

I'm in a doctor's office. The haze of the medical lab is gone. Damien is gone. A leather chair rumples under my thighs. I'm wearing the blue dress I got at the flea market with my friend Andy two months before. I have my hair. And the coldness is gone, now nothing more than a nightmare.

Was that all a dream?

The doctor comes into the room and sits at his large desk in front of me quietly reading my chart. His white lab coat has a blue CryoLabs logo branded across the breast. He rocks back and forth in his chair rhythmically, never taking his glazed-over eyes off my folder.

It seems as if he's about to fall asleep when he says, "Rosebud? Like in the movie *Citizen Kane*?" The north-of-middle-aged man leers at me, skeptically. "As I said before, this has to be an emotionally charged word for you. Not a nostalgic, ironic reference."

I try to respond, but my mind aches, having been torn in so many directions. Two seconds ago, I was naked, covered in red mucus, sitting in a glass cage with a grinning man named Damien. And now I am in a doctor's office, having an inane conversation about the word "Rosebud."

My response seems unnecessary as the doctor continues with little pause. "This is your trigger word. Your tether. The tool that will allow your brain to make sense of what has happened to your body. This process won't be easy. It's vital this word means something deeply important, or your body may reject it."

Rejection. That's it. That's exactly how I feel. Like a transplant patient's body refusing its new foreign heart.

"Well? Is Rosebud an emotionally charged word for you?" the doctor asks.

Someone grabs my hand. I know who it is before I even turn. I feel my skin melt into his. His eyes find mine. It's Max. Not imaginary Max or angel Max. This is My Max. I fall in love with him all over again.

"It's not ironic," I tell the doctor, not daring to tear my eyes away. The reality of that dark abandoned lab and Damien slides deeper into the recesses of my mind. This room and Max are as real as it gets.

I think harder—trying to remember—knowing with every fiber of my being that the word Rosebud is important to me. To us. Then, in an instant, it comes to me. "He gives me rosebuds. The discarded ones that most people overlook and throw away. He saves them." Max's nose wrinkles, attempting to abate his tears, as he holds my cheek in his palm proudly. "It's our thing," I say confidently.

Everything comes flooding back. I remember that I'm dying. Or I remember that I died. I can't decide. I remember my last moment and that darkness. That horrible darkness.

I can't breathe.

Max guides my eyes toward his. I melt. "Remember why we're here, Al." I search my brain for answers to questions I'm barely able to form. "Remember Rosebud," he urges.

I know the answer. It's right there. It's in the blue CryoLabs logo etched into my memory. I researched. I raised money, a shit ton of money. I signed papers. I made a choice.

I chose to freeze myself.

"We prefer 'Cryogenic Preservation Therapy,'" the doctor parrots. "After you pass, your body will be preserved using a patented nitrous solution and then carefully maintained in one of our state-of-the-art facilities around the country."

I laugh as a tear skips down my cheek. "You make it sound like a trip to the spa."

The late nights of research I did before I got here fill my thoughts. People have been freezing themselves for decades. It's expensive but an option for anyone who has the means to make it work. The science is there. Cryogenics is real.

"When is she going to be brought back to life?" Max asks naively. The doctor shifts, annoyed. We all know the answer. Though I get why Max asks again—that sneaking hope.

"Well, first there has to be a cure for Alabine's lymphoma. Also, while CryoLabs is the leader in developing how to resurrect a preserved human, we don't know how to do it . . . yet. At the moment, we just know how to preserve her. I'm legally obligated to tell you, it might never happen."

"If you don't know how to bring her back to life," Max continues, "then what's all this about a trigger word?"

"We assume some things about what the process will look like," the doctor responds, seemingly impressed by the question. "For instance, we shave the heads of those going through preservation in order to put in a port." He points to a spot just behind his ear. "We've found that's the most effective way to deliver the nitrous solution with minimal cell death. We believe that will be the most effective way to warm up the body upon resurrection as well."

My hand intuitively touches the spot behind my ear, but there is nothing there. As I imagine this doctor shaving the head of my newly deceased corpse, I clutch on to my now thin but still long brown hair that I fought so hard to keep through a year of cancer treatments.

"You know all that, but you still don't know how to bring someone back." My intonation is somewhere between a question and a statement, so the doctor doesn't quite know how to respond. It's okay. I don't need him to. I know the answer.

I'm putting my life in the hands of a science that doesn't even exist yet. All this could be for nothing. The savings I depleted. All that crowdsourced fundraising. The time spent at extra doctor appointments when I could've been with Max, living the little that was left of our life together. It could still never happen. I could remain a preserved popsicle until the end of time. But it's my only chance.

And then, even if I do miraculously come back, I'll be alone.

"Yeah, I'll be super dead by then." Max laughs, reading my mind through his watery eyes. I can't help but laugh along. Trying to hide his tears, he buries his face in my hands and kisses them. I pull him up to my lips for a real kiss.

He backs away, only an inch, his breath still slips across my cheek. His rich amber eyes meet mine with an intensity I've rarely seen in them. "Rosebud. Remember Rosebud, Al."

And just like that, I was back in my glass coffin with Damien. My hair was gone, replaced by the small metal port behind my ear and the coldness in my stomach.

I wasn't breathing.

Damien grabbed my arm to keep me from falling over. His touch—a poor substitute for Max's—wrenched me further away from the doctor's office and back into the cold lab. I felt sick.

"What the hell was that?!"

"It's okay. You're okay." Damien responded with well-intentioned solace that was entirely worthless to me in my chaotic and confused state.

"Where is Max?!"

Damien's curiosity was piqued. "Max?" He then raised a flashlight to my eyes. As my pupils dilated, he put my hand on his chest and emphasized his breathing. Like a baby curled against its mother, I instinctively matched my breath to his, and I found myself calming just enough to process the facts.

It seemed impossible. That doctor's office wasn't just a memory. I was there. I lived it. Again? For the first time? I couldn't decide, but it didn't matter. All that mattered was now I was back here.

"This isn't real. This can't be real."

"This is very real, I'm afraid," Damien said. "You had what's called a 'Lucid Memory.' It may be based in a memory, but it's more like an incredibly vivid dream. A normal side effect. Your brain's way of pro-cessing your two lives."

"My two lives?"

"It's very important that you understand what happened to you, that you understand that this—right now, right here, no matter how shocking it is—is your life. And at this moment, you're in grave danger of cryogenic psychosis." I tried to understand what he was asking of me. He saw my confusion. "You'll go crazy if you can't accept what happened."

Finally the words came to me. Tears dammed in my eyes as I ad-mitted what felt like my deepest secret:

"I died."

These haunted words pushed out of me in a breathless whisper. I remembered—not much—just enough. The word: *Rosebud*. My tether. It worked the way the doctor predicted. It helped me to under-stand and realize.

I died.

Damien gently held my trembling hand. "You did."

I searched his face, desperate for compassion for the life I lost, the life I no longer could have, but instead I only found Damien smiling.

"Didn't you hear me? I died!"

He nodded. "And now you're alive. Welcome back, Alabine Rivers. We've been looking for you for a long time."

"Looking for me?" My head pounded with questions. With more than questions, with pain. This was all too much. The coming back to life. The Lucid Memory. I wanted to understand it all, but all I could do was groan.

Damien pulled himself out of the glass container with an ease in his movement that I wasn't sure I'd ever regain. He reached back for me. "We have to move. There's a lot to do and quickly. Before they find us."

First there was a "we"; now there was a "they." My curiosity over-rode my pain. "Wait. Who's trying to find us?"

"The people who don't want us to bring you back."

2

AND THAT WAS IT. I was alive.

In pain, excruciating pain, unable-to-think-straight pain, but alive. There was absolutely nothing I did on that cold morning to miraculously make me come back to life. I didn't flip a switch or press a button. Obviously I had planned for it a century before. Paid good money for it. But I didn't choose that morning or that lab to come back to life. That was all decided by someone else. In the end, I was quite unimportant in the actual act of being resurrected.

Damien held my weight around his shoulders as I limped down the wide hallway. He gently ushered me into a dark and sterile room that was much smaller than the lab. Running along the walls were tidy rows of chairs that looked like what you'd find in a dentist office. There was a small monitor in front of each chair, and thin metal arms boasting various medical tools protruded from the sides.

Carefully, Damien sat me into one of these chairs. An unnatural pain vibrated through my bones. I felt like I'd been hit by a truck that was still rolling over me, smothering me into the hot asphalt. Breathing, or even thinking, took all my focus.

"Just wait here. The process will start soon," Damien said before turning to leave.

Panicked, I reached out and grabbed his hand. "Where are you going?"

He smiled. It was the kind of genuine smile that makes you instantly know everything will be okay. "Don't worry. After all I've done to find you, I'm not going to just leave you. I'll be back soon." He patted the arm of the chair like it was a trusted old dog. "This will fix that pain you have. It's an important part of the revitalization process."

And then he left. And it was silent.

Then, in that moment of silence, I realized . . . *holy shit*, in the time I was on ice, science figured out how to resurrect a preserved body. This was the most important discovery in the history of humanity, and I was living, breathing proof.

It's not that cryogenics promises immortality. Despite what some people believe, it isn't simply raising corpses from the dead, and the world will never be at risk of a zombie apocalypse. After resurrection, you're a perfectly normal person. Time takes the same toll it always does. There comes a day that everyone must meet their maker.

Cryogenics is a pause button.

It can't save you from a sudden heart attack or a fatal gunshot. It doesn't cure old age. God still lays claim to those. Instead cryogenics is mostly for people like me: terminally ill patients destined to die before their time. For us, it is hope. Hope for a second chance. Hope for a cure to be discovered. Simply hope for more time. And still, its discovery changed the world.

At this point, I feel I should make it clear that my life wasn't always about pickled bodies and preserved death. I wasn't raised to be the person I became. This all was quite the diversion from what I had thought my life would be. I don't want you to think I was some sort of special human born to be the heroine of a Kafkaesque nightmare. I wasn't.

That said, my first life wasn't ever truly ordinary either. My parents made that impossible. My life in 2018, in the months before I was diagnosed, was filled with work. I was a low-level staffer in the campaign office for Jessica DeWhitt, who at that point was merely an unknown state senator in Illinois. I helped manage her social media presence alongside a stable of other idealistic Gen Zers. Unfortunately, despite my desperation to stand out, no one ever noticed me. Jessica's campaign manager kept calling me Alice.

Though annoyed, I let it slide. Remember, I thought that I had all the time in the world to have bad jobs because one day I would be running things. My dream was to become Jessica, a daring woman pushing the boundaries and breaking the rules. Someone people listen to. A leader who changes the world.

Then, on one otherwise unremarkable day, my dreams were shattered when someone in the crowd hurled a smoke bomb at us during a rally. The perpetrator was part of a growing group of loud protesters who followed us from town to town preaching that Jessica was stealing jobs and giving them to immigrants and automated machinery. The smoke bomb was a marked escalation from the usual chanting and sign touting.

Luckily for me, I inadvertently stepped in between this man and Jessica right when he threw it. I felt a sharp pain and was then engulfed by a cloud of blue chalky smoke. People screamed. A security guard grabbed me and herded me inside along with the other staffers. Jessica was crying. At first, I thought she was hurt.

Turned out I was.

The projectile had deflected off my body just enough that the only damage Jessica suffered was to her $3,500 white pantsuit. But that was enough. Jessica was furious. As we all regrouped, she told her campaign manager, Peter, that she was going to drop the jobs bill. The signature plan that made so many of my generation, including me, fall in love with her. And now she was dropping it for a pantsuit. I was the one bleeding.

After that moment, I no longer wanted to be her. I swore I was going to be better. I didn't yet comprehend at all the courage it takes to stand for what's right when your life is at risk. That little lesson would catch up with me much later.

Eventually Peter noticed I was bleeding and called a medic despite my protests. He said Jessica wouldn't want me bleeding on the flyers we just had printed.

Now here is where I owe a grand public thank-you to that man who threw the smoke bomb that made me bleed because that unwanted medic who came to tend my wound just happened to be Max.

That's the truth behind the oft-glamorized story of how we met. I was so invested in self-pity around losing my role model that it took a full twenty minutes of Max bandaging me up before I realized he was flirting with me.

"You're lucky, it could be worse" was finally what he said that got my attention. I was furious.

"How could you possibly look at me and think that I'm lucky? I'm actively bleeding for a woman who doesn't even know my name," I said bitterly. "Apparently I'm worthless and pathetic and should just curl up in the corner and die. No one would miss me."

"That's not true . . ." Max paused for dramatic effect, trying to hold back a grin. "You're not actively bleeding anymore."

That adorable excuse for a joke finally alerted me to the fact that he was flirting. Surprised, I leaned back and took him in. He had broad shoulders, rich amber eyes, and perfect brown skin. He was Indian-American and quite cute, but honestly it didn't matter what he looked like. I was not in the mood to be flirted with. I wasn't in the mood to be a person, let alone a woman.

"Are we done?" I asked, annoyed.

"I just need your name and phone number." I rolled my eyes. His face dropped. "It's for the paperwork," he said, coldly holding up a clipboard of forms.

I blushed before finally stammering out, "Alabine Rivers." He scribbled my response on the form. "I'm sorry," I said, trying to save at least a slice of dignity.

"It's fine. Hope your day gets better." The subtlest *fuck you* tone tinged his goodbye. As a fellow passive-aggressive ninja, I was quite impressed. He turned to leave.

How different everything would've been if I'd let him walk away.

"Wait," I called after him. He turned back.

Time lurched into slow motion. Without realizing it, I stopped breathing for a moment. Even through his annoyance, he radiated comfort and safety. I thought he looked like a real adult, an odd thing to think as we were roughly the same age. I decided that I wanted to be in his orbit. To know more about him. I needed him to stay.

"Uh, it still hurts," I muttered, trying to think of an excuse quickly. "Can you check to make sure the bandage is on right?"

Max scoffed. "I know how to put on a Band-Aid." He sat back down, rightly insulted. I was really nailing this repartee. "It's fine," he said before pausing, feeling something on my neck.

In the silence, I cleared my throat. "One more favor. Would you mind telling my boss I need some rest? I really can't take more of her right now. Maybe I could stay out here with you?" Max's brow furrowed, trying to gauge if I was flirting back. I was. Clumsily. Neither romance nor friendship was a top priority for me. Until Max, I had always settled for vaguely attractive guys who put in a bit of effort so I didn't have to.

Telling the story later, Max remembered that he agreed to my plan and told Peter and Jessica that I should go home to rest. I remember that Max refused, and I had to go to the staff meeting and listen to Jessica complain about how hard it was to run on progressive platforms in red counties. But my memories are a little unreliable, so I'd trust him.

What we both agreed on is that I told him he could use my number for non-form-related uses, if he so desired. He said he would and left. But not before he told me to get a swollen gland on my neck checked out. I thought nothing of it with the carelessness that only healthy young people unknowingly possess. Maybe if I had gone right away, I would've caught it before the cancer spread to my lungs. I only went to the doctor weeks later when other symptoms developed.

It was then that my entire world became about frozen pickled bodies. I didn't ask for any of this. I was a typical, stubborn, privileged girl from the early millennium who knew loss and pain but never knew true suffering.

I didn't want to die. I wanted to live my life with Max. Grow old with him. If I ever had a choice in any of this, that would have been it. I certainly was not prepared for the new life that lay ahead of me.

These memories stuttered through my mind, hazy and half broken, as I sat alone in the strange chair where Damien had dumped me. I was trying desperately to remember who I was and where I came from. It was coming back in drips, but I wanted a flood.

In a flash, the screen in front of me lit up with a prerecorded video. The silence in the room was shattered by the oppressively loud and uninspired intro music. The screen's glare was so bright I had to squint through my outstretched fingers to make out the image of a woman with pearly white teeth.

"Thank you for choosing CryoLabs as your life-extension provider."

Her words stuttered, and her perfect smile pixelated. The video was rife with glitches and sound dropouts. My heart beat harder in my chest as I was once again confronted with evidence that something about this new world was off.

A red laser blinked across my eye followed by a high-pitched confirmatory *ding*. Through the speakers, an automated voice said, "Alabine Rivers," mostly mispronouncing my name. Before I had a moment to panic or question what was happening, relief came. A wave of contentment and relaxation overtook my senses. The throbbing in my head subsided. The bone-crushing ache that permeated my body melted away.

I exhaled.

"Our patented Revi Serum will help your body adjust and keep you from rejecting your new life." Pearly Whites smiled at me from behind her pixelated partition like the annoying infomercial she was.

It was only then that I saw the three-inch-long needle at the end of one of the robotic arms. As it origami-ed itself back into the derelict dentist chair, I realized that my new pain-free euphoria was thanks to whatever serum this needle had injected into my skull through the metal implant behind my ear. I tried not to think about it. It was easier not to think about it.

Pearly Whites then gestured toward a small pad on a new robotic arm that slithered out of my chair like a centipede. She casually instructed me to put my hand on it. I obliged, not even questioning it. Why would I? She had taken away my pain and lulled me into complacency.

I was far more trusting than I should've been.

My hand gently rested atop the appointed pad. Suddenly, a clasp locked around my wrist. There was a loud noise followed by pressure and burning.

I screamed. The lights flickered.

The clasp released my weak and trembling arm. After sitting in a moment of shock, I forced myself to turn my wrist over. Barely visible under my skin was the outline of numbers:

47931

I touched the sore incision. A bit of blood trickled from the wound.

"This is your ID. Remember those numbers." Pearly Whites's saccharine tone was starting to piss me off. "It is for your protection. Thank you for your cooperation with law enforcement and a continued respect of current residents. Remember, this is *their* home."

The video glitched again.

Something was very wrong. A feeling in my gut told me to run.

"And now," Pearly Whites said like a magician with something up their sleeve, "in the bin below, you will find your cure."

Her words hit me like a ton of bricks. My only memories at that point were dying of cancer and being in the hospital trying not to die of cancer. Cancer killing me was all I knew about myself.

"Welcome to your life, happily ever after." Pearly Whites winked. Just below the monitor, a small slot popped open like a toaster and a container slid out.

But it was empty.

Frantic, I looked back up to Pearly Whites for some explanation. The video only glitched as she smiled. After a long silence, it occurred to me that Pearly Whites was stuck on a never-ending loop.

"Damien," I called out softly. There was no response. "Damien!" I tried again, louder this time, but with the same result. Reluctantly, I pushed myself out of the chair onto my still unsteady legs and hobbled to the door.

The rusted squeal that rang out from the door's large hinges echoed through the empty hallway. I looked both ways and saw the same half-working fluorescent lights. Debris and broken glass were everywhere.

"Damien!" My voice ricocheted off the dark and dusty walls. Despite Damien's assurance, I somehow found myself alone with no idea what had happened to the smiling man who brought me back from the dead, and no idea what I should do.

Directly across the hallway was a faded poster. A CryoLabs advertisement that featured a diverse group of cloyingly happy twenty-somethings. The tagline read, "Find Happiness in Your Second Life." As intriguing as the poster was, my focus was taken by the dull orange spray paint sloppily scribbled on it: "Stay Dead Scum."

I couldn't stay there a moment longer. Right or left, it didn't matter just so long as I was headed someplace else.

As I delved deeper into the building, my initial suspicions of the lab's abandonment were confirmed. Every hallway was trashed. Broken glass. Graffiti. Words littered the walls like "Kill all cold cuts" and "Fuck Devil's Touch" and "We Will Remain."

Through all the vandalism, I could still make out that, in its prime, the building had functioned like a hospital. Various mazing hallways connected what must have been hundreds of rooms, each with a different purpose.

As I lost myself among the winding hallways, my grip on reality began to slip. I felt like Alice tumbling through Wonderland, wondering about this strange new world and why I'd been dumped into it like this. From what little I could remember, I was supposed to come back to life when there was a lymphoma cure, but the bin was empty.

So why was I alive?

It wasn't long before I heard scuffling footsteps and distant chatter. At first, I thought it was just in my imagination, but then I concluded that I wasn't alone. There were other people in these haunted halls. Maybe the voices belonged to the "we" who Damien was with. Maybe they were the even more mysterious "they" who didn't want me brought back.

I had to find Damien.

I turned the corner, then immediately stopped dead in my tracks. My jaw dropped. I'll never forget the sight. A huge glass door lay in front of me. Through it was what looked like a warehouse. There was a uterine-pink hue to the room. Hovering on the ground was a thick fog indicating the room's subzero temperature. It was like a shipping fulfillment center, but this contained only one thing: human bodies. Thousands of bodies, more than I could count, were hanging in bags. All still frozen. Humans hoping for a second chance at life on display like fish at the grocery store.

The scope of cryogenics was far greater than I ever imagined. When I decided to do it, people thought I was crazy. The only person I had heard of freezing themselves was Walt Disney, and even that was just a rumor. In that warehouse, I was confronted with the massive number of people who chose as I did. Whether they did so before or after me, I had no idea. My head started throbbing again.

I was leaning against the wall to catch my breath when someone came up behind me. Hoping that Damien had found me, I turned around to instead see a person dressed head to toe in body armor. A helmet covered his face, which didn't much matter as I couldn't take my eyes away from the very large gun in his hands.

He froze, seemingly as shocked to see me as I was to see him. Neither of us quite knew what to do next. I was trying to determine if he was a "we" or a "they." Behind us, an audience of a thousand frozen bodies watched our standoff.

"May I help you?" As soon as the words came out of my mouth, I knew how dumb it sounded. I assumed he was embarrassed for me too, but he didn't show it. Instead he pointed that very large gun at me.

"Get down!" he shouted. There was an intensity to his voice that I only knew from movies. It was then that I rightly assumed he was a "they."

No one had ever pointed a gun at me before. I quickly raised my hands. "I'm sorry, I think there's been some kind of mis—"

Suddenly, he grabbed me by the neck and dropped me to my knees, his fingers crushing the air from my throat. Instinctively, I gripped his wrist and tried to pry myself free, but he didn't budge, and I realized this was just the beginning. His foot cocked back, about to stomp me down to the ground like a bug.

In the second grade, I was in a fight on the playground. Some tall, skinny girl with curly blonde hair wanted to hold hands with my crush. So we fought. She quickly had me on the ground, kicking me in the stomach. Alas, Blondie's size-one light-up sneaker couldn't compare to a grown man's steel-toed boot.

I clenched my eyes shut, bracing for impact. Then I heard a crunch and yet surprisingly felt nothing. In fact, the man's hand went limp around my throat. I opened my eyes as my attacker's body slumped to the ground beside me. Standing over both of us was a petite but muscular woman with a pistol.

"'May I help you?' Really?" She snorted. With a lunge, she grabbed my arm. Perhaps a smarter person would've felt relieved, but I just saw another stranger with another gun. I pushed her off and slithered away until I hit against the huge glass door. A part of me wished I was back in that warehouse, frozen again, hanging with the rest of the bodies. At least they were safe.

"I'm getting the hell out of here. You can come with me or you can die." With that, she left. The distant shouting got louder. My head kept pounding. Then, from someplace far away, but not far enough, I heard gunshots. That's when the room flooded with a bright red flashing light and an alarm blared a deafening wail. The man on the ground, my attacker, stirred from his momentary unconsciousness. I hesitated, but only a moment, before stumbling out.

"THIS IS A SECURITY LOCKDOWN" sounded on a loop from the building-wide speaker system. The automated voice was oddly calm. I looked up and down the hallway but didn't see my mysterious rescuer until she yanked my arm and pulled me along at a brisk jog that I struggled to match.

"Keep up, Rivers!" she shouted.

She knew my name. I didn't know hers yet, but I assumed she was with Damien. We weaved in and out of hallways and stairwells that all looked the same. Soon I was unable to breathe. That relief I had felt in the dentist chair quickly eroded, and in its place was a grinding ache.

"Wait. Stop," I begged breathlessly. She paid no attention and kept running. I fell to my knees coughing. Blood splattered on the ground in front of me.

I knew this blood. This blood was the most familiar thing in the world to me. It was a result of the blood vessels in my lungs bursting. It was a result of my cancer.

Max's absence shot through me. That he wasn't there to hold me and hug me and tell me that he loved me was almost worse than the proof of my unrelenting and still uncured disease.

The woman ran back and dragged my collapsed body behind a concrete pillar. She covered my mouth to prevent me from coughing.

"Be quiet!"

Shuffling footsteps approached; then a blur of people ran by. I could make out someone dressed like the woman beside me, in jeans and a camo jacket, and two people with shaved heads like me.

The woman recognized them and shouted "Charlie!" Not a second later, there was a barrage of gunshots. The people who had run by crumpled into a bloody heap on the floor. I quickly looked away.

After a moment, three men in black armor and large guns marched past. They didn't see us. Thank God. Their gloved hands felt for a surviving pulse from the bodies on the ground. They found one. A single gunshot rang out. If I'd had any breath in me, I would've screamed.

Then they left.

We sat still for a while, the woman beside me in shock. Meanwhile, my vision tunneled, and I grew weaker. A weight inside my chest made even shallow breaths impossible.

"I need a doctor," I pleaded. Despite the urgency in my voice, this woman continued to stare at the wall. I clung desperately to consciousness. "Please, I need a doctor!"

Finally, she snapped out of her trance and returned to her same sharp tone. "Do you see any doctors around here?" She grabbed a syringe out of her bag and, before I could protest, violently stabbed it into my thigh. "That's the last one I got, so enjoy it."

I did. My vision cleared as life filled me once again.

"Who are those people with guns?"

"The bad guys" was what she said. What she meant was *Shut the hell up.*

She then yanked my arm, and we were off again. I forced myself not to look back and see the pile of bodies on the ground.

Whatever she had injected me with was potent enough for me to be able to keep pace with her. It wasn't long, though, until we turned a corner and saw the exit at the end of the long hallway. Even better, Damien was in front of the large metal doors that led to our freedom.

He rushed down the hall as soon as he saw us. Without a word, he held my face in his hands, inspecting my eyes for signs of life. "Are you okay?" he demanded more than asked but then didn't wait for an answer before whipping around to my rescuer. "Gina! We're trapped. The doors are locked."

"Damn it!" she shouted. "We don't have time. We have to move." Gina grabbed the crowbar from Damien's hand and worked to pry the locked doors apart.

Damien stepped toward her. "We're still waiting for Charlie. She's got Hobbes and Laughlin and—"

"They didn't make it." Gina's blunt tone poorly masked her grief.

Damien softened. "I'm sorry."

She tried the crowbar again, putting every bit of her anger into freeing us from this death-infested building, but it was a Herculean task. The doors didn't budge. Whatever plan had been in place, it seemed to be going desperately awry.

It was then that I noticed there were two other people standing in the hallway with us. A tall Black man. And a young Latina girl, no more than thirteen. They also had shaved heads and metal implants behind their ears. We stared at one another, looking for some sort of realization or rationalization that didn't come.

"Hi. I'm Al," I finally uttered with a meek and awkward wave.

The young girl slowly walked over. "Minnie. Like the mouse." I couldn't help but smile. Her innocence was so refreshing in this new world of guns and blood.

The man nodded his head. "Avon Williams."

"Are you both . . ." I wasn't quite sure what the rest of my sentence was. *Dead? Used to be dead?*

"Awoken?" The man named Avon responded. "Yes. I think."

"Awoken?" Minnie asked, beating me to the question.

"People who were frozen and resurrected. People like us . . ." Avon's voice trailed off, heavy with this realization that he now belonged to this word too.

"There's a name for that?" I asked, astonished that resurrected people were such a regular occurrence that the group had earned a proper name.

Suddenly, bullets dented the locked metal doors behind us. Down the hallway, an armored soldier ran toward us, shooting wildly. Minnie screamed. We all took cover as best we could. As she dove, Gina's pistol fell off her belt and slid into the center of the hallway.

Damien yelled, "Avon!"

Avon jumped into action and made a break for the gun. He slid across the slick floor, dodging bullets and scooping up the gun along the way. Ducking behind a desk for cover, he aimed Gina's gun and, with one shot, nailed our attacker square in the head.

Even though I had been one, I'd never actually seen a dead body before. Not in real life. As I stared at the dead man, I felt strangely calm. Death was familiar now. I pictured the darkness the dead man saw when he exhaled his last breath. The moment before, he was a thing, and now his consciousness was absorbed into the darkness. It was eerily beautiful.

Avon, his gun trained down the hallway, shouted to Gina, "Why are we being chased? Who are they?"

"Who are you?" I added.

Gina glared at me. "We're the people risking our lives to save yours. Good enough?"

I was about to snap back with something snarky, but thankfully, Avon responded first. "No. Unfortunately, that's not good enough."

"Bringing people back from cryo isn't exactly legal anymore, Avon."

Damien spoke calmly. "We don't think that's right. So we break in, steal your bodies, and bring you back to life. I'm Damien Grey, and this is Gina Han."

Gina added, "We're Resurrectionists."

That name also meant nothing to me at the time. Later I would learn that they were part of an underground group of activists. A rag-tag rebellion that was disorganized and decentralized. Their name started as a derogatory slur that was then adopted by the group and reappropriated as their official name. A real *fuck you* to the powers that be.

Another soldier came around the corner. Avon had him dead before he could even take a step. More for the darkness. It was hungry.

Behind me, Gina grunted, making little headway against the steel doors that were trapping us in our corridor of death. Out of the corner of my eye, I saw Minnie desperately looking around—at the door, the walls—and then her eyebrows rose. With determination, she scurried over to an unlit panel near the door. She was so small, no one else seemed to notice. I watched her as she expertly popped off the cover and revealed a tangle of wires behind it. After she fiddled with them for a minute or so, the screen lit up. She pressed it, and the doors magically opened. A surprised Gina fell to the ground on the other side.

The adults stared at this child with awe and confusion. She simply shrugged. Damien's curiosity drew him to the lit screen like he had never seen one before.

"Let's go!" Gina ordered. I didn't hesitate and ran out as fast as I could. The large doors slammed shut behind us.

Finally I was outside.

For the first time in one hundred years, the sun beamed down on my face. The warmth wrapped itself around my cheeks, and I breathed real, fresh air. Wind rustled through the leaves of a nearby tree. The birds flitted by, having no idea the hell that existed inside that building. Out here was peace. Or so I thought, until I opened my eyes.

All around us were the ruins of an abandoned city. Though we appeared to be in the downtown of a major metropolis, we were the only souls in sight. The city wasn't destroyed. No buildings crumbling; no rats scurried through piles of rubble. It was just empty, save for the plants pushing their way through concrete cracks.

It was as if one day everyone had just picked up and left.

"Where are we?" I asked. An unpowered traffic light swung idly in the breeze.

Damien, who was a few steps ahead, walked back toward me. "Indianapolis."

I gasped. *How can this possibly be Indianapolis?*

He held out his hand to me. "Come on. We have to get out of here."

I wanted to take his hand and leave this horrible place. But before I could, I doubled over coughing. Damien's eyes followed mine to the puddle of blood in my palm.

"The woman on the video," I stuttered breathlessly, "she said there was a cure?"

"This place was looted of easy-to-carry valuables like pills ages ago. Don't worry, Al. We'll get you the cure. I'm not going to let you die again so easily." He smiled. I was exhausted to delirium, my teeth were stained with blood, and yet I couldn't help but smile back at him. He put my arm around his shoulders and guided me away from the building. "I would give you another Dreno shot, but we don't have many left and you might want it more later."

"I'm dying," I said. More to myself. Confirming what I knew to be true.

"You have time." Damien nodded. "This cryo process is pretty lethal to cancer. So, you're sick. But you're not at death's door anymore."

"How long do I have? If we don't get the cure?"

"We will."

"How long?" I demanded.

Damien looked deeply in my eyes for a moment before breaking away. He shook his head and shrugged. "A few weeks, I'd guess. It'll escalate quickly. Quicker than the first time." He offered his hand to me again. "Don't worry."

Only a person who had never died before could say that.

He led us toward Gina and the other two, who were piling into a secret compartment under the floorboards of a cargo van parked behind a tree. There was another van there, and I remembered Charlie, or, more specifically, I remembered Gina's face when she saw Charlie and those other Awoken gunned down. Focusing back on the first van, I pushed the image out of my mind.

"Where are we going?" I asked Damien.

"Chicago. There's a camp there led by Wade Lovett. Our leader. And he can't wait to meet you."

"So, it's safe?" I asked, putting off my real question: Who was Wade, and why would he, or anyone, want to meet me?

"Well, safer, at least." Damien chuckled. "And from there we can get your cure."

My mind was reeling. A cure *did* exist. I could be cured. It seemed more unbelievable than an abandoned Indianapolis or even coming back from the dead. I could actually live a life free of cancer.

"What year is it?" Out of all my questions, this was the pertinent one I thought to ask. Behind it, I was really asking how far away I was from the world that I knew. From the people that I knew. Would living a life free of cancer even mean something?

"2121," he responded, with empathy in his voice that made me think he knew exactly what I was really asking.

"So, everyone I knew is gone. Max is . . ." I couldn't bring myself to say it. *Max is dead.* I would never again feel Max's hand on my cheek. Never hold him or wake up curled into his arms. *What good is a new chance at life if it's a life without him?* I thought.

Damien held my hand, pulling me from my spiral of despair, as he guided me into the van's secret compartment. "You're here. You're alive, Alabine Rivers. That's something."

With that, he closed the floorboards, shutting away the light.

FRED WONG

Cryogenics Debate Turns to Bloodshed

By FELIX WICKER

The world stands in disbelief today as Minneapolis police confirm the murder of Fred Wong. Mr. Wong, a Minneapolis native, was a controversial figure, known for being the first human successfully resurrected from cryogenic preservation earlier this year.

Last night at 11:04 p.m., Mr. Wong was shot in the head twice by what the police have identified as a sniper rifle used from the top of the AT&T building. Witnesses say Mr. Wong was still conscious when his security team carried him inside the apartment building at the southeast corner of 32nd and St. Patrick's Avenue.

Within minutes, Mr.

Wong was brought via ambulance to Christ the Redeemer Hospital, where he was declared dead on arrival.

The sudden and violent death of Mr. Wong has sent shock waves across the globe. He represented hope for those who see the emerging field of cryogenics as a new wave of human ingenuity. Vigils are being held in his name in 32 different countries, and a march is planned for Saturday to protest the growing violence against the cryogenic movement.

Mr. Wong first died of a viral pneumonia in July of 2023. Upon learning of his imminent death, he contracted with CryoLabs Industries to preserve his remains.

Over a decade later, Mr. Wong was chosen to be the first human awoken from preservation after numerous ani-

ASSASSINATED

mal resurrections and a very publicized selection process.

Many condemned the resurrection of Mr. Wong as an affront to nature and launched an effort to overturn the landmark Supreme Court case *Green v. Board of Health* that legalized human resurrection in 2031. That decision brought the world into a new era of humanity where death is not necessarily the end. While "anti-cryers" have not yet been successful in reversing the law, the upheaval in the Senate during the last election, along with Mr. Wong's assassination, signals that public opinion is shifting against cryogenics.

The plaintiff in the Supreme Court case and public face of the pro-cryo movement, Mr. Green, spoke at a rally last night on the steps of the Minneapolis courthouse. "We will not be scared into submission. We will continue to fight for the rights over our own bodies and for our loved ones who no longer have a voice. I will not stop until every person has the right to live."

In a press conference this morning, Senate majority leader John Howard first condemned the actions of the shooter but went on to say that the motive was a noble one. "The growing fear and division in America is due to the unnatural road this country has decided to walk."

Minneapolis police, meanwhile, prepare for the upcoming rallies that are sure to bring protesters on both sides. The chief of police tried dissuading any further violent actions in a press conference this morning. "We are a peaceful city. Let's keep it that way."

3

IT WAS PITCH BLACK under the floorboards of the cargo van where they stowed us. Squeezed in shoulder to shoulder next to Avon, I could hardly move. Minnie was crammed in on the other side of him. We lay there in silence. The smell of sweat and fear staled the air. Over the hum of the engine, I could faintly make out the sound of the van's radio. The DJ kept laughing, at what I couldn't tell, but it was the laugh of a man who didn't have a care in the world. I clung to the sound with every fiber of my being.

We were fugitives. The word seemed overly dramatic, but who else gets shoved into a secret compartment inside a run-down van? And still, I couldn't wrap my head around it.

The others might be actual fugitives, but not me, I thought. My deeply felt terror pushed me to find some reasoning. They killed those men, the cops or soldiers or whoever they were. Gina and Avon killed them. I hadn't killed anyone. If we were caught, I'd be able to explain myself. And Minnie, she didn't do anything wrong either. We were innocent. I could protect us. Or so I believed.

Making sense of this new world was overwhelming. Some things, like the van, were so familiar. There was even a Ford emblem on the hood. And besides Indianapolis being eerily vacant, it too looked normal. Normal buildings. Normal roads. In a way, the world seemed just as I left it, and still it felt so foreign.

The incision on my forearm from the implanted numbers rubbed against the rough metal floor. Though I tried, there wasn't enough room for me to reposition, so I embraced the sharp pain as a feeling of claustrophobia ran through me.

My eyes eventually adjusted to the darkness and I could see more of the secret compartment. It was dark. Cold. Too small for the number of bodies that occupied it.

Avon, this man who I was so uncomfortably and intimately pressed up against, appeared to know more of this world than I did, despite the fact that he too had been brought back to life only a few hours before. He was in the same boat as Minnie and me, and yet he didn't seem to be capsizing. Avon was difficult to read. Even in the face of taking someone's life he maintained a stoic and calm expression. His chiseled features and disarming eyes reminded me of the likenesses painted on a pharaoh's sarcophagus. Timeless royalty. Like he was destined to etch his way into history books.

"I lost to cancer, how about you?" I asked in a futile attempt to strike up conversation. There was no response. So, I tried again, "I really didn't expect—"

"Be quiet. Or do you want to die?" Avon snapped. I stopped talking.

Sometime later—I'm not sure how long passed in silence—Minnie's hushed voice rose to a level barely audible over the sound of the van. "Did you see anything after you . . . Did you see a light or go anywhere?"

My heart dropped. So young to lose the hope that there's more to life after death. She needed her parents to comfort her, but all she had was Avon and me.

42

"No. There was nothing," I responded, trying to sound sympathetic but probably sounding more scared.

"Me neither," Avon added, to my surprise. "Which is why we need to be quiet. I don't want to die again. Not for a long while."

Dying again. A terrifying thought.

In the dim light, I made out a small gold cross necklace around Avon's neck. "How do you have that?" I asked, jealous that I didn't have any souvenirs from my first life.

"I can't remember," Avon whispered. He touched his necklace. The gold cross tumbled effortlessly between his fingers like it had seemingly done countless times before.

No one spoke again for what felt like an eternity of bouncing around in the dark. In that stretch of the timeless passing of minutes, I focused on the radio from the van's cab where Damien and Gina were. The music was soft and soothingly hypnotic, lulling me into an uneasy sense of rest.

My eyes stayed fixated on the small amount of light reflecting off Avon's necklace. I was desperate for something that would connect me to life back then. To Max.

Then, I remembered what Damien had taught me. I thought of *Rosebud*.

DING.

I jump. The loud phone alert is sure to give us away.

Except I'm no longer under the floorboards of the van. I'm on a couch. Sitting next to Max. I watch him as he mindlessly texts someone with a small smile. My body swells with contentment and happiness. That other life becomes nothing more than a distant memory. A bad dream.

Finally Max looks over and sees me watching him. "Sorry," he says before putting his phone down and going back to watching TV. Some late-night host joking about a senatorial candidate's platform of restricting the age at which you could own a smartphone: "If the world isn't already ending, it's about to." Max laughs along with the studio audience.

I watch him. I want him. I need to tell him something. It's on the tip of my tongue. But I don't want to ruin the moment, and to be honest, I can't exactly remember what it is I need to tell him.

We have been on three dates at this point. Well, four, if you count the time we went to the library, but it was cut short when a man suffered a heart attack and Max had to perform CPR. It doesn't count if he makes out with a stranger more than he does with me. So, three dates. We've kissed good night sweetly on my stoop twice. And I already am falling head over heels in love with him. I'm so overwhelmed by this feeling that I can't breathe. Some people might find this time in a relationship exhilarating. I suppose to some extent it is, but in the case of love, I like proof and facts. Likely a side effect of being my parents' child, where love was more of a puzzle to be solved than a certainty.

We are curled under a brightly colored quilt, a kantha, that his mother gave to him when he moved out of their family home. It's beautiful. I run my hands over it, partly admiring the craftsmanship and partly giving my hands something to occupy themselves with when all they really want to do is to reach out and pull Max toward me.

My hand finds his under the blanket. He turns to me, shocked. Not in a good way. Shit. I read the entire situation wrong. I start stuttering something incoherent, trying to back my way out of this massively uncomfortable mess I've gotten myself into.

While I'm mid-mumble, he wraps his hand around my neck in one swift movement and pulls me into a kiss. A sigh stretches through my body. It's a really good kiss. My mind stops racing as he slides me onto my back and we both start undressing, lips never parting.

Wait.

I'm not sure if I say it in my head or out loud, but Max stops either way. He looks at me. "Is this okay?" I nod, so he goes back to kiss me again.

Wait, I say (or think) again. This time I pull away. Max stops and sits up. "I'm sorry. I didn't mean to push you."

I want this. Really, really want this. But instead I say, "I need to tell you something first." *What the hell am I doing?*

Max stares into my eyes, awaiting this big important declaration that's about to issue from my mouth. Jesus, Alabine, this better be worth it.

"I have cancer." It comes up as quickly as vomit.

Oh, right. That's what I came to tell him tonight. He looks at me dumbfounded, clearly wondering if this is a joke; it's not. "I found out on Thursday. That lump on my neck you found . . ." I trail off, not knowing what else to say. "I wish I met you before it, you know, spread everywhere."

He just continues to stare at me. No emotion. I did the same thing when the doctor told me. I stared at her, not even thinking about what she had just told me. I was thinking about my grocery list, not the fact that I was just told I had cancer. I wonder if Max is thinking about tomatoes.

"I know you didn't sign up for this," I continue, looking for some sign of recognition or acknowledgment. "My doctor has treatment plans. She's optimistic. I'm optimistic."

Max does nothing. Not a muscle twitches in his whole body. I broke him; I broke this poor young man by springing heavy news on him like this. We could be having sex right now, and instead I dropped this decidedly not-fourth-date information.

Might as well keep going.

"I'm sick. And I'm probably going to get sicker. So . . . I just wanted to give you your Get Out of Jail Free card before we went further."

Suddenly, Max grabs my hand in his, stares deeply into my eyes. "Whatever happens, I'll always be there for you." He takes my breath away. I swear I hear a Celine Dion song belting in from another apartment. It's like a dream. I love this man and he loves me and he's going to help me fight—

"Wait." This time, I definitely say it aloud. "That's not what happened."

"What are you talking about?" Max puts his hand on my cheek reassuringly.

It all starts coming back to me. "You didn't say that." The Celine Dion music stops. "I wanted you to, but . . . you left."

Max stands up, appalled that I would suggest such a thing. "What? I would never just—"

Before he can finish his sentence, we are thrust back to a moment earlier. Max stares at me, mouth agape. This time, Max doesn't reach out and grab my hand. I try to hold his and he pulls away. I hang my head, knowing exactly what's coming.

"I'm sorry, Al. I watched my sister die." He told me about that on date number two. How close he was with his sister when she died tragically of some really long and drawn-out illness. He still has nightmares about being unable to save her. "I can't do this. Not again." The final nail in the coffin.

We sit in silence a beat longer. Some emotion that I can't identify fills my body. It's sympathy and understanding. No. It's anger. Actually, scratch that, it's full-on rage. I grab my bag, button my pants.

"I'm sorry," Max says, trying to quell the building volcano that's about to explode.

When I get to the door, I whirl around for my final goodbye and shout, "Fuck you!"

Except it's not my voice.

.
.
.
.

It was Gina's. And I was back beside Avon. The van was stopped.

Let me tell you, the whiplash in coming out of these Lucid Memories is insane. I'd never fully get used to it, but especially in those early days, part of my brain felt stuck in this other life. It was the way I could be with Max. And then, just as I'd been given a respite from the taxing new world, I was thrown back into reality—torn once again from the man I loved. It was a lot to handle. Trying to piece together two separate lives.

Slowly, I was able to gain my bearings under those van floorboards and figure out what was happening.

We were in trouble.

"When did a patrol station get here?" Gina slammed her palm against the steering wheel in frustration. There was a small roadside booth with a long barrier stretched across the highway. It was unimposing, but Gina and Damien clearly felt threatened.

"We need to report this," Damien said. Fear penetrated his voice, which normally carried a comforting ease to it. I heard a click followed by a high-pitched noise and a moment of static.

"Han to Lovett," Gina said.

Avon shifted. "They have ham radios," he whispered to himself with a tone of astonishment that I didn't understand. In my time, two-way radios were still easy to come by. I didn't know they were now outlawed for nonauthorized citizen use—their scramblers even more so.

"Lovett here." The voice coming back over the ham radio was deep and intense.

Lovett. Wade Lovett. The leader Damien told me about who couldn't wait to meet me. In his voice, I could feel his power. His control. It was both terrifying and comforting. He sounded like a leader. Perhaps the kind where you better like where he's leading you because you don't have much say in the matter.

"There's a patrol station with two armed officers on 94 North," Gina reported.

"Where are you?"

"Two hours south of the city. We need transport permits, Wade."

There was silence for a moment. "Helen Smith lives in Braddock," Wade Lovett finally responded.

"Chris's mom? She'd just turn us away if she doesn't call the police first. She hasn't helped us since Chris went missing."

"Tell her we know where her daughter is."

"Do we?" Gina asked suspiciously. There was no response.

"I'll tell you where she is, rotting away somewhere. Likely killed by the Territorial Army," Damien said with a quiet defiance that made me certain the radio wasn't transmitting.

Wade's voice then crackled through with a direct order. "Tell Helen we've found Chris and that she's safe and sound."

Gina responded without pause: "Yes, sir."

I didn't fully comprehend what they were planning, but this was a clear lie. I wasn't the only one who felt unsettled.

"Do you trust them?" Minnie whispered.

I didn't. I didn't trust Wade Lovett or Gina, who blindly followed his orders. Damien even admitted that they were breaking the law. I thought about running to the cops. There were two in that patrol station. I wasn't a fugitive. Not in my mind. Not yet. And I was starting to believe the longer I stayed with these people, the more likely I was to be mistaken for one.

"They're shooting at the people shooting at us," Avon said. "That's as much trust as I need."

He was right, of course. While I was condemning these people for what they were doing, a small part of me knew that I was certainly benefitting from it. That soldier's bullets would've hit me too if Avon hadn't killed him. I should've been grateful, but the idea that I really was an outlaw because of who I was, regardless of what I'd done, was too alien for me to process. So I justified my decision to stay hidden under those floorboards by telling myself that it wasn't about trust; it was simply survival. I believed that everything would sort itself out if I could only explain my situation to someone in charge.

———

WE ARRIVED AT HELEN Smith's house a bumpy hour later. Avon, Minnie, and I didn't say another word the whole time. Silence is golden after all. And I was tired. So very tired. When we arrived, I planned on asking Damien for another shot of that stuff. Something to relieve the pain in my lungs.

The van pulled to a slow stop. I tried to hold it back, but I coughed and sensed Avon's judging eyes on me. I felt the tacky blood on my chin.

Sunlight came flooding in as Gina flung the floorboard open. She pulled me out without a word and forcefully escorted me out of ear-shot of the others as I wiped the blood off my face. Damien helped Avon and Minnie out of the van with much more tenderness than I was receiving.

Gina had changed out of her rugged denim cargo pants and jean jacket and was now wearing a long-sleeve, poufy pink dress. She looked uncomfortable, but I didn't dare question her reasons.

"You'll tell everyone your name is Alice tonight. Say nothing about yourself or your first life." Disdain coated her words, and she didn't even wait for me to respond before storming off toward the house in front of us.

"I hate that name," I muttered to myself. All I could think of was Peter, Jessica DeWhitt's campaign manager. He used to call me Alice all the time. I stopped correcting him after my crush on him and my idolization of Jessica DeWhitt wore off. Still, it infuriated me. I saw Alice as the name of someone who was destined to be a nobody, for-gotten and unloved. Someone who became complacent in her medi-ocrity and was actually happy to be an Alice. Apologies to all the Alices out there. I know that this is entirely absurd.

That night, Gina wanted me to be an Alice. Unspecial and unre-markable. Fine.

I looked up at the house. Helen Smith's house. Even from the back,

I could tell it was nice. An idyllic cottage. Pristine, clean, quaint, and inviting. Flower boxes lined the windows, and a lush fairy garden wrapped around the front. It was a wooded area, so the neighboring houses that surrounded us were barely visible through the trees that still clung to their leaves. The air smelled like honeysuckle and cold fresh water. I swear I heard a babbling brook, but that might have just been an overactive imagination as I've since looked at a map and found no such water nearby. The home's facade promised safety, even for one night. We just needed to get inside.

Damien was the one who knocked on the door. A Black woman in her mid-forties answered. This was Helen. She wore a manicured blue dress with a lace apron draped perfectly over her full skirt. There was a polished beauty about her.

The hope for a warm welcome was immediately put out of my head when I saw that she wouldn't open the door more than a foot. "No. I said no more. I told Wade. I'm done." Her eyes darted from side to side, scanning for a nosy neighbor. "You get out of here now."

"Please, ma'am, we need transport permits," Damien pleaded with her.

"Absolutely not." She tried to shut the door, but Damien pushed his hand against it. Fear shot into Helen's eyes. "You better leave, and don't come back."

"They'll die."

"That's not my fault," she quickly rebuked him, like she knew the guilt bait was coming. She didn't have any room left in her heart for guilt. It was filled to the brim with fear and grief.

I didn't want her to turn us away. More than anything, I wanted inside that house. All that waited for us on the road was more guns. More secret van rides. I needed a break. We all did.

Helen pushed the door hard against Damien's hand. "Chris told us to come here." Damien said it quickly and confidently. This was the lie. The lie that Wade ordered.

Helen stopped. She stared at Damien, a completely different

woman. Tears welled in her eyes. "You've found her? You found my baby?"

Damien nodded. "She didn't want us to tell you because it could put you in danger." He was a good liar. Too good. A rock fell into the pit of my stomach when I realized he smiled at Helen the same way he smiled at me. I knew I didn't trust Wade or Gina. Now Damien, and his smile, seemed suspect. Despite the relief that washed across Helen's face, I didn't speak up and tell her the truth. The promise of a safe bed bought my silence.

"Oh, thank God! Come in. Come in now." Helen pushed her door open and ushered us all across the threshold.

The inside of Helen's house perfectly matched the outside. It was lovely. The room smelled of cinnamon and sugar. Minnie immediately spotted why. The kitchen counter was filled with baked goods of all kinds. Buttered tops glistened in the setting sunlight.

Helen chuckled, full of rediscovered maternal warmth. "Well, go on then."

Minnie didn't need to be told twice. She beelined for the kitchen and began stuffing her face with whatever she could. Only a semblance of decorum kept me from doing the same. I was starving. A slight nod from Helen encouraged Avon and me to join Minnie's feast. We dove in. I ate like I had never eaten before, or at least not for a century, ravaging the spread of pastries in front of me.

"This is Avon, Minnie, and Alice." I caught Gina's eye as she told yet another lie to our unknowing host. My concern easily subsided with another bite of something cherry-filled with a sugar-crusted top.

"No reason to eat like wild animals," Helen chided us. "You got time. Can't leave tonight. People would find a van traveling alone at night very odd. You wouldn't make it two miles after dark." Helen then grabbed Damien by the arm and pulled him out of our earshot. She cried softly as they spoke, Damien undoubtedly fleshing out his lie assuring her of her daughter's safety.

As my stomach filled, I took in my surroundings. The decor was simple and classic. Wood floors, lofted ceilings, and soft colors. A small tin crucifix was nailed to the wall next to delicate lace curtains. The kitchen opened to the dining area that held a wood table, beyond which was a quaint living area with a couch and two armchairs facing a crackling fireplace. It was quiet and still, like we'd stepped into a painting.

And then I noticed something very strange: there was no TV, no computer, no electronics of any kind, in fact.

Helen's home was the first glimpse I had into the normal of this new world. How people existed outside the bullet-riddled warehouses of mummified bodies. What the future really looked like.

Much to my surprise, there were no AI robots or flying cars. It was the opposite. Priorities had dramatically shifted from what I had known growing up in the early part of the millennium. A conscious rejection of screens and technology. Apparently the future was analog.

After taking a particularly good bite of Danish, I noticed a framed photograph lying in front of me on the kitchen counter. It was a formal portrait of Helen with a stunningly beautiful young woman: Chris, I assumed. A crumpled-up tissue lay next to it. Wanting a better look at the girl I knew to be dead, I picked up the photo.

"Don't touch that!" From across the room, Helen marched toward me, interrupting her conversation with Damien. She tore the photo from my hands.

"I'm sorry. I didn't mean—" My apology was cut short when I felt Avon pointedly grab my shoulder. A gesture that conveyed, *I'll handle this.*

"She seems like a brave woman," Avon said earnestly.

Helen softened, releasing a bit of her chokehold on the picture frame. "I wish she were less brave." There was a deep sadness in her voice that was vaguely disguised by disappointment.

Avon's face softened, and color filled his cheeks as they widened in a smile. "My mother said the same thing when I was drafted. 'Let others be brave.'" He hovered in this memory of love from another life.

Helen placed the picture facedown on the counter. "The military at least has honor in it. But this . . ." Her hand remained resting on the back of the photograph.

Avon reached toward it. "May I?" he asked. As tears formed in Helen's eyes, she removed her hand. Avon took the photograph and walked it over to the wall where a picture hook hung empty. Gently he returned it to its original place.

Helen watched Avon's every move, touched by his gesture. Then her eyes widened and she filled with dread as she realized, "You don't even have wigs on."

Minnie looked up from her plate of sweets as we all curiously watched Helen dig through her closet to pull out an old cardboard box. She riffled through until she found three wigs, then offered the pile of hair to Avon.

As he took the wigs, she held on to him. "When you see Chris, tell her I love her." Avon nodded, accepting this unachievable task solemnly.

Helen walked away. Once alone, Avon leaned momentarily against the wall, in pain. Unable to hide it anymore. Like me, he was sick. We needed those cures, and Helen held the ticket for us to make it to Chicago and get them.

After some discussion between them, Damien gave Avon a shot like the one Gina had given me. Avon closed his eyes in appreciation of the relief that came. "I can almost forget that I'm still dying," he told Damien, who chuckled.

"Relax." Damien patted Avon's shoulder. "Let it do its job. Your body's been through a lot." Then they started talking in hushed tones. I couldn't hear them, but I had a feeling they were talking about me as their eyes would dart quickly my way.

Soon Damien brought a wig over. It was a short and choppy blonde number. Decidedly not the long dark brown hair from my first life.

"It's to hide the, uh—" He was too nice to say it.

"Big shiny bald head?" We both smiled. "Not a good look for me?"

"You pull it off. But it's a major giveaway that you're an Awoken. That and the implant." He gestured to the metal device behind my ear. "Without wigs, you're a target."

It was then that I understood that Helen was committing a very serious crime by harboring us. Multiple people were risking their own lives to save ours. I felt guilty, but told myself I shouldn't. I didn't ask to be awoken in a time when it was illegal.

"I'll wear it, but I'm really not a blonde," I joked.

Damien put it on my head and adjusted it. Then he smiled. "It works for you, Rivers." Though he was joking, it was nice to hear. I hadn't lost my vanity yet, you see. That would still take quite a bit more time to get beaten out of me.

As he adjusted the wig, he looked at me with such hope and promise, reminding me of what he had said in the lab: *We've been looking for you for a long time.* After everything that had happened since, I wasn't sure I wanted to know what he meant.

His hand, invitingly warm, lingered on my face for a moment. I had forgotten what human touch felt like. While my Lucid Memories of Max felt so real while I was in them, they were only a figment of a dream once I was back in reality.

I fought the soothing warmth and pulled away, still feeling uncomfortable with the ease of Damien's lie. I understood why he'd done it. He was following Wade Lovett's order. And honestly, I probably would've done the same thing. It was the only way to get inside Helen's safe house. It was for my benefit—mine and Avon's and Minnie's—not his.

Damien's smile dropped when he saw I was concerned. He opened his mouth to speak, but just then Helen approached. She handed Damien transit permits, yellow slips of paper that somehow meant my life or my death. Helen instructed us to take some of the pink bakery boxes full of baked goods in case there was an inspection.

"Thank you, Helen," Damien said with a nod.

"I really hope you all can stop this soon. It's a peaceful world out there except for this nonsense." She said it like a teacher, scolding her pupils.

"Peaceful?" I asked incredulously. Her warped perspective floored me.

"People in this country are content with the lives God gave them, Alice." My false name scraped through Helen's gritted teeth. "We live fulfilling lives. Happy lives. And then we die. That's the natural way of things. Your kind threatens the hard-won order our country fought to secure."

"We're not the aggressors here, Ms. Smith," Damien gently defended.

"Tell that to those poor innocent people you blew up at Eavesman Square not two weeks ago." Helen held a restrained rage in her voice. "More than a hundred miles from here and missing posters clutter our light posts. Put there by people looking for hope that will never come."

She glared at Damien, then me, before walking off. She'd won this exchange, that much was clear, though I didn't quite understand how. In the ensuing silence, Damien was left a bit stunned. An apprehensive guilt was palpable on his face as he stared off.

"What's Eavesman Square?" I asked.

"Nothing. A bad decision we made." He tried to walk away, but I grabbed his arm and stopped him.

"You have to tell me more than that, Damien."

He paused to consider before nodding. "The government was decommissioning a cryo facility just outside of Columbus in a populated rural community. In that facility were thousands of bodies in stasis, waiting for life. We thought we could stop the decommissioning. We didn't. All those bodies were discarded like trash." He swallowed his building anger. "And then a lot of people in the town died. There was a bomb. Wade's plan—"

"Wait, your leader blew up all those innocent people?"

"It's complicated." Damien sighed.

"Doesn't seem all that complicated to me," I spat back, understanding Helen's anger.

Damien shook his head. His eyes cast downward. "Wade's a good man. Great, even. He's a hero among the Resurrectionists." It sounded more like propaganda than actual belief. Regurgitated lines.

I thought about innocent people dying in an explosion set by these Resurrectionists. And then I thought about those thousands of bodies, bodies like mine, that would never be allowed another chance at life. Maybe I should have been more grateful they had woken me up and I had not suffered a different kind of fate. With all those thoughts in mind, I simply and earnestly offered, "I'm sorry."

Damien gave me a half-hearted smile and walked off to load Helen's bakery boxes into the van. As I watched him, I wondered who these Resurrectionists really were. And more specifically who Wade Lovett was.

Just keep running away from the bullets. That's what I kept telling myself over and over.

Across the room, Helen turned on her simple radio. The only piece of technology in the entire house. And it stood in a prominent position at the center of her sofa table. She sat and wrote in a ledger as she listened to the soft music. The dulcet tone of the radio DJ occasionally interrupted the music with a kind word to his listeners and introduction of the next song.

"DJ Raheem here as always on UA52, sinking into this beautiful evening with a tune or two that I hope gives you a nice still moment at the end of a productive day. Life is good. And we will remain."

It could've been a scene from the mid-twentieth century. DJ Raheem's voice effortlessly embodied his message of peace and contentment. I was comforted by the simplicity, the familiarity, and took a seat next to Helen. She eyed me briefly, suspiciously, then went back to her work.

The radio looked strangely simplistic. A speaker took over much of the box face. There was no tuning dial—no screen or other display showing what channel she was listening to. There was only a volume knob. It was quite a beautiful machine that looked handmade. I rested my chin on my hands and let the music wash over me.

It wasn't long before Helen closed her ledger. "There's pillows and blankets in the closet. Make yourself at home. Just be off first thing before my neighbors are up, you hear?" And with that she turned off the radio and went to bed.

While Gina and Damien finished loading the van, Avon, Minnie, and I collected pillows and distributed them around the room. We found our various spots, on couches and overstuffed armchairs, where we could sleep. Finally, allowing myself to feel the weight of my exhaustion, I collapsed onto the floor next to Minnie, who had snuggled into the couch.

The shock and fear and anger I'd been holding tightly in my muscles spilled out of me. My pulse, which had been racing all day, started to normalize. Everything up to then had been adrenaline-fueled chaos. I hoped to fall asleep quickly, but in the vacuum created by releasing my physical stress, questions filled my thoughts. What conflict had I found myself in the middle of, and how could I get out before it sucked me in? Most important, what kind of life was I even fighting for?

A life without Max.

Minnie reached over and held my trembling hand in hers, stilling it. She smiled softly; then her brow furrowed in pain. The look in her eyes echoed the same fear of death that I felt. Minnie had never been given even the chance at a full life. And here she was, dying all over again.

She was so young, just needing to be tucked in by her mother, and I was a lousy stand-in. I felt like a scared kid myself, but Minnie didn't know that. An intense feeling of responsibility and protection overcame me. I thought about what a mother might do in that moment. I thought about doing the opposite of what my own mother would do. I held Minnie's hand, and we both fell asleep.

MISSING PERSON

Claudette Pearl, age 41, black hair and a birthmark on her right ankle. Last seen on December 1, 2121, at Fred's Postal Shop on Eavesman Square before the terrorist attack. CCTV shows her running away from the initial blast. We believe she may have been taken to an emergency response tent in the surrounding area, perhaps in an unconscious state. We have faith our loved one has survived and are doing everything we can to find her. If you have any information on her whereabouts, please inform the police or nearest emergency response center. Thank you, and God Bless the United America. We will remain.

Cash Reward.

4

MINNIE MORALES WAS BORN in 2020, less than a month after I died. She had the kind of childhood I always dreamed of, filled with love, family, and security. She was destined for a great life. The poster child of Generation Alpha, Minnie was accepted at eight years old into a special STEM program where her talent with computers flourished. She was declared a genius, and the *LA Times* even wrote an article about her when she became the youngest person ever to win a national hacking competition. Google started recruiting her when she was ten, but when she was eleven, she was diagnosed with a rare disease that caused her organs to calcify. An incredibly painful and fatal illness without a known cure. Her only hope lay in the growing movement of cryogenics.

Minnie lived in a time when America prospered. The tech boom had led to a surge in medical advancements, sparking a golden age of science that brought about countless lifesaving innovations—none more so than the discovery of how to resurrect a preserved body.

In 2028, CryoLabs successfully resurrected a cryogenically frozen monkey, Arnold. It was the headline of the millennium. Arnold the monkey found similar fame as Dolly the cloned sheep from the 1990s. With all the attention came the same condemnation. People like Minnie watched the global debate unfold with bated breath. Now that animal trials had proved successful, there was a fight over the legality of resurrecting a human. The world split into factions: those who believed cryogenics to be the next evolution of humanity and those who believed it to be a horrible affront to God and the natural order.

In 2031, six months after Minnie's terminal diagnosis, humanity was forever changed with the landmark Supreme Court case *Green v. Board of Health*, which legalized the revitalization of preserved human bodies. Minnie celebrated at a march in downtown LA perched on her father's shoulders, chanting "Our lives, our rights." At that point, assisted suicide wasn't legal, so Minnie had to spend a very painful two and a half years dying. Then, once legally declared dead, Minnie was preserved, waiting for a cure to be discovered that would allow her a second chance at life. From one generation of Moraleses to the next, the responsibility was passed to wake and care for Minnie once she was eligible for resurrection.

As cryogenics became the go-to choice for those desperate enough to need it, the opposition voices grew louder. Popular opinion of cryogenics continued to evolve over the decades, swinging back and forth between acceptance and abhorrence, each new generation bringing their unique perspective colored by the events of the time. Regardless of one's belief, both sides agreed on one thing: resurrecting humans signified the largest change for humanity since the dawn of time. It meant neither God nor nature decided who lived and who died—humans did, at least to a point. If you had the money and the will, you could circumvent death itself. However, from the very first resurrection, there was a pervasive belief that those who were brought back—the Awoken—were somehow tainted, no longer human.

Unfortunately, generations later, Minnie's inherited guardian—her grandnephew—legally terminated his custody. Minnie was orphaned in her preservation bag, damned to remain that way indefinitely. That was in 2082, when cryogenics was widely demonized.

The very same decade, during that wave of public opposition to cryogenics, Avon Williams was preserved. Born in 2058, he was technically the youngest of us. He died in 2088, when he was thirty years old. Avon didn't like to talk about his first life, especially his time as a soldier. He was very close with his family: his mother and younger brother, Joshua. They were poor, as was much of the country in the 2060s after the Second Great Depression. Avon was drafted into the army at age fourteen. He was skilled and thus tracked for special ops before he was eighteen. In the 2080s, the country was embroiled in the North American War, a bloody civil war, with the western states who were backed by Canada, and Avon fought on the front lines.

His mother hated that he was in the army. There was an infinite number of ways for her beloved firstborn son to be sacrificed in the name of patriotism. Avon was a natural leader of his brigade and had an aptitude for military strategy. In 2085, while in Colorado on a top secret mission, Avon was badly injured by a roadside bomb and required a blood transfusion. The blood was tainted with a nasty mutated strain of malaria. At the time, the treatment was a pill taken daily for a few years. Effective, manageable, and potentially curable if the medicine was sustained for as long as necessary. Unfortunately for Avon, the pill patent was bought by Revi Solutions, the massive pharmaceutical company that, among many other things, sold cryogenic preservation services. They increased the cost of the pill to drive up their cryo business. Too poor to afford the medicine, Avon was forced to undergo cryo while his family saved up the money for the years of malaria treatment he required. Avon legally euthanized himself with the expectation that he'd be brought back within a few months, a common practice that was termed a "death loan."

When I was alive, cryogenics was only an option for the rich and privileged. I had to raise $200,000 on GoFundMe, and that was after Max emptied his savings account. Preservation was expensive. But in Avon's time, advancements in cryogenics had made it cheaper than ongoing medical treatment. So cryogenics became a method relegated to the poor who couldn't afford cures. In the 2080s, the association with lower-class people degraded public opinion on cryogenics even further. The government capitalized on this hatred to unify the war-weary country against a common enemy: the Awoken. Unnatural, unseemly, and unwanted.

In late 2088, months after Avon's death, a new Supreme Court case overturned the *Green v. Board of Health* decision. Resurrection was declared illegal. Avon was one of the last people to be legally frozen, and he was not brought back to life as he had planned. It's estimated that almost five million bodies were already in stasis across the country when the law suddenly changed. Trapped forever in death.

There were thousands upon thousands of bodies still frozen in the cryo facility where I was stored. Each one had a story. But we were the three whom Gina and Damien chose to bring back from the dead that day. There were supposed to be five. Another Resurrectionist team led by a woman named Charlie Wells was tasked with bringing back two other Awoken. As Gina and I witnessed, they didn't make it out.

Five were chosen by the Resurrectionists. Five out of thousands. And I was one of them. It was clear why they wanted Avon, the military stud that he was. Even why they wanted Minnie, a technological genius to turn the tide in a world that had forgotten technology.

But I was nobody. I was still an Alice when I died. I didn't have a specific skill set besides being above average in eliciting social media engagement. I didn't have time to make a name for myself. No, I didn't take the time to become the person I wanted to be.

So why me?

That question burned in my mind when I woke up on the floor of

Helen's house. It was still dark outside. Everyone around me was asleep, strewn across the room. I saw blood on the hem of my blanket and realized I must've coughed myself awake, as I had so many times before. I was shivering, dampened with sweat.

God, I hate cancer.

Out the window, the glow from a bright streetlight drew my attention. It was both eerie and serene and seemed like a dream. In my sleepy state, I found myself standing next to the window looking onto the still street.

The houses sat peacefully in the night as bits of snow fell gracefully to the ground. There were fields filled with perfectly placed rows of deep green kale barely peeking out from the snow-dusted ground.

This was the world I had expected to wake into. Maybe I envisioned more flying cars and robots in 2121, but a version of this utopia was what I'd hoped for when I signed that CryoLabs paperwork.

Looking out the window, I had a thought that maybe I didn't deserve to be in Helen's world. Maybe the darkness, the cold pit in my stomach, tainted me. Maybe they were right to want to keep me out.

I found myself absentmindedly tracing the outline of numbers under the skin on my wrist. The pain on the incision had dulled, but there was something lingering. It took a moment for me to realize that I felt shame. I was marked with an identity outside of my choosing, and I hated it. I pulled my sleeve down tight and adjusted my blonde wig, further securing the dried-out adhesive to my scalp.

Outside, I noticed a vibrant red quilt on the fence post in the front yard. It flapped gracefully in the breeze. I thought I must still be dreaming because I knew that quilt, and it knew me. It was Max's quilt, the one his mother lovingly made for him.

My feet were cold. Cold and wet.

That was how I realized that I was unexpectedly outside, barefoot on the icy ground. The quilt vibrated with life as my hands ran across the colorful stitching.

Suddenly, Max was in front of me. My heart raced with love and anticipation. He smiled as he offered me his hand. It seemed so simple. I could just go with him. Then I'd be home. In a world that I knew. A world in which Max still existed.

I knew that this moment couldn't be real. I hated that this couldn't be real. I snapped out of it.

I was indeed standing barefoot in Helen's front yard. Snow fell onto my nose with an unwelcoming chill. Max and the quilt were gone. In their place was now a small boy in pajamas. I was unsure if I was still dreaming, remembering, or if he was really standing there.

"I like your face," the small boy in pajamas said to me in that bluntly curious way kids talk. "How old are you?" I froze, worried that if I moved, something terrible would happen. "I'm five and three quarters," he told me proudly. The boy climbed up the fence posts to match my height. "I've seen your face before."

He reached out and put his hand on my cheek, feeling around for its familiarity. I found myself relaxing under his gentle touch. This kid, even if he was real, wasn't a threat to me. He had a sweet face with dimples and innocent blue eyes. In fact, he reminded me of a little boy I used to babysit. For a split second, I forgot about the guns and dead soldiers.

It was only a split second.

As the five-and-three-quarters-year-old boy was feeling my face, he touched my hair. Except it wasn't my real hair. The wig slipped off my head. The boy stared wide-eyed. Neither of us said anything.

Then he screamed.

"What's going on?!" The shout came from across the street. The boy's father, dressed in overalls for the day's work, came rushing toward us.

I should have run. I should have hid. I would have done a million other things, if only I'd known better. I didn't. Like the small boy in his pajamas, I thought I was just innocently enjoying the early-morning snowfall.

But I wasn't. I wasn't like them at all.

When our eyes met, the father stopped in his tracks. What started as annoyance at his kid quickly morphed to petrifying fear. No one had ever looked at me the way this man did. I was the monster under the bed, disgusting and terrifying. The last thing in the world this father wanted or expected to see standing next to his little boy.

"You're one of them," he stuttered, half bewildered and half accusatory. He pointed at me like I was some wild bear. I didn't know what to do except quickly put the wig back on my head and run.

As I retreated into Helen's house, I glanced back at the boy. The terror on his face is still emblazoned in my mind. He reached out for his father to hold him.

"Did it touch you?!" the father shouted. The poor boy nodded. The father backed away aghast, then began shouting for help, shattering the pristine silence of the sleeping neighborhood.

Once inside, I slammed the door behind me. Gina immediately jumped up, pistol in hand. She saw me standing at the door. "You went outside?!"

"They saw me . . . what I am. I think we have to go."

"You think?!" Gina yelled as Helen came storming in from her bedroom in a pink nightgown and matching hair cap, screaming for us to leave her house. I watched helplessly as Damien jumped into action. Avon scooped up a half-asleep Minnie in his arms. The world whirled around me as I struggled to see what to do in the chaos I had inflicted.

We all ran out the door toward the cargo van. The screaming from the street was louder, and now other voices had joined in.

I helped Minnie into the van's floor compartment. She arched in pain. Avon was climbing in behind us when Gina thrust a pistol into his hand.

"In case." She closed the hatch. We sped off.

Meanwhile, the dozens of shouting people stormed Helen's house. Police sirens weren't far behind. But by then we were gone.

"What were you thinking?" Avon didn't wait before jumping on me. "You went outside? Are you crazy?"

I was too shocked and embarrassed and guilt-ridden to respond. I told myself that this was their mistake. I shouldn't have even been there. I hated this world, and this world clearly hated me. All I could mutter under my breath was, "I'm sorry."

I closed my eyes and thought about Max, and *Rosebud*. Anything that wasn't that moment or that compartment. I thought about what it felt like when I wasn't so alone.

It worked.

Just like magic, I'm no longer under the floorboards. I'm in my apartment, and it's pitch black. I know it's my apartment because of the smell. The Thai restaurant on the ground floor always fills my tiny, cluttered home with aromas of seafood and peanuts.

I run my hand along the wall until I find the light switch. The lights come on and reveal a man standing in my living room. I scream.

"Sorry! It's me. It's just me," the intruder says. It's Max.

"What the hell?" I shout before breathing a sigh of relief.

Max is holding a bouquet of flowers. Rosebuds speckle the floor. "I got the super to let me in. She said it was really romantic." He pauses, doubt creeping into his voice. "Although now I think this is also something a serial killer might do. And by the look on your face, you think so too. Just know that I thought I was being romantic."

"Romantic?" I try to calm down and accept that I'm not about to be murdered. For a brief moment, I contemplate laughing and falling into his arms. Letting him hold me and stroke my hair and heal me by simply loving me. I need his comfort more than anything else in the world right now. But then I remember he left. So I say, "What are you doing here? You don't get to do this, Max."

"I know. I'm sorry. This is just . . . hard for me."

"Hard for *you*?" Screw him.

"I know. That's just it. You deserve someone brave. Braver than me." He inches closer. I want him to leave. "I should leave. If I had an ounce of selflessness, I would. But I had to tell you that even though I'm nowhere near good enough for you, I'm not going anywhere unless *you* want me to. I'll be there every step of the way. If you want it. If you want . . . me."

"I don't." I'm surprised at my own steadfastness. Especially because I'm so tired. Exhausted. And cold. Was it snowing outside? *No.* Back to Max. "You're already looking at me differently. I'm just the sick girl to you now."

Max stands there, staring at me. "Al, please . . ."

My resolve grows in the face of his hesitance. "Stop! I'm not one of your patients for you to come in and save."

"I know," he says, stepping two feet closer. He's now only an arm's length from me.

With every step closer, I feel my wall crumbling. I realize I'm fighting back tears. I'm so tired, and my willpower is waning. "I don't always want to be the sick girl to you. I want to be the fun girl. I want to go dancing with you, Max. And have awesome crazy sex. We haven't even had sex yet!"

"I know," Max repeats in a tone that implies he's well aware.

Then it all hits me. Over a week since that horrifying appointment, and I finally grasp what the doctor told me. I'm sick. Really sick. And . . . "I don't want to die," I finally confess as I collapse. Max catches me and gently tucks a piece of my hair behind my ear as tears stream down my face.

"I know," he repeats back to me softly.

I don't want to die. The words roll over and over in my head as Max wraps his arms around me. I want him to make it all better. But he can't.

"No. No!" I push him off me and stand. "You left!" Max clings to my waist. "Let me go, Max. There's nothing you can say." I rip myself off him and take a few steps away. I can't bear to look at him. I want him to leave and never come back.

Then I hear music.

I turn around to see that Max is playing a song on his phone. His lips tighten with determination. I know the song: "Sorry," by Justin Bieber. Not my favorite. Regardless, playing any kind of music in that very specific moment is an odd choice. I don't know quite how to respond. To his credit, my anger subsides a bit to make room for confusion.

"Just leave," I beg weakly. He doesn't. Instead he starts moving his shoulders. Then his hips. He stands up off the ground and rocks side to side. He's dancing. Much to my astonishment, he's completely, seriously dancing. In my living room. The smell of shrimp pad Thai filling the air. Tears in both our eyes.

I'm trying to find a way to still hate him. Trying not to get pulled back in. But then he breaks out in a smile and spins around, and I forget about the cancer.

He offers his hand to me. "I want to dance with you, Alabine Rivers."

I try not to, but I can't hold back the bubble of laughter that comes out. He looks absolutely ridiculous and insanely hot.

"You're crazy," I say. He shrugs as he bites his lip. Surrendering myself to the absurdity, I let the music overtake me. I throw myself into him, and we start dancing. We press our bodies into each other's. I resist until I can't. We kiss.

I suddenly remember that I will die fourteen and a half months later. I remember that I will wake out of this memory into a barrage of bullets and hate. Even still, I let this moment of us dancing surround me. I touch his skin and absorb every good feeling I can. Later that night, we sleep together for the first time.

After that, he is there for me through everything. Every doctor's appointment. Every scan. Every night. My Max.

Watching him asleep in bed next to me, I wonder how, if this is only a memory, it can feel so real? Past and present blurring together without a wall of time. I could get lost in here. Lose reality. Lose myself in Max. But it's a trap. This is not my life anymore.

Max is dead.

Wake up.

5

THE UNITED AMERICA MOVEMENT took over the country in a calm and legal manner. No bullets flew; no trumpet of surrender sounded. The new political party started gaining power in the late 2020s. Even I was unknowingly aware of an early offshoot of their movement in my first lifetime; the man who threw the smoke bomb at me was an avid follower.

In the years and decades after I died, the UA party won more and more elections until by 2050 they held the Senate majority. They weren't far right or far left specifically. They offered an answer to lower- and middle-class fears of tech automation taking over blue-collar work and built a strong luddite platform. Promising a fairer distribution of wealth and a healthy middle class, they united people under wholesome family values and moral superiority with an emphasis on rural and agricultural importance in a technology-obsessed world.

It was a party for everyone that took a little from Republicans and a little from Democrats and fundamentally disrupted the political conversation. They were pro-nationalism and anti-immigrant while also being anti-racist and pro-environment. It was sort of ingenious how they warped the long-standing rhetoric behind these big issues to sway people from all backgrounds to their beliefs.

Most of all they preached anti–Silicon Valley rhetoric. Their mantra was natural over engineered. Human over machines. "The Natural Order," they called it. From my early-millennia perspective, it appeared to be a twisted neo-hippie faction. Certainly not the high-tech authoritarian government I expected from watching sci-fi movies. Sure, they used controlling tactics, but not all of their policies were destructive. In fact, once in power, they intensely regulated corporations, thus leading the world in the fight against the changing climate.

Women played an important role in UA leadership from the beginning. It was a large and passionate subset of the female voting bloc who truly cemented the faction's rise to power. The party promised that women would be listened to, respected, and have a voice in government in a way unparalleled in American history—certain women at least. A new cabinet position was formed that could only be held by women, Secretary of Homelife. This high-level representative would be consulted on everything from declarations of war to budget allocations, determining the effects on family life. One word from the Secretary of Homelife could dramatically shift global politics. That change in governmental power created an empowering ripple effect across the new country. Men were no longer seen as the head of the household. However, feminism shifted from the *women can do the same things men can do* philosophy that I knew so well from my time to the belief that women and men are naturally different and suited for different responsibilities. A mind-set that seems desperately flawed to me but generally is accepted and an element of society that most United America women are proud of.

This was the Natural Order.

Keeping in line with that philosophy, cryogenics was in the UA's crosshairs from the beginning, an obvious threat to the Natural Order. It was a hot-button topic around the world, one that impassioned people on both sides. Look, I get it, bringing people back from the dead, what could seem less natural? If it took decades to change popular opinion about stem cell research, I wouldn't expect an overnight global acceptance of resurrection. Change is terrifying.

Each country had to decide how it would react to this earth-shattering innovation. The legality of bringing a person back from the dead was the moral issue of the millennia. The world divided along ideals: those that restricted or even banned resurrection and turned away from technology, and those that embraced medical advancement and bodily autonomy. It was the age-old debate of nature versus science, and cryogenics was the crucible.

At first, in the 2030s and '40s, America was pro-cryo, and it became widely used. But as the UA gained power, opinion shifted. Fear of cryogenics fed the UA's rise, and the UA's rise fed the fear of cryogenics. For every new body frozen, fifty more people showed up to protest the so-called abomination. Domestic terrorism increased tenfold. Although stemming from both sides, the violence pushed moderates into the arms of the UA, which promised to secure peace.

One side believed they were saving lives; the other believed they were saving souls.

The question on everyone's mind: Should it be within our power to bring someone back from the dead? And that question without an answer created the vacuum in which the UA took control.

By the mid-2050s, the first UA president was elected: President John J. Howard, a charismatic and serious man who in every way upheld the values the party professed. The country was dangerously divided, and people believed Howard could unite everyone. It's hard to argue that they didn't do a damn good job of it, at least at uniting the vast majority of people. Hate crimes were so harshly punished that they quickly ceased. Under the Howard administration, if you were a hardworking citizen committed to raising a patriotic family in the way of the Natural Order, you were accepted. Although, he accomplished this not by celebrating and normalizing our differences, but by convincing people that each American was indistinguishable from the next. It was effective. Children were taught not to take pride in their different heritages, religions, or races, but instead to see themselves as the same. As American. No other subcultures would be tolerated. There was a pervasive feeling of wrongness in being different. Fear of rejection led people to shed any other identity.

The United America identity prevailed, but the cost was high.

If you didn't subscribe to the UA identity, if you didn't try to be *normal*, you were reeducated. Undocumented people were deported en masse. Borders were closed. Restrictions were levied against individual rights, trade, technology, and scientific advancement. After I was awoken it was difficult at first for me to tell who was considered normal or not as the distinction didn't follow the cultural rules I grew up with. It took years for me to learn the specific characteristics that make up an ideal United America, but a rural-living, God-fearing person with a lot of children seemed to be the core of it.

Not everyone was on board with this new vision for America. The states west of the Rockies banded together and refused to ratify the new United America constitution, hurtling the country into a civil war that turned into the North American War. Canada, furious with United America's new isolationist policies that tanked their economy, formed an alliance with the United Western States. Strengthened by their northern allies, the West successfully separated from the rest of the country, but Canada ended up losing a chunk of territory, including Toronto, in the war. Avon was part of the initial invasion and occupation of Toronto.

It wasn't an easy start for United America. They lost half the country and plunged into a major economic depression. But the North American War solidified the country's new identity.

Without the western states, the new ruling party used their supermajority in the Senate to fundamentally change the way the government functioned, starting with eliminating presidential term limits. As a symbol of unification, they changed the flag to one that replaced the fifty stars with UA insignia.

I'll never forget the first time I saw this new United America flag.

In the early-morning hours, we drove the long country road from Helen's house to the patrol station whose presence had derailed our journey the day before. In my haste to escape, I had dived headfirst under the floorboards and was lying on my stomach. Quite uncomfortable for the bumpy journey, but if I craned my neck just so, I was able to see outside through a small opening behind the van's wheel well. For miles, it was only road and sky. Snow-covered fields of crops. The occasional passing car, which made my heart pound with fear that the angry mob had caught up to us.

Helen will be okay, I thought to myself. *She has to be okay.*

And that's when I saw it. The red, white, and black UA flag waved mockingly atop a high pole. We had reached the patrol station that stood between us and the supposed safety of Wade Lovett and his refugee camp in Chicago. Shivers went down my spine. The American flag I knew and had pledged allegiance to every morning in elementary school was no more, replaced by this imposter.

It's funny how things change. Now when I see the old American flag, it looks strange. I hardly recognize it. As if someone reached into my memories and stole what was.

A loud knock made me jump. It was the signal from Gina that we were approaching the patrol station. In that knock was a not-so-subtle *Shut the hell up, or else*—an order I was happy to oblige. The van slowed to a stop. Avon crossed himself and said a small prayer. I simply held my breath as prayer had never much worked for me before.

I watched through the little gap as two patrol officers approached the van. I couldn't see much of them except that they both wore tan uniforms and had guns.

"Mornin', miss." The officer's voice carried a thick accent that was undeniably American but not quite from a region I could place. It was hard to make out the mumbled conversation between Gina and the two men. Blood filled my ears as nerves overcame me.

It had to go well. We had risked Helen's life. This had to work. Gina would show them Helen's transit permits and we'd be on our way. Two minutes, tops.

As the conversation continued out Gina's window, the other officer's slow footsteps wrapped around the van before stopping at the back door. The doors opened with a thud, and I had to keep myself from gasping. We were still hidden beneath the floorboards, but all that stood between us and discovery was the thin veil of a metal sheet. After the encounter with that boy and his father, I knew that we'd be killed if discovered.

A pair of black boots stepped up into the van. The officer started rustling around, inspecting the pink bakery boxes. Our cover.

"They got doughnuts, Vince!" Black Boots called out. The glee in his voice belied his youth. He was clearly younger than the officer speaking to Gina. Crumbs from a freshly bitten doughnut fell through the floorboards. Not a moment later, he jumped down out of the van and closed the doors. That was all it took. Doughnuts. We were clear. We were going to make it to Chicago after all. The three of us took a collective exhale.

Remember, I had never been in a situation like this before. I made the painful mistake of allowing hope to fill me. Since then, I've learned hope is the enemy. You make foolish decisions in pursuing the comfort of hope.

A radio crackled just outside the van. At first, I worried it was Gina's radio and that Wade's deep commanding voice would give the whole game away. Actually it was much worse.

A woman's voice broadcasted across the officers' walkies, "Helen's Bakery was raided this morning with a cargo van spotted fleeing the scene with suspected Awoken smuggled inside. Move to apprehend."

My heart jumped into my throat.

"Hands up! Get out of the van!" Vince, the more senior patrol officer, shouted. His gun was pointed directly at Gina, her face outside of my view.

"Hold on now, Officer," Damien said. "There must be some mistake." Even I knew his charms would do no good here. The doors in the front cab opened, and they both got out. They were about to die, and we would be soon to follow.

"Search the back again!" Vince shouted at his black-booted subordinate. Not a second later, the van doors flew open, and Black Boots jumped inside. He tossed the pretty pink bakery boxes around. I reached out for Avon's hand, but instead I grazed the pistol Gina had given him. I somberly realized that we wouldn't go down without a fight.

I thought of Max. I was tempted to retreat into another memory. To get far away. But I couldn't. I could only think of Damien and Gina and the danger they were in because of us. I locked eyes with Minnie, who was frozen in fear.

And then there was silence. For a moment.

The floorboard above Minnie ripped open, and light flooded into our hideout. Black Boots's gloved hand shot down and grabbed Minnie by the collar. He pulled the screaming thirteen-year-old from her hiding place. I reached for her, but Avon held me back. Black Boots hadn't seen us—only Minnie—and he was content with his one capture.

Damien shouted when he saw Minnie dragged out of the van, "Please don't!"

Vince didn't care. "If it's an Awoken, shoot it, son."

I readied myself to hear the thunderous gunshot that meant Minnie's death, but it didn't come. Avon quietly pushed the floorboard above him open and climbed out. He then gestured for me to follow.

Outside, Damien and Gina were on their knees, held at gunpoint by Vince. The younger officer held Minnie by the shirt, gun pointed at her head. This was Black Boots. He seemed almost as scared as Minnie, and only a few years older.

I looked to Avon. He always had a plan, a fact that would save my life time and time again, and this time was no exception. He slid his pistol into my hand. I shook my head desperately. Growing up in a time of frequent mass shootings, I hated everything that had to do with guns and had never even held one before. Of course, none of that mattered anymore. It was life or death. Avon reached over, turned off the safety, and placed my finger on the trigger. That was the only gun lesson I received. He slowly and quietly unlocked the side door, signaling me to go out on his cue. He then tiptoed toward the back of the van, where the doors still hung ajar.

Meanwhile, Black Boots fumbled with his gun as he withdrew a small blacklight device from his belt. He pointed it at Minnie's arm and revealed the numbered ID, branded into her wrist. "I got an ID tag here, sir," he confirmed in a wavering voice.

Vince cocked his gun, pointed right at Gina's head. "You goddamn Resurrectionists. It's an Awoken, kill it!" he ordered. I held my breath and looked to Avon for a cue. He was silent, not taking his eyes off Minnie.

"I . . . it's a kid, sir," Black Boots said with uncertainty.

"It's dead. An illegal. Shoot it!"

Finally Avon nodded to me. I squeezed my eyes shut and jumped out of the van with my gun pointed directly at the young officer. "Stop!" I shouted. It was enough of a distraction. Avon ran over and tackled the officer away from Minnie.

Vince spun toward me and fired. From the ground, Damien kicked Vince's legs out from under him, causing his shot to miss and shatter the van window behind me. Gina grabbed the dropped gun and unloaded before I could even blink. She pulled that trigger with all the rage she could conjure. Vengeance for Charlie Wells fueled that fatal shot.

Behind me, Avon and the young patrol officer were locked in a brawl. Even in his weakened state, Avon moved with a devastating grace. Black Boots was no match for him. In a matter of moments, the officer was pinned to the ground, his mouth pressed into the dirt and arm twisted behind his head. Avon's face was calm as he looked down at his captive. Unlike Gina, there was no anger in his gaze. He was a trained weapon.

Meanwhile, I couldn't look away from Vince. His eyes were still open. The darkness swirled behind his lifeless pupils. It recognized me. I shuddered and had to force myself to turn away.

Minnie ran over to me and wrapped her arms around my waist, sobbing and trembling. I soothed her and adjusted the wig on her head. All the while, I felt the cold presence of Vince's fresh corpse behind us.

Gina hustled over toward Avon. "Well done, Williams." The bloodied young officer held in Avon's unwavering vise grip came to terms with his fate. The realization that he was about to die was unmistakable. It oozed out of his every pore.

Gina lifted her gun and aimed it at him.

I don't remember walking over there. I just remember finding myself between Gina's barrel and Black Boots's head. Protecting him.

"Get out of the way, Rivers!" Gina was furious. Damien cautiously stepped toward me with a look of utter confusion that was echoed on Minnie's face, even behind her swollen, tear-filled eyes.

I cleared my throat. "There's been enough killing, don't you think?" My voice shook with uncertainty. The truth was that everything happening was so far out of my realm of understanding. I'd never seen so much violence, so much death. I thought it was my place to stop more from happening. Even though I knew he was on my side, Avon scared me. Gina scared me. At that time, I didn't know what to do with that fear except protect Black Boots from them. From us.

Gina pointed to Vince's dead body. "None of this would've happened if you hadn't snuck out of Helen's house. His blood is on you."

"That's enough," Damien barked.

Gina whipped around, her rage finding a new target. "Her? She's the one you've been fighting to find all this time?" She raised her gun again and pointed it at Black Boots, with me still in the middle. A poor disguise for her actual desire to point a gun at me. There I stood, trembling in fear, in between two people who hated me.

"Please," I begged before quickly discerning that mercy wasn't going to convince Gina. "He's more help to us alive than left dead on the side of the road. If we get caught again, we can trade him. They know about us now. Those travel permits mean nothing. We need him." I kept talking, offering more reasons to spare the stranger behind me, hoping that one of them would resonate with Gina. All I wanted to say was, *Please just let him live.*

Eventually Gina held up her hand for me to shut up. I did. She glared at both me and Damien. "Wade will decide." She stormed off.

The young officer behind me exhaled deeply. Damien brushed past without a word but squeezed my arm, which was still tingling with adrenaline. He and Avon tied up our prisoner and put him in the back of the van.

WE CONTINUED OUR JOURNEY to Chicago, now with a hostage in tow. There was no need to hide us under the floor anymore. If we were stopped again, our only hope was to trade Black Boots for our lives.

Avon wouldn't look at me. Only Damien made eye contact, but he didn't smile. He was trying to figure me out, trying to figure out why I would possibly want to save this man.

Looking out the shattered window, I watched this new world zoom by. A picturesque blue sky dotted with chirping birds hovered over lush fields. The landscape was broken up only by an occasional farmhouse that looked straight out of a pastoral painting. The highway was mostly empty, save for the passing pickup trucks. Billboards with ads from a world long gone were crumbling and faded.

The future continued to surprise me.

Life was good in this world for those who were wanted in it. It's just that I wasn't wanted. Coming to terms with that was the first hurdle I had to overcome. I never felt so alienated just for being alive.

Inside the van, Avon riffled through our hostage's pockets. He pulled out a small leather wallet and thumbed through. Some things fell out onto the floor, and I picked them up. One item was a picture of Black Boots and a girl. His girlfriend, I guessed. She was pretty. They looked happy.

Another item was a gun license on which I learned that Black Boots's real name was Ralph Jones and that he lived on Block A7 in Oak Lawn, not far from where I grew up. I wondered what that looked like now, how different Block A7 was from the neighborhood I once knew. I tried putting the items back in his pocket, but when I leaned in, Ralph lurched away from me.

"He thinks you're infected," Damien said to abate the confused look on my face.

"Cancer isn't contagious." *Maybe he doesn't know*, I thought. Some people don't. I reached out again, and once more Ralph cringed in fear of my touch.

"He doesn't think cancer's contagious," Damien clarified. "He thinks that *you* are contagious."

My brow furrowed. In Ralph's eyes was the same fear that I'd seen in that young boy, the same anger I'd seen in his father.

"I'm not going to hurt you," I explained sincerely.

In response, Ralph spat on my shoes. "Millions of folks died. Because cold cuts like you thought you deserved a second life more than the rest of us deserved a chance at a first one." His words pushed out through clenched teeth.

Minnie turned to Damien, looking afraid not only of the world around her but also of herself. "Is that true?"

"There was an infestation about a decade ago," Damien explained. "A new kind of drug-resistant microscopic fungus that wiped out almost a quarter of the world's population. Most people think Awoken are to blame since they seemed impervious to it. They think that the spores developed during the cryogenics process and then killed the living."

"Even though scientists proved that wasn't true," Gina added from the driver's seat, a chip on her shoulder at all times.

"Anarchist lies," Ralph grumbled.

"Everyone already hated the Awoken," Damien added, ignoring Ralph. "This just gave them an excuse."

Avon shook his head. "I knew some people were against cryo, but I never thought it could get to this," he said.

I tried to imagine the world from Avon's perspective. I felt like an alien on an unrecognizable planet. But Avon was only two generations removed from his time. His family might have still been alive.

We rode in silence for a while. I watched Ralph. He hated us—that much was abundantly clear—and though it took me a long time to name it, there was also disgust in his grimace. If he were given the opportunity again, he would shoot each and every one of us. There would be no more hesitation.

"We're coming up to the city limits," Gina announced from the front.

I looked out the window, and my heart broke. If this was Chicago, it was a mere shadow of the city I knew. Like Indianapolis, it was deserted. Only it wasn't Indianapolis. This was Chicago. My home. The place where I grew up, went to school, and fell in love with Max. It simply had been forgotten. My memories, my loves, my years, they were all gone. Replaced by vacant streets and eerie silence.

"How could everyone just . . . leave?"

Damien turned around. He saw the pain in my eyes. "The infestation. It took a long time to figure out what it was and where it came from, but it spread like wildfire through densely populated areas. So, people moved away from the big cities."

"'An Acre and a Purpose,'" Ralph stated proudly, regurgitating some propaganda campaign. "'Every person has a place.'"

"Even me?" I asked him.

"Every *person*," Ralph reemphasized. "God knows what you are."

Damien cleared his throat, uncomfortable. "The upside is that cities are now an ideal place for our camps. Even though the spores are mostly gone, people are still too scared to enter city limits. Everyone lives in small country towns now."

"The people who are left," Ralph punctuated.

"If you hate us so much, why didn't you just shoot Minnie?" I asked. Ralph lowered his shame-filled eyes. "Or why didn't that other guy just shoot Damien and Gina? If we're really that bad, he would've."

"He could've shot Minnie," Damien clarified. "I don't know why he didn't. But they couldn't have shot me and Gina. Not unless we shot first. He would've been arrested for murder. As citizens, we have a right to a humane arrest and a trial. Not you or Minnie or Avon, though."

I looked at Ralph and pointed to my wrist. "So, these numbers and the Frankenstein bolt in my head are all that separates us? Gives them a trial, and you the right to shoot me?"

"You died," Ralph responded, meeting my eyes. "Your life isn't valid. That's what gives us the right to shoot you. It's not killing if you're already dead."

The confidence with which he spoke rattled me. I turned back to the landscape rushing by, trying to make sense of this world I now inhabited, very much against its will. What Ralph didn't know was that I didn't want to be there just as much as he didn't want me there. I didn't want to be unwanted. Hated. Alone.

Then I saw it out the window. Something that made me forget about everything else. Most people would've barely noticed the faded and forgotten billboard on the side of the highway. But for me, it changed the whole meaning of my existence.

"Gina, stop the truck," I demanded. Gina didn't listen. She kept driving. I had to see it again. "STOP THE TRUCK!" This time, I didn't wait for her to obey. I grabbed the handle and flung the door open as the van barreled down the highway.

"Al, no!" Damien reached for me, but I jumped out of the van just as Gina slammed on the brakes. I tumbled down the pavement, entirely unaware of the scrapes and bruises left by the rough surface. Once I found my feet, I ran down the empty highway back toward the billboard. Behind me were the distant shouts of the others running after me, but I didn't stop.

And then there it was. Plain as day. I stopped running. I pulled the hot and itchy wig from my head and stared at the mammoth billboard, completely stunned. In the cold air, my heavy breath turned to steam.

Damien walked up behind me. "Alabine. I can explain."

The billboard was my face. A picture of me. My Instagram profile photo, actually. I remembered Max taking it. My face fifty feet tall. And my name. The slogan read "Alabine Rivers. One Life. All Rights." It was an old CryoLabs advertisement. The canvas peeled off the frame with age and disrepair, but there was no mistaking it was my face up there.

Furious, I turned back to Damien. Gina and Minnie stood beside him. Tears streamed down my cheeks. I tried to speak but couldn't. Minnie's mouth dropped as her eyes darted back and forth between the billboard and my face. "You're Alabine Rivers!" she exclaimed in the same way that someone would say, *You're Elvis!*

Gina stepped forward nervously, hand clutched around the pistol at her waist like a security blanket. "Get back in the van. We're not safe out here!"

I couldn't move. I could barely stand. "Why is my face up there? Why did you bring me back, Damien?!"

Gina had had enough. She pointed her pistol at me. Damien protectively jumped forward. "Gina, no!"

She didn't lower it. "Van. Now, Rivers."

I started laughing—it surprised me as well as the others. "You think that scares me?" I felt possessed. I was done with this nightmare. Done with the dead bodies and scared children. Done with the apocalyptic cityscapes and patrol stations. Most of all, I was done living in a world without Max.

I rushed toward Gina, took the barrel of her gun in my hand, and pushed it against my head. "Do it!" I screamed.

Damien stepped toward me cautiously. "Al, don't!" he pleaded with genuine care in his voice. My mind raced. I didn't want to be there. I wanted everything to go back to the way it was.

"Put me back under," I begged Gina, falling to my knees. She was my best hope. She didn't want me there either. "Put me back!"

"It doesn't work like that, Al," Damien said in the calmest voice he could muster. He knelt next to me. "Please. Let me explain."

I didn't want him to explain. I didn't want to understand. I shook my head violently, reaching toward Gina's trigger finger. She tried to pull away, but I wouldn't let go. I wanted Max. If he was in the darkness, that's where I wanted to be too. As horrible as it was, at least things made sense in there. There was nothing. I was nothing. That's what I wanted. I squeezed Gina's hand tight around her pistol.

And then the darkness came.

AN ACRE AND A PURPOSE

ARE YOU DISPLACED FROM AN INFESTED AREA?

ARE YOU A LAW-ABIDING CITIZEN?

ARE YOU INTERESTED IN ENROLLING IN A UA-SPONSORED
FARMER TRAINING SCHOOL?

THEN YOU ARE ENTITLED TO AN ACRE OF LAND!

DO YOUR PART IN THE FIGHT AGAINST DEVIL'S TOUCH.
RELOCATE TO THE COUNTRY WITH A LAND GRANT AND MONTHLY
STIPEND WHILE ENROLLED IN AGRICULTURAL COURSES.

ALTHOUGH WE ARE APART, WE REMAIN UNITED.

EVERY PERSON HAS A PLACE.
CLAIM YOURS.

6

THE DARKNESS WAS MUCH more temporary than I'd hoped.

A small red flower. My fingers traced the outline of its petals as my consciousness dragged itself back to the world. It looked like it came from the field of poppies where Dorothy fell asleep on her way to Oz.

Except this flower wasn't real. It was on the bedsheet covering the mattress. I didn't know where I was or why, but immediately I knew my name and remembered Max. This wasn't like the last time I was brought back from the darkness because this time I hadn't died. I was knocked out.

I tried to sit up too quickly, and a throbbing pain shot up the side of my neck.

"Easy. Let me help you." Damien was there. He put his arms around my back and lifted me up.

"Ouch" was all I could muster in response.

Damien sympathetically winced. "Sorry about that."

I reached up and rubbed my sore neck, bruised by the blunt force that had rendered me unconscious. "Something tells me this was Avon's doing, not yours."

Damien sighed and sat on the edge of my cot. "You really scared me, Al. I told you I would explain everything." He spoke like I had betrayed him. Oddly enough, I felt like I had.

My whole body ached. I did not have the energy to explain why I had held Gina's pistol to my head, to describe the look in the small boy's eyes when he realized what I was, or to convey how the darkness in Vince's eyes had called me toward it. I couldn't bring myself to articulate the crushing feeling of being so alone and not knowing how to live in this horrible world without Max. So I didn't say anything.

In our silence, I took in the strange room. The walls were cloth—mismatched cotton bedsheets stitched together into tent form. The sparse furniture that was there was unmistakably Ikea. A century into the future, and Swedish flat-pack furniture still reigned supreme. The dull warm air carried the taste of burnt wood and ash, and the lack of ventilation told me that it wasn't some forest outside the flap; we were inside a structure.

"Where are we?" I asked.

"We made it to the camp in Chicago," Damien replied. "And don't worry, that patrol officer is alive. He was brought to Wade. I'm sure they'll just detain him for a bit before sending him home." I grimaced as Damien pulled dirt out of the scrape on my knee. "Wade wants to see you now if you're feeling up to it." Damien had a hesitation in his voice.

"What I'm feeling up for is a large cup of coffee and binging TV in bed all day." As Damien's brow creased, it occurred to me that binging TV might not make any sense to him. "Never mind." As much as I didn't want to meet Wade Lovett, I had questions and Wade had answers. It was time to reveal the man behind the curtain. "I'll go," I confirmed. Damien nodded and stood. He seemed distant. "Is everything okay?" I asked. "You said Wade is one of the good guys, right?"

Damien's eyes widened with forced enthusiasm. "Yes. He is. He's important to us, to all Resurrectionists. And he's done a hell of a lot to protect the Awoken. He unified a movement that was disorganized and on the brink of collapse after the infestation. He's a legend." Damien took a deep breath and concluded: "He'll want to keep you safe. Just like I do."

There was a reverence, which I admired, in the way he spoke about Wade, but there was something else there too. He was holding something back.

Damien offered me his arm. As he pulled the tent flap open, I nervously clutched on to him, and we walked out together.

It was a parking garage. Makeshift tents lined the aisles as far as I could see. A large falling "IKEA" sign on the wall confirmed that the camp was constructed in the underground parking garage of an abandoned Ikea.

Despite the hundreds of people crammed into the concrete cave, it was eerily quiet. If people spoke, it was only in hushed tones. The electricity seemed to be working as people cooked in toaster ovens plugged into extension cords. Small fires made from scrap wood were used for warmth. Clothes hung to dry on lines stretching from tent to tent. Soot and mildew clung to the concrete walls and the area rugs that carpeted the floor.

As we walked down the main stretch, I noticed that the camp's population was mainly young adults in their twenties or thirties. Almost all of them were Awoken, as revealed by the metal implants behind their ears. A few of them were over fifty, but most were younger. Cryogenics was a game for the young who had the possibility of a full life in front of them. Some were bald or had hair that was still quite short, like me, while other Awoken had longer hair. Length of hair was an indicator of how long they'd been awake.

There were children too, some even younger than Minnie. Whatever plan for guardianship that had been put in place by well-intentioned parents before their deaths had been long forgotten. And as helpful and caring as the Resurrectionists were, they weren't babysitters. They were a militia. This world wasn't set up for these children, and I couldn't imagine why someone would want to wake a child into this kind of life.

Scattered among the Awoken were Resurrectionists. Dressed mostly in durable denim clothes like those Gina wore, they stood out due to the guns they carried. They were watching, protecting, and generally keeping order in the camp.

Besides me, there were 814 souls in the camp that day. That number would soon be burned into my memory forever.

Their eyes followed us as Damien and I walked through the endless rows of tents. I realized they were looking at Damien. We'd pass, and they'd smile and wave at him. He'd nod back, clearly well liked. I clenched on to his arm a bit tighter.

Eventually we arrived at a tent that was substantially larger than the rest. This was Wade Lovett's tent. Damien stopped outside the entrance.

"Are you not coming in?" I asked.

"You'll be okay. I've got some things to take care of, and Wade only asked for you. Don't worry." He spoke to me like I was fragile. I was. He pulled open the flap, and I walked in.

IT WAS A WARM and tidy room, sparsely decorated with a large wooden table in the center. In the far corner were two dark chairs atop a fur rug. The room exuded a very specific authoritative, masculine warmth.

A fitting environment for the man who stood at the center of the table. A strong, tall, handsome man with a hint of gray just starting to make itself known in his otherwise black hair and beard. I didn't need an introduction. This was Wade Lovett, the camp's leader.

Standing with him at the table were four others. The two men on the ends I didn't know, but the two people closest to Wade were Gina and Avon. Relief washed over me. I felt better, safer, near Avon.

They all looked up when I entered, interrupting their meeting. Wade smiled, immediately recognizing me. There was a small glint in his eye like he was looking at a shiny new weapon he couldn't wait to use. Even so, he was different from what I expected. Warmer, I suppose. With a kinder face.

"Well, hello, Ms. Rivers," he said, his voice soothingly deep. "Thank you for coming." He rolled up the maps that were spread across the table, then looked to the others in the room. "That'll be all for now."

The two men I didn't yet know began collecting their things. One was young and handsome, and the other was older and even taller than Wade. They couldn't keep themselves from staring at me, watching me curiously. Studying me. They walked out of the tent, followed closely by Gina, who left with little more than a glance.

Wade extended a hand to Avon. "It's been a pleasure. We're lucky to finally have you."

"Excited to get to work, sir," Avon responded, shaking Wade's hand enthusiastically. He had already been brought into the leadership's inner circle, which I was glad to see.

Avon went to leave, but I grabbed him with perhaps a bit more desperation than I intended.

He stopped, softened, looked me deep in the eyes, and squeezed my arm. "You can trust him. I do." His earnest tone comforted me, albeit only a little.

I nodded nervously. Then, before letting him go, I playfully whispered, "Did you judo-chop me or something?"

He chuckled. "Something like that." He left. I was now alone with this stranger, having no idea why I was there.

"How are you feeling?" Wade walked around his table and sat in the wooden armchair that might as well have been a throne. He gestured for me to sit in the matching one beside it.

"Tired," I replied. I felt so many things, but tired seemed the easiest emotion to convey. Wade laughed heartily.

Despite Avon's assurances, and as much as I wanted to, I didn't trust this man. He'd ordered Gina and Damien to lie to Helen about her dead daughter. He clearly was willing to do whatever it took to get his way, and there was no doubt in my mind that he had killed people before. I wasn't sure if he was like Avon, stoic and calm in the face of taking another life, or if he enjoyed the kill. Time would tell.

As I took my seat, I noticed a Japanese-style room partition in the back corner. It obscured a neatly made bed and a large desk with tangled electronic equipment on it. The microphone in the middle of the table led me to believe that this was the ham radio Wade had used to communicate with Gina when we were on the road.

Wade didn't speak right away. He was treading carefully. I felt his hesitation, like one would have before making the opening move in a chess game. I decided to make the first move.

"Do you have the cure for my cancer? Damien said you'd have it."

Wade pressed his wide fingertips together. "I thought we would, but things fell through. We used to have an abundant stockpile of medicine and Dreno shots given to us by our allies in Canada. Unfortunately, after President Redden took office in January, our supply lines were cut off. We've been burning through our stores ever since. But I have a plan. Tomorrow we will leave for—"

"I'm sorry, not to be rude, but I don't care about your new president, or your Canadian allies, or your plan," I responded matter-of-factly. "I had a plan. To be awoken when there was a cure for my cancer. If you don't have my medicine in hand, then I'd like to go back. Back under. I don't want to be here. Not in a world like this one."

Wade shifted in his chair. "Yes. Gina told me you felt that way. I'm sorry to say, you don't have a choice. We don't know how to put someone through the cryo process anymore. It's been illegal for half a century, and the technology has been lost to us. We hope to be able to do it again one day. For now, I'm afraid you're stuck with us."

"What if I just convince Gina to shoot me," I snapped back, surprising both of us with this threat. "I'm sure if I got her alone, without

Damien or Avon, I could annoy her into pulling that trigger. If I die, it will be on my terms."

Wade replied, deeply serious, "If you die again, you'll stay dead."

I bit my lip to keep it from trembling, but tears came to my eyes all the same. I didn't have the energy to keep up this facade. I was barely able to stay sitting upright. The dam broke.

"Since coming back to life, I've been shoved into secret compartments and screamed at and shot at! This camp looks like a freaking UNICEF commercial. My face is on a billboard! I mean, what kind of fucked-up world is this? And on top of all that, I'm still dying! There's a cure, but you guys don't have it. Either by bullet or cancer, it seems you only brought me back just to die again! Why the hell did you wake me up into this nightmare?"

"Because we need to turn the tide. We're losing, Alabine."

"Losing what?" I asked, trying to catch my breath between sobs.

"Everything. Since there have been people like you, there have been others who are frightened by your very existence. Those in power have stoked that fear to unify the common man against a common enemy." Wade pointed at me. "You. If the people of this country had their way, every single person who has been cryogenically frozen would be killed. Whether already awoken or not. The law of the land is 'shoot on sight.' No questions asked."

"Exactly!" I exclaimed through my tears. "So leave us be. Don't wake us up yet. Bring us back when it's legal again. When opinions have changed, and we aren't so hated. When we can actually live our lives."

Wade looked at me like he regretted something—or, no, he was disappointed.

"Opinions don't just change on their own. Someone has to fight for what's right." His tone carried a disbelief that he had to point this out to me. "There isn't any more time. This current president, Billy Redden, who you 'don't care about,' is hell-bent on extinguishing this movement and all of you with it once and for all. He had the audacity to destroy an entire cryo facility that held thousands of preserved bodies—people like you waiting for their second chance."

"Do you mean Eavesman Square?" I remembered my conversation about it with Damien at Helen's house. Wade nodded. "If cryo is illegal, why didn't they just do that years ago?" I asked.

"Oh, they've tried, but until Redden, they never were successful," Wade said with a weary expression. "For decades, the Supreme Court refused to sanction the decommissioning of cryo facilities. It's illegal to resurrect people, yes, but the bodies in those facilities paid good money for preservation, and so preservation couldn't be taken away. If anything in this country still holds weight, it's the mighty dollar. The buildings can't be touched." He shrugged. "Or they *couldn't* be touched. Redden's army of lawyers found loopholes: land preservation, danger to surrounding towns. Bullshit reasons. They've stacked the courts and are finally accomplishing what this country has been desperate to do for decades, whether people would admit it or not."

He dropped his head into his hands, revealing more of his exhaustion than he perhaps intended. After an exhale, he looked up. "The Awoken are the last remnant of a different world. One that revered technology and scientific achievement. Ideas that now terrify people. Redden feels it's not only his right but his sacred duty to rid the country of these old-world tombs."

The thought of hanging helplessly in my bag only to be executed because people were scared made me want to throw up. My life, all those other lives, snuffed out like candles without hope or choice or a fighting chance.

Wade leaned toward me. "Redden started slow. Testing the waters to see how far the public would let him go. Sure, people hate the Awoken, but it's hard to swallow stories of murdered children, regardless of who they are. Redden knows the public would much rather be blissfully unaware of what's really happening." Wade shook his head. "First they targeted small facilities with just a few hundred bodies.

When we would get word of a decommissioning, the closest Resur- rectionist camp would rush in and wake up as many people as they could. But the government still killed thousands. When there wasn't any public outcry, Redden proved he could get away with it. Then they announced Eavesman Square. It had far too many people for us to wake in time. So I decided to try and stop them. I thought we could stop them . . ." His words slipped away to regret.

"Helen said that innocent people died." There was empathy in my voice.

Wade took a breath, collecting himself. "Unfortunately, yes. Four- teen citizens died in the blast. And twenty-two are still missing. I'll carry each of their souls on my heart for the rest of my life. But eleven thousand six hundred forty-two Awoken were murdered when Presi- dent Redden decommissioned that facility. And he's promised he'll do more. Millions of Minnies, of Avons, of you, all set to be wiped out."

His passion was disarming. I couldn't hold eye contact with him any longer, having to avert my gaze like a scolded child. Wade squeezed my arm, encouraging me not to disengage.

"Make no mistake, Alabine. This was already a war, it has been since the beginning. Only now Redden has made it a genocide. And if we lose, millions will die." Wade paused and sat back in his throne. "Maybe you're right, and I shouldn't have brought you back like this, but we've run out of time and options. I thought I could stop them at Eavesman Square. I was wrong." He looked deep into my eyes. "You're our last chance."

"Me?" I quietly asked. "What can I do?"

"You have power in this world, even if you don't see it yet. People will listen to you. That's a privilege and an obligation. Soon you'll come to realize, like I have, that we will never be able to do this on our own." He let those words hang between us before continuing. "I do have a plan, as much as you may not care. I promise you that I will get you your cure. That and so much more, Alabine Rivers."

I sat there in silence, trying to process everything he was telling me. My fingers once again found themselves tracing the outline of the numbers branded into my skin.

"I never asked for any of this, you know." I'm not sure why I felt it necessary to say that to Wade, but I did.

He reached out and held my hand, stopping me from rubbing the numbers. He squeezed firmly, reassuringly. In that moment, I couldn't help but accept his stern comfort.

"The question is what are you going to do now?"

I thought. "I don't know. The way that boy looked at me. Even Helen at times." Lost in the memory of their faces, I cringed at the idea of this being my life.

"You know, Helen Smith was also skeptical at first. Scared and unsure, just like you. Despite those hesitations, she's done such good for this movement. Her daughter, Chris, was a passionate person who didn't even personally know any Awoken, but grew up during the infestation and saw the injustices firsthand. She couldn't sit idly by and watch. At a very young age, she joined us, and her mother eventually came around too. Like the rest of the country will if we only convince them."

"How? By lying to them like you told Damien to lie to Helen?" I asked bitterly.

"No. By telling them the truth."

It was obvious that Wade deeply believed everything he was telling me. I might have thought this was a chess game, but it wasn't. It was poker, and he was showing me his hand.

"Why do *you* do it? Risk your life for people like me?" I asked, trying to find a way to trust him.

Wade rhythmically tapped his knuckle on the armrest and strained his jaw, deciding whether he should reveal this intimate part of him. He eventually nodded to himself, having made the decision.

"My wife died. Toward the end of the infestation. We thought we had made it through the whole thing unscathed, but then . . . she got sick. They were so close to discovering a cure. She only needed a few more months, then they would've been able to heal her. Cryo could've bought her the time she so desperately needed, but it was illegal. I tried everything, absolutely everything I could, but I failed. I couldn't save her." Choking back his emotions, he tapped his knuckle faster and faster until he abruptly stopped. "Most of us aren't like Chris: honorable for honor's sake. Most of us are here because we want a kind of revenge; we've lost someone, or know someone who is an Awoken. Some of us are here because we don't fit into the mold this country prescribes, and this is our way of fighting back. We all have our reasons, but we're united in our belief that that every living thing deserves a long, fulfilling life. Nobody should take that from you, or my wife, or anyone, just because it scares them."

I watched him as he slipped away into the absence of his love. Grief gripped him. He looked fragile for the first and only time.

Finally I said, "I'm sorry." There were probably other, better words, but I couldn't find them.

"You came here asking me for a cure for your cancer, but I think you also hoped I could give you something that doesn't exist. You won't be normal ever again, Alabine. Not their version of normal. You're an Awoken. There's no cure for that. At least not one that fits in a bottle."

That truth pulled like a hook between my ribs.

He smiled kindly. "But maybe I have something for you that's even better." He walked over to a chest in the corner. A moment later, he returned with a small metal safe. After unlocking it, he took an item out of a velvet pouch and offered it to me.

It was a phone.

An iPhone.

Confused, I slowly reached for it. With a nod of approval from Wade, I pressed the power button. The familiar logo lit the screen. It seemed to take eternity for it to boot up. Then, suddenly, it did.

My mouth fell open.

On the screen I saw something I never dreamed I'd see again—a photo of me and Max. I looked up to Wade for an unspoken confirmation of what I knew to be entirely true.

It was Max's phone.

"I'm not sure what you remember," Wade said. "Or if you've been having Lucid Memories already, but hopefully this will help. Only you can open it. I'm not entirely sure how, but that's what I've been told by people from your time."

The phone was pristine. It looked exactly how it did before I died, meticulously cared for over the century. Yes, I knew how to work this phone—I had a million times before. I remembered the moment we decided to add each other's face IDs to our phones.

It scanned my face and, with a click, unlocked.

On the phone, I was astonished to find hundreds of photos, voicemails, and text messages within the six-inch device. On this phone was our entire life together. Not just a memory. This was real.

Wade sighed, relieved the phone had responded to me. "There's a message on it for you."

The only app on the first screen was Voice Memos. I opened it. The one at the top read "LISTEN TO THIS FIRST." Numb, I clicked play.

"Hi. It's, uh, me . . . Max. Duh."

I burst into tears and laughter. I forgot Wade was there. I forgot about everything and lived in those audio waves. I hadn't thought I'd ever hear Max's voice again, and there it was.

"This phone contains my entire life. Everything that happened after you died. A lot has happened." My mind raced with images of us together. Kissing and holding each other. Smiling. Crying. Living. "I always said you were special, but . . . Al, your death started it all. I didn't plan it. I just told the world how much I loved you. How could I have known? You became the face of a movement. Something so much bigger than either of us. The right to control our bodies. And we won. A *big* court case. I'm talking the Supreme Court, Al. It's now legal to bring people back from cryo."

My Max. Max Green—as in *Green v. Board of Health*. After my death, he used our love story to publicize and humanize the fight for cryogenic rights. Because of him, it became legal for the first time to bring a person back from the dead. He made my life mean something in a way that I never could. In a way that I never did.

"Things were supposed to get better—and they did. But they're sliding back now. People are scared. And that fear is turning to anger. This fight is just beginning. I know now that I can't do this without you. I don't want to do anything without you. So, I've decided to die."

His words hit me like a ton of bricks. Everything was spinning. "Assisted suicide is still illegal, so in order to be legally preserved, I had to get sick. Measles or dysentery, I'm not actually too sure what I was given. It's all very Oregon Trail." I couldn't help but laugh as tears blurred my vision. He was always such a dork. "I'm doing cryo so we can be together again. I love you. And I miss you. More than you will ever know." Then his voice deepened. "If you're listening to this, it means that I'm out there, dead, but waiting for you. Find me, Al. See you soon."

That was the end of the message. I looked at Wade not knowing what I could possibly say. Luckily he decided to go first this time.

"Yes, Ms. Rivers. I know where Max is. And we're going to bring him back."

PART
TWO

SUPREME COURT OF THE UNITED STATES

No. 1—October Term 2031

MR. MAX GREEN, MRS. MEI HAN, MR. HARPER CROWLEY, ET AL., PETITIONERS *v.* BOARD OF HEALTH OF CHICAGO, COOK COUNTY, ILLINOIS, ET AL.

Although it is not as far-reaching as some members of this bench feel is their entitlement, the decision of the majority amasses an obscene amount of power for the most dangerous branch of government, the judicial branch. It is not within the constitutional or ethical scope of this bench to determine what constitutes a life after expiration and what rights are due that soul.

The question of this case is quite simple: To what degree should man play God? We have seen time and time again that legality is not at issue here. It is not for courts to regulate the morality of men, and it is certainly not the role of this Court to claim to have knowledge of what happens to a man's soul after death. However, the majority's decision far outreaches even a semblance of restrained scope of the judiciary and has completely abandoned even the pretense of neutrality.

In this case, not only have we pruned away the sweet fruits of God-fearing trepidation, we have attacked the very root of life's meaning. By allowing mankind to revive deceased persons, especially with no other decree of law or congressional approval, which has been unsuccessfully sought, we have hacked away the mutilated plant's remaining healthy limbs and are left a withered and bare specimen.

Alas, since the majority of the Court feels that it is within our reach to allow such a condemnation of our humanity, I dissent.

7

IN ONE INSTANT, MY whole world broke open. I wanted to scream, to cry, to dance until my feet could no longer hold me.

Nevertheless, Wade continued.

After promising to bring Max back from the dead, he went on to tell me how important the story of Max's love for me was; important not only to Awoken and Resurrectionists, but to the whole country—even the world. Our love was that of legend, like Antony and Cleopatra. Max became the leader and founder of the civil rights movement that would become the Resurrectionists.

It all began a few years after I died when a promising new experimental treatment for lymphoma became available. Even though bringing someone back from cryo had become scientifically possible, it wasn't yet legal. Across the country, every state health board rejected petitions to resurrect preserved bodies.

Desperate for us to have a life together, Max wouldn't take no for an answer. He, along with others like him who had loved ones in cryo, sued for the right to bring us back from our frozen stasis.

Max, brilliant man that he was, knew it wasn't just about the court; it was about the people. He stepped into the spotlight and went on a publicity tour, telling the whole world about me and how I tragically died. He told the world how much we loved each other. We were star-crossed lovers with only death keeping us apart. In doing so, he convinced the world that I, and by extension everyone like me, was deserving of life.

With public opinion on his side, Max pushed *Green v. Board of Health* all the way to the Supreme Court. In October 2031, the court handed down a historic ruling declaring resurrection to be legal. An earth-shattering win for humanity, borne on the back of his love. And even those in the country who did not agree with the decision found inspiration in the love Max held for me.

Tragically, by the time resurrection was legalized, the promising new lymphoma treatment was found to be less effective than Max had hoped. It would've given me only a few more years. Max wanted a lifetime together. So he left me on ice, waiting for a real cure to be discovered. That wouldn't happen until 2063, long after Max froze himself.

Despite our personal destiny to remain separated in death, Max Green changed the lives of so many others.

It has always seemed a little ironic to me that Green became a name history would remember, like Roe or Brown. Max's great-great-grandparents gave themselves the name during the British occupation of Calcutta, but Max never much looked like a Green, something he used to joke about.

Regardless, because of Max Green, Alabine Rivers became a household name as the personal story behind a civil rights movement. Without me lifting a finger, my face became a symbol of freedom, hope, and choice for generations.

I only heard bits and pieces of what Wade was telling me. My mind couldn't get past the fact that we were going to find Max. My Max.

The possibility that I wasn't going to be alone in this horrible world consumed every part of me.

Our meeting was eventually interrupted with an urgent matter that Wade had to see to. I walked out of the tent in a stupor, relishing the comforting glow of Max's phone. The picture on the lock screen was from my best friend Andy's twenty-third birthday party. We were in her backyard. Edison bulb string lights, mason jars, and recycled wine bottles filled with flowers intimately decorated the lush garden. A real Pinterest wet dream of early-twenty-somethings trying to play adult and have a cocktail party. The rim of a champagne glass was at the bottom of the frame. I'd given Andy one of those karaoke microphones for her birthday, so for most of the party we belted out Adele and Disney songs while Max mainly stuck to Garth Brooks. That night, Andy officially gave Max the best friend stamp of approval.

As I stood alone in the parking garage turned refugee camp, the photo reminded me of everything I had lost, the subtle luxuries I'd had at my fingertips that I took for granted. The taste of grilled guacamole burgers overtook me.

I felt a squeeze and looked down to find Minnie's arms wrapped around my waist, her head buried in my chest.

"Gina told us you'd woken up, Al." She pulled away, remembering that I was not only someone she knew, but also someone she knew *of*. "Or should I call you Alabine?" She giggled. "This is so weird. You're Alabine Rivers!" It was odd to hear her say my full name like that. "My mom had a book signed by Max Green that had your picture on the cover." She studied my face. "You look different."

"I feel different," I replied as I squeezed her into a tight hug.

Then Avon walked up. We exchanged knowing smiles as I rubbed my sore neck jokingly. *When my pride is less bruised, I'll thank him*, I thought to myself. If he hadn't stopped my suicidal hysteria, I would never have learned about Max. Now there was one thing in this world that I needed to live for.

"So, you know?" Avon asked.

"Yeah, I guess," I said, running my fingers across Max's phone. Then I pretend-flipped my nonexistent hair and put on a sarcastic grin. "I'm like famous or something." Avon and Minnie laughed.

"I don't know about famous," Avon said. "But I did learn about you and Max Green in history class."

"You are definitely famous!" Minnie refuted. She then grabbed my hand and pulled me toward a large tent at the center of the parking deck. Awoken waited in a long winding line pouring out of the entrance. "I scoped out the food as they were laying it out," Minnie declared proudly. "Don't fill up your plate at the beginning with the salad and stuff. There's bacon and sausage at the end."

I was starving, and yet I couldn't bring myself to follow Minnie into that tent. "You guys go ahead. I'll catch up."

Minnie looked up at me, worried. "You sure?"

Avon recognized my expression. "Let's give her a moment, okay?" He absentmindedly rubbed his gold cross necklace as I did the same with Max's phone, turning it in my hand. Both were tokens from the lives that we were ripped from. All I wanted to do was dive into that phone. Learn everything I could about Max's life after I was gone. Dream about the moment when I'd see him again.

"Save me some bacon." I touched Minnie's cheek gently. She leaned the weight of her head into my palm. Avon squeezed my shoulder in solidarity before guiding Minnie off toward the food tent.

Not too far away, I spotted our cargo van. After Avon and Minnie were settled in line, I made my way to the respite of the van.

Avon's pistol was sitting on the front seat. I very gingerly moved it over before sliding in behind the wheel. With the bang of the door closing behind me, I had the privacy I needed. The silence was truly golden.

However long I spent by myself in that van poring over Max's life, it wasn't long enough. I don't think any amount of time would've satisfied me. There were thousands of photos. Hundreds of videos. Audio messages. Written notes. His entire diary. Max himself was inside this phone, and he'd left it all for me.

I clicked on a random photo in the sea of thumbnails. It was Max with a large group of protesters in front of the White House. He looked stoic and serene in the chaos. He had a beard, which I wasn't used to seeing. Max stared directly into the camera. In his eyes I saw a spark of something I'd never seen in him before: purpose.

After his sister died, Max had decided he wanted to become a doctor. Disillusioned in college, he thought he might be able to make more of an impact as a nurse. Then, after a semester of nursing school, he dropped out to become a medic. He said it was the only way he could actually save lives, but I believed that he kept limiting his dreams because his parents never pushed him. They were happy enough with their second-generation immigrant son being a medic. Max hated it when I blamed his parents for his choices. He often asked me if I was simply embarrassed by his career. I told him I wasn't, of course. Don't get me wrong, he was a great medic—he saved countless lives, just like he wanted. Maybe it was me projecting, but I believed deep down he wanted more. He deserved more. And finally, in that photo, I saw the version of Max who demanded more.

Standing next to a bearded Max was a pregnant woman, her mouth open wide, frozen for eternity in a guttural shout. I would later learn that this was Mei Han, Gina's great-grandmother. She was a co-plaintiff in Max's Supreme Court case, fighting for the ability to resurrect her husband, who was preserved a few years after me. This picture documented the roots of the Resurrectionists. The early pioneers in the fight for the rights of their deceased loved ones.

As I stared at the photo, I thought about what Wade had said: *We will never be able to do this on our own.* He was right. I needed Max, yes, but in staring at that photo, I realized that we all needed Max.

I scrolled back in the timeline of thumbnails with a specific date in mind: January 30, 2020. The day I died. There was a photo of our hands. Mine pale and lifeless. His lovingly wrapped around my skin and bones. That was the last photo of us together. I don't know if I was alive or dead.

The next photo was of Max standing in a park. There were people I knew but couldn't quite remember milling about around him. Max was in the distance, staring off in thought. Quite alone in a sea of activity. It was a stunning shot. I never found out who took it. I'm so glad they did.

It was my funeral. The funeral I'd planned for months. With no body to bury, it had to be unconventional. There were the paper lanterns I wanted lit in a circle on the ground. Some purple chiffon I'd picked out was draped across the tree limbs and blowing in the breeze. The whole scene was beautiful. Max did a great job. The guilt of leaving him alone flooded through me. He had already lost so much in his life. I hated that my death caused him more pain.

I was so wrapped up in the phone I forgot my surroundings and felt Max next to me in that quiet van. I felt at home.

Then there were gunshots.

At first, they sounded far off, perhaps on another level of the garage, but within a few short moments they were right outside. Automatic guns, and lots of them by the sound of it. I frantically looked around to see where they were coming from but could only see the cement wall in front of the van.

Then I heard, "Let me out." The voice was eerily close to me. I turned around to see the silhouette of a man.

It was Ralph. The goddamn patrol station guard whose life I saved had been tied up in the back of the van this whole time. Silently sitting in the dark, watching me as I cried over Max's photos.

There wasn't a moment to process as more screams erupted just outside the van. Before I could open the door to see what was happening, Ralph threw himself at the metal barrier that divided the cab from the back. I jumped. His face was pressed up against the thin sheet of metal that separated us.

"Let me out. I don't need to die with you." There wasn't fear in his eyes. Instead I saw confidence that he held the upper hand.

The screams outside the van were so loud I couldn't think. I had no idea what was happening, who was shooting or why. That very strong instinct to run away from the bullets was aching for me to listen to it, but instead I flung open the van door to go find my friends.

However, as soon as my feet touched the ground, someone pushed me back into the driver's seat and slammed the door shut. It took me a beat to get my bearings and realize that it was Gina. Blood pulsed from a bullet wound in her shoulder, but she showed no pain, only determination.

Through the van's closed window, she shouted something. Between the screaming and the gunshots, I could barely hear her, but I understood that she wanted me to drive away. To abandon everyone I knew in this world and leave.

"No! I'm not leaving!" I shouted back, unable to bear the thought of Minnie having a similar wound in her shoulder, or something even worse. I had to get to her.

Gina started shooting at someone behind the van, then lunged out of sight. Terrified, I grabbed Avon's pistol on the passenger seat and tried to remember my lesson—safety off.

Suddenly, a man in a black mask and full body armor tore open the door and grabbed me from behind. I screamed as he pulled me out of the van. I heard the bang of a gunshot, and the man released his tight grip on me, falling to the ground dead. Gina had saved me once again.

For the first time, I was relieved to see someone die. This world was already changing me. For better or worse, I'm still not sure, but I was adapting. Coldly studying the dead man, I realized from his uniform that these people were the same "them" we first encountered at the cryo facility. Behind the masks, these were UA soldiers, sworn protectors of the country.

I pushed myself up and ran toward Gina at the back of the van, and that's when I saw the entire floor of the garage. It was overrun with soldiers, and they were massacring the camp. Bodies strewn about the ground. Some Resurrectionists, but mainly Awoken. There were children lying facedown in pools of blood.

From what I could tell, they weren't just spraying bullets into the crowd. The kills, though massive in number, were targeted. I saw one soldier grab a young woman, an Awoken, who'd collapsed on the ground. She looked about my age, and judging by her hair length, she had been alive for a few months. The soldier studied her face. I thought he was simply going to help her up and let her go on her way, but he raised his gun and aimed it directly at her head. Her hands jerked up to shield her face. It didn't matter. He brutally executed her at close range.

Gina yanked my arm and pulled me out of my shock. "They're here for you," she shouted over the screams of terror all around us.

It didn't make sense. I struggled to focus on Gina and push the gunshots and pools of blood out of my mind. "How the hell do they know I'm here?"

"It doesn't matter. If you don't get out, they'll kill everyone."

It occurred to me that the soldiers were checking people before killing them. Checking them to see if they were me.

Gina grabbed my chin and pulled my face into hers. "They're taking prisoners to Montrose to interrogate them. Do you understand?"

"No . . . What?" I was so dizzy. Gina leaned out from behind the van and shot twice. "What's Montrose?" I asked but got no response. I don't think she heard me.

She pointed toward a caravan of unmarked black vans that were being filled with prisoners. I scanned the line of hostages for Minnie or Avon but couldn't find them.

"They're taking Wade!" Gina shouted.

That's when I saw him. Bloodied, restrained, still fighting as hard as he could until he was wrestled into the van. The Resurrectionist leader, caged like an animal.

"If they find you, there's no more reason for him or the others to be taken alive." Gina shot off a few more bullets before turning back to me. "Get out of here, Rivers!" She pushed me back toward the van and ran off into the badly lost battle. It was suicide, and she didn't even think twice. She was a true soldier who believed in her cause. Loyal to the end.

Channeling some of her courage, I didn't hesitate. I didn't think. Immediately I scrambled back into the van, tripping over the dead soldier's body on the way. How was I possibly going to escape without being caught? Or shot? Suddenly, I couldn't breathe again. However, this time it wasn't emotional paralysis; it was the cancer that was not so slowly eating away at my body. I coughed and gagged for breath.

"Turn yourself in."

I jumped at the sudden and nearby voice. It was Ralph in the back. I had completely forgotten he was there. Again. "The UA government will cure you. They wouldn't let Alabine Rivers die."

He was being too obvious. He thought he could play off my fear of dying to get me to sacrifice the lives of so many to save my own. It didn't work. I was resolved to get the hell out of there and save what lives I could.

As soon as I could take one shallow inhale, I turned the keys in the ignition and screeched toward the exit ramp. Ralph yelped as his body slammed into the side. I swerved to avoid a blockade of armored cars. Bullets ricocheted off the vehicle; then I felt a sharp pinch in my forearm. I'd been shot, but I hardly noticed at the time with all the adrenaline surging through my body.

Racing through the levels of the garage, I started smelling smoke and then saw flames all around me. The UA soldiers were lighting the garage on fire. Up ahead, there were other Resurrectionist vans trying to make their escape. It gave me hope that we'd actually be able to do this. Then one of the vans ran over a spike strip and crashed into a wall. We continued toward the garage exit, which was flanked by

Humvees. Another van was gunned down and burst into flames. There were still two other white vans like mine that continued to break through the barricades on each floor as we made our way to the surface.

The exit was heavily guarded. Charging through the relentless onslaught of bullets that shattered my windshield, the three escaping white vans rammed through the gate. My van flew through the air before slamming into the ground. The tires sparked against the asphalt, and I gripped the wheel with every ounce of determination I had, trying to maintain control. In the side mirrors, I saw four Humvees in pursuit. Two veered off to chase one of the escaped vans that went down an alley, one followed the other vehicle, and one stayed on my tail.

If this was the Chicago from my time, the streets would've been packed with traffic. But this was not that Chicago. The streets were completely empty. A flock of pigeons was the only obstacle I had to avoid.

I knew these streets. The Ikea was new, and there were other buildings that weren't there in my first life, but it was similar enough. I had gotten really drunk at the bar on the corner that I sped past. I was groped by a stranger at the movie theater where I took a sharp turn. Amid all the chaos, I was shocked by the emptiness of my hometown. It was a surreal dreamscape. Memories of friends and family, of mundane days and careless nights. Memories of a life never fully lived echoed through the empty streets as I whirred past.

We'd driven dozens of blocks, and I no longer saw our pursuer, but I didn't trust that we had successfully lost them. I remembered a cut-through to the highway out of town. It was one that traffic apps never even knew about, so I'd often take it to avoid rush hour. A small alleyway that connected one big avenue to another. It was coming up. It was so close: safety and freedom and just one tiny second to breathe. I swerved around the corner.

The rosebud rests perfectly on my porcelain sink. The red of the petals is rich and deep. It reminds me of blood.

Blood. Whose blood? Am I bleeding?

The petals are tightly entwined with one another. Perhaps one might be sad that this beautiful specimen of a flower will never bloom. That it was cut down in its infancy and never allowed to open and fully become what it was born to be. But I see something entirely different. I see petals that are never forced to separate. They can spend their entire lives feeling safe, wrapped around one another. They meet their end entirely unaware of the flower they could have become if life had gone differently. They're happy in their ignorance.

I look up from the rosebud and see myself in the mirror. Though I appear normal, I'm somehow surprised by the reflection. My long thick brown hair is pulled back into a messy bun. I'm wearing my favorite pj's: Max's shirt. It still smells like him, though, so I guess I haven't yet appropriated it as mine.

Then I'm drawn to touch a spot just behind my ear. Something's missing. The soft hairs electrify under my fingers. The thing that's missing unnerves me, and yet I can't quite remember what it is that's lacking. My fingers get tangled in my messy, unbrushed hair.

I pick up the rosebud. I smell it. It reminds me of Max. I don't need to be reminded of him. He's right there. I lean out of the bathroom and see Max sleeping in my bed. He's shirtless next to the ruffle of bed linens where my body was just a few minutes before. And where it will be in a few moments more.

But I take a beat to look at him—watch him as his chest rises and falls. Everything outside of the room feels just like a bad dream. This is real. This is happening. This is true.

Ouch.

I never saw the brick wall.

Slowly, things came back to me as my senses cleared. I heard sounds first. The rhythmic ding indicating the van door was ajar. The click of the blinker. The sound of DJ Raheem's voice on the radio:

"Weather up and down the coast will be sunny, though parts of the country can still hope for a white Christmas."

Eventually the blur of light filtered through my eyelids. I fell onto the pavement. Everything hurt. Even my palms burned when they touched the asphalt. I tried putting weight onto my left arm, and I collapsed as if it weren't even there. Using one arm, I hoisted my weakened limbs through the twisted door frame as my battered and bruised knees scraped against the rough ground.

A luxury apartment building was built right smack-dab in the middle of my cut-through. And I'd crashed right smack-dab into the side of it.

Flopping onto my back, I looked up at the sky. It was overcast and yet jarringly bright. It was easier to close my eyes. I must've fallen asleep because when I opened my eyes again, the sky was noticeably darker. Almost dusk. I had lost track of the days now. In my old life, I was obsessed with time. How old I was, how long until summer break, how much time I had left to live. Now time seemed like a nuisance.

My body was running purely on adrenaline at that point. I pushed myself to a feeble stand. Damien had said that I had weeks before the cancer caught up to where it was when I died. I was confident this crash would speed up that timeline.

The pursuing Humvee never found me. I cradled my wounded arm and finally saw the gunshot wound—a deep gash along my forearm with burn marks on either side. It sat just above the outline of the numbers that had been etched under my skin. The bullet had grazed my arm and luckily hadn't gone through. It had mostly stopped bleeding, but it still hurt like hell.

In the sky, a pillar of black smoke rose from the direction of the garage. There was a smell in the air that I'll never be able to forget. So many people brutally murdered. Burned alive. The tragedy washed over me, and I started to panic. I had to push the feelings down. I couldn't take it all in. Not yet.

If I ever doubted who to trust, I didn't anymore. I knew everything I needed to know about the "they" Damien had referred to. "They" were monsters. The United America government was perpetrating mass genocide in broad daylight. I swore that they'd pay for what they did.

Shivering from the cold, I looked around, not having any idea what to do next. No one was coming to save me. Not Damien. Not Wade. Not Max.

Shit, I thought, *the phone*. I threw myself back into the van. Thankfully, it was there among the shattered glass. Thinking to save the power, I turned it off.

The van was obviously undrivable, so I looked around for supplies that I could take. I had to get moving, and quickly.

Under the seat next to the phone was the pink and poufy dress Gina had worn on our drive from the cryo facility. I needed a bandage for my arm, so I went to rip the dress but quickly thought better of it. Unlike the bloodstained white dress I wore that Damien had given me, Gina's dress was clean. I wrestled my way into it, then ripped up the fabric of the white dress and used that to bandage my arm. The long pink sleeves held the makeshift bandage tight.

Next to where I found the phone and dress on the floor among the shattered glass, I saw my blonde wig. Under that, I found Avon's pistol.

I checked around the cab for any other useful supplies. There was a single Dreno shot in the glove compartment, which I immediately gave myself. The relief was instantaneous.

Just then, I heard moaning from the back. Ralph. I'd forgotten about Ralph. First, I considered leaving him. *But leave him to go where?* I thought. The only souls I knew in this incredibly dangerous world were either dead or captured. Ralph was all I had. The idea was fucking depressing.

The phone in my hands was a reminder that I had Max too. I only had to find him. He would know what to do. His purpose in life had been to make sure I could live again, and now it was my purpose to bring him back. For everyone. I didn't know where Max was, but Wade did. The image of him being hoisted into the black van flashed into my mind. Wade was in Montrose, so that's where I had to go.

I grabbed Avon's pistol.

The van doors were crumpled from the crash, but I was able to pry them open. Ralph lay there on the floor. His hands were tied. A few remaining pink boxes from Helen's Bakery were strewn about. Ralph had dried blood on his head. He squinted as his eyes adjusted to the rush of early-evening light. Then he saw me. Blonde crop-cut wig firmly in place, standing tall and assertive. Looking like a badass. At least that's what I hoped he saw. I needed his respect if I was going to convince him to help me. And the only way I thought I could get that was through a healthy dose of fear.

"Get up." To my surprise, he listened and pushed himself to a sitting position. He looked at me for my next command, I hesitated, and in that hesitation, he began to see through my charade. He leaned forward with a slight smile, slowly building the courage to take me on. I saw it, and I had to shut it down.

So I pointed the pistol at him before he had a chance to speak. My hands trembled. I knew I wouldn't be able to still them, so I didn't waste any effort trying to hide it.

Ralph threw his hands up. "Whoa! Wait a second. Do you even know how to use that thing?"

"Do you want to find out?" The power dynamic was shifting. Guns tend to do that. "Those black vans back there, they're taking my friends to Montrose. Where is Montrose?"

Ralph scoffed. "They're not your friends. They're just using you. They're terrorists, Alabine Rivers."

The heat of anger flooded my face. "Don't say my name. You don't get to say my name." The anger flowed from my face down my arm and to my finger. I cocked the gun. It would've been so easy to shoot him. Until that moment, I always thought that only bad people could shoot someone. It would've been so easy to take his life right then and there.

I didn't shoot him. Instead I deepened my voice. "Tell me where Montrose is."

"North. Outside Milwaukee. It's a big government center. You'll never make it there."

He was right. I didn't see how I could possibly make it to Milwaukee on my own. I wasn't strong enough. I didn't yet believe I was strong enough. When I was young, my aunt often told me that I couldn't do anything on my own. Her words still haunted me. I needed Max to help me die. I needed Damien to bring me back. I had no faith at that point that I could do much of anything by myself.

Although I hated to admit it, I needed Ralph. The world now worked very differently from how it had when I knew it. I needed a guide and the protection I'd get by just being with him.

"You'll take me," I confidently commanded.

He looked me square in the eye. "I'd rather die."

Slowly, I crouched down and got directly on his eye level. His breath quickened as I leaned in closer. "You don't know what death is. It's a void. A nothing. There's no memory, no thought. But there's still time. It's not that you stop existing. You do exist, just as nothing. Trapped forever as the darkness consumes you. I know what death is. Trust me when I say, you wouldn't rather die."

In Ralph's eyes, I saw fear overtake his stubbornness. And yet still, with a tremble in his breath, he replied, "I won't help your kind."

So I tried a different tactic: an out-and-out threat. "Will you help that pretty girl? Block A7, Oak Lawn." It was the address I'd seen on his ID card. A new worry filled his eyes. I smiled, finally feeling like I had the upper hand. "Oak Lawn is a lot closer than Milwaukee. Bet I can get there all by myself and find her with no problem at all." His shock told me my threat was working.

"You're bluffing. You wouldn't hurt her." He studied me like he never had before. Trying to read me. "You're not good at this."

"I'm good enough."

I reached toward him. He scampered back as quickly as he could. He was exponentially more scared of me infecting him with the supposed fungus I carried than he was of the gun. And I played him perfectly.

"Please. Don't touch me," Ralph said quickly, trembling. My hand was only inches from him, and he was backed into a corner.

"It's easy to be brave if it's only your own life at risk; it's much harder to risk the lives of those we love."

Eventually Ralph nodded. "Okay. I'll take you."

I'd won. I don't think I'd ever convinced anyone to do anything before. I felt a rush of pride. With Ralph's help I would find Wade, and he would take me to Max.

Once I stepped back, Ralph safely wriggled his way out of the van, still handcuffed with a zip tie. He stared at me. I stared back. Our tenuous partnership was by no means ideal, but I felt better knowing that someone was going to be by my side. Even if it was the enemy.

I was already a different person than that scared girl Damien woke up. I knew what I had to do. And of course, in the back of my head, I knew I had saved Ralph's life before. Surely that must've meant something to him.

My eyes softened. "Okay then. Which way?"

8

WE HEADED NORTH OUT of the city on foot. Every car we passed, I checked the ignition for a key. My hope was to drive to Milwaukee and skirt through checkpoints using Ralph's badge. Unfortunately, while some cars were unlocked, none had keys, and I most certainly didn't know how to hot-wire a vehicle.

After an hour or two of walking, I was exhausted. I needed sleep. What I really needed was to not have cancer, but sleep would also do. I hadn't slept properly since I was dead. The relief from the Dreno shot had started to wane, and with it the bloody coughs resumed. If I didn't stop somewhere soon, I was going to collapse. It wasn't just the cancer and crippling exhaustion; I needed a moment to breathe, to think, to process. I would've just found some abandoned building to camp in, but I didn't know what to do with my captive. Looking at Ralph, I could tell he needed rest too. It was hard to believe that it was only that morning I had stepped between him and Gina's gun.

I dragged both of our tired asses through the empty dark streets on the outskirts of the city, looking for someplace safe to stop. Occasionally, after I coughed up another gross clump of blood, I caught Ralph looking at me with a hint of sympathy. Maybe there was some humanity left underneath that handsome Nazi Youth exterior. I was desperate to find it.

With each passing block, it seemed less and less likely we'd find a car to drive to Milwaukee, and thus less and less likely I'd get to Wade in time. I allowed myself to believe that Avon and Minnie, and maybe even Damien, had also been taken prisoner because the thought of them burning alive in that garage was too much to bear.

A few miles out of the city, we came across train tracks. We followed the tracks until we got to a rural train station. It was small but pristinely maintained. The schedule was printed on a sign. There was a North Midwest line that left the next morning at 8:05 a.m. and would take us exactly where we needed to go—Montrose.

Nearby I found an unlocked old Chevy parked behind a building. With a plan for the next morning settled, I decided to shut Ralph in the trunk. He was less than happy about that decision.

"I'll suffocate," he pleaded.

"Just don't." My retort wasn't very clever.

I popped the trunk and ushered him in. After making sure he was locked up tight, I tucked myself into the backseat. It wasn't my first time sleeping in the back of a compact, so my body easily slid into the grooves of the worn-out cushions.

I took a breath. Then another. My arm ached. In the quiet, my brain finally processed that I had been shot. It didn't feel the way I had thought it might. The wound burned, almost like I could still feel the heat from the bullet radiating through my skin. The same question kept circling around in my head: *Can this really be my life?*

Though I desperately wanted to sleep, when I closed my eyes, the horrific image of all those dead bodies lying on the ground in the parking lot filled my head. I was overcome and could no longer hold back my tears. Those people died because of me. All of them. The children.

Those 814 souls in that camp were plowed through like weeds so the UA soldiers could find me.

I had no idea, yet, how many had died or were captured or if any escaped. I held on to a sliver of hope that Minnie was in one of the vans that broke out of the garage and made it to safety. Or, if she was captured, that one of the men behind the intimidating black masks and full body armor wouldn't be able to bring himself to torture a child.

My tears were for me too. For being brought into this nightmare. I didn't want any of it. I didn't choose it. Maybe it was stupid of me to think I'd wake up and just continue my life like nothing had happened, like I hadn't died. The hate in Ralph's glare haunted me. That I had to hold a gun to his head to get him to help me was devastating. To him, I wasn't human. To him, my life wasn't worth his help to save. What kept me going was the belief that Max and I would be reunited. That thought made everything worth enduring. I had to keep living—for him.

As the trauma from the day sank into me, my sobbing became uncontrollable. Like a junkie, desperate to survive the night, I pulled Max's phone from my pocket with a trembling hand. After turning it on, I scrolled through the videos, picking random ones that fell under my finger, needing to see his face, his smile. Those eyes.

One video I watched was him sitting in our living room and talking diary-style about a terrible date he went on. He was blaming me because I made him promise he'd try and find someone else after I died. He ordered the fish because she ordered fish, and he hates fish, so he didn't eat it, which made her feel self-conscious, so she didn't eat. Neither person said more than a few words the whole time, and now he was on the floor of our apartment eating a taco from our favorite truck down the street.

Even through the unrelenting sadness, I laughed.

After that, I watched countless videos and photos of Max leading rallies, giving speeches, and inspiring crowds of people. It was a side of

Max I always believed was there but never truly saw for myself. He was a leader changing the world, like the leader I had always wanted to be.

If only the Max I saw in the phone were next to me in that old Chevy, he would know exactly what to do next.

Eventually I fell into a restless, nightmare-filled sleep.

THERE WAS SCREAMING, AND the world started shaking. I woke up drenched in sweat, the ghastly shrieks rattling in my ears. At first, I thought they were the screams of the children being burned alive; then I realized it was Ralph in the trunk, shouting at the top of his lungs and kicking. The whole car jerked with each strike. I bolted upright, only half remembering where I was. My eyes were swollen from crying myself to sleep. I heard a voice—a man just outside the car. Terrified and caught in that haze between dreaming and reality, I jumped out of the car. It was already light out, clearly later than I had intended to wake. And it was very cold. Ralph's kicking and shouting intensified. I looked around for the man I'd heard but didn't see anyone. It was just as empty as it had been the night before.

"Here for you. All day. Every day. We will remain."

The voice was familiar. I looked up to where the sound was coming from and saw a billboard. It was a brightly colored ad for the radio station UA52 with a picture of a man whom I thought was LeVar Burton but then realized was actually DJ Raheem. His face, like his voice, exuded a serene, innocuous calm. A much-too-loud speaker at the base of the billboard was broadcasting the phrase on a loop to the now obsolete morning rush hour. I breathed a sigh of relief.

Clearly unaware the muffled voice he heard was an unmanned recording, Ralph continued shouting for help. When I opened the trunk, he frowned, realizing that in place of his would-be daring rescuer it was only me, silhouetted against the morning sun.

We were about half a mile from the train station. I pushed Ralph to walk quickly, not knowing what time it was and how soon the train would be coming. Feeling the dried blood on my face and seeing Ralph's similar state of dishevelment, I decided we needed to clean up so as not to draw attention.

There was a water spigot down a small alleyway within sight of the train station. I turned on the valve, sending a gush of cold water into my hands.

"Go on then." I gestured Ralph forward to the water.

He looked at me. There was a glint of appreciation in his blue eyes. "Thanks," he said, his voice lifted. It was the first we'd spoken to each other all day. After our quick rinse, we both were respectable enough to pass by unnoticed. Without the dirt and blood, he looked like a normal kid, not some evil villain.

To get to Milwaukee, I needed his help. I knew that, but it was more than that; I really needed him to *want* to help me. Within that hope was my desperation to find a semblance of decency in these people.

I offered him one of Helen's doughnuts, now stale, that I had stashed in my pocket. He took it gratefully and shoved it in his mouth, hardly chewing before he swallowed it down.

"Thanks again. And for yesterday. For stepping in front of that gun. I should've said that earlier." He wasn't looking at me, only staring at the doughnut crumbs on his fingers, but I accepted his sincerity all the same.

I didn't say anything, worried if I said or did the wrong thing I would scare away his humanity again. My gaze turned to Ralph's zip tie handcuffs. "You'll need to take that off."

"I'd love to. How do you suggest doing that?" Ralph held up his bound hands. I looked around for something sharp, but the streets were surprisingly clean. The only thing was the water spigot and a pipe coming out of the wall.

"That." I pointed to the pipe. "Wedge yourself in there and pull them apart so you can slide your wrist through."

Ralph scoffed.

"I wasn't joking. Here—" I stepped toward him, and he scurried away from me, frightened. I held up my hands as a signal that I would respect our truce and not touch him. I softened my tone. "Then do it yourself. Quickly, please."

Ralph cautiously made his way over to the extruding pipe. It took him a while, struggling against the metal to pry his wrists free. He was trying—I had to give him that—and when he finally succeeded, he didn't run. The Dreno had worn off entirely, and my body was screaming with pain, so I appreciated it more than he knew.

As we approached the small station, the train was already there, sparkling in the sun. At this point, I was no longer surprised and instead found comfort in the fact that things in this world looked an awful lot like they would have in my time—except cleaner. A woman in a quaint stewardess uniform and heels stepped off the train and flipped a sign from "Arriving" to "All Aboard."

I adjusted my wig, making sure it was securely on, felt for the pistol hidden in my pocket, and then headed for the old man in the ticket booth, Ralph trailing just beside me.

"Just don't say anything, okay? If I get a hint of something going wrong, I'll run straight for Oak Lawn."

"Rebecca," he said. "If you're going to threaten her life, might as well know her name. I was supposed to propose to her next week, you know." This bit of personal information surprised me. It was like we were friends. I missed having friends.

"You still will. This will all be over soon." I held out my hand. "Wallet." Ralph reached in his pocket and gave it to me.

The old man in the ticket booth was reading the newspaper. He didn't look up when we approached. My heart was pounding, but I plastered on a smile.

"Hello, sir. My boyfriend and I would like a ticket to Milwaukee. Or two tickets, please. One for each of us." Not my most convincing, but my voice didn't shake, thankfully. The old man plucked his gaze off his paper and looked up at me quizzically. I froze, smiling so wide my cheeks ached.

"There's no stop in Milwaukee, miss," he said with a suspicious leer. *Shit.* I knew that. All cities were basically shut down—why would I want to go into the city?

Feedback from the loudspeaker interrupted our awkward misunderstanding. *"All aboard for 8:05 North Midwest."* A few melodic bells signaled the end of the announcement and the imminent departure of our transport.

"Right. Montrose," I corrected, remembering our actual destination.

The old man's intense gaze was riddled with suspicion. "Two thousand."

It took me a moment to understand him. "Two thousand dollars?" I asked, unable to hide my surprise. I opened Ralph's wallet, hoping there'd be very large bills, but there were only quarters.

Before I had time to freak out, Ralph took his wallet from me and said, "Here you go." He handed two silver coins to the old man. It was then I noticed they weren't quarters. They were larger, like silver dollars, and had a big "1000" stamped over the UA symbol. I couldn't believe it. Ralph was helping.

After the old man begrudgingly handed us our tickets, we hustled onto the train and quickly sat in the two closest seats. The train lurched forward and pulled away.

I gazed out the window at the distant city I used to call home. It looked just like it had before. The same skyscrapers stretched above the sea of buildings. However, the eerie stillness made it clear that I didn't belong there anymore. Not in this city. Not in this century.

"Apologies for stepping in back there, miss." Ralph smirked, having a grand time mimicking the old man. "Just thought you could use a little help."

"Thank you." I meant it. He paused, seemingly touched by my earnest response, then nodded. I thought that perhaps it wasn't so hopeless to believe some part of him was still good.

The train ride was two hours to Montrose, where the government center was. We were finally on our way. The only issue was that I had no idea what I'd do once we got there. I needed a plan.

Max always had plans. It's why I thought he'd make a fantastic doctor if he could only believe in himself long enough to try. I wondered what Max would do in this situation but came up with a blank. It was hard to picture him in any sort of trouble, running from the law. If I wasn't living it, I'd not be able to imagine it for myself either.

The early-morning light filtered through the train window. It was quiet. We had boarded at the first stop, so we shared the commuter train with merely a handful of other passengers. Ralph quickly dozed off, exhausted from his restless night in the trunk of that Chevy. It was quiet. The only interruption to my thoughts was the ever-more-familiar voice of DJ Raheem, softly projected through the train's speakers.

"Hello, good morning, and good day, my fellow citizens. What a be-a-utiful day it is, whether you find yourselves basking in the sunshine-drenched plains or sipping a cup of warm tea listening to the pitter-patter of icy raindrops along the eastern coast. Either way, this promises to be yet another wonderful Tuesday in our great nation."

His narration and the ensuing light piano scored the scene passing outside the window. A sprawling countryside with rural communities every few miles. The train stopped at each one, and more passengers ambled on. These towns were very similar to one another, similar to Helen's town. Quaint. Rural. Idyllic. Crops in various stages of harvest stretched from farmhouse to farmhouse. Tractors and trucks seemed the preferred mode of transportation. On the train, the commuters dressed in sharp business suits discussed their farms back home, complete with a cow or two.

In between these sparsely populated towns, literally in the middle of nowhere, were massive corporate complexes. Little towns themselves, each named after a corporation. Some that I recognized: Coca-Cola. Tesla Ford. And some that I didn't: Elias. Patriot Manufacturing. Not only had the people moved out of cities, but businesses had too. These massive offices were connected to the towns that supplied their workers via the well-established train system.

People made their daily commutes from their country homes into the corporate complexes that still ran the world. They completed early-morning chores, then went to their manufacturing or sales jobs. Younger single women were a part of this dance in proportion to the men, but married women were decidedly absent. I later learned that once women started a family, they were promoted to head of the household, even receiving a government-issued salary, and would stay home to care for the homestead. It was a different way of life than what I had known, to say the least. The mundane desk jobs that inundated my time had faded away for this new kind of living. The middle class was thriving in a way it never had in the history of America. People seemed happy.

It was the first time I got to see the men and women of this new world—really see them—not as an Awoken but as one of them. I wanted to understand more of this world I was trying to blend into. What struck me first was how everyone seemed so similar. There was no poor town versus rich town. There was no white-collar worker versus blue-collar. Not that I could see, anyways. Outwardly, there was no class hierarchy at all. Everyone was comfortably middle class.

The commuters even all dressed alike: the men in their nice suits, thin ties, and brimmed hats; the women in their effortlessly elegant dresses and stylish uniforms. They all talked and read their newspapers as the train glided through the pristine landscape.

After dozens of stops, I eventually came to notice that amid all the uniformity, there was quite an apparent racial diversity. Black, brown, and white people—practically clones in every other way—boarded the train in equal droves. Pleasantly surprised, I wondered if the systemic segregation and divisiveness that had permeated the country in my first life was miraculously a thing of the past.

It's a peaceful world out there except for this nonsense. Helen's words echoed in my mind. Maybe she was right. Maybe United America was truly united.

Ralph stirred from his sleep and looked at me. There was less hate in him now. He seemed more perplexed than angry with me.

"There's such diversity here," I noted to him, my reluctant tour guide in this strange world.

"What do you mean?" He looked around with a cop-like suspicion.

"There's so many different . . . kinds of people," I clarified uncomfortably, worried that I was acting ignorant in some way.

Ralph snorted. "There's no diversity. We're all American." He sat back in his chair, satisfied that all was well.

"So am I," I responded.

Without a word, Ralph turned away to his window, so I turned to mine and watched Helen's peaceful world pass by. I couldn't help but marvel at the part of this world that was untainted by the horrors I'd experienced the last few days. It seemed impossible that the two worlds coexisted, this one of racial harmony with a booming middle class and my world of guns and fear. What I didn't fully understand yet was how, in fact, this peace could only exist because of those horrors. If only the people in my train car were confronted with what had just happened in Chicago. If only they knew what was sacrificed for their happiness.

The train continued along. The closer we got to the Montrose terminal stop, the more people boarding the train wore white coats with a "Montrose UA Center" logo stitched on the back. ID badges that touted the UA insignia dangled on lanyards around their necks.

The first man I saw in a Montrose Center uniform was an older man, maybe mid-sixties. He was clean-shaven, and wore a simple hat that flattened down what was left of his gray hair. I watched him for a while, expecting a cunning government operative of the place that had imprisoned Wade, but he was just a simple man, reading his newspaper like the rest of the men on the train. He probably was a dad, maybe even a grandad. His daily commute was more than an hour long.

And still, I wondered whether if I revealed who I was, he'd shoot me then and there.

When he looked out the window in boredom, I peeked over his shoulder and saw the headline on his newspaper: "President Redden to Christen National Park." Although I wanted to read more about this man Wade hated so much, the page was turned to an article about the winners at the county fair.

After more than ten stops, I began to find my mind wandering. I was still very aware that I had to keep an eye on my hostage, but the passing trees lulled me into a feeling of security. Ralph had fallen asleep again. I watched him breathe slowly and rhythmically as his eyes fluttered with a dream. The sun-warmed window invited me to lean my cheek against it. Raheem had introduced a new song that spotlighted a smooth saxophone whose notes slid easily into my ears. My body still ached. From the crash. From being shot. From being brought back from the dead. I owed myself this moment of peace.

I didn't mean to, but I thought about Max. And then, before I knew it, I thought about *Rosebud*.

There are butterflies in my stomach as I stand outside the two-story Victorian off Elm Street. The bright robin's-egg blue paint has faded to a muted gray that's chipped around the windows. The spring days are starting to stretch and offer a colorful glowing sunset at dinnertime. Which is why I'm there at the Victorian off Elm. Dinner.

But I can't have dinner. I'm not supposed to be here. I need to be watching. I can't remember what or who. I shouldn't—

Max squeezes my hand, a bit tighter than usual. He's nervous too. We smile at each other with an unspoken *Here we go*. He looks so handsome tonight. I have a sinking feeling in my stomach that I will need to cling on to this memory someday. So I take in every fading flicker of light as it streaks across the lawn. I take in the smells, the feel of Max's hand.

He leads me up the porch stairs to the large stained-glass entryway. He opens the door and walks right in, but I stop at the threshold. He turns back to me with his hand extended.

"You can't back out now."

I'm not backing out, though it's not a bad idea. I'm just stunned that he so confidently walked into the house without even a knock. I haven't had that kind of freedom since I was seventeen and lived with my aunt, before I moved out. Since then, I've always had to knock before entering a house I don't live in. Not here. Here, Max is always welcome. And so am I now, I hope.

Inside it smells divine. A perfect balance of sweet and spicy aromas fills the house. Instantly I'm transported to another world. The striking decor of bright rugs and paintings with gold accents only intensifies the sensations. A statue of a Hindu god peers skeptically at me over his flute.

Max and I have yet to really have the race talk. He's mentioned his Indian heritage as backdrops to stories, but never like, *Hey, so I'm Indian and you're white, let's discuss.* I think about it, of course, but don't know how to bring it up without seeming insensitive. After our second date, my best friend, Andy, told me, "You guys will have the cutest babies." I spent the next few days picturing our adorable brown-skinned, blue-eyed babies. I don't even have blue eyes, so I'm not really sure where that idea came from. A part of me wonders if it's kinda wrong to fantasize like this, which is probably why I don't talk to him about it even though we talk about everything else.

A woman's heavily accented voice shouts from another room, "You're here already?" A short woman dressed in jeans and a colorful sari appears in the hallway. She exudes motherliness, loving and warm with just a dash of judgmental expectation.

Max's hand releases mine. He bounds forward and wraps his mother in a big hug, lifts her off the ground, and spins her halfway around. She playfully pats Max's back and tells him to put her down.

Her wide grin shouts, *All of the sacrifices I made to raise my children were worth it to be greeted like this by my son.*

The love Max has for her radiates from his soul. He only knows one way to love: all encompassing. That's how he loves his mother.

I shouldn't be here.

The thought echoes through my body. At first, I assume this desire to flee comes from a normal fear of meeting the parents. Every girlfriend goes through this. But then I remember that it's something else. Something bigger. My brain keeps telling me: *Watch him closely.* But it's not Max whom I'm supposed to be watching.

Max introduces me to his parents, and we exchange pleasantries. His mother is nicer to me than I thought she'd be. In my mind, I am the white girl there to steal her son away. But his mother declares unabashedly at the dinner table, "The last person Max dated was Muslim. And the person before that was a boy! Did he tell you about that one?"

In fact, Max had told me about Danny, the librarian he dated a few years before. I stalked him on Instagram for a few days and could see why. Danny was carefree, fun, and gorgeous. Max told me that Danny helped him out of a deep depression after his sister died. Personally, I think it's because he feels a need to protect the women he dates, so dating a guy relieved him of that responsibility. However, when I suggested that to him, Max disagreed and said that he simply thought Danny was amazing.

He has not, however, told me about the Muslim girl. I'll have to remember to ask about her later. More late-night stalking is in my future.

"You're not his worst rebellion," his mother concludes. Max's father shakes his head but does not look up from his plate.

I notice an empty chair just across the table from me and stare at it. *Someone should be sitting in that chair.* This feeling is strong, and yet I can't remember expecting anyone else at dinner besides the four of us.

Max turns to me. "I'm so sorry." The conversation is just normal family banter, which is nice to be a part of. "It's not a rebellion, Mom. I date the people who I'm attracted to. I love Alabine." My body tenses. I didn't know Max was going to tell his parents he loves me. They don't know I have cancer. I hope he doesn't spill those beans too, just to make a point. I'm enjoying being normal for a night.

His quiet father finally looks up from his plate. "Good. We came to America so you would be American. This girl is as American as you can get. I approve." His mother raises her glass in agreement. I shovel more rice into my mouth while his father's statement catches in my chest.

I have never thought of myself as being particularly American. In my mind, a true American is a flag-waving, pickup-truck-driving cowboy who drinks beer. I'm none of those things. Perhaps, from their perspective, that's the point.

"Not that we were looking for your approval, but good to know we have it." Max squeezes my hand under the table. I gasp. *Is he supposed to be touching me? Didn't he tell me he couldn't touch me or he'd get sick? Or was that someone else?* I look back at the empty chair across from me. It's different from the other chairs around the table. This one is upholstered in blue velvet while the others are wood.

Max's mother puts another helping of food onto my plate, which I'm happy to accept. "So, tell me about your family, Alabine. Are you as much a pain in the butt to your parents as my son is to us?"

"Mom, please. Leave her alone, and let her eat." Max knows the tumultuous relationship I have with my family, so ever the knight in shining armor, he's quick to come to my rescue.

Except I think I'm actually okay and wouldn't mind telling them. My heart flutters with the desire to share myself with them. To sink myself into their parental affections. To possibly be loved by them even a fraction as much as they love their son.

"I don't really know my parents. My dad's dead. My mom's still alive, but I don't hear from her much. I was raised by my aunt. We weren't ever that close. She was pretty strict, although she would tell you that I was impossible. We were starting to get closer after I went to college, but then she died too, about two years ago, so it's sorta just me now." I see Max's mother's face fall with each additional detail I provide. She quietly returns to her seat and sits solemnly. All the warmth is sucked away from the table.

"It is not good not to have a relationship with your parents. With your mother. Family is important." Max's mother says this more to herself than to me. "A person is damaged by these things."

Oh no. I messed up—miscalculated.

"I'm sorry, I didn't mean that I don't like family. I do want a family. Kids and all." Max's mother doesn't look at me. I try to continue, but suddenly a man walks by the table. Not Max or his father. Another man.

I watch this person go to the corner of Max's parents' dining room, just beyond the blue velvet chair. He has his back to me as he whispers to a very tall man with bright white hair. I can't hear them. I have no idea who they are or why they're here.

"Excuse me . . ." I say to the man in the corner, but he doesn't hear me.

Max grabs my hand. "Al's not damaged, Mom!"

No one seems aware at all that these two strangers are huddling in the corner. Perhaps even more shocking, no one has noticed that the dining room table is now in the middle of a train car.

Most shocking of all, Ralph's seat is empty.

.
.
.
.

Ralph was gone. I looked around frantically for my missing hostage. The train was much fuller than it had been before. Almost every seat was now occupied by commuters. They watched my alarm with increasing suspicion as I whipped around, desperate to find Ralph.

Maybe he went to the bathroom?

Only I knew he wasn't in the bathroom. Best-case scenario was he had made his escape. Worst case was he'd given me up and was marching back with a host of armed guards by his side, ready and willing to take revenge.

I shuffled out of my seat and ran up the hallway. A stewardess collecting tickets blocked the way. I tried to duck around her and accidentally stepped on her toe. She yelped, then instructed me to "sit down at once."

Ignoring her, I continued to push my way through until I heard a deep voice behind me. "Is there a problem here?" A man in the same tan patrol officer uniform that Ralph wore stood menacingly behind me. I clutched my wig, praying it wouldn't come loose.

"Just looking for my boyfriend, Officer." Everyone noticed my voice quaver. Things were about to escalate. I backed away slowly.

Then the officer grabbed my elbow. "Why don't you come with me, miss." I tried to think quickly. I could fight, but what about the other men there? I could take the stewardess, but the businessmen were clearly watching with a bellicose curiosity. I could run. Plead for mercy. I could . . .

"There you are, dear." Ralph. It was Ralph! Thank God. "I went to the washroom while you were napping. Is everything okay here, Officer?" The officer looked to the stewardess, who nodded. He then released me. Ralph gently helped me away. Careful, as always, not to touch me.

Walking down the aisle, I wanted to fling my arms around Ralph and thank him for saving me. I refrained, mostly because he would think I was attacking him with my Awoken germs, but I also wanted to wait until we got farther from our skeptics. I had every intention of showering him with my gratitude once we sat down. However, when we got to our seats, Ralph didn't sit.

"Keep going." His tone was severe enough that I didn't dare question him. I stayed quiet as we passed into the next car. He started walking faster.

Fear surged through me. I looked behind us to see if we were being followed, but I saw no one. I tried to read some sort of intention in his face as Ralph pushed us through another door into the next car.

"Ralph, what's going on?!" I demanded. The clamor of dishes and plates overtook the soundscape, and I looked up to see we were in the dining car.

"Nothing," Ralph responded casually. "I just wanted to get us away from those jerks and grab a cup of coffee." He sauntered over to the bar and took a seat.

It was a cute little café like you'd see on old-school trains. The walls were decked out in textured bright red wallpaper, and the ceiling was painted a dusty gold. Along one side were booths, and along the other was bar seating with a barista making all kinds of caffeinated beverages. From the liquor bottles behind the coffee paraphernalia, I surmised that the car turned into a bar after a certain hour.

I went to join Ralph at the bar, but before I did, I took a good look around the room.

This was when the game changed.

In my first life, I wasn't known to be the most observant person in the world. I was the kind of person who looked for sunglasses already on her head. But in those two traumatic days of my new life, I had begun to adapt. I was quickly evolving into another person. It's said that in trying times, you meet your true self. I'm not so sure that's right. I think I actually am the person that I was in my first life. For better or worse. Trying times beat you into the person you have to be to survive. It's not who you are; it's someone entirely different whom you have to become. Or die. A lot of people never get to be their true selves, unadulterated by trauma and fear. I was lucky in my first life.

When I looked around the room, I saw two people whom I recognized but could not place immediately. Both required time and space to process. I had neither.

The first was a young Black woman sitting at the far side of the bar. She was strikingly beautiful and strangely familiar in a world in which no one was familiar. She wore her long hair slicked back in a low bun. Her white coat said "Montrose UA Center" across the back in large, stitched lettering. Around her neck dangled a lanyard with an ID badge. She had captured the attention of two men who were also employees of the center. Most people in that train car were Montrose Center employees as we were nearing the end of the line. I focused on her face—that's where the familiarity lay.

A picture of her came into my mind. She was with another beautiful, though slightly older, woman: Helen. This woman in the café train car was with Helen in the picture. This woman was Chris! Helen's missing and assumed-dead Resurrectionist daughter. Sitting just there in the same train car as me, an apparent employee of a government center.

Could she have joined the UA? I wondered.

Then, it occurred to me that this might have been the intention all along. It needed to look like she was dead because she was actually undercover. That was the only rational explanation I could come up with. Wade must've known but not told anyone else for her safety. It wasn't a lie after all.

I had no idea what to do with this huge piece of information until I noticed the second familiar person in the room. A transparently pale man. The very man whom Ralph sat next to at the bar and pretended not to know while ordering his cup of coffee. He wore small glasses that half covered his haunting light blue eyes, and he had such blond hair it was practically white. He also had a lanyard with an ID badge, but his had big red bold letters that read: "Security."

I had never met this man, and yet I knew exactly who he was. A weight dropped into my stomach. Ralph had set a trap, and I was walking right into it. There was no time to process the betrayal or stupidity I felt for believing that Ralph was a good person.

This man sitting next to Ralph was familiar to me because I'd seen him one time before—in Max's parents' living room. It was Ralph who rudely walked through and interrupted our dinner, and this man was the one he talked to in the corner. I still don't fully understand how the brain processes the various lives of an Awoken, but while I was in Max's parents' house having an uncomfortable dinner, some part of me actually saw Ralph leave his seat and go speak to this man who ran Montrose security.

And Ralph told him exactly who I was.

There was no time. I had to think fast. They were probably waiting until after we got off the train to arrest me so as not to cause a scene. The man would then inconspicuously grab my sleeve, careful to not touch my skin, and whisper something in my ear to keep me from screaming and causing mass panic in a train station full of ordinary people just going about their ordinary day. They'd bring me in quietly and be heroes. But now I was one step ahead. If I acted quickly.

I sat next to Ralph and sipped the badly burnt coffee. My mind raced. I had less time than I thought as the conductor announced over the speakers that we were arriving in Montrose Center Station. Ralph smiled at me. I couldn't muster the acting chops to smile back. I suppose I just looked worried, which was to be expected.

As we stood up to leave, I grabbed the pen and receipt on the counter next to me. I scribbled a note as fast as I could without Ralph or the Pale Man seeing me.

When we walked toward the exit, we passed by Chris. I only had one shot at getting this right. With all the deftness I could summon, I slipped the note into her unsuspecting hands and walked by without glancing back. I desperately wanted to, but I knew I couldn't. So I prayed instead.

Metro Express CAFE
Please pay cashier
12/16/2121
0059 to go

LG Latte 230
+ Sub Oat Milk 30

UA Tax 5
TOTAL 265

they have us.
-A.R.

Thank you. Come Again.

9

THERE WAS A DELIBERATE order to the chaos. Commuters exited
the train with a choreographed precision embedded into the cultural
subconscious. The sea of suits was suffocating. As an outsider unaware
of the intricacies of the flow of traffic, I let Ralph guide me through
the crowd until we found ourselves standing on the Montrose Center
train platform.

We were underground—that much was clear. The station was
white and pristine and filled with the bustle of daily life. It looked the
most futuristic of anything I'd seen in the last few days. Still no flying
cars, but a digital scanner tracked ID badges, and purposefully visible
security cameras lined the walls.

"Let's regroup there." Ralph pointed toward a café just outside of
the security checkpoint. It was quite busy with the morning commuter rush. People buying their bagels and coffee. I wondered if they
knew that at that exact moment, while they sipped their espressos and
nibbled their croissants, people were being tortured in the shadowed
bowels of the building.

Maybe they all just didn't know. I wanted to give them the benefit of the doubt. But if they were told, would they even put down their pastries to stop it?

As we walked toward the café, Ralph's eyes never darted back to the Pale Man, who kept two paces behind us. Still, anticipation hung like humidity in summer air.

Fairly quickly, I became fed up with the charade and abruptly stopped walking. It took him a few steps, but Ralph soon noticed and stopped too.

"Alabine, what are you doing?"

For an instant, his eyes flicked to the Pale Man standing behind me. That was all I needed. Just that one glance to confirm my suspicions. Don't get me wrong, I was nervous, terrified, and felt as if I were going to puke. But I didn't. Instead I turned around and confronted my shadow standing perfectly still mere feet from me.

"If you're gonna do it, then what are you waiting for?" I asked the Pale Man. His ice-blue eyes revealed nothing. He neither acknowledged me nor looked away.

Ralph shuffled forward. "What are you talking about? Let's get something to eat. You'll feel better."

Ignoring Ralph—he meant nothing in this—I continued addressing the Pale Man. "At first I thought you were holding off because you didn't want me to make a scene on the train. But now what are you waiting for?"

The Pale Man continued to stare silently. I believe I saw the edge of his mouth curl up for a moment. He was enjoying this: the cat confronted by the mouse.

"Are you waiting for a signal?" I asked, my anger starting to rise. "Then you'll tear my wig off and reveal me to be an Awoken. Maybe you'll paint me as a terrorist about to blow up the station!" People passing by were gawking as my outburst continued. "You'll figure out a good headline, I'm sure."

Ralph cleared his throat. "Please, Alabine, you're going crazy."

Maybe I am, I thought. If I explained it aloud, it seemed absurd. *I think you're going to turn on me because I saw you talking to each other in Max's parents' living room in 2019.* It was quite possible I had gotten this all terribly wrong. My heart was beating so loudly I was sure both men could hear it.

"Sorry, sir," Ralph offered the Pale Man. "She's not from around here. We'll just—"

The Pale Man held up his hand. Ralph immediately stopped talking. I quietly exhaled. I wasn't crazy. Validation felt good, even if the outcome wasn't in my favor.

I laid out my terms. "I won't give you the headline, but I will come with you. I won't fight. I won't try to run. You win." They stared at me, trying to figure out my game. I hoped they didn't figure out that I had no game. I only knew two things. First, there was no other way out of this that didn't involve more bullets, and I really couldn't take any more bullets. And second, most important, surrendering was my only chance to find Wade.

The Pale Man offered a slight bow of his head in agreement and pointed us toward the center's entrance.

We passed through the security checkpoint. Without a word, the Pale Man took Ralph and me around the corner to a back hallway that led to a bank of secure elevators. After a fast elevator ride that reminded me of the one in *Willy Wonka* and gave me an inopportune craving for chocolate, we arrived at a waiting room.

I stepped off the elevator onto a marble tile floor. The ceilings were dramatically high, and the furniture was chicly sparse. There were neither windows nor art on the walls. Bold striped wallpaper provided both an elegance and a sense of imprisonment. The sole focal point of the room was a pair of massive double doors. They spanned floor to ceiling and were embellished with gold inlay.

Suddenly, the Pale Man grabbed my body and started running his hands all over me. It took me a moment to realize he was patting me down. In my first life, I'd always effortlessly moved right through security, so was unfamiliar with the sensation. Even though he was careful not to touch my skin, it was still alarmingly aggressive. He quickly found the pistol in my pocket and took it.

Then, as soon as I remembered that Max's iPhone was in my other pocket, the Pale Man's long fingers found it. I tried to snatch it back, but he was too quick for me. He looked at it with a creased brow.

"Don't!" I lunged for him.

Like a snake, he counterattacked, striking my arm and spinning me around into a choke hold. My legs kicked helplessly. He held me by my neck just off the ground as I fought for breath. A glint of concern came to Ralph's eyes.

Just as I started to black out, the Pale Man released me. I collapsed to the ground, gasping. When I looked up, weak and trembling, the Pale Man was already on the far side of the room. He tucked Max's phone into his pocket and slipped through the massive doors.

Once we were alone, I pushed myself to my feet. Rage filled my body, a deflection from the devastation of losing Max's phone. I glared at Ralph, waiting for him to gloat about tricking me into capture, but there was no gloating. He avoided eye contact and quietly sat in a nearby chair. He was still that young nervous patrol officer from a rural town who had just enough humanity to disobey an order to shoot a child but not enough to step in when I was being choked to death. When it comes to doing the right thing, inaction is so much easier than action.

Turning to the doors at the end of the long waiting room, I wondered what, or who, was on the other side. And more important, what they wanted with me. I knew what I needed from them. My phone back, for starters, as well as safety for myself and Wade and any other captives they had. I didn't yet know what I could give them in exchange. Wade said I had power in this world, but it certainly didn't feel that way. A sneaking thought kept pushing itself into my mind. If they offered, if they had the power to put me back under cryo and promise my safety, would I accept? Two days ago, it was all I wanted. But now, with Max out there waiting for me to find him, how could I?

It was up to me to convince them to show us mercy—all of us—by proving to them that we were all human. I had to convince them that we deserved life. It was naive, but I had to try.

"I didn't think they'd hurt you, you know." Ralph cleared his throat.

Before I could reply, the massive double doors pushed apart, and a smiling, bright-eyed, middle-aged man with salt-and-pepper hair strode through. Ralph and I both stood. It seemed like the thing to do, though I now wish I'd kept sitting in a small act of defiance.

"Alabine Rivers. As I live today." This man approached me with wide arms like he was about to embrace me in a big hug. Instead he stopped a few steps in front of me and clapped his hands together with a laugh. "I can't tell you what a surprise and absolute pleasure it is to meet you."

He introduced himself as Gene Minchin—United America's secretary of science. He then pointed through the double doors to a massive specimen of a man in a military uniform, whom he identified as General Tom Standard, leader of the Territorial Army.

"Oh, and of course, you've already met Aldy." Minchin gestured toward the Pale Man. "Our stalwart head of security who I believe is the man we have to thank for our chance meeting this morning."

"It wasn't him," I corrected. "Ralph here is who brought me in. I definitely wouldn't be here if it weren't for the actions of this young patrol officer."

Ralph's face dropped. Good. I wanted him to know that I blamed him and only him for whatever fate was about to befall me. In him, I sensed the guilt for betraying me was growing. My subtle gibe worked. The subtext, however, went entirely unnoticed by the upbeat secretary.

"Well, who'd a-thunk it?" he said, noticing Ralph standing there for the first time. "Thank you for correcting me, Miss Rivers."

And that's when it happened.

Minchin reached forward and grabbed my hands. Like a true politician, out of politeness or to seem more approachable, he squeezed my hands with a *please excuse me* laugh and patted them in a way that reminded me of a charming, bumbling Hugh Grant in a rom-com. Normally this would've been an unmemorable gesture, and yet my heart fluttered. I was being touched.

Gene Minchin, Secretary of Science, wasn't scared of touching me. The last few days had shown me how terrified Ralph was of my skin. He thought one touch would infect him with a horrible disease. It was constantly on his mind, and thus mine too. Gina said the idea that Awoken carried this terrible disease was wrong, but that the government kept touting it as the truth. Minchin *was* the government, the secretary of science, for Christ's sake. Above anyone, he should've been keenly aware of the dangers I posed. And yet he touched me.

After a beat, Minchin let go of me and offered his hand to Ralph to shake. "Congratulations, son." Ralph's lips tightened. He was quite aware that Minchin had been holding my hands only a moment before. Meanwhile, the secretary's outstretched hand awaited a response. Ralph twitched, but he couldn't bring himself to do it; duty only pushed him so far. Instead he brought his hand to his head in salute.

It was awkward.

Minchin seemed unfazed. He lowered his hand and turned back to me. "We have a lot to talk about." He gestured toward the large conference room where Aldy and the general were waiting. We started walking, his hand on my shoulder. Ralph was following just behind until—

"That'll be all, Officer," Aldy barked from the corner, a devilish smirk behind his words. I looked back at Ralph. He stood there, stunned, like an abandoned puppy. Minchin kept ushering me forward until we were in the room. The massive doors began closing. I didn't know what to feel. I didn't have warm feelings for Ralph, but I was very aware this was going to be the last moment I ever saw him. He was, at least, the devil I knew. These new people were strangers, and terrifying ones.

I opened my mouth to say something, but nothing came out. We stared at each other with blank faces. Then I remembered his plans that I'd interrupted.

"I hope she says yes."

He didn't smile. If anything, he looked even more worried. Like he realized he might actually care what happened to me. Maybe. Just before the doors sealed closed, Ralph stepped forward. "Goodbye, Al. Good luck." Then the doors shut.

THE CONFERENCE ROOM WAS unlike anything I'd seen before, in either life. It was impossibly grand. Massive and sparkling with tinted windows that looked out over a vast utopian landscape. However, the warm yellow sunlight was overpowered by an unnatural bluish tint that covered the room. Plastered along one wall, hovering over us, were dozens of digital screens.

Yes. Real-life TV screens.

Since arriving in Montrose, I'd sensed that this building was different from the rest of the country, and now I was confronted with the enormity of it.

The lack of technology was a signature characteristic of this world, and yet this room looked like it was out of a science fiction film. The imposing wall of screens flickered with security feeds and data reports. Weather forecasts and agricultural trends. Satellite images of people crossing the street with information on it that looked like wanted posters. This was closer to the future I had once envisioned waking up to, albeit much more sinister.

I'd thought this world had forgone technology for a simpler life, but I'd assumed wrong. While stripped away from the common man, technology was reserved for those in power. And worst of all, they made people believe it was their decision. Everyday people like Helen and Ralph didn't miss computers or phones. They didn't want them. Little did they know, those who ruled over them remained reliant on the very tech they disavowed.

While taking in my surroundings, the three men watched my every movement. I felt their eyes on me. Each presented his own unique threat. Aldy was simple enough, no more than a hired gun who liked hurting people. Though scary, his choices would be predictable. The other two men I needed to understand more.

Secretary of science wasn't a cabinet position in my time. In this new world, however, it was an important role, with the power and prestige that I associated more with a secretary of state. Only important people were appointed, and their names were remembered by history. The secretary of science position was vital from the beginning of the UA restructuring, but it became more so after the strange fungal spores killed millions. Despite its title, the position was more to regulate and control scientific achievement than to inspire it. The country was satisfied simply benefiting from the substantial advancements made in the previous century. It was the solemn duty of the secretary of science to curb the dangers of human ingenuity and maintain confidence in the administration's control by constructing a careful narrative that fed into the country's fear of the "unnatural." Minchin was a celebrity, and his ego radiated from his impressively chiseled cheekbones.

The third man in the room was top brass in the Territorial Army, a term that meant nothing to me at the time. Long after that meeting, I learned that in the middle of the twenty-first century, the police force was demilitarized to the point where they didn't even carry guns. What seemed like a sweeping success for police reform advocates was but a Trojan horse for something much worse. First the National Guard slowly assumed an authoritarian presence on our streets. When lawsuits limited their growing power, smart politicians created a new, well-armed "peacekeeping force" and called it the Territorial Army. That very force, basically police on steroids, was what had raided Wade's camp at the command of the man standing in the corner, General Tom Standard.

His close-cropped black hair, linebacker shoulders, and permanently affixed sour grimace made him look the part of merciless military general perfectly. That day, I only had an inkling of how evil this man was. Of who this man was. He was simply a stern man sitting silently in the corner. I'd learn much more about what he was capable of in the months to come.

"Please. Sit." Minchin offered a chair at the table that faced away from the wall of screens. "Oh, and before I forget . . ." He casually placed a phone on the table in front of me: Max's phone. I stared at it, worried if I moved too quickly he would snatch it back. "Aldy never should've taken it." Minchin smiled sweetly.

Slowly, I took the phone off the table and returned it to my pocket where it belonged. The grip that had been around my chest since Aldy plucked Max's phone from me relaxed. I had no idea if Minchin knew what it was or whose it was; his expression indicated neither.

Minchin looked me up and down me like he was hungry and I was a juicy steak. "Can I get you a coffee?"

Coffee sounded amazing, but I hesitated. Maybe they had poisoned it. Maybe laced it with a truth serum. Both of those things sounded ridiculous, I decided, like out of the spy novels my aunt loved to read. I accepted the coffee.

With a wide toothy grin, Minchin strode over to the long buffet. The porcelain clinked as the coffee steamed and hissed under the heat. Soon the room began to smell of deep vanilla and cardamon. I was spellbound by the rush of pleasure to my senses. Aldy and the general, who had still not uttered a word, watched Minchin silently.

The secretary sauntered back to me with a cup and saucer in one hand and a sterling silver pot of coffee in the other. He placed it before me and poured the thick stream of hot black deliciousness. I may have been drooling.

It was as satisfying as I had imagined. With one sip, the days of sweat and blood and guns melted away. I felt human again and took a deep breath.

I wanted to be the first person to speak, but I only got out a few syllables before my words slipped into a garbled coughing fit. The bitter coffee mixed with the metallic taste of blood. My cancer was like a newly minted older sibling acting out, reminding the parents that they're still top dog. The darkness was reminding me that it was my true enemy.

"Oh, dear," Minchin said with saccharine pity. "That just won't do. What is it you are sick with, again?"

"Classical Hodgkin's lymphoma," the general surprisingly, and correctly, offered from across the long table.

Minchin pressed a button on a speaker in the center of the table. "Darla, dear. Can you ask the lab for the classical Hodgkin's lymphoma treatment? Send it up to Conference Room A, 'toot sweet.'" He chuckled at his overexaggerated butchering of the French phrase.

I didn't speak, afraid if I did, I'd break down sobbing at how simple it was for this man to just order my cure like McDonald's fries. It didn't seem real. Hope coursed through my blood, convincing me with each heartbeat that I was about to be cured.

"That'll take just a moment. While we wait, I have about a million questions to ask you. I'm sure you must have as many for me. Now, I know my wife would beat me senseless if she knew I wasn't deferring to a lady, but would you be so kind as to allow me to begin?"

I cannot stress enough to you how much I hated this guy. Not simply because he was the only face I had to put to the Redden regime that wanted me and my friends dead, but also because of who he was as a person. The pomp. The fake gentility. His politeness came from a place of dominance rather than sincerity. I swallowed my annoying instinct to smile in the presence of authority.

He took my silence as approval, no surprise there, and clicked on a small recording device. I assumed it was just recording audio, but it did seem oddly complicated for that, so it could've easily had a small camera as well. I found out much later that it did.

"Secretary Gene Minchin sitting here with Miss Alabine Rivers on December the sixteenth, 2121." After this introduction, he turned to me. "Obviously, because we're here together right now, I'm aware of who you are. Do you know who you are?"

"I'm Alabine Rivers," I responded matter-of-factly. I knew what he was getting at, but I wanted him to work a bit more for it.

"Indeed. And do you know why that name holds enough weight to get you a seat at this table?" He said it like I should thank him for the honor of being there. As if I had any other choice.

I thought for a moment, but not too long. I had met men like him before, and men like him always preferred answering their own questions. So, before I could be interrupted, I simply said, "My story is a legend."

He slapped his thigh. "I couldn't've put it better myself. A true-to-life King Arthur back from the annals of history and here in the flesh and blood."

"Now I have a question for you," I said.

"Oh, I didn't think this would be a back-and-forth repartee." He leaned back and crossed his legs. From Psych 101 I took at Northwestern freshman year, I gleaned that he was feeling defensive. "Please, go ahead."

"I know who I am. I know what Max did. I represent everything you despise. So, Secretary, why do you seem so happy to see me?"

"You're a smart girl. I imagined you would be." He paused and exchanged his fake smile for an even faker look of concern. "The truth is, I'm scared, Alabine. I'm scared for the good and decent people of this country who have entrusted President Billy Redden with their protection. They go about their lives, not ever having to think about the troubles out there." He clicked his tongue. "But now this group of militants, who illegally and without your permission ripped you back from the dead, want a war that will bleed out onto the front lawns of these good and decent citizens." He struck the table with his finger to emphasize certain words. It was effective. "Finally, after a century of fighting, they are on their last leg, wounded and desperate, like a cornered wild animal. I'm scared of what they will do. These Resurrectionists have already shown that they are willing to take as many lives as needed to seize power and destroy this world as we know it."

The man liked to talk in hyperbole. Most politicians do. I came to terms with the annoying fact that he was good at this game. He stood up and calmly paced back and forth as the tirade ran on.

"So why am I so excited to meet you? Well, I'd be pleased as punch to meet King Arthur, but that doesn't mean I'd support a monarchy. I believe in the person, not the cause. I believe in *you*." He smiled wide. "You're a national treasure. We love your story because it represents love, freedom, and unity. The very pillars this country was built on." He leaned over the table, inching uncomfortably close to me. "Now this country needs you more than ever. I think you may be the only person living who can resolve all this without another drop of blood spilled."

"Are you offering a truce?" I asked. The idea of ending the violent raids like the one in Chicago was all too appealing.

"I'm offering you a way out," Minchin corrected. "If you, *the* Albine Rivers, spoke against these terrorists, it would mean the end of all this pain and suffering." He slapped his hands together. "Poof! Think of the innocent lives you would save." He sat back down in his chair with a sigh. "I love this country with all my heart, and I know you would too. We have something truly special here. Look around! People are happy. They are thriving!" He held out his arms as if a crowd of people had just erupted into applause.

There was silence.

Then I cleared my throat, summoning as much courage as I could. "I have looked around, Secretary, and I've seen what's been sacrificed for your peace."

Before Minchin could respond, the massive door opened, and a slim woman slipped in. She wore a pleated pencil skirt, and her red hair curled up into a neat ponytail. The click-clack of her heels on the tiled floor echoed through the heavy air. Minchin kept his eyes on me. While he assumed I was distracted by the redhead, I noticed a shift in his gaze. For a split second, his expression twisted from over-the-top positivity to something much harsher. A cruel leer.

When the redhead was almost to Minchin, he snapped back on his Dr. Jekyll and held out his hand. "Thank you, Darla." She gave him a small bottle. Without even a glance to me, she turned and walked out. Minchin's eyes glimmered with the upper hand. "Well, here you are, my dear." He read the instructions on the bottle as he walked around the long conference table and hovered close to me. "One pill twice a day for two weeks."

He popped the cap off the bottle and poured a single red pill onto his palm, examining it between his fingers. There was my cure. First, I considered that this could be poison or some other trick to kill me. If they wanted me dead, Aldy's gun seemed a much easier method. This was clearly a chess move to gain my trust.

One pill, twice a day, two weeks. The words rang in my head. Minchin offered the pill to me. I was worried my hand was shaking too much, but slowly I collected myself, calmly reached forward, and plucked the red pill from his fingers.

It was beautiful.

I quickly popped it into my mouth and felt the chalky texture on my tongue. I brought the porcelain coffee cup to my lips and took a sip. It was still hot. The pill slid effortlessly down my throat. Now was not the time to celebrate. I had to maintain some semblance of composure, so I offered a simple and sincere "Thank you."

Then I pulled my focus back into the room and remembered what else was important to me besides that glass pill bottle. I remembered Aldy in the corner with his gun. I remembered why I was there.

"Where are my friends?"

"That polite patrol officer?" Minchin asked. "He went back home. I'm sure we could—"

"My friends from the camp in Chicago. The camp that you attacked." My accusation languished in the momentary silence. Our facade of gentility threatened to crack.

"Now, Miss Rivers, that's not all entirely fair. *Attacked* is a strong word. My understanding from General Standard here is that a welfare check was being performed and many illegals were found in horrid conditions."

"Welfare? They burned people alive! For what? To find me?" My words began to slur together as anger mixed with deeply felt guilt. "How did you even know I was there?!"

Minchin chuckled knowingly. "Your so-called friends are not as impervious to corruption as you might think." This took me by surprise. He was insinuating that someone gave me up. That there was a leak within the Resurrectionists or the Awoken who saw me in camp. Minchin continued before I had time to consider this new information. "Miss Rivers, please. I do not want to argue. We can at least maintain civility, can we not?"

"Civility? You killed children!" I jumped to my feet, remembering with each syllable the horrible images of children lying dead in their own blood. Imagining Minnie to be one of them. Recalling the feeling of her arms wrapped around my waist. "You killed my friends!" My voice echoed against the towering ceiling, reverberating for a moment until it faded to silence. Tears welled in my eyes, and I trembled from the release of emotion.

Minchin slammed his hand down on the table, revealing his anger for the first time. "They are not your friends, Miss Rivers. They are terrorists blowing up innocent citizens in the name of so-called civil rights."

Eavesman Square. The "mistake," as Wade had called it. I didn't have a comeback quick enough, so Minchin sat back and a hateful grin etched into his cheeks as he reveled in his victory of shutting me the hell up.

In my silence, he continued, now calmer, back to the dominating politeness that he so adeptly embodied. "They may not be your friends, Alabine, but you do have friends here. I would like to be your friend. I've offered you something those terrorists haven't been able to. Your health." He shook the bottle back and forth, taunting me with the clinking of pills against the glass.

"Let me get this right," I said as I exhaled, utterly exhausted. "You'll give me those pills, but only if I . . . what? Join you here in Oz?"

Minchin nodded. The part of me that was terrified of the darkness and dying again was telling me to take the deal. But it didn't take more than a moment for a much louder part of myself to start talking.

"If that's your grand plan, then I need to stop you there and tell you that it's fucked. No deal." I only believed my words as I said them, surprised by my own courage. "Besides, I've already been promised a cure by a man I like a hell of a lot more than you."

"That man wouldn't happen to be in one of my detention cells, would he?" Minchin spat through clenched teeth. "It seems your grand plan is the one that's fucked right now." He said "fucked" with an emphasis that conjured an image of violent sex. "We've only treated you with kindness. Alabine, what can we do to gain your trust?"

What did I want? This was my chance. I had come into this room with a hope that I could change his mind about Awoken and get him to willingly release Wade and the others. That hope was now extinguished, but he was asking me what I wanted. So I racked my brain. *What would Max do?* My eyes narrowed as it came to me as simply as can be.

"Admit publicly that Awoken aren't a threat to anyone. That cryogenics didn't actually create a deadly fungus or infestation or whatever you call it." As much as I wanted nothing to do with this fight, or this world, here I was, diving in headfirst.

Minchin was speechless for a moment. I suppose this wasn't on the top of his mind of something I might want. He smiled his phony annoying grin. "You want me to lie to the citizens of this country. I could never do that. Not even for you. I apologize—"

"It's not a lie, and you know it. You, the secretary of science, are not scared to touch me. You held my hands for a full minute just moments ago. Tell the truth, and I'll join you."

Minchin sat back in his chair, deep in thought. I couldn't tell if I'd caught him in a mistake or if he intended for me to know. He gave no indication how he felt. Slowly, he reached forward and stopped the recording device.

Now, there were two things that happened well after I sat in that chair. First, my asking him to admit that Awoken weren't infectious was edited off that tape. I know this because I am certain I said it before he stopped the tape. So, despite the reports to the contrary, the tape was doctored. Second, the following five minutes were never recorded and thus forgotten by history, but not by me. They were the most important five minutes I spent in that room.

This is when he told me everything he knew about the infestation—Devil's Touch, as he referred to it. How scientists couldn't figure out where the spores came from or why people's bodies had such a weak immune response to it. It wasn't a virus. It acted like a mold that started as a skin infection before spreading to the brain and central nervous system. The microscopic fungus ate away at a person's bones as it took over a body. Its victims died horrible deaths, and it easily spread from person to person through physical touch. A cure was developed eventually, but well after billions of people around the world died.

It quickly became clear that Devil's Touch affected Awoken at a much lower rate. That's where the rumor was born that Awoken must've caused it, as they were surprisingly resistant to its ravages. People were already untrusting of Awoken and believed them to be unnatural. Although it didn't stop the Resurrectionists of the time from bringing people back from the dead, resurrecting a human had been illegal since the 2080s, a quarter of a century before the infestation started. Those who had been resurrected were seen as lower than dirt. When the fungus came about, it was all too easy to push blame onto the Awoken.

As Gina said, people were looking for an excuse. They believed the fungus was something Awoken carried with them from death. Hence, the Devil's Touch.

The truth was that due to the cryo process, an Awoken person's skin changes slightly to be softer and more elastic. It heals quickly, and so Awoken were infected at a slower rate. Babies and young kids also weren't as affected, thankfully.

However, by the time the mechanics of the fungus came to light, the blame on Awoken had taken root. The president at the time was more than happy to push the lie and stoke the fear, as it meant finally ending the cryogenics movement entirely. That was when the mandate to shoot an Awoken on sight was made law, all because of an out-and-out lie.

That was a decade before I was awoken. Societies around the world changed their ways and moved from the cities to the more spread-out countryside. While no vaccine ever worked, it was extremely rare that a person would contract Devil's Touch anymore. Even if they did, there was a fairly successful treatment.

The only lasting effect Devil's Touch had on this earth was that Awoken were still paying the price for people's willful ignorance. This war, if that's what you want to call it, between UA forces and Awoken had nothing to do with an infestation and everything to do with maintaining control during a time of utter tragedy.

Minchin admitted all of this to me, albeit with a positive and propagandized slant that I don't feel like repeating. I didn't give a shit. Nothing mattered in the face of the atrocities to which he had just admitted and casually justified as a necessary evil.

It wasn't until after Minchin finished speaking that I realized I had tears rolling down my cheeks. I was horrified that anyone could act this way while simultaneously patting himself on the back. He earnestly thought of himself as the good guy. In my first life, I knew the government did terrible things. I went to protests. I condemned wars. Jessica DeWhitt's fall from grace taught me that even well-intentioned leaders were unforgivably human. But I always assumed the real bad guys knew they were doing bad things and twirled their metaphorical mustaches while stripping rights away. I was wrong.

The monitors behind me continued to cast a reflection of their bright haze on the glass table. I didn't see him do it, but when I looked down to wipe the tears off my face, Minchin turned back on the recorder.

I looked up with the most strength and defiance I could summon. I wanted no misunderstanding. "I'll never join you."

Minchin tried not to smile. "I'm so sorry to hear that. I tried. You can't say that I didn't try."

That's when Aldy came for me. I didn't just let him take me this time. I'd learned too much. This time I fought back. I landed a few good punches and scratches, but his thin wiry body was quicker and stronger than mine, and I was no match for him.

The only way our young country will survive and withstand the
test of time is if we stay true to the values that brought us together in the first
place. A United America man must build a *family*. A United America woman
must raise and nurture that family. There is no room for deviance or difference.
Previous iterations of this country fought over our ideals for too long, each
subgroup seeing only the truth and facts they wanted to see. A melting pot
does not work. We've decidedly turned away from all that. Now we believe
in the same truth. There is only one identity—the United America Identity.
There is only one culture—the United America Culture. There is
only one people—the United America People.

We will remain united.

—President John J. Howard,
first Patriots' Day address, 2062

10

THE PAST IS A fickle thing. It both doesn't exist and entirely makes us who we are. It's subjective and changes with time. Memories shift. Emotions dull or heighten. Two people can experience the same event but come away with different accounts. What is the past if not a story we tell ourselves to justify our present.

Lucid Memories make the idea of the past even more complex. They aren't your past when you're in one. They're immediate, and yet still just as unreliable for determining the truth.

In the beginning of my new life, I wasn't just having Lucid Memories; I was also getting back normal memories of my first life, specifically when something sparked them. A smell. A taste. Or a feeling.

After I fought Aldy and found myself half conscious on the cold ground, I was overwhelmed with a memory from my childhood.

I was six, lying on a concrete floor, my face pressed so hard into the rough surface that I struggled to breathe. Terror radiated through me. My father and I were trapped in the small basement closet that enclosed our hot-water heater.

My father pushed against the closet door with all his might, fighting against someone trying to break through. The banging was so loud it seemed as if the whole house were going to collapse around us. My father was crying and shouting. I remember seeing a refraction of light in his glasses as they slid down the sweat and tears on his nose. His head was bleeding, and mine too, from when he fell while carrying me during his mad dash down the basement steps.

We were trapped like rats, futilely trying to hide from the intruder. I was terrified, imagining a monster with fangs and claws on the other side of the door. My dad, a tall skinny man, was our only hope for survival, and he was losing. There was a loud slam. My father shouted "No!," then shoved me to the ground. His full body weight slumped over me, pressing my head into the concrete. I couldn't see anything at that point. All I could hear were my father's shouts. Terror of what was about to get us seized me. I prayed to God that my dad would be strong enough to protect me.

The pain intensified as he pressed harder against my cheek. "Daddy, you're hurting me," I quietly pleaded. He didn't respond as he continued to battle for our lives.

It wasn't minutes but hours later, after I had passed in and out of consciousness, that I finally realized there was no one on the other side of that door. No monster. No robber. No one at all.

He was diagnosed with paranoid schizophrenia before I was born. Deemed to be "functioning," whatever that means, he held a prominent professorship at the University of Chicago. Most people who knew him had no idea. Back then, healthcare wasn't really set up to help people with these kinds of serious mental health issues. It wasn't until the person committed a crime that the state took interest.

After that horrible night, my father checked us both into the hospital. I left a few days later; he never did.

My mother had left us long before then, and so from age six until I went to Northwestern at seventeen, I lived with my aunt, his sister, a nice enough woman who wasn't prepared to raise a traumatized child. We fought a lot. Our relationship was always tenuous at best.

I remember going to visit my father in the hospital a few times. I had such high hopes for our visits. That he'd be the father I wanted, and not the father in that closet. Sadly, he spent most of our time together yelling about the government sending "bad men" to get him. Eventually my aunt stopped taking me to see him, and I hated her for it.

I was thirteen when my father died. I had never cried so hard, all the while hating myself for mourning a man who put me in the hospital. To my friends, I put on a facade of anger and told them I was relieved when he died. Finally I wouldn't be burdened by him any longer. That lie made me even lonelier and more isolated. The truth was that I loved him. He was an amazing father, and I don't mean in spite of his diagnosis. Every part of him was a good father. So much of who I am is because of him. Sure, some of the bad, the obsessive and broken things, but mostly the good in me is him. I've always known that, but it seemed too complicated of a feeling to get across, so instead of grieving, I turned to anger. People understood my anger. I don't think they would've understood that really I just missed my dad.

Now that I'm older, I can bring adult rationality to the events as I know they happened, but I will always feel the emotions ingrained in that memory as if I'm still six years old, hiding from the monster in the basement. That's why it's still the most terrifying memory I have.

Max was the only person I'd ever told that story to. My aunt, friends, and countless therapists asked me again and again, but I couldn't bring myself to tell them. Only Max, and only after I realized we would never be able to fully love each other until I unearthed this memory. After that, we were forever imprinted on each other.

I must've blacked out after Aldy punched me. When I opened my eyes, I found myself lying facedown in a very different room. I calibrated myself away from the memory of the hot cramped closet and remembered Aldy and his gun. Quickly, I looked up, expecting him to be hovering over me.

Instead I saw Gina Han.

It can't be, I thought. *Gina Han is dead.*

I moaned as I tried to make my eyes focus.

"I told you not to get caught." Hearing her unmistakable sharp tone, I knew definitively it was her. She was alive. And pissed, as always. Relief stretched through my bones and threatened to lull me back into unconsciousness. With Gina there, it meant I was safe. She turned away and announced, "She's awake."

When I squinted open my eyes again, other people were huddled around Gina, staring down at me. I didn't recognize any of them but could tell by their clothes they were Resurrectionists.

I reached out to Gina, and my hand hit up against a Plexiglas wall. It felt terrifyingly familiar, like I was back in that cryo facility with Damien, being awoken for the first time. Trapped in a glass coffin.

"Welcome to hell, Rivers," Gina said.

A heavy guttural groan was all I could offer in response. I summoned enough strength to push myself up to a sit. The large room was oppressively bright, and there wasn't a single window in the whole space. There were two rows of cells whose transparent walls spanned from floor to ceiling. A small metal box with a red light was attached to each door. Presumably the locks. Along the ceiling were dozens of security cameras pointed right at us. Every now and again, they'd pan slowly to the left, or the right, or eerily tilt down. The presence of the controller sitting in some not-so-distant room was palpable. We were constantly being watched. At the far end of the aisle between the cells was a single, nondescript closed door. The exit.

There was no one else in my cell with me. Most of the cells in the room were, in fact, empty. Gina's cell was next to mine. In with her, crammed shoulder to shoulder, were more than a dozen other Resurrectionists. They all looked pretty beaten up. Black eyes and swollen lips. Blood stained their clothes, and they looked like they hadn't slept or eaten in days.

Daring myself to hope, I scanned the room. Across the aisle on the other side of the room was another cell packed with people, Awoken prisoners. To my surprise and delight, Minnie and Avon were at the front. They stared at me, their hands pressed against the cell wall. I smiled so wide it hurt my bruised cheek. Minnie jumped up and down and hugged Avon, who reached into his shirt and brought his golden crucifix to his lips, thanking God.

I really didn't think God was the one to thank that any of us were still alive.

"She's okay! You're okay?" Minnie shouted. I had heard Minnie's sweet voice in my head over and over since the raid. How wonderful it was to hear in real life. I nodded to her, trying to hold back tears and project strength.

After being apart, I realized how much I had come to care about these people. They were my friends. My only friends in the entire world.

My feelings of happiness quickly vanished when I took a wider look at all the Awoken in that cell, and it was clear, like the Resurrectionists next to me, they had been tortured. Just as I had feared. There weren't many Awoken. Less than ten in that tiny cell. All beaten and bloodied. I wanted to scream. I wanted to punch something. Most of all, I wanted to break out of this cell and hug them.

Avon saw the look of dread on my face. "We're okay. Don't worry." He always had a knack for reading my mind and knowing exactly what to say. I felt immeasurably safer back in his company. Nevertheless, I knew he was lying. They weren't okay. None of us were.

"Wait," I whispered, realizing who was missing. "Where's Wade? Where's Damien?" Frantically, I looked around both cells and couldn't see either of them. People's faces darkened. Minnie's smile dropped as concern filled her eyes.

No. It can't be.

Just before I broke into tears, I heard, "Here." Wade's deep voice cut through the crowded Resurrectionist cell.

Bodies parted, allowing me to see Wade kneeling on the ground. *Thank God*, I thought. Wade was alive. Of course I was relieved because he was the only person in this world who could reunite me and Max, but I was also glad to see him because I'd come to care for him. He was a good man. Like Damien said.

Damien.

It was then that I fully took in the scene and saw that Wade was kneeling over Damien's body. He was in bad shape. A massive head wound was ruggedly wrapped in a ripped strip of T-shirt, soaked in blood so red it was almost purple. I pressed my hand against the cell wall.

"Is he . . ." I stopped. Unable to bring myself to say it.

"Alive." Gina's voice carried a sympathy that felt strange coming from her. "He goes in and out of consciousness."

I tried to focus on the good part of the news that Damien was not yet absorbed into the darkness, into nothing. Damien was still inside that body. Somewhere.

"I don't understand," I said to Wade. "What happened?"

Wade stood up solemnly from Damien's side and walked toward me. His gait carried a new limp. Slowly, he sat down just on the other side of the transparent wall. "They wanted information."

"On me?" My cheeks reddened.

Wade nodded. "At first."

I had to look away, but in doing so, I caught sight of Minnie. She was hurt and in pain, and that too was my fault.

"I was glad they did, it told me you had gotten out." The care in Wade's voice was reassuring. "And none of us knew where you were, so there wasn't any risk. But when they stopped yesterday, I assumed, correctly it would seem, that they had found you. Then they started asking about our other camps. Their whereabouts and how many people we had."

"Traitors!" Gina shouted as she slammed the door with her fist.

Wade's voice remained calm as he explained to me, "A few of our people never came back. We assume they traded their freedom for information."

"Fucking rats." Gina paced like a caged tiger.

"Our people aren't coming back either," Avon said with a haunted tone. "But it's not because they gave up secrets, it's because they're being exterminated."

No one dared respond. Wade simply nodded.

Avon said "Our people" like it was us versus them, even in here. At the time, despite everything that had happened, part of me felt more like a Resurrectionist than an Awoken. I was used to being the person trying to help. Here, I was the person who needed help, but I still felt like the them to Avon's us.

"What'll they do with that information?" I asked.

"We've survived this whole time by living in secret hideouts," Wade responded. "We're all going to die if we don't get out. If we don't warn them, it will mean the collapse of the entire movement."

Gina stopped pacing. "It'll be a fucking massacre." Her words hung heavy for a beat. Then she kept pacing.

"And Damien?" I asked, tears coming to my eyes. Looking at Damien's mangled body, I doubted he'd survive much longer. The idea of losing him and his warm smile was unbearable.

"I'm not sure," Wade responded. He pressed his palm against the Plexiglas. I released a shuddered breath and met his hand with mine. We couldn't touch, but it still meant the world to me. "We have to get out while he, and the entire Resurrectionist movement, stand a chance."

It seemed impossible. There was no breaking out of this place. I wondered if I could try bargaining with Minchin again. Then I remembered.

"Actually, I might've done something."

Before I could say any more, Gina whistled and Wade turned

expectantly to the door at the far side of the room. A few seconds later, it opened. A group of masked guards marched down the aisle. Everyone in the cells jumped up, so I did too. The soldiers dragged a half-conscious Resurrectionist by his jacket collar, leaving a trail of blood in their wake. They unlocked the cell and threw the man inside. Then they grabbed two new people, an Awoken woman and a Resurrectionist man. Both screamed and fought to no avail. Everyone in the cells just stood there as they were taken, eyes glued on the ground.

"Stop! You're hurting them!" I slammed my hand against the walls.

It was no use. They dragged these two people toward the exit. Taking them to be tortured. Unlike everyone else, I kept screaming for them to stop. I quickly learned why I was the only one. Before leaving, one of the guards peeled off from the group, stormed into my cell, and punched me in the side as hard as he could.

All the breath flew out of me. I crumpled to the ground.

"Are you okay?" Wade quietly asked. I nodded even though all the muscles in my abdomen spasmed. The door at the end of the room closed and locked. The screams of the two captives suddenly went silent.

"Start the count," Avon announced to the eerily still room. I noticed a few people start tapping their thighs rhythmically.

"What count?" I asked, still trying to catch my breath.

Wade leaned as close to me as he could. "Every three hours on the dot, they come to get more of us," he told me quietly. "We count so we'll be ready. And now that you're awake . . ." His voice purposefully trailed off.

"Now that I'm awake . . . what?" I asked, worried I already knew the answer.

Wade held his finger up to his lips, indicating for me to be quiet; then he pointed at the cameras watching us. He turned to Avon and Gina and nodded to them. They nodded back and began speaking in hushed tones with the people around them.

"Wait. What are you doing?" I didn't need an answer. I knew what they were going to do. When those men came back in three hours and opened the cells, they were going to charge the guards and try to escape.

"No. Just wait. I have a plan. I—"

"Al, please," Avon whisper-shouted. My panic was going to alert the guards on the other side of those cameras. Avon intentionally turned his back to the camera pointed at his cell so he could plead for me to go along with the plan.

I couldn't go along with their plan. Rushing the guards like that, trying to get out of this massive center, they stood no chance. They were going to die, but that didn't matter to them. They thought they were dead anyways.

"I told you," Wade said determinedly. "Everything depends on this."

Terror filled me, imagining Minnie and Avon slaughtered by those masked guards. They didn't yet know what I did. I had to find a way to tell them.

Not wanting to give the security cameras anything to be suspicious of, I carefully picked my words and lowered my voice.

"I met her on the train," I said. Wade locked eyes with me, unclear of my meaning. "I know you were all worried about her, but she's okay." My words were a nonsensical jumble. I hoped to be cleverer, but I didn't have the time or energy to invoke some sort of secret code. Gina and Avon both looked at me like I was crazy.

Thankfully, Wade didn't dismiss me so quickly. He focused with a curious intensity. He didn't understand, but he wanted to. So I continued: "Wade, I assumed you knew she was okay. You didn't lie after all. I'm sorry I didn't believe you. I told her we said hi."

It clicked. I watched the realization spread across Wade's face. He understood I was talking about Helen's daughter, Chris Smith.

He stepped forward with a knowing glint in his eye. "You're right, I knew where she was." Gina and Avon followed our coded conversation with confused looks. They didn't matter. If I could convince Wade that I had set up a plan for Chris to rescue us, he'd call off their suicidal escape attempt. "But I wasn't sure she was okay. Are you certain?" Wade asked.

Now I was getting lost. He knew where she was; this meant I was right: Chris was indeed secretly undercover, and Wade knew it, but I didn't understand what he meant when he said that he wasn't sure she was okay. When he saw that I had lost the meaning, he added, "I haven't heard from her in a long while."

Then I understood. He wasn't sure if she was with us anymore. He was worried she might've flipped. What he wanted to know was if I was sure she was on our side. If I was sure she was coming to our rescue.

The truth was I wasn't. I hadn't spoken a word to this woman. She might not even have read my note scribbled on that old receipt. Hell, it might not even have been Chris. The more I thought about it, the less I was sure of anything.

"Are you certain?" Wade punctuated each word the way a general would when speaking to his soldier. If I confessed that in fact I was not at all certain, Wade would've kept the plan in motion. People would've died. Minnie would've died. So I did the only thing I could think to do.

"I'm sure." I lied.

Wade exhaled. It was long and filled with relief. He looked up and nodded to me gratefully before turning to the room. "Sit down. All of you."

"But, sir!" Gina's protestation was met with a stern look from Wade, so she sat along with everyone else. People stopped tapping their legs. Stopped tracking the seconds until the guards came back. And we waited. For Chris to save us. For a miracle.

No one spoke for the rest of the three-hour period. Time continued to march on, as it ever does, and yet everything felt stagnant. Wade didn't leave my side that whole time. Gina wore a rut in the floor pacing back and forth. Avon clutched on to Minnie as though she would fall into an abyss if he let go. And Damien—well, with Damien, I could see his heartbeat in the blood oozing out of his head. He didn't have much time. At one point, he stirred and started mumbling. I thought about calling out to him but then worried that it'd upset him. So I stayed quiet. Sitting on the floor, holding my legs, hoping I was right about Chris.

Eventually, as expected, the door at the end of the long hall opened, and a troop of guards escorted in the man who was taken a few hours before. I held my breath, hoping I had done enough to stave off the doomed plan of attack. They unlocked the cells, and the man stumbled back in, limping and bloody with swollen eyes. The Awoken woman wasn't with them. She never came back.

While the cell doors were unlocked to return this man to captivity, Avon and Gina watched Wade with a soldier's intensity. Waiting for him to strike. All the Resurrectionists were suspended in the same breathless anticipation. Waiting for the call to battle that wouldn't come.

The masked guards dropped the man in the cell, grabbed another two prisoners—kicking and screaming—then left. No one said a word, not even me this time.

The man who was just brought back lay in a fetal position on the floor. I'd seen him before in Wade's tent. His name was George. In that tent, he was commanding with charisma and certainty. Wade was grooming him to become a leader of his own camp. Now he looked no older than a high school boy as he pushed off the ground and propped himself up in the corner, shivering, blood trickling down his face.

Eventually George looked up and into my eyes. He was scared. He needed strength, which I couldn't give him. I didn't have it. The world started spinning around me as panic inched its way through my body. The taste of sweat and blood and fear was suffocating.

Needing a fix, I closed my eyes, but I promised myself that I wouldn't check out entirely. I had to keep a part of me in that cell.

Believing I could control it, I thought, *Rosebud.*

My fingers feel the cell's concrete floor beneath me, but I sense Max is nearby. I worry that if I see him, I'll slip away.

"Keep your eyes closed," Max whispers tantalizingly in my ear. "It'll be more fun like this." I feel his breath on my neck just before his lips kiss it. My skin prickles with goose bumps under his touch.

I scratch my fingernails on the concrete floor to keep myself anchored in reality when all I want is to let go and leave this cell. Feel something good. Forget all about George's pained gaze.

"I can't stay," I whisper to Max, relishing his touch.

"I know." His soft lips find mine. He kisses me.

"I'm not strong enough. I don't know what I'm doing." I breathlessly confess. My eyes are still closed; he brushes his finger down my chin, then my neck. I want to see him. I want to open my eyes and take him in completely, with all my senses. I start to forget the cell. The security cameras watching our every movement. The bloodied people around me. They all start to fade away.

"Don't you dare," Max commands with a coy smile.

"Why not?" I ask playfully, fluttering my eyes open, trying to sneak a peek. He covers my eyes with his hand, keeping them closed.

"Because you know exactly what to do. If you don't trust yourself, trust me. You have power in this world." Then he grazes one hand up my leg while the other falls from my face and runs down my forearm. A shock of pain surges through me when he touches the scab from my gunshot wound.

I open my eyes with a jolt.

Back in the cell, Max was nowhere to be found.

Three more hours went by. The guards came and went. Two more prisoners taken. Another Awoken never to come back. I wasn't at all sure if Chris was coming to save us anymore. I wanted to trust Max, but then I remembered. He wasn't real. I needed to trust in myself, and yet with each passing minute, I was betting with Damien's life and the lives of all the Awoken in camps across the country. I couldn't maintain this fraught hope for long—no matter how desperate I was to prevent their ill-fated plan to storm the guards.

Soon enough, I started coughing blood again.

One pill twice a day for two weeks.

Panicked, I thrust my hand into my pocket. Much to my surprise, I felt the glass pill bottle clinking around in my dress safely next to Max's phone. My cure. Trying to be sensitive to all the wounded around me, I slipped it from my pocket unseen and unscrewed the cap.

Except no pill tumbled into my hand.

I frantically looked inside the bottle. There was a folded piece of paper where the cure for my cancer once was. I squeezed my fingers inside and pulled it out. It was a business card for Gene Minchin, Secretary of Science. On the back, he had scribbled:

Call for a refill.

The ultimate checkmate. The message could not have been clearer: *Join us or die.* I felt the darkness laugh, but I wouldn't let it tempt me. My cancer cure existed. I'd had it. I was going to get it back.

I should have torn up the card; instead I secretly tucked it back into my pocket. Not that I planned on calling. I didn't want to call. Even so, I couldn't throw away the option.

In an effort to gather some sort of strength by falling into Max's life, I wanted to look at the phone, but I didn't want to spend the battery, which, last I'd looked, was down to 3 percent. I wanted to think of *Rosebud* again and wrap myself up in Max's arms and be warmed by his body. Maybe get lost in a memory of a dinner date, where I'd be able to eat and drink to my heart's content. God, was I hungry.

So many hours passed in silent anticipation. Languishing in that cell morphed into a dream. I wasn't sure what was real anymore or how long I'd been there. It seemed as if the world outside had sputtered to a stop and no one knew we were still in here, burdened by this relentless continuing on. I kept wondering how much time would have to pass before I accepted the obvious truth.

Chris wasn't coming to save us.

"IT'S BEEN MORE THAN three hours," Avon quietly announced to Wade. He had kept count, all this time. Now, for some unknown reason, no guards came.

Wade stood and slowly walked toward the cell wall. He looked up at the security cameras that sat still, pointed directly at him, unmoving. Wade squinted as he tried to discern if there was still someone watching on the other side.

Then there was a loud clank, and just like that, all the little red lights on the locks turned to green. No one moved. No one breathed. We all froze in a stupor wondering if this was some sort of trap.

Wade pressed his hand against the glass and, with the ease of turning the page of a book, pushed the door open.

Avon followed suit. It was as if all the power had gone out. No alarms sounded. Nothing had changed at all except now the doors were open. Now our way was clear.

There was no time to question it. Wade took a step out. That was the starting pistol. The rest of us sprang into action. From each of the cells, people began running toward the exit door. Some stayed behind to help the wounded to their feet.

Quickly, I fought the flow of traffic to get to Minnie and Avon. I threw my arms around them, pulling them into a giant bear hug. It was too short. We didn't have time for a proper reunion. Avon signaled me to hoist Minnie onto his back. Carefully, I helped Minnie's tiny body latch on to Avon's shoulders.

"I'll be right behind you!" I shouted. Avon nodded and ran toward the exit. Even after being tortured, and still sick with malaria, he had such an impressive and understated strength.

I rushed into Wade's cell and helped him lift Damien's limp body. Wade was a large man, so while he didn't exactly shrug me off, it was clear he didn't need my help. Before I stepped away, Damien's eyes fluttered open, and he smiled at me.

"Told you I wouldn't let you die, Rivers." It was good to hear his voice, cracked and breathless as it was.

"Right now, you just worry about yourself," I told him.

With Damien tucked in his arms, Wade took off after the others. I looked around to make sure everyone else had gotten out okay. Down the hall, an Awoken man was still struggling to limp to the door.

Wade passed him and shouted, "Rivers! Samson! Let's go!"

I scurried up to this Samson person and offered him my shoulder, which he gratefully took. With me to assist him, he was able to hobble faster, and we made it out the door.

Finally in the hallway, I tripped almost immediately, taking us both to the ground. Samson grunted in pain.

"I'm so sorry!"

I looked back to see we'd tripped over a dead guard. His head was unnaturally bent to the side. Only a few days before, I had never seen a dead man, and it hadn't gotten easier. This one was up close and personal. Through the slit in his helmet, I saw his eyes bloodshot and dull.

The darkness inside me roared in recognition of its kin.

Samson nudged me with his one good leg to get my attention. "We gotta catch up." He spoke with a soft Caribbean accent that momentarily made me think of warm beaches and frozen cocktails. I scurried to my feet, then helped Samson to his, and we continued down the hallway.

We passed through a control room where the security cameras were monitored. The screens were black, and in each of the three chairs were dead officers. Their throats slashed.

Perhaps on my own, I would've caught up to Wade and the group, but with Samson and my weakened, beaten, still atrophied muscles, I struggled to maintain a fervently-trying-to-escape pace. To navigate our way out, we followed the echoing sounds of shouting and scuffling feet made by the group ahead of us. Each time I heard a shout, I hoped it came from an unlucky UA officer who found himself in the path of our secret escape and not from one of our people. My hopes were confirmed as we passed from room to room, finding a trail of dead guards in the wake of the stampeding horde.

In a utility hallway, there were a number of bodies on the ground. As we hobbled by, one of the bodies coughed. I stopped. There was someone still alive. In pain. Struggling to live. I wanted to turn and look at him, to hold his hand as he passed into the darkness. He was about to be alone for eternity, not even having himself for company. But I didn't turn around. I kept going. If not for myself, for Samson.

Eventually we came to a propped-open door, and through it I saw our group. I took a deep breath, relieved this escape from hell was almost over.

We pushed our way through the door and reunited with the battered group of ragtag refugees and rebels. Everyone was weak and weary but free. We had made it out alive and undetected.

Samson thanked me before wrapping his arms around a friend and limping away. People were excitedly pouring themselves into the four vans there waiting for us.

I maneuvered my way to the center of the group, trying to spot Minnie and Avon. The first person I found was Wade. I tapped on his shoulder. He turned around, grinning from ear to ear. As the people around us wildly celebrated our newfound, though still tenuous, freedom, Wade and I shared a moment in silence. He beamed with pride.

Finally, he said, "Well done, Alabine. Very well done." Tears came to my eyes, and for the first time in days, they were tears of joy.

A woman walked up to us, interrupting our moment of peace. I immediately recognized her from the train. It was Chris. Now up close, I saw how young she was. Maybe only twenty or so. She handed something to me. I looked down and saw the receipt I'd given her with my note on it.

"It's good to finally meet you," she said with a lift of hope in her voice.

"Yeah, you too." I thought of Helen and how happy she'd be to learn her daughter was alive. If Helen herself was still alive, that is.

Wade patted Chris's back. "Chris has been undercover for almost a year. She's been using her position here to secretly communicate with our allies in Canada and broker a deal for supplies. Food, weapons, antibiotics. For your medicine, Alabine."

She smiled bashfully. "I had to rush some things at the end, but it's all set up. They have enough supplies to last us for years. They just need to know where and when to deliver it."

I heaved a selfish sigh of relief. Wade was going to fulfill that promise to me, which meant he'd keep the one about Max too. Everything was falling into place.

Behind us, people continued to file into the vans. "Where's Minnie? And Avon? How's Damien?"

Wade laughed at my onslaught of questions. "They're in the vans. We should hop on too before Chris's cover expires and we're discovered."

"It's okay. Breathe. There's still some time left." Chris squeezed my hand, then ran off to help others into the vans. But in the quick moment before she left, I noticed her eyes dart over to the door behind us from which I'd just emerged. At least, that's what I remember seeing. It was so quick and so subtle that I didn't think much of it at the time.

Wade put his hands on my cheeks and looked deeply into my eyes. "You see, you *can* do this." I started to believe him. "There is so much we can do. So much we will do. We're going to change the world. Together." He pulled me forward and kissed my forehead.

What happened next transpired so quickly I can barely remember the series of events to recount them coherently. What I know is that suddenly there was a loud noise and I was on the ground, awash in blood.

It wasn't until after I hit the pavement that I realized it was Wade who had pushed me down as he lunged forward. Gunshots rang out. Instinctively, I covered my head. When I looked up, Wade was a few paces behind me, fighting two officers. There were three bloody holes in Wade's broad back. But by the way he was overpowering these men, it seemed inconceivable that he'd been shot. He moved like a massive lion hunched over his prey. Among their tangled bodies, a final two gunshots cut through the cold air. These shots were dealt by Wade, who had wrested the guns away from the officers.

By then, Avon, Chris, and some of the other Resurrectionists had gotten to Wade and pulled the dead officers out from under his body. Wade collapsed to his knees. That I remember with absolute certainty. Forever emblazoned in my mind is the image of Wade's muscular body kneeling on the ground. His back was to me as he breathed deeply and slowly, blood streaming down his shirt. He reached up and grabbed Avon's arm and said something to him I didn't hear. Avon nodded. Then Wade looked back to me, his breathing becoming ever more labored. He didn't smile. He didn't frown.

He was a king.

And that's how Wade Lovett, beloved leader of the Resurrectionists, died. Wade Lovett died saving my life.

Right then and there, I made a promise to myself. His death would mean something.

PART
THREE

IN MEMORY OF WADE LOVETT

Sunday, December 22, 2121

Hello, and welcome. There's a lot of familiar faces out there, as well as some new ones. For those who don't know me, my name is Chris Smith. I've been a part of this movement since I was thirteen. I joined the day the law was passed that mandated Awoken be shot on sight. Even as a child, it didn't make sense to me how, in an advanced and thriving society such as ours, we could classify any life as unlawful. I knew I needed to do something about it. My heart inspired me to find this group; Wade Lovett inspired me to stay. Over the years, he became like a father to me. My own father died during the infestation, so I don't have many memories of him. From what I've heard, that perhaps is for the best. My mother and I never saw eye to eye. She hated that I joined up and tried having me reeducated, worried how it would look that her only child had become political. She's never forgiven this betrayal. So, I was honored to count Wade among my chosen family. Unlike my parents, Wade loved me unconditionally. Like he did for so many of you, he taught me how to fight for what's right, how to think for myself, how to dream of a country we can be proud to call home.

We didn't always agree on everything. God knows he often asked too much. He pushed me to the very limits of my comfort and sanity. Wade was a man of principle, and men of principle are often, let's say, difficult people. I know he wouldn't want me to smooth out his rough edges now that he's gone. He cared too much about the truth for me to do that to him.

Before he joined the Resurrectionists, Wade was a leader without a calling.

Without Wade, the Resurrectionists were good intentions without an engine. The movement needed Wade, and Wade needed the movement. Luckily, they found each other. And together they did remarkable things. For the first time, Wade secured international allies. He then took the splintered Awoken camps from Georgia to Maine to this one in Detroit and united them and their leaders under one banner. He thrust the need for Awoken rights into mainstream conversation in a way it hadn't been for decades. As you all know, this has been met with strong opposition from the new administration. But in the most challenging time this movement has ever faced, Wade provided the leadership we needed to survive. What was before a rudderless and powerless group that would've fizzled out after the infestation is now feared and listened to. Thanks to Wade and his vision.

Wade died for love. He died for what he believed in. He would not have wanted it any other way. Sacrifice was never something that frightened Wade. He told me over and over, "A life without sacrifice is not a life of worth." I used to hate him when he said that, but now I've come to realize he was right. The only thing Wade would've regretted about his death is that he hadn't yet accomplished all he wanted. In his mind, he hadn't yet done enough. I always saw what he did for us—for our country, for every single Awoken, for wayward little thirteen-year-old me—I always saw that as enough. And still, he did more. And still, he never saw it as enough.

So, let me say now, Wade's work will not be put aside. It was enough because we will finish what he started, and we will make it be enough.

11

THE SCREAM CAME FROM a place so deep inside of me that it was unrecognizable. Savagely guttural. Ugly and primal. Wrenched out of me like a heart from one's chest. Its sound reverberated against the tile walls of the shower stall and more resembled an animal's wail than any noise that could be created by a more highly evolved being. Of course it was accompanied by tears, but they seemed inconsequential among the downpour of water and washed down the shower drain all the same.

Since watching Wade die, I had robotically moved through the steps that took us from Montrose to a remote Awoken camp in Detroit. Leaving that cursed building, I put one foot in front of the other, following the people around me, until I was on a boat to Grand Rapids. From there, we drove to an abandoned underground train station in the north of the desolate snow-covered Detroit landscape. All the while I didn't say a word, instead using every muscle in my body, every ounce of focus, to hold myself together.

Arriving in Detroit was a blur. We trudged through untouched snow down wide empty streets that hadn't seen a soul in years. The buildings looked down on us like gods: stoic, unfazed by human affairs. This urban capital that once teemed with life and the busy goings-on of humanity now lay silent, having surrendered to nature. A bird flew overhead, completely disinterested in everything happening below. It comforted me to see how inconsequential we were. The city was hers now.

We made our way to the hidden train station entrance. Nothing more than a hole in a plywood-covered wall.

Once we were safely tucked inside, a kind older woman guided me into a bathroom and helped me undress. She then left and closed the door. The old woman stood vigil just outside and protected my solitude from curious intruders. I was alone. Left alone to scream. Scream for Wade sacrificing his life for mine. Scream for losing the hope of finding Max along with him. Scream for fear of what was going to happen to me next.

The shower water was blissfully scalding hot. With every droplet, the death and darkness I'd seen over the past few days washed down the drain. My trembling hands instinctively reached for hair and instead found my bald head. With a painful vigor, I scrubbed my scalp using the aggressively floral-scented soap until every speck of grime fell off. I scrubbed and scrubbed until my scalp was so raw that it burned; like if I could just get clean enough, I'd step out of the shower a new person. A different person. Sadly, when the steam evaporated, I found the same ghostly Alabine staring back at me in the mirror, the same one I first saw in the glass reflection only moments after being brought back to life. A terrified girl, scared and scarred and utterly lost.

The old woman eventually came back in and helped me dress. I might not have emerged the new person I'd hoped, but I had to admit that I felt better having finally bathed for the first time in a century. The red goo from my preservation bag was finally rinsed off my skin along with the dried mud and clotted blood. The old woman held my hand as I stepped into jeans, wool socks, scuffed white sneakers, and a long-sleeve wool tunic that covered both my scabbing gunshot wound and ID numbers. Finally, I put the blonde wig on my head, covering the metal implant behind my ear.

The air was crisp and cold, but with my body still warmed from the hot water, I was comfortable enough in the clothes the old woman brought me. I never learned her name. We didn't speak. Before she left, she hugged me.

I wanted to run away, simply disappear, to be washed down the shower drain along with the soapy hot water. No one would've much cared or even noticed, not really. As I contemplated my inconsequential existence, my fingers traced the ID numbers under my skin and then inched their way up to my sore gunshot wound. Eventually my thoughts circled their way back to the subject that had consumed me since Montrose: Wade.

He saved my life, and now he was dead because of me.

On top of everything, I had no idea how to find Max without Wade. But he was out there—Max was out there waiting for me. That was enough to keep me going. To keep me from throwing in the towel and choosing the darkness over this hell I was living. My desperation to find Max and avenge Wade was all that kept me upright.

Of course my coughing, night sweats, and labored breathing returned as cancer spread through my body, slowly resuming its habit and rituals like some family returning home from a long vacation. Thankfully, the unmistakable feeling of imminent death had yet to take over. Though exhausted, I still had life's energy in me. Whatever healing process happened during cryo, it was still working, despite the recent trauma my body had endured. Damien had said it would take a few weeks for the cancer to consume me again, and it'd only been a few days of this new life. I had time. Still, I kept Minchin's business card secretly tucked away in my pocket. Not that I had any idea how I would call him. Max's phone sure didn't have Wi-Fi signal or cell service, as those were relics of a former world. Still, Minchin's card was my secret security blanket.

The days leading up to Wade's funeral were busy and chaotic. I needed time and space to heal, but it was difficult at first to find either in my new home. It was a smaller camp than the one in Chicago and run by an eccentric and enigmatic woman named Eliza Shift. For a while, that was the extent of my knowledge of the camp. Eliza and Avon tried to get me to take an interest and participate in their meetings to plan for the future of the movement. It's not that I didn't want to. I wanted to help them find Max, and now I also wanted revenge, but there was something else much more present that took my entire focus.

I was determined to keep a very injured Damien from joining Wade in the darkness. His name wouldn't be added to my list of people to avenge. Not if I had anything to say about it.

There were two instances when I thought Damien died.

The first time was on the boat that took us across Lake Michigan from Montrose to Grand Rapids. Damien's head wound was impossibly deep. I swear I could see his brain matter. As we bounced around on the tormenting waves, Damien's body became still and all color left his face. Miraculously, he was still alive when we made it to camp, but barely.

The second time was the following morning. He began hemorrhaging, and it didn't seem like he was going to make it. I stood there, helpless, resigned to the idea that I was about to watch Damien die. Then an Awoken man named Noah, a surgeon in his first life, swooped into the makeshift hospital room like an angel. With the limited medical supplies available, he performed emergency surgery to repair the artery in Damien's head. Dr. Noah stopped the bleeding and successfully staved off infection.

Noah was a handsome man in his early forties. He was always clean-shaven and exuded more charm and poise than anyone else I'd met. Two years before he saved Damien Grey's life, Eliza's team woke him specifically for his skills with a scalpel. In those two years, he saved countless other lives. Noah was born in New York City eight days before the Twin Towers fell and died in New York on the fortieth anniversary. He underwent elective euthanasia, finally a legal avenue in 2041, due to a terminal pancreatic cancer diagnosis. He was awoken before the Redden administration came to power during a time when the Resurrectionists' medical supplies were still abundant. Unlike mine, Noah's cancer was cured, as promised, shortly after he was brought back.

After the worst was over with Damien, Noah left the day-to-day care to me. We had holed up inside a rundown train car that had been converted into a bare-bones hospital room. Despite its limitations in every conceivable light, I was thankful it existed. It was a safe place for Damien to fight for his life. I helped however I could, changing bandages and refreshing IV bags. Mostly, I just kept Damien company and tried to keep his spirits up, which in turn helped me. Tending to Damien kept me from suffocating under my grief. With him I found the space I needed to begin to heal.

I don't remember the day of Wade's funeral. I don't remember going, though I know that I did. Someone gave me a simple black dress to wear that I ended up keeping for a long time. It reminded me of Wade and his sacrifice. Whenever I thought of giving up, I'd look at that dress and push myself to keep fighting.

Of course the loss of our leader hung heavy over those of us who'd arrived from Chicago, but it was a tragedy for people in the Detroit camp as well. Many of them knew him or of him. Memorials to Wade popped up around the camp. Candles were lit. Prayers were said. He was a mammoth of a man, and his death caused an earthquake.

The only beacon of light amid the doom and gloom was Minnie. Her smile. Her laugh. Her enviable resilience. Despite Wade's death and Damien's injury and her rapidly worsening disease, Minnie happily immersed herself in the school established by the camp. She was much more carefree than our situation seemed to afford. It was life-giving for me to see her simply act like the child she was.

Whether I was ready for it or not, life was marching on. Without

Wade. Without Max. I was happy enough to watch it pass without me too. Simply the thought of leaving the safe bubble I'd carefully built around Damien would send me into a panic. Though I wouldn't tell anyone, I wasn't able even to walk through camp without breaking down into tears.

One day at a time, I told myself.

Finally, after a week in Detroit, two days after Wade's funeral, I found myself smiling for the first time since arriving. Damien was eating lunch—roasted chicken with crispy skin so salty I could smell it. We were talking about my messed-up family. Damien, wounded and all, was distracting me from Wade and death and being hunted, and thankfully, it was working.

"My mother was young when she had me," I told him. "Not even nineteen. Though she told my dad she was twenty-one. He was a young physicist, and she was on the janitorial staff at the university. Her name was Miranda Pickett. She was gorgeous. My dad carried a photo of her with him every day." I smiled, thinking about that photo. "My dad always wanted a close family and kids. So, my father convinced Miranda to have a baby. He wanted to be loved, she wanted the stability he offered. Ergo, I was born."

"The world was never the same," Damien said with a smile. I laughed a full-bellied laugh that took over my body. Unfortunately, the effort it required made me cough up blood. Damien casually handed me the napkin off his lunch tray. "You were one big happy family," he concluded.

"If only," I responded. "Miranda left when I was still a baby. My father wasn't the easiest man to love." I wasn't ready to dive into my dad's psychosis with Damien yet, so I left it at that. "It's awful for me to say, but I think she found out he didn't have as much money as she thought. My family came from old money, but that was squandered generations before me. All that was left was the house, and then that was lost after my dad died." Damien watched me silently, totally engrossed. I felt myself blushing at the attention. "Those are the excuses I tell myself, but really I just don't think she liked being a mom. At least not yet. She had a couple kids many years later. It seemed like she was a good mom to them. Didn't leave, at least." I shrugged.

"That must've been hard." He tucked a stray curl behind his ear. The concern in his eyes made me uncomfortable. It made me want to open up about my past in a way I had done before only with Max. I changed the subject.

"Tell me more about your family."

His face lifted. "Growing up with two older sisters was wonderful. They'd put lipstick on me and dress me in all sorts of outfits. I was like their real-life doll." His Virginian accent was always strongest when he'd reminisce about his childhood. "Father quickly put a stop to it whenever he found us, swearing he'd send us to one of those reeducation camps, but he didn't find us all that often." Damien took a large bite of his chicken.

He called his parents Father and Mother like those were their proper names—not *my* father and *my* mother. Oddly formal, especially for Damien. His childhood sounded so simple and normal. I could have lost myself for hours in the storybook recounting of his life before joining the Resurrectionists. It was a life I so desperately wanted for myself. I wanted that future with Max. I couldn't imagine how Damien could leave all that serenity behind and choose to join this fight, willingly, no matter how noble the cause.

In the background, a small radio played DJ Raheem's broadcast. I know it sounds silly, but I had come to find comfort in Raheem's easy positivity and mild music. Damien and I always had him on in the background in our healing bubble.

"Hello, good afternoon, and good day, my fellow citizens. Raheem here, as always. It's four in the afternoon, time for violin hour."

Living underground was like being in a time vortex. It had been a week since we escaped Montrose, but it felt like months. We had fallen into a comforting routine. Four o'clock meant Minnie would be getting out of school. It also meant, "Time to change your dressing."

With a patient's obedience, Damien wiped the chicken grease off his hands and shifted forward to the edge of his bed as I collected the things I would need: gauze, tape, ointment, and antibiotics. Violin music played softly from the radio. Slowly, he unwrapped the white linen bandage. I watched him out of the corner of my eye while I carefully injected the syringe of antibiotics into his IV bag. The gauze on his wound now only showed a bit of dulled red.

"It's looking better," I offered. The feeling of accomplishment flooded through me as I remembered how hard I'd worked, at Dr. Noah's instruction, to heal him. He would live—that was evident in the coagulated bloodstain. With Wade's death, I thought that we all needed a bit of good news in this shit of a world, and that was going to be that Damien would live.

Slowly, I peeled back the bandage. The wound was above his left eye. A deep gash stapled together. With care and a delicate touch that I'd honed in the past few days, I applied the thick white ointment and covered it with a fresh sheet of gauze. Then I wrapped the long linen bandage back around his head as if he were a mummy. Medical supplies were very limited. They had fallen victim to the same broken supply chain that made medicine for me and other newly revived Awoken so hard to come by. The promised caravan from Canada had yet to materialize, so I was extra careful with the amount of everything I used. Down to the very last thread.

Damien watched me while I tended to his wound, never taking his eyes off my face. I looked down at him, and our eyes met for just a moment. He quickly looked away.

I cleared my throat, then asked, "So we're even now, right?" with a cheeky grin. "A life for a life, my debt is repaid." The *Mulan* reference went unnoticed.

"Rivers, I brought you back from the dead. You put a Band-Aid on a scratch. We'll never be even." His smile stretched from ear to ear.

"Well, then, my continued gratitude will have to suffice." I paused as I finished tying up the bandage, consumed once again with how close Damien had come to the darkness. "I imagine you'll want to go home and never look back after all this."

Damien's brow creased. "Certainly not. It'll take more than this to scare me away."

"Why? You're not an Awoken. You don't even have any in your family. You could be with your sisters. Warm and reading a book, not sitting here bleeding, having almost died."

He thought deeply for a moment. Something was on the tip of his tongue that he was trying to find the right words to say. He shrugged, giving up on that thought and finding another. "I like being a part of something. I never felt that I had a purpose in this world, like I was born to do something, but I hadn't yet lived up to it." His words strongly resonated with me. He too was an Alice, trying to find a way to make his life meaningful. "So when a colleague of mine at the research lab where I worked started hinting that he was a part of the Resurrectionists, I jumped at the chance to join and was hooked. I felt at home for the first time in my life. It's intoxicating being a part of this movement, being a part of history. That's why I stay, I guess. The movement. Changing the country. Doing the right thing in this beautiful broken world." He was staring off into the ether, perhaps into the world he believed he could make.

Just then, Minnie came bounding in with an armful of books and a salami sandwich. The girl was always eating. She wanted to soak in every ounce of life she could. Dying young will do that to you. Moreover, she was acutely aware that death might come again, and soon, if we didn't get her medicine. It was incredibly frustrating to know that her cure was out there; we just couldn't get our hands on it. Not until Chris's Canadian allies came through.

I sat down on the bed next to Damien, readying myself for an onslaught of stories about how school was that day, as had been our routine. Minnie dove between the two of us. Damien melodramatically winced, pretending that she'd hurt him. We all laughed together.

Suddenly, the darkness lurched inside of me. My body flushed cold. I wondered why it had chosen this moment to remind me it was there, a moment when I was happy for the first time since Wade's death. Perhaps that was the perfect moment to remind me that happiness was fleeting.

As if on cue, Avon walked into the room, his face weighted heavy with worry. Minnie stopped her story, and we all stared at him.

"I'm sorry, Alabine, something's happened. We need you in One."

One was what they called Eliza Shift's quarters, where she held the important meetings with camp leadership to decide strategy and plans. I had been avoiding One, and Eliza, since we got here. The ostentatious and charismatic leader of the Detroit camp had tried speaking to me on several occasions, but I wasn't ready to dive back into the world of guns and raids yet. In this bubble of safety I had constructed around Damien, I felt normal. I was myself. To Eliza, I was *the* Alabine Rivers. Even in our glancing exchanges, it was clear that she was a big fan of me and Max and knew our story well. I didn't think I was strong enough, not after everything that had happened, to be the person she expected.

Until that moment, Avon had diligently intercepted Eliza's advances toward me, respecting my need for time to heal, but something had changed. I saw it in his face.

"Now?" I asked. Avon nodded. A rock dropped into my stomach, dread at having to leave that room. I reminded myself that going with Avon wasn't some chore I didn't want to do. I wanted to be in those meetings. They were deciding what to do next. I had to save Max. However, with each passing day, it still never felt like enough time. I still wasn't ready. Maybe I never would've been ready.

Slowly, I pushed myself up from the hospital bed and walked toward Avon.

"Good luck," Damien said. I looked back at him, and he was smiling softly. "You'll come back here after you're done?"

"Those bandages won't change themselves." All I wanted was to stay with him and Minnie and forget about everything else. Instead I left.

OUTSIDE DAMIEN'S TRAIN CAR, in the main station that this camp molded into a home, was a mess of noise and chaos. All the camp's children had just gotten out of school. Boundless energy and joy radiated from their little bodies. Pushing through the skipping rhapsody, in a stark contrast, a group of people worked in unison to haul two recently killed deer carcasses. As they passed in front of me, the gamey smell of dying flesh and bullet-singed fur filled my nose. If the darkness could smell like something, that would've been it. It also made me realize I had yet to eat that day.

It wasn't the first day that I'd forgotten to eat. Gina, of all people, brought it to my attention at Wade's funeral: "After all we went through to get you here alive, Rivers, don't starve yourself to death out of self-pity." She had a point, although I remembered that lack of appetite was another side effect of my lymphoma.

Only a few hundred Awoken called this abandoned train terminal home, making it much smaller than the Chicago camp. However, in comparison, Chicago seemed like the Ritz, with its toaster ovens and rug-clad floors. The Detroit camp was cramped and smelled of stale urine.

The main area where most of the residents mingled lay beneath a beautiful tiled mosaic that splashed across the towering ceiling and told the story of Eve's fall from grace. The lustrous red of the apple had faded and dulled from centuries of wear. The slender, tastefully nude female body stood imposingly in the center of the ceiling. Eve's long brown hair worked in tandem with an orange maple leaf to cover what parts of hers were deemed unsuitable for public consumption. Pouring down from the tree was a golden chandelier. The brass arms spanned an impressive width. While some of the lights worked, most of the bulbs were broken or missing. The effect was a dimly cast iridescent hue that unevenly lit the station's expanse.

The space felt old. At some point, I found a plaque that established the building was built circa 1908. In another time, this room would've been quite the majestic sight. This was no longer that time. Now it only provided a secret and safe, if not the most sanitary, sanctuary for these few hundred refugees and the Resurrectionists who protected them.

At the Chicago camp, people were housed in various tents and makeshift structures. Here, it was entirely open. People slept in groupings on the floor with only blankets to cover them. Every wall was lined with nests of sheets and pillows. Warming fires blazed in trash cans scattered around the station. There were multiple staircases leading to various platforms, each one just as packed with people as the last.

The platforms surrounded a row of tracks, most of which were empty. From what I could tell, the tracks were mainly used as a playground for the older children. They were too dark and dirty to commandeer into appropriate living spaces. The track in the very center, however, had a broken-down train on it. The train cars were clad in such a rusted metal that it was difficult to imagine they once shone silver.

There were nine cars. Avon and I walked briskly from the sixth car, the hospital room where Damien was, to the first car, where Eliza lived. Aptly named One, it also served as a meeting place with her advisors.

At the back of the train was a car that had been converted into a library, much to my delight when I first arrived. Next to that was a schoolroom that always had children running in and out. Eliza built the library and school, for which she specifically resurrected teachers, as a symbol that this camp meant to do more than simply survive. The attempt at normalcy provided an unsettling comfort. I couldn't decide which was worse, only scraping by in hopes that life would get better, or accepting that this was all life could be for Awoken, so we should live it up as much as we could.

Directly behind Damien's car was another medical car. When we arrived, one medical car was cleared out for all the injured people from Montrose. Now Damien was the only one who remained. Samson, the man with the Caribbean accent who I helped limp out of the Montrose facility, was the last to leave. The interrogators had rammed a one-inch-thick metal rod through his shin when he couldn't give the details of Awoken camp locations. He'd walk with a limp for the rest of his life. The truth was, he didn't know them. He confided in me that when the pain got to be too horrific, he made up a camp and its location just so they'd stop for a moment. The fake admission convinced them to keep him alive for more questioning. In the end, that one-inch metal rod sort of saved his life.

He and Damien kept each other company as they both healed. Samson was a part of our bubble for a while. We learned that he was awoken before the fungus spread and lived a full year out in the open. After the infestation hit, he was forced to go into hiding. Eventually he found a home with Wade and the Chicago camp. All three of us became close in those few days in the hospital car, but Samson and Damien became especially close. The two of them were calling each other "brother" by the time Samson healed enough to leave and join the rest of our group on an upstairs platform.

That upstairs platform became New Chicago. All of the refugees from Wade's camp made a home there, where Gina guarded the group like a mother cat watching over her kittens. The Detroit camp was more than welcoming, but you can't blame us for not wanting to disperse into the general population; we had been through so much together.

As Avon and I walked the length of the train, we passed the kitchen and dining cars. I promised myself I'd get a big dinner after the meeting in One. Perhaps there would be more of that salty chicken Damien had for lunch. Suddenly, all I could think of were potato chips. The really salty, greasy ones with ripples on them perfect for scooping into some large tub of sour cream dip. I could almost taste them on my lips.

"Before we go in—" Avon stopped walking. Thrust out of my potato chip fantasy, I found myself standing in front of the train car with a giant red number one painted on the side. Avon touched my arm and pulled me aside. I could tell he was nervous about something. Unlike me, Avon rarely seemed anxious about anything.

"Is everything okay?" I asked, fearing the worst.

Avon nodded, searching for words. "In there, we have to decide what we're going to do next. Wade told me his plan, and I'm going to push for it. I'll need your support. Your opinion means a lot to those people in there."

Avon's tone was very serious. My instinct was to make some sort of joke and lighten the mood, but thankfully, I decided otherwise. "Of course. Wade's plan was to get Max. He said the future of the movement depended on it."

There was more Avon wanted to say, I could see it in his face. All he said was, "It's more complicated than that. But yes, that was a part of his plan."

I reached out and touched Avon's hand. "I'll support you, Avon." He exhaled and smiled. From the beginning, Wade had brought Avon into the Resurrectionist leadership. It's why he was awoken to begin with, to help lead. I felt safer knowing that Avon would be making decisions along with Eliza.

At Avon's invitation, or perhaps more like insistence, I stepped inside.

Immediately, I was hit with a wall of warm air. A nice respite from the cold drafty camp. But the warmth had an oppressiveness about it, almost smothering in its comfort. The sensation was followed by a wave of chaotic energy. We had walked into an active war room, and I was caught completely off guard by what was about to happen.

"Leave everything! Go now!" Eliza Shift shouted desperately into a handheld two-way radio. The cluttered room was abuzz with people darting this way and that. Unrolling maps, plotting routes, and shouting at one another.

Avon left my side and dove headfirst into the chaos. "What's going on?"

Chris grabbed his arm. "Another raid. A camp in Nashville."

My heart leapt as images from the raid in Chicago haunted me, my memories amplified by the sounds coming through Eliza's radio. Screams. Gunshots. Death.

"They're everywhere!" The voice transmitting from the other end was a terrified woman. Her desperate cries cut in and out of the radio's static and the hostile background noises. She screamed a guttural battle cry, then shot multiple rounds off. "Help us!"

"Madge!" Eliza shouted into the radio. "Get out of there!"

"Tell them to run," Avon demanded as he leaned over the large table in the center of the room. "Don't fight. They don't stand a chance!"

Before Eliza could transmit any more messages, Madge screamed again. This time it wasn't a battle cry; it was a cry of pain. "No, God! No!" The puttering *whoosh* of a flamethrower overtook her pleas. Then the radio went silent.

The entire room stilled. The chaotic energy dissipated as everyone turned and stared at the vacant radio. Slowly, Eliza reached up and clicked off the handset.

Avon crossed himself and muttered a prayer. "That's the second one today."

"Fifth since Montrose," Chris added.

"What the hell is going on?" I quietly asked. The somber room turned to me.

Eliza's grief morphed inconceivably quickly to excitement. "Alabine

Rivers. Welcome. I cannot tell you what an honor it is to have you here." Her smile brought her out of whatever hell was on the other side of that radio and back into the train car. She walked around the table and put a hand on my shoulder. I shifted out of her embrace, uncomfortable with the familiarity.

I knew very little about her. She had unkempt graying blonde hair that she tossed up in a messy bun like a nest on top of her head. Her skin had the kind of mottled tan that proved she was a proud worker bee, not just the queen, very willing to break a sweat to get the job done. She wore army fatigues under an expensive tailored vest that made her look like a futuristic space pirate.

"That was a raid?" I asked, shocked.

"Our suspicions were right that some of the captured Resurrectionists in Montrose traded information for their freedom," Avon explained. "They gave away the locations of, we have to assume, all the Awoken camps around the country. The Territorial Army has been raiding camps ever since. We've lost a lot of people."

"What about us?" I asked, terror spreading through me with each thumping heartbeat. "Should we evacuate? Was that why you said there was no more time?" Repressed images of children drowning in pools of their own blood overtook my brain.

Avon put his hand on my arm with a compassionate touch. "It's okay. No one who was questioned knew about this camp. Chris didn't even know. Only Gina and Wade. We're safe here."

"We're safe." I repeated the phrase over and over so I could hear it out loud, so it could firmly take root in me. I didn't question why this camp was different somehow, more secret than the others. It didn't matter, so long as we were safe.

"We've sent messages to every camp telling them to find new homes immediately," Eliza announced.

Chris scoffed. "A hundred camps. About five hundred Awoken in each camp. Plus Resurrectionists. It's an exodus disaster of biblical proportions."

Ignoring Chris, Eliza leaned closely into me. "They'll be fine. Don't you worry. We know what we're doing." She winked. I hated when people winked like that, even if they had the best of intentions.

"Eliza, they won't be fine," Avon said in his most serious voice.

She smiled in a passive-aggressive way of dismissing him. "Please, let's all take a breath, and a seat."

Eliza guided me toward the seat next to hers at the cluttered table. As she did, I finally took in the strange train car. The long narrow room was filled floor to ceiling with stacks of memorabilia. A Mets flag was folded on top of a Civil War–era map of America. The peeling floral wallpaper hid behind towers of boxes stuffed with other such items. It was a chaotic shrine to American culture.

A homesickness came over me surrounded by artifacts from my time. I missed seeing baseball games at Wrigley Field. I missed my best friend, Andy, and the adventures of our youth. Eliza's room reminded me of all these things in a way that only gave me a hunger for them.

In between the mess of items was Max—or, more specifically, his face. And mine. We were everywhere. Framed photos hanging on the wall, posters, and newspaper clippings all told snippets of the century-long fight for Awoken rights. One framed picture was the same one of me that I had seen on the billboard: "Alabine Rivers. One Life. All Rights."

Another was a poster for a movie released in 2042. A biopic that told the story of the cryo movement with a forty-year-old Finn Wolf-hard as Max. It was weird to see Max cast as a white guy, but the bottom of the poster boasted that Finn won an Oscar for it, so it seems he did a good job.

Eliza's shrine to American culture was inherently impressive, if not a bit telling of her obsession with history, culture, the cryo movement, and . . . me. It struck me how different her train car was from Wade's tent. I'd expected the same austerity and restrained comfort. I'd expected Wade. A rush of sadness filled me as I came to terms with the fact that this new leader was very different from the one we had just lost.

After Eliza sat me in a chair, she hovered uncomfortably close. "I didn't have a chance at the funeral to tell you how sorry I am about Wade. He was a great, albeit stubborn, man. Years ago, I knew him well, and to this day I very much respect him. If it weren't for the radio system he established between camps, we wouldn't even be able to forewarn these people. Find comfort in the fact that his legacy lives on." She stared deeply into my eyes with an intense care, then asked, "How's Damien?"

In that moment, I realized she was playing her own game of chess. I preferred Wade's, or even Minchin's, game to Eliza's. The two men were much easier to read, while Eliza's strategy was to lure you in with kindness and compassion in order to get what she wanted. I had to be on my toes; her maternal energy was disarming.

"He's fine," I responded curtly, then stood, walked back around the table, and sat next to Avon. That was my opening move. I knew why I was there. The people in this room were the ones deciding the Resurrectionists' next step, and I needed to make sure that it involved waking Max up. I didn't know how much of a fight I had in front of me. I didn't know whose allegiances belonged to whom. So, I steeled myself.

Around the table were some faces I recognized, others I didn't. On one side were Avon, Dr. Noah, and Wade's lieutenant George, the man who was taken for questioning while we were in detention. His face still showed the bruises. Next to him was another Resurrectionist man who was in Montrose with us as well—he was the other man, along with George, whom I first met in Wade's tent what seemed like a lifetime ago. I can't remember his name anymore. He was older and very tall.

I was half surprised that Gina wasn't there. Then again, she wasn't as interested in these larger movement decisions. Wade's death hurt her deeply, so she distracted herself by focusing on our Chicago group.

On the other side of the table were Eliza and two of her lieutenants. All three women were tall and stunningly beautiful. The one who introduced herself to me as Diana, Eliza's number two, had long brown hair that made me miss my own. I tugged vacantly on the blonde wig covering my head. Like all of Eliza's lieutenants, these two seemed like Amazonian warriors: exquisitely feminine in their commanding strength and unwavering ideals.

Then there was Chris. She was seated at the head of the table with her boots kicked up, rocking back and forth on her tilted chair. I hadn't spoken with her since Montrose. Since Wade's death. To be honest, I was avoiding her. Avon told me he had relayed Helen's message of love, and in doing so he also told Chris what happened that horrid morning when I exposed us all, and how, as a result, we weren't sure if Chris's mother was even still alive. Although I'm sure Avon carefully chose his words, Chris now knew the truth that the whole thing was my fault.

But even more disturbing than that, the image of Chris's eyes darting to the door just before two officers came through and killed Wade kept replaying over and over in my head. As did Wade's coded comment to me that he had concerns about Chris's loyalty after being so long undercover. Whether it was guilt over my own actions or suspicions over Chris's, I avoided direct conversation as long as I could. Seeing her in that room, I had to constantly remind myself that she was one of us.

Avon had kept me updated on Chris's regular contact with Canada, working out a way to get the supplies, including my cancer medicine, across the border. She must be one of us. She'd proved herself to be one of us, *right?*

Eliza took a gulp of something out of a large pewter mug. "All right, now that our party is complete, let's continue. We unfortunately don't have the time to indulge in the pleasantry that tradition dictates, and we must instead 'duke it out,' as they say, with the information we have now."

There was a formality to her cadence that I wasn't expecting, given her disheveled surroundings. The more she spoke, the more I correctly guessed that she came from a wealthy upbringing, though those days were now far behind her. The Eliza I saw when we first entered, trying to save a woman in the last moments of her life, was drastically different from this smiling politician eager to make a good impression on me.

Eliza continued, "As you heard on the radio, things are not going well out there. We must decide what our response will be. Diana, will you bring Alabine up to speed?"

Diana stood. "A few weeks ago, Wade led a group of Resurrectionists to try and stop the UA forces from decommissioning a cryo facility outside Columbus."

"Eavesman Square," I said, nodding. "Wade told me."

Eliza leaned forward. "Did he tell you that because of his, shall we say, ill-advised attack, almost two dozen civilians died?"

I swallowed. "He did."

George, the bruised lieutenant from Chicago, passionately interjected. "What went wrong at Eavesman Square was not our fault. The Territorial Army escalated the situation. We didn't set off that bomb. We didn't even bring explosives."

"But Wade said it was his fault," I muttered, confused.

"Wade took responsibility for all of it because it was his decision to challenge them that led to the civilian casualties. The UA set off the bomb and blamed us. It was only afterward that Wade realized that was Redden's plan all along."

"And you guys fell right into it." Eliza closed her eyes in frustration. "Redden made us look like radical terrorists and got exactly what he wanted."

Diana cleared her throat, attempting to bring us back to the matter at hand. "Regular people don't like to think about us—Awoken, Resurrectionists, or even death. It makes them very uncomfortable. Eavesman Square forced them to see us, and they saw exactly what the president wanted them to see: extremist revolutionaries. Monsters. The public relations success for Redden's administration allowed them to obtain court approval to decommission a much larger facility in Atlanta." She pointed at Atlanta on the map on the table.

Looking at the map, I noted some of the state lines were drawn in different places from what I knew from my first life. Very interestingly, the land from Detroit to the north of Toronto was part of United America. And perhaps most surprisingly, the western UA border ran through Colorado. The states past the Rockies were now their own country.

My eyes fell back to Diana's finger hovering over Georgia.

"They registered the land under environmental protection," Chris moaned from her end of the table. "It'll be a national park. Built on the ashes of murdered innocents."

"They're wiping out half the deserted city and eighty thousand Awoken with it," Avon said. "And it's all perfectly legal."

"Eighty thousand?" I tried to imagine a facility that big. Remembering the storage warehouse of bodies I saw in Indianapolis, this would've been at least twice the size. "How can we stop them?" I asked.

"Wade had a plan." Avon stood up solemnly, first addressing the room, then turning directly to me. "To wake you up. Then Max. With you both at the head, he'd convince as many Awoken camps as possible to join us in a march to meet Redden on the steps of the Atlanta facility where the eyes of the world would be watching. Where you and Max, with thousands of Awoken and Resurrectionists behind you, could make a passionate plea to the country. Show that we're not terrorists. That we're just people. The same thing your story did for this movement a century ago. It's one thing to kill eighty thousand people when you think they're inhuman. But with the march we'll make them look us in the eye. Wade believed that with the two of you reunited you had the ability to—"

"Change minds." I remembered Wade telling me that part. "He thought in order for us to turn the tide in this war, we had to fight to change minds."

Avon nodded.

"It's a foolhardy plan," Eliza said, sitting back in her chair. "Marching up to the enemy is a surefire way to get everyone killed. People don't change their minds that quickly."

I looked away from the map and up to Avon. "It does seem dangerous. Why there? Then?"

Avon opened his mouth to answer, but Dr. Noah gently touched his hand, stopping him and offering his own response. Noah was the person in that room closest to my time period, and with a shared context, he thought he could help me understand. "There isn't internet or even TV anymore. It's just radio and newspaper now, and both are effectively controlled by the government. Publicly available mass communication is nonexistent."

Chris laughed sardonically. "The whole decommissioning will be broadcast live on UA52. They're already running ads. It's gonna be a lavish Patriots' Day celebration with all the pomp and bullshit befitting this administration. That's the only shot at speaking to the nation. It's the only shot at convincing people to leave us alone. We have to take it."

"Okay." I sighed, contemplating the enormous task in front of us. "Then how do we find Max? With Wade gone . . ."

"Max is as dangerous to the UA as he is important to us," Eliza jumped in. "They targeted the Atlanta facility to begin with because they think Max is there."

My stomach shot into my throat. "Max is in the facility they're about to blow up?"

Before I could spin into panic, Chris kicked her boots off the table and rocked forward. "He's not there. Our predecessors planted this misinformation in the UA's registry decades ago."

Eliza clicked her tongue. "A good ruse to be sure. And one that is finally paying off."

"Paying off?" Avon scoffed. "Eighty thousand people are about to be blown to smithereens because of it." Eliza sat back, properly chastised. The silence in the room was heavy with anticipation of an explanation or apology that she never gave.

"Max Green's true location is in the main cryo facility here." Diana's finger moved up the map from Atlanta and landed gently atop New York City. Words continued to flow out of her mouth, but my mind screeched to a halt.

Max was there. I couldn't believe it. Max was right there. Dead. Sleeping. Waiting. There. The secret of his location hadn't been lost with Wade, like I had thought. Though I couldn't yet remember why, I knew in my bones that New York was the most special place in the world to Max and me. Now it would be all the more special; it would be the place we would reunite after death and a century apart.

"The largest CryoLabs facility in this country is in Brighton Beach," Eliza said with a smile. "It's said there are almost a million preserved bodies in there. And we know that Max is one of them."

I flushed beet red. Wade's plan was a good one. First to New York to save Max, then a march in Atlanta to save eighty thousand others. Marches for civil rights are a fundamental part of the history of this country; they've worked before. It was a risk, but with Max by my side, we could do anything.

Avon put his hand on my shoulder, and with that single touch, I knew he was about to end my joy. "Just this morning, likely due to our escape from Montrose, President Redden announced that the decommissioning of the facility in Atlanta will be moved from his birthday a month from now to January first, Patriots' Day. In one week." He paused. "Al, there isn't time to get Max."

"Wade's plan was to get Max," I responded like a stubborn child. "You just said so. Wade promised me."

Avon exhaled. "It'll take time to travel undetected, on back roads and only at night. Then to find and power up the cryo facility. Then to wake up Max and give him the medical treatment he'll need. At the end of all that, there isn't enough time to make it all the way down to Atlanta, let alone organize the camps for the march. If we go to New York, if we go get Max now, we lose our one shot at speaking to the nation."

"Wade's plan relied on Max," I said again, anxiety overtaking me.

"Yes, and my plan only relies on you," Avon punctuated.

I shook my head at the absurdity of it. "I can't convince people on my own. I've never done that before. Max was the one who inspired this whole movement to begin with. I was dead. I had no say in the matter. It was all Max."

"And *you* inspired Max," Avon responded emphatically. "You can inspire everyone if you try. Marching with thousands of Awoken behind you, we can show the world that our lives mean something. That you can't just discard eighty thousand of us without a second thought and then go play with your kids like nothing happened."

Eliza slammed her mug down with a *clank*. "If we go to Atlanta, it will be another Eavesman Square but worse. The facility is eight times the size. The entire Territorial Army will be there. It's too risky."

"Unlike Eavesman Square, this won't be an armed attack. It will be a peaceful march." Avon turned to me. "Eighty thousand people are guaranteed to die in that facility if we don't at least try. They won't slaughter us with the world watching."

"Of course they would," Eliza responded.

"I agree," I said. "I've met Minchin. He has no hesitation in killing us and will just make the world see what he wants. Don't overestimate his humanity."

"And don't underestimate your power in this." Avon stared me directly in the eye. "You *can* do this, Al." I lowered my gaze.

Eliza emphatically rapped her finger on the table. "There's nothing we can do for Atlanta. We have to focus on protecting ourselves now, the ones already here. We need to focus on getting Max. With him and Al reunited, it changes the game, changes the narrative. It gives hope to all those camps out there on the brink of collapse."

"Hope doesn't matter if everyone in that facility is executed!" Avon shouted. "Hope means nothing if our lives are still disposable. When the camps come to Atlanta and march with us, we'll be together. We are stronger together. We will show the world our worth."

Eliza threw her arms up, exasperated. "We've survived this long because we're hidden and separate. That's always been our tactic, and it's worked so far." Eliza's two lieutenants banged their mugs on the table in support.

"We've survived this long because we aren't actually fighting," Chris retorted. "We're hiding. The old man's plan was to change that."

Avon turned from Eliza back to me to try again. "Alabine . . ." he pleaded. This was it, the moment he said would come. He needed me to support him, back him up like I'd promised. The only problem was, I couldn't.

"Please, don't put this on me." The desperation in my voice was palpable.

"Don't you want to stop running? Stop hiding?" Avon asked.

Of course, I thought.

"Well, until we stand up and demand to be heard, it won't stop. Not for the camps. Not for the Awoken in that facility." He paused. "Not for you or me. Not for Minnie. Not for any of us." Avon emphasized every syllable.

Eliza stood up, and her height suddenly felt intimidating rather than maternal. "I don't care what plans you or Wade put in place. Going to Atlanta is a suicide mission." Her voice was deep. She wanted to be taken very seriously.

Chris leaned in. "No offense, lady, but this isn't your call. I know Wade liked you, but you're a stranger to me. Wade was our leader; I follow his plan."

"Wade's dead," Eliza said coldly. All of the compassion and flowery language about Wade's legacy was gone. I couldn't tell if Chris was about to cry or throw a punch. The two women stared each other down until Eliza stepped back. "Fine. You're right, this isn't my call. It's Alabine's."

Time itself stopped in that moment. Everyone turned to look at me. It was like one of those classic nightmares in which you have a test for a class you've never been to. And you're naked.

"Her?" George asked the question everyone had in their heads. Me included.

Eliza winked at me. Again. "Yes, George, of course. Alabine Rivers was and always has been the head of our movement. Now that she's awake, she should take over leadership."

Chris laughed. "Max was the head of our movement. Wade wanted Max. He only agreed to get Alabine first after Damien Grey convinced him."

This hit me like a punch to the gut. Doubt crept into my mind. *Was that true?* I wondered. *Did Wade not even want me?* My confidence that I should have a seat at that table quickly eroded.

"Well, Max isn't here," Eliza said.

Chris stood up but still was much shorter and had to continue to look up at Eliza. "Wade wanted Avon to carry out his plan. That was his last order before he died." We all looked at Avon, who held his ground stoically.

"Sure he did," Eliza said with an eye roll. "Wade certainly was an idealist, but I don't believe he'd actually put someone like him in charge."

Chris slammed her fist on the table. "What does that mean, 'like him'? Avon is more of a leader than you will ever be!"

"Stop," Avon commanded. The bickering room fell silent. "As formidable as Wade was, he doesn't get to just appoint another leader. You all must choose if you want me. I will follow Wade's plan to march to Atlanta and have Alabine speak to the nation in front of as many camps as will join us."

Eliza sensed my skepticism and turned toward me, avoiding eye contact with Avon in an attempt to not recognize his authority. "If everyone goes to Atlanta, we'll be stoking a fire we can't extinguish."

I felt my own eyes on me from the framed poster hanging on the wall. And I felt Max's eyes. If only he were there. I looked back and forth between Chris and Eliza. Then, finally, I looked up to Avon, who was deep in thought, eyes cast downward at the map on the table.

"Avon, we need Max. I can't do what you're asking me to. Not alone. We'd all die with those eighty thousand. If we could just get Max first, then at least—"

"There's not enough time. This is our only opportunity to show the world who we are."

"And that opportunity is worth *all* of us dying?" I asked, half meaning it to be rhetorical.

"Yes," Avon said with such certainty that I felt myself persuaded. Only for a moment.

"No." The word came from my heart and out of my mouth before I could process what I was saying. "We need Max. We can't save those people in Atlanta or any of us without him. In the phone he left me, I've seen some of what he did back then. He was amazing. Let's get him first, then we can decide what to do next." The authoritative tone in my voice wasn't difficult to summon. There was no question in my mind. It was the right decision, not just for me but for everyone. Wade believed so too, despite what Avon said. Max was the key, not me.

"There. It's decided," Eliza said with a sneer.

Chris chortled. "Nothing has been decided. You're the only person who declared Alabine our leader."

"Well, right now, I have the guns and the food and the shelter," Eliza responded. "You're all guests in my domain, and I say Alabine is our leader and calls the shots." She paused, perhaps thinking, perhaps for dramatic effect. After looking around the room, she smiled. "Let's take a vote if you want it to be decided more democratically."

Chris agreed.

I looked up to Avon, who didn't return my gaze. Instead he focused intently on the map on the table. It seemed a very conscious choice on his part not to meet my eyes. I realized we were opponents. I had come there to support him, and now we found ourselves on different sides of the issue.

Eliza, initially hunched over the table, straightened her back and stood tall with the solemn air of official and sanctioned business. "All those who want to follow Avon into war, remain sitting. All those in favor of Alabine as our leader, stand with me."

Diana and the other Amazonian lieutenant stood. No shock that they took Eliza's side, but their move officially set in motion this vote for control over the Resurrectionist movement, Avon or me. It all happened so fast, and I wasn't sure if I was a pawn or a queen.

Then, after a weighted beat, George stood up. Much to everyone's surprise. This floored me. I thought he'd be steadfast to Wade, always his trusted man.

George cleared his throat as the room looked to him for an explanation. "None of us would be here if it weren't for Alabine and Max. My grandmother was an Awoken. She would've never had my mother if cryo didn't save her. We owe them our loyalty."

Eliza smiled and patted George on the back. He shirked off her touch, uncomfortable at the temporary alliance. Noah, Avon, the older Resurrectionist, and Chris remained seated. There were four sitting and four standing.

Then there was me.

"Alabine?" Eliza asked in an expectant tone. She thought she'd won. She assumed I'd stand and vote for myself, but when the time came, I froze with the decision.

Finally, Avon looked down at me with pleading eyes. "We'll wake him up," Avon said. "We just need time, Al."

"I've never had time, Avon." Then I stood up. The final vote swinging the decision in my favor. It felt as if a chasm opened between me and Avon.

"Good," Eliza declared with a smile. "We leave for New York tomorrow evening." The excitement that filled my every bone found an uneasy host. I hated that I had gone against Avon.

The meeting wrapped up shortly after that as people went off to plan for the departure. Chris ushered Avon off quickly. Too quickly for me to pull him aside and try to mend the rift this had caused. He and I had been in this together from the beginning.

If only I could get him to understand, I thought.

As the people filtered out, I was left alone in the tent with Eliza and her people. All strangers. I felt sick. I had flinched and, without even realizing it, changed the world.

"Rest up, Alabine. By the end of this week, you and Max will be back together." Eliza winked.

12

REST WAS ABOUT THE furthest thing from my mind as I left One. I headed toward Damien's train car so he could help me make heads or tails out of what the hell had just happened. Soon enough, though, I stopped. Instead of seeking solace with Damien, I decided I needed to speak to Avon first. So I turned away from the train and ventured toward the upstairs platform, New Chicago.

On the way there, my mind spun. I had just been elected leader of the Resurrectionists. That said, only five people voted for me and I was one of them. It didn't really give me a mandate to make decisions on behalf of tens of thousands of people. But regardless of the how we'd ended up where we did, an entire room of people listened to me. They called me their leader. It was a dream I'd had since I was a child, to be listened to. To make a difference. It's why I got into politics. And yet I had this voice in the back of my mind whispering that I didn't deserve it.

The area the Chicago refugees had sectioned off for themselves was up a series of staircases and through to the other side of the tracks.

Having stayed every night in the medical car, I had only been over there once before, so I almost got lost. Eventually I found my way by following the unmistakable sound of Gina's hearty laugh. It was inter-mixed with a general din of friendly conversation and the clatter of dishes.

They were all having dinner, or had just finished, by the looks of it, when I approached. The air smelled of pork and rosemary, which at first made me want to puke thanks to the cancer. Then I remembered I needed to eat and hoped there might be some scraps left over.

Gina and the others lounged on deerskin blankets and makeshift pillows around the fire while a small radio played soothing music un-der the curation of DJ Raheem's familiar voice. Unlike the rest of the camp, which used trash cans for their fires, here they used metal lids on the ground. It gave off a more romantic camping vibe and felt less like an encampment under the highway. I looked around at these peo-ple and was glad to see all of their faces. I was home.

Minnie ran up to me and threw her arms around my waist. I hugged her back, tightly at first, which I quickly released when I felt her wince. I wondered if I might be able to convince Eliza to find her some Dreno.

She looked up at me. "Did you see Damien?"

"No, I haven't yet. Is Avon here?" I looked around the small platform.

Gina leaned back from her conversation with the other Resurrec-tionists. "Thought he and Chris were with you." She chewed open-mouthed on some pork.

"Yeah. They were." I sat.

A few feet away, Minnie dove back into the rumple of fabric that was her bed and turned on a flashlight, illuminating the mess of elec-trical wires that entangled the sheets. Minnie was beyond thrilled when she found the camp's stash of broken equipment and frayed wires gathered from around the abandoned train station. Trash that had now become her cherished treasure. Ever since, she had spent most of her free time tinkering with the various monitors and cables. She yawned about as wide as her mouth would allow her. Those wires didn't stand much of a chance of being tinkered with for very long that night.

Thankfully, I found a pot of wild boar stew on the fire that still had a few spoonfuls left. And even better, there was a large piece of crusty bread on the ground.

"May I?" I asked Gina, who granted permission with a grunt.

I took a bite, worried I was going to throw it up. Thankfully, it went down easily. Without seeming too much like a starved kitten, I scarfed down my dinner. It was salty and savory and warm, everything I needed. Only a full glass of red wine would've finished the meal.

While I ate, Gina simmered next to me in silence. She chewed on a bone like one would smoke a cigarette after a big meal. People around us were engaged in various conversations, but they started to dwindle off and retire to their respective beds. I scanned the camp for Avon or Chris and didn't see them.

However, I did see George when he walked in with an Awoken woman. He offered me a slight knowing nod of his head. A gesture acknowledging what had happened in that train car. It wasn't just a dream. He intimately draped his arm around the woman he was with, and they slunk off into the shadows together, enviously curled into each other's embrace. I didn't know her name, I didn't know a lot of the names of these people, and yet still, we were indelibly bonded.

Gina flipped over to face me. "You're not your usual chatty self, Rivers."

We'd barely spoken ten words to each other since Wade's death. I didn't push it. I knew she didn't like me very much. When I was younger, especially when I was in high school, I hated when someone didn't like me. It ate at my soul, and I would try everything I could to change that. But as I neared death, I learned to let it go.

Even after everything we'd been through, Gina's disdain for me had anything but waned. After Wade's death, Gina expressed her grief through angry outbursts. So I mostly steered clear of her. This initiation of conversation was the olive branch I'd been hoping for.

"How'd the summit go?" she asked.

"Fine. Avon just left quickly, is all. I wanted to talk to him."

Gina turned the pork bone around in her mouth and gnawed on the other side. Briefly, I was reminded of how strange she had looked in that poufy pink dress she wore in order to blend in while on the road. In her denim jacket and cargo pants, she looked much more herself.

"Did you guys get into a fight?" Gina asked with only mild interest.

"We disagreed. And everyone ended up doing what I thought, so . . ."

"Of course they did. You're Alabine Rivers," she said with a sneer.

I didn't feel like rehashing the debate in an attempt to get Gina on my side, though I did consider it. Instead my mind wandered from Avon's annoyance with me toward the person who backed Avon. "What do you think of Chris?"

"Wade sure liked her a lot." Gina paused to think. "Chris sacrificed a lot for this movement. Her relationship with her mother, for one." She looked at me, trying to figure me out. "Why do you ask? Did she disagree with you too?" Her tone fell back into mockery.

"Chris said in the meeting that Wade didn't want to wake me up. That it was Max he wanted."

"That's true," Gina replied quickly. "Damien convinced him to get you first. I, for one, was adamantly against it."

"You wish I was still dead?"

"Don't you?" she asked, referring to the whole holding-her-gun-against-my-head-and-asking-her-to-shoot-me incident. I lowered my eyes, trying to ignore the darkness I felt gurgling in my belly as I remembered the moment it almost claimed me again. Gina continued, "We knew that facility you were in was still being watched. We never raid monitored facilities. It's too risky. But Damien was adamant. He scoured the logs of your facility and that's when he identified Avon and Minnie, both of whom Wade had on his wish list of assets to find. A military savant with a vendetta, a technological genius, *and* Alabine Rivers all in one place. Damien convinced Wade that it was worth the risk. I didn't agree. We lost good people because Wade listened to Damien over me."

I clearly remembered the people shot to death in the darkened hallways of the CryoLabs facility. They were the first of the countless dead bodies I had encountered.

"You mean that woman. Charlie?"

Gina nodded, swallowing her emotion. It was clear this Charlie meant something to her and that bringing me back to life was what ended Charlie's.

The guilt and sadness I'd carried for days felt too heavy to keep holding down. So, I didn't. "I'm sorry, Gina. For Charlie. And for Wade." Only two of many people who were in the darkness now so I could live.

Not that I expected her to respond in any meaningful way, but she didn't move a muscle. Gina continued to stare off into the fire. Eventually she pushed herself up from her recline into an energized crouch. She then pulled the bone out of her mouth and tossed it aside, finally surrendering to its inedibility.

"My great-grandmother knew your Max, you know. She was a co-plaintiff on the Supreme Court case," Gina stated very matter-of-factly. "They protested together and became good friends. She always said how great of a man he was. So, yeah. In the Alabine-versus-Max debate, I'm team Max."

"Me too," I muttered under my breath.

Just then, Minnie called out for me. Pushing myself up from the warm inviting fire, I walked over and knelt beside her. She was tucked into her bed, half asleep. Wires, exploding from the inside of old-school headphones, sprawled across her chest as she continued to fight her exhaustion.

"I made something for you today." She reached into her blanket folds and pulled out a white cable. "They have a bunch of these wires in the camp, and I tried to find one for your phone, but they were all for future models. So, I stripped them and made this. It should work."

It was a phone charger. Back home, I'd had a drawer filled with countless of these. But now I took it from her hands with the reverence one would pay a holy relic.

"Go on. Try it." Minnie beamed up at me.

There was a plug on the wall not too far from her bed. She was already using it to charge her flashlight, which she kindly unplugged so I'd have room. I grabbed the phone out of my pocket, grazing against Minchin's business card in the process, and plugged it into the charger. After a suspenseful beat, the phone lit up with the familiar, life-giving power-charging display. I burst into joyous laughter. Minnie joined in.

"Now you can look at it anytime you want," Minnie assured me. However, even with all the excitement, she was unable to stifle another massive yawn that overcame her.

"Thank you, Minnie. You're the smartest person in this whole camp, you know."

She smiled and rolled her eyes. "Duh." Then she snuggled back into her bed and turned off her flashlight. "Good night, Alabine."

"Good night," I replied. Then I looked down to the phone. My plan was to go as long as I could and fall asleep after hours of poring through Max's life.

Before I began, I looked around, trying to find the pile of my things I'd left somewhere. When we arrived in Detroit, we were each given clothes, shoes, and blankets, as well as a canteen and soap. Because I had been staying with Damien, I just used what I found in the medical car, with Minnie bringing me a change of clothes every now and then. My pile of these rations sat largely untouched in the far corner. I scooped everything up and brought it back to the wall next to Minnie and the charging phone.

There was a poorly stuffed sack that was supposed to be a mattress and a deerskin blanket to go on top. Leaning myself against the cold tile wall, I slipped out of my oversized wool tunic and threw on the long johns I found in the linens. Once settled in, I turned on the phone.

The countless videos still took my breath away. Mostly they were selfies, video diaries in which Max would speak to me in direct address. There was a part of me that wanted to go back into the depths of the phone when I was still alive. Before the video diaries. Our life together. The memories I had were anything but intact, and this phone would fill in every gap I could possibly imagine. But after considering it, I realized I wasn't ready. Not yet.

So I looked once again into the future I never thought I'd see. Max's life without me. My eyes strained against the now unfamiliar harsh light emanating from the screen. It was such a comforting pattern in my first life, sitting in bed, fighting sleep with only my phone to keep me company. I settled uneasily back into the routine and began watching Max's videos as quietly as I could so as not to disturb the sleeping camp.

I wondered how he imagined I would be when I watched these. Alive in the future. Happy? Safe? With him? Whatever imagined version of me he was speaking to, this phone clearly had become a sort of therapy for him. In the diaries he made, he would process my death, or brainstorm ideas on the movement, or debrief after a big rally, reluctant to believe how well it had gone.

One video that caught my eye was Max backstage at *The Daily Show with Trevor Noah*. We loved watching that together. At first, I assumed he was in the audience, but it quickly became clear that he was that evening's guest. He was giddy with excitement as he showed me, the currently-dead-but-possibly-one-day-alive me, around his dressing room. There were flowers and a massive Toblerone chocolate bar.

"I'm so nervous," he confessed. "I keep wondering why people care what I have to say, but then I remind myself that I'm just the messenger. It's you they care about. When I talk about you and us, they keep listening. Let's hope they listen long enough to actually do something."

While Max's moments backstage before and after the interview have been memorialized, the actual interview has been lost to history. I've never been able to find it. However, I did find a photo of Max sitting in front of Mr. Noah, who has his hand clasped over his mouth looking at Max with a mix of astonishment, amusement, and respect. Max has his head hung, one hand clutched around his heart and his other extended high above him clenched in a fist. It became a meme in its time, used both in jest and sincerity to convey an intensely held belief.

Then I watched a video from a few months later. Max filmed himself in our bed watching *SNL*. He was in tears laughing at a skit where a young Middle Eastern comedian I didn't recognize was portraying Max. A white actress whom I did recognize from when I was still alive played me, resurrected. The bit was about me meeting Jesus in the afterlife and leaving Max for him. I couldn't hear most of it over Max's laughter, but it seemed kinda funny. The Max character consistently tried to prove he was a better man than Jesus by listing all the amazing and very real things he'd done in his life. The Jesus character would respond with a miracle of some sort, culminating with him turning water into wine and the me character saying, "Ohh! I love wine! Gimme gimme gimme!"

Then the end of this video shocked me. Somewhere in our apartment—in Max's apartment—a woman called out, "Pizza's here!" Max's smile instantly dropped, and he quickly stopped recording the video.

I tried not to think too much about it. Maybe she was just a friend. Maybe she was only the pizza delivery person. But probably she was his girlfriend of some sort. My heart sank. I was the one who had told him to move on, and I knew for a fact that he really didn't. I mean, he died to be with me. So I did my best to push that woman's voice out of my mind and pour myself into more videos.

The chronology progressed until 2030, at which point all the remaining videos showed the date "1/1/2000" and were listed in no particular order. Maybe the phone was just too old at that point and wasn't supported anymore. I remembered that happened to my aunt's old phone when she refused to upgrade. Maybe Max began importing the videos from another device and there was a data corruption in that process. I wasn't sure. I tried to figure out the right sequential order, but the further I dug, and the sleepier I got, the harder it became to determine the timeline.

As my obsessive viewing continued deep into the night, and everyone around me was far into sleep, the humorous and lighthearted videos gave way to more serious-toned ones. Max increasingly appeared to be run ragged. He grew his beard out, really embracing the whole rebel look. I watched protest after protest, some where police shot tear gas canisters into the crowd. In many, Max was actively bleeding. In many more, he was expertly tending to someone else's wounds with care.

I clicked on the last video in the list. I wasn't sure when it was from, but the Max in this video was a very different Max from the one backstage at *The Daily Show*.

He sat at a desk in a room unfamiliar to me. The camera was haphazardly framed, so I could only see his shoulder and a part of his face that was further covered by his hands. He rubbed his mouth methodically, almost compulsively. Then he began speaking:

"There was another bombing of a cryo clinic this morning. Two people died. A ten-year-old girl is in the ICU." His voice sounded strange, different, altered. He stopped rubbing his face but left his hands over his eyes and took a deep breath. "It's hard, Al. Made harder by the fact that when shit like this happens, it feels like you die all over again." He turned to the side, and I could only see the back of his head. He looked up to the ceiling. "I miss you a lot today, Al. I miss your eyes. And your skin. I miss how you would try to make me laugh. I miss laughing." He chuckled to himself. It sounded robotic. Emotionless. Suddenly, he leaned across the desk and into the phone's camera. His eye was mere inches from the lens and filled most of the screen as the focus stuttered in and out.

And then, without a word, he stood up and walked out of frame. I had to listen to this next bit over and over again with the volume turned up as it was so quiet and distant. But what I eventually settled on was: "It's heavy. This crater in my chest. I hate it. I want to kill them all."

The video ended, and the image froze on the empty room. Only Max's thumb could be seen in the corner of the frame as he reached in to hit stop. I stared at that image, stunned, entirely unsure what I'd just witnessed.

With all my heart, I willed Minnie or Gina to wake up. I would've taken the company of anyone, but no one stirred. I looked around for Avon and still didn't see him in the sea of blankets and pillows strewn across the ground. So in the absence of someone who could come and hold my hand—and with a desperate need to be with Max, *My Max*—I pushed a thought into my head as clearly and strongly as I could:

Rosebud.

.
.
.

"What do you want?"

The lights are warm on my face. I have to be careful not to look directly at them, but their positioning just above the woman makes it all too enticing. Immediately my eyes water with the overwhelming luminescence of the bulbs. I shut my eyes tightly and through the darkness can still see the golden halo burned into my retinas.

"Alabine?"

I open my eyes. The woman sitting in front of me is beautiful and well groomed in her red power blazer. I have a passing thought that her heavy makeup actually hides her natural beauty, but she probably already knows that and is very intentional with her makeup application. There's only so pretty a girl can be in this world and still be taken seriously.

"What do you want?" she asks again.

An entrancing camera lens stares at me from just over her shoulder. I watch the iris expand and contract as it adjusts its framing. The depth of its blackness is haunting.

"I want to live, Nancy." I adjust my cardigan, which is slipping off my shoulder, revealing my bony, emaciated arm. I'm in the thick of treatment, and it's taking its toll. Unlike journalist Nancy in the red blazer, I need every drop of makeup caked onto my face to look even somewhat like a human.

"You've said that beating your cancer is highly unlikely at this point. Have you given up hope?" Nancy asks with a journalist's detachment.

Coming with the hard-hitting questions there, Woodward.

"I'll never give up hope. I'm going to my treatments. I'm enrolling in every trial I qualify for. My oncologist is fighting alongside me every day. We're all doing our best. But as we know, sometimes our best is not enough. That's why I'm working on a backup plan."

Nancy smiles politely. It's a display of empathy, sure, but she is also making a mental note of the good sound bite I just gave her. I was in politics for a hot minute; I know how to do an interview. A fact she just realized. She sits back in her chair, eager to coast through the remaining talking points, and perhaps even end early, so she can get another almond milk latte before heading back to the office to oversee the edit in time for the five p.m. broadcast.

She's not thinking she'll win any local Emmys with this simple feel-good family story. However, with a compelling enough angle and the good sound bites I can give her, she'll be able to stick it to her boss, who's been passing her up for the important assignments because she turned him down when he tried to sleep with her at the Omaha Marriott last Christmas.

Kidding. I don't really know what she's thinking. But that's probably not too far off.

"So, let's talk about this backup plan. It sounds like science fiction." Nancy used the words *science fiction* so that I might parrot them back to her in yet another good sound bite. Interviewing 101.

"It seems a lot like science fiction, Nancy." Signed, sealed, delivered. "But cryogenics is very real. And very expensive." I laugh. She smiles and silently laughs, as decorum requires, while also not audibly overlapping my words for the edit. The expense of preserving my body was why Max called Nancy's news station to begin with. Hopefully, pleading my case on TV will inspire people to donate. The executives were more than eager to give me a platform. A dying girl pleading for her life on the evening news is good TV. I just need to tee it up. "My boyfriend started a GoFundMe that we're so grateful went viral."

It's only then that I notice Max standing behind the lights. Of course he is—where else would he be? I knew he was there, and yet seeing him in the dark behind the bright lights takes me entirely off guard. A feeling of utter loneliness consumes me. I want him near me. Beside me. Holding me.

The black camera lens zooms in. I see the shift in the internal mechanisms. It focuses. Getting closer. *The darkness is always getting closer to me.* I have the thought that I need to find Max, but he's right here. Or is he in New York? Is he dead? Am I?

I reach out to him.

"There he is. Max. My Max. He's done everything. Put this whole interview together. The fundraising campaign." My fingers strain to reach for him. He's so far away—a century away. I turn to Nancy. "Is it okay if he comes on?"

Nancy's mascaraed eyes widen, and she shifts in her chair trying to stifle excitement. "Of course. We'd love to have a shot of both of you." She turns to her cameraman. "David, can we just—"

Max says from the shadows, "No. No. It's okay."

I put on a smile, trying to hide my desperation. "Max. Come on. Please." My fingers are like magnets, trying to dislodge themselves and fly across the room to him.

Nancy cranes her neck to see Max behind her. "Are you sure? Would be great for the piece. Endless love and all. People really respond to that."

I try to radiate courage. I try to show him in my eyes how desperately I need him to sit by my side and hold my hand.

"No." Max shakes his head. "This is really about Al. She should be front and center." He slinks back into the shadows.

I can't believe it. And then I feel my phone vibrate in my pocket.

"Well, front-and-center Alabine, what's the best you can hope for if you do end up preserving your remains?" Nancy asks.

Still furious at Max, I sneak a look at my phone. A number with a St. Louis area code pops up on the screen. I should just ignore it. Probably spam. But something urges me to answer. Who do I know in St. Louis? No one I can think of.

"Do you mind?" I ask Nancy, gesturing to my phone.

"We really are almost done," she impatiently responds as the possibility of her almond milk latte diminishes.

Ignoring her, I slide off my couch. "This won't take a minute." I walk past Max without even glancing at him. I'll deal with him later.

I dodge around the news crew and equipment and shut myself in the bathroom. Quiet and alone, I answer the call, but I don't say anything, half expecting a robocall voice to start up. Instead I hear breathing on the other end.

"Hello? Alabine?" The woman's voice is familiar, though I can't quite place it. "Alabine, it's me. It's Miranda Lewis. Well, you know me as Pickett, but it's Lewis now."

Everything in me twists so hard it hurts. I lean against the thin bathroom door and slide down until I'm sitting on the ground. I can't find the air in my cancer-ridden lungs, but eventually I pull together enough strength to ask, "Mom?"

"Hey, baby. I saw Uncle Neil posted an article about you on Facebook. Is it true?"

Uncle Neil isn't a real uncle. He was a good friend of my father's who became hard to get a hold of once my dad was hospitalized. Uncle Neil is, however, very active on Facebook and never misses an opportunity to comment on my photos "Looking good!" with a winky face. Uncle Neil is a little gross.

Miranda, my mom, clears her throat. "Cancer, Alabine? You could've emailed me."

"I know. I'm sorry."

There's a soft knock. "Al, you okay?" It's Max. I elbow the door hoping he gets the message: *Go away. I hate you for abandoning me. Also, no, I'm not okay, my emotionally unavailable mother called me. Break this door down and save me.* Of course I don't say this out loud, and it's a lot for an elbow to the door to convey, so he doesn't get the message.

Miranda continues, "This whole freezing-yourself thing . . . It sounds like something your dad would do, if I'm honest."

"Since when do you care what Dad did?" The tone in my voice intensifies. I always cringe when Miranda talks about Dad.

"That's uncalled for, Alabine."

"I know. I'm sorry." My second apology in as many minutes. From the floor, I pull the towel down off the drying rack and wrap it around my head. I don't know why. It's comforting.

"Aunt Marie would've never let you go through with it. I wish she was still there with you."

Me too. "You never called after she died. I thought you'd call."

"You seemed to be doing fine. Plus, you got all that money from her."

"There wasn't much money, Mom." Neither of us speaks for a moment.

"It's strange to hear you call me Mom. Marie was much more of your mom than I ever was. After all your dad did to me, it was good she could step in. You know, your father would be prosecuted nowadays with the 'me too' people and all." I cringe again, but I know that she isn't entirely wrong. I always held in the back of my head that what he did was not okay. She was nineteen. He was twenty-eight. She was young, and he was her boss, in a manner of speaking. So, yes, it was icky, but that ickiness is absolutely the last thing I want to be thinking about, curled up against my bathroom door, mad at my boyfriend, dying of cancer, with a news crew in my apartment.

Miranda cleared her throat again, shifting her voice into a positive, almost enthusiastic cadence. "Anyways. I'm calling because I know a great journalist here in St. Louis. Young handsome guy who's gonna be a prime-time anchor real soon. He said he'd want to do a piece with both of us on your cancer and the freezing yourself. It'd be on the nightly news!" Her excitement has nothing to do with helping me get attention and raise money for cryo. I am simply her ticket to be on the news.

"I can't really travel right now. My treatments and . . . I'm just pretty weak." I pause. She says nothing. "You could come here. It'd be nice to have the extra help. I'm sure Max could use the break."

"I can't do that. With the kids and my work. I'm really busy, Albine." I'm not sure if she wants me to curiously ask what she's busy with, but I don't bite, so she continues: "If you can make your way here, you can stay on the couch. Probably would have to be soon, though. I'm not sure how long we have this guy's attention for."

I've had just about enough at this point.

"Jesus, Mom. I'm probably going to die, and all you can think about is the attention of some local news jerk-off?" I yell so loud that I wonder if Nancy hears it. I don't need her including this as a part of her story. Angry dying girl doesn't engender as much sympathy, or donations.

"Cut me some slack. I'm hurting here too. I just found out my daughter has cancer."

"Yeah, must suck for you. But as you said, I was never really your daughter, so at least you've got that going for you."

I hang up the phone, hopefully before she could hear the shaking in my voice that betrays the tears trickling down my cheeks. I sit there in stunned silence. On the one hand, I can't bring myself to hold her accountable for what she says; she's been wronged a lot in her life. I believe that deep down there is love in what she says to me.

On the other hand, I fucking hate her.

Just then, a business card slides under the door across the bathroom tile. I pick it up and read "Nancy Hanna, NBC 5 WMAQ Chicago." Outside the door, I hear her say, "Email or text if you can think of anything you'd like to expand on. I can always add quotes during my on-air report."

I flip the card over. For some reason, I expect to find handwriting on the back. Some special little note just for me.

Call for a refill.

But it's blank. All of the rage against Miranda for saying those horrible things to me, and against Max for not coming to sit with me in the interview, and against the doctors for not curing me—all that rage comes bubbling to the surface as I jump to my feet and fling the door open.

Nancy is right on the other side.

"Get out!" I scream. She freezes in shock. I could hit her. I want to. I want to punch her in her overly painted orange-blush cheek.

Max steps in. "Al, they're leaving. I told them to leave." He rubs my arm, and I immediately shrug him off.

"Well, aren't you my goddamn hero?" I see the look of judgment on Nancy's face. "What? Too much for a five o'clock segment, Nancy?" I pull off my cardigan and hold out my skin-and-bone arm. "This is what dying really looks like. David, can you get a shot of this?" The cameraman doesn't even look up at me and continues to pack his equipment, eyes cast down. I turn back to Nancy. "Well, now do you think I should give up hope?"

As she watches me in silence, I see her expression change from shock, to pity, then to disappointment. She turns to Max and shakes his hand. "Thanks for your time." After one final glimpse of me, she follows her crew out my apartment door.

Max looks at me. "Are you okay?"

"No, I'm not fucking okay, Max! You left me back there when I needed you."

"I don't like going on camera, Al. You know that."

I push out a loud exhale. The truth of my deeply felt anger finally bursts out of me. "That was my mom just now on the phone. She knows I have cancer, and she wants to go on TV with me."

Max steps forward, clearly wanting to hold me. "Jesus, Al." He moves to hug me, but I push him away. He reaches for me again.

"Stop!" I shout. He stops.

He doesn't take his eyes off me. I don't take my eyes off the ground. We stand there at an impasse. I want to shoot up through the ceiling like a rocket, through each apartment above ours, into the sky, and keep going and never come back into this moment or this body or this life.

"No. I won't stop loving you." Max lunges forward and wraps his arms around me. I start sobbing as we collapse to the ground. I kick and push and wiggle against his embrace, testing him to make sure he doesn't let go. He doesn't.

I cry. And cry. And he just holds me. He starts kissing me all over my face. They're rough passionate kisses. I feel his skin fusing with mine as we become one person. His hands coil around my arm until our bones meld together and his arm is nothing more than an extension of mine. His heart an extension of my heart and able to carry some of the load.

Feeling somewhat whole again, I slowly stop crying. I take a deep breath and let it shudder as it comes out of me.

"I thought she could call me just once and have it be about me. I'm dying, and she makes it about her and what my dad did to her. Now I'm her ticket to get on TV, and it's almost like I owe it to her."

Max pauses, taking me and all of my sadness in. Then he smiles softly and says, "She'd probably just promote a horrible MLM company she's a part of. 'Sure, my daughter's got cancer but look, you can buy this eyeshadow and become an associate for the small price of your soul! Act now!'"

I laugh. We breathe together. In and out.

"I'm really sorry about the interview," Max admits. "I just freeze up being put on the spot. I'm sorry . . ."

I grab his face in my hands and pull him close to me. "I don't want to do this alone."

"You are alone." His bluntness takes me by such surprise it reminds that this is not real. That he didn't really say that. I feel the deerskin blanket wrapped around me. Max caresses my cheek. "I don't matter. You do. Remember that."

I woke up with a jolt. A familiar cold sweat covered my entire body. My blanket was drenched with my body's futile attempt to rid itself of disease.

How much of that Lucid Memory was real and how much of it was my current life bleeding into it, I didn't know. Regardless, feeling Max's lips on mine was life-giving. I ran my fingers across my mouth, trying to glean any remaining warmth I could.

Out of the corner of my eye, I noticed a wisp of movement among the sea of sleeping bodies. It was Gina, silently sneaking toward the steps that led down to the main platform. Through the darkness it was hard to see any details, but she moved as if she didn't want to be seen.

In the pit of my stomach, I feared that she secretly knew where Avon was, and they were plotting. Scheming to stop my plan to wake Max.

It was freezing as I dragged my heavy and sore body out from under the blanket. Quickly and quietly, I slid on my scuffed white sneakers, wishing they too were made of deerskin, then wrapped around my shoulders a large coat that Eliza had given me shortly after we arrived.

This coat was among the better offerings. It fit me perfectly and went all the way down to my knees to stave off the chill.

The long corridors of the train station were even more ominous and mazelike at night. Following Gina, I kept my distance, assuming that even the slightest noise would reveal me. Soon it became clear that she was headed for the street exit, piquing my curiosity even more.

The blustering wind pummeled down the stairwell that led toward the cold and snowy night. After the exit door closed behind Gina, I peered around the corner and considered the steep incline. I hadn't left the station, not since we arrived. With a deep breath, I braved the ascent and found myself surrounded by the dark night. Gina was nowhere to be seen.

I stood for a moment. My body was aching for me to forget it and go back to bed. I needed rest. Just before giving up to seek the warmth of the camp, I spotted Gina's footprints perfectly preserved in the freshly fallen snow. While desire for sleep desperately tugged at me, suspicion over Gina's middle-of-the-night escapade drowned out any other thoughts. I trudged off through the snow.

Wandering through the dark and still street, I found the fresh air rejuvenating. I had to be careful not to slip on the patches of ice that were hard to see even in the bright light of the full moon. Above me, thousands of stars and even the Milky Way itself gleamed bright. I'd never seen the sky so clear, especially in the heart of a city. When I looked up to the magnificence, light snowflakes tickled my eyelashes and melted on my nose.

A sound broke through the silence. Thinking that Gina had discovered me, I darted behind a tree, only to watch a family of brightly colored orange foxes prance down the empty street. As I watched them, the echoes of bustling traffic and crowded sidewalks seemed not just from another time but from another world. In yet a hundred more years, I imagined that the buildings would be covered in vines and trees, unrecognizable as monuments to mankind's old way of life. In the meantime, the city rested peacefully in its obscurity. Disuse looked good on it.

After rounding the first corner, I thought I started to hear music drifting on the wind. It made the dreamlike quality of my journey intensify to the point that I couldn't remember if I ever woke up. Or if being in the bathroom of my apartment talking to my mom on the phone was the reality and this was the dream.

Step in step with Gina's footprints, I heard the music grow louder with each passing block. It swerved out of intangible dreamlike reverberations and materialized into full melodies. A singer's smooth, rich voice cut through the cold air, belting out a slow sultry tune. It hypnotized me. My time in this new life had been filled with the music from DJ Raheem's radio show, which was calming but lacked much else. In contrast, this song echoing through Detroit's abandoned streets was moving, emotional, and passionate. I let it fill my soul as I continued my slow and weak yet steady march.

The snow began falling in heavier drafts, and I lost the outline of Gina's footprints, so I just continued to follow the music, hoping it would lead me to her. Through the blur of white, I saw a freshly painted red door in the back of a nondescript building. The strange and beautiful music was playing just on the other side. As I reached out to open the door, someone grabbed my arm. With a gasp, I turned around and saw Gina.

"What are you doing here, Rivers? Go back to the station."

"What is that music?" I asked, compelled by this growing mystery.

Gina pulled me a few steps away from the door. "It's not safe out here. If someone saw you—"

"Who's gonna see me? The foxes?" I joked. Gina clearly wasn't in the mood. I sighed. "I thought you might know where Avon is."

"I don't." She started yanking me by the elbow toward the street. "I'll take you back."

Just then, the red door opened. Hazy blue and yellow lights poured out of the room like the particles couldn't stand being contained for a moment more. The music was no longer muffled, beating out through the open door with every note.

A slightly drunk Eliza stood in the door frame. "You know, someone said there's a girl outside who looks just like Alabine Rivers, and I thought, 'Well, maybe it *is* Alabine Rivers!' So I came out to see. Good on you, Gina, for bringing Alabine to our little sanctuary."

"We were just leaving," Gina responded.

"Nonsense. Come in!" Eliza wrapped her arm around my shoulder and guided me inside the mysterious building.

Stepping over the threshold, I entered another world. The lights were dim, but I could see that the room was crowded with people. Unlike the deserted city outside, this place felt full of life. Shadowed bodies swayed like trees to the music, couples wrapped in passionate embraces. The welcomed warmth that radiated through the room was manufactured not by a heater but instead by the closely packed bodies. Around me, no one seemed to much notice or care that I was lurking. Some eyes glanced at me but only for a moment before they turned away again.

Captivated by the magic in the air, I didn't even question what this place was or why it existed. The struggle and strife I'd been overwhelmed by the past few days were all but a distant memory. The people here wore elegant outfits: sequined dresses and sparkling jewelry. I hadn't seen such elegance in this lifetime.

"Can I get you a drink?" Eliza asked me.

The craving I'd had since dinner for a glass of red wine turned in my belly. I went to accept but quickly took a finger to the ribs.

"We really should be going," Gina insisted.

Before Gina could sweep me aside, I spotted Avon across the room. At first, I couldn't believe it. It was hard to see anything in the dark and crowded room, but Avon's height made him stand out. After all my searching, Avon was there! I slipped out of Gina's grip and weaved my way through the dancing toward Avon. He was dressed in a suit and danced slowly with someone draped across his shoulder. His eyes were closed. He seemed peaceful.

"I've been looking for you for hours," I shouted over the music.

Avon's eyes flashed open. "Alabine." He muttered like he'd just woken from a dream. "What are you doing here?" He was more shocked to see me than I expected. Before I could understand why, his dance partner looked up. It was Dr. Noah. He wore a slimming tuxedo with no tie, looking irresistibly dashing. They were locked in an intimate embrace. I smiled at the pair, caught up in the love that surrounded them and how it reminded me of Max, but neither smiled back. Instead Avon wore a horrified expression.

There was so much I wanted to say to him. I wanted to jump into my excuses and explanations for why I didn't support him in the meeting, but his expression somehow made me feel even more guilty. I wondered if he was embarrassed that I'd seen him and Noah together. The utter horror in his eyes took me by such surprise that I didn't know what to say.

Not wanting silence to mistakenly speak volumes, I offered a quiet "I just wanted to talk about today . . . but we can talk later."

From behind me, Gina grabbed my arm, as she had done so many times in the past, and pulled me away. Avon didn't say another word. I don't think he even breathed.

We found Eliza sprawled out on a low deep-cushioned couch with her arm intimately draped over Diana's shoulders. She drank a whiskey cocktail out of a small glass flute.

"Avon wasn't up for a chat?"

"Not really." I looked down to my feet, trying to find the best way to ask my question before deciding there was no good way, so I blurted out, "Is it illegal to be gay?"

Eliza gently twirled Diana's hair in her fingers. "Not illegal, per se, but no one is anymore. Publicly, I mean. If I walked into a diner holding hands with Diana, we wouldn't get thrown in jail, but we certainly wouldn't be served, at least not anything edible." Eliza squeezed Diana's hand. "Out there, we're not encouraged to take pride in our differences or else we'll be reeducated. It's the Goldilocks standard; they don't want us to be too different. Too gay, too dead, or even too dark-skinned. Poor Avon's got the brunt of all that." She clicked her tongue in a show of sympathy. "You'll get along in this world fine if you're *just* right. So here we are, relegated to the underground to flaunt our sins."

"Uniting America has had its casualties." Diana slurred her words through her teeth. She playfully lowered her voice and mockingly intoned the same UA slogan that Ralph had quoted days before: "'Every person has a place.'" Then Diana giggled as she ran a finger across Eliza's cheek.

"Resurrectionists, Awoken, even people in the nearby towns have found a respite here in the Hideaway," Eliza said with pride in her eyes as she surveyed her sanctuary. "Now you see why only Gina knew of our location."

Even under the colored lights, I could see Gina flush red. She looked to the ground. "We should go."

Nodding in agreement, I said my goodbyes and followed her to the exit. We left the smell of booze and sweet perfume and trudged back to our encampment. All the while, my mind lingered on my brief conversation with Avon. Regret seeping into my thoughts like poison.

For most of the walk back, I didn't say anything. Gina didn't either. She walked a few paces ahead. As we approached the door that led down to the train station, Gina suddenly stopped. I did as well, expecting her to turn back to me, but she didn't. We both just stood there in the snow.

I filled the space. "Look, I'm sorry. I don't think I should've been there. I didn't mean to offend anyone." Gina remained silent. "I won't say anything if that's what you're worried about."

Then Gina turned around. I recoiled, expecting her to unleash a tirade, but she didn't. Instead she wore a look of compassion. "I know you're trying, Rivers, but if you're in the position where people are going to follow what you say, then you need to start understanding their experiences, not just yours. You're still barely coming to grips with being hated, but Avon . . . Avon has always been hated. He gets what we're trying to do here and understands these people more than you ever will. That's why Wade chose him. Your innocence is a danger to all of us."

Watching Gina disappear down the long stairwell, I wanted to shout after her. Defend myself. Or better yet, I wanted Max there to yell at Gina on my behalf. Stand up for me being a woman and how more women should lead, not fewer.

My mind continued to build walls around my fragile self-worth, grasping at anything it could to keep me from admitting to myself that I knew Gina wasn't doing that at all. I briefly considered reversing my decision and agreeing to Avon's plan to organize a march in Atlanta. In the end, I never did.

Instead I walked down those steps, crawled back into bed, and dreamed about the next evening when we'd begin the journey to Max. But my thoughts were haunted by the horrified look in Avon's eyes as I drifted off to sleep.

Dear Joshua,

I'm alive.

I can't tell you how I'm alive, or where I am right now, in case this letter gets intercepted. So just know, I'm okay. I realize that you may no longer live at the home we shared and will never read this. Or, God forbid, you may not even still be alive, but I had to write you just in case. I needed to let you know that I am awake, and I am okay.

I hope this is welcome news to you, little brother. I have to believe it is. I need something to fight for. Something to keep me going.

I don't know how it all went so wrong. Please believe me when I say that I don't blame you or Mama, but Jesus, after I came back with malaria, I thought I was only going to be on ice for six months, and then to wake up almost forty years later! It's a lot to bear. Let me say again, I don't blame you. I know there was a reason you didn't wake me up when we'd planned. The laws changed. Or you didn't have the money. It doesn't matter.

We had our differences, Lord knows, but I do not believe you would've just left me for dead. I know you did everything you could. You and Mama loved me and wanted what's best for me. I didn't make that easy on you. Sometimes the world is just too crushing for people like us, with not a dollar to our name and too dark for our own good—but especially for men like me. I fondly remember the nights you, me, and Henry would sit on that stoop until the early hours of the morning, hypothesizing and dreaming about the world being different. Better. Without the draft or the Depression.

Where Mama could own our house, and we wouldn't have to feel so out of place all the time. Although it would've been naive to expect the country would turn into that dream we had on the front stoop, it's disheartening to see how far it has fallen for those who don't fit into President Howard's American identity. I'm astonished the sacrifices the people of this country willingly made in pursuit of a better life. The cost was too high.

Thankfully, there's a lot happening here, so I've been keeping busy and not dwelling too much on the past. Still, I can't help but think about how four decades is a lot to miss. You turned sixty last month. Sixty! I can't believe it, baby brother. I've thought about you and Mama every day since I woke up. Do you have children? Maybe even grandchildren? I hope you married that sweet girl Rosie who you were dating when I deployed. That was literally a lifetime ago, so perhaps not. You weren't one to settle down. But if not Rosie, another girl. A tall woman who looks great in a dress and has a purple tint to her favorite lipstick. And hopefully she cooks garlic green beans the way I used to, just how you like them. I wish that for you, Josh.

Unlike you, I'm the same. The chills still haunt me. And the stomach cramps. Did I mention? I'm still sick. Luckily, I've yet to break into a fever. They hope we'll find medicine soon. We just need to get our hands on it.

I won't tell you what death is. Only know that my faith has been shaken, I can't lie to you and say otherwise.

I have my necklace. It's impossible to imagine Mama sneaking it into my preservation bag, so I assume that was you, dear brother. For that, I thank you from the bottom of my heart. I find myself absentmindedly rubbing it between my fingers like I used to. The necklace is my proof that you did care for me, and leaving me in death was out of your control.

What a sad note I'm writing! As with most of my life, I'm struggling to find the light in a dark place. It's all made worse by loneliness. I feel like I'm back in the West, but without the camaraderie of my troops. There are a few people who might become friends in time. As close as I can ever let friends be.

Oh, don't listen to me. I'm fed and clothed. Plus, I have work to do. But I do look forward to the day this work will no longer have to be done. I'm tired. Exhausted, really.

I love this country with all my heart and am honored to have fought and died for her. It's just getting harder each day. Love has always been a self-destructive thing for me. Something I give and don't expect anything back in return. Love continues to be the ruin of me. Maybe my love for this country is the same. Maybe I finally need to accept that and move on. I want to be an American. I want America to want me to be American.

I keep writing that I'll see you soon and then have to erase it. It's not true. I likely won't see you anytime soon, if ever again, and you know how much I hate to say a thing I can't make good on. So, I'll just say, I hope you have a good life. I hope you've had a good life. I miss you and Mama dearly.

All my love,

Avon

13

WE PLANNED TO LEAVE at sunset for New York. For Max. I woke up that morning restless. Tired and sore from sleeping on the ground after my midnight hike across the city, sure, but I bolted out of bed, pushing through the pain and exhaustion, excited to get everything ready for our journey. Eliza said it would be a three-day trip, starting by boat and then continuing by van, to get from Detroit to New York City.

Sunlight streamed into the lofted upstairs platform through a row of vent grates that lined the ceiling. I looked around for Avon, hoping to see him among the Chicagoans, but couldn't find him.

In the corner, huddled around a fire that cut through the damp morning air, Samson was talking to Diana and Gina. When Diana saw me, she handed me an empty backpack.

"For your food and supplies in New York. We're organizing parcels with various sundries. They'll be passed out down in the main area. So, pack everything you want to take with you, but leave some room." There was trepidation in her voice, and a shadow in everyone's eyes.

They were afraid. Afraid of our impending journey. Afraid of New York.

While all cities now carried with them a reputation of being cursed, New York City was the most infamous. The city was ground zero for the infestation. It was where it all started. People were so terrified, not even Awoken dared return.

Samson had the most to fear. Standing around the fire with Gina and Diana on that cold morning, he told us about living in New York during the infestation. As the death and rumors spread, he saw the change in how people looked at him. Before the infestation, he experienced bigotry and hate, but after, the hate mixed with fear. I knew the look he described. I had seen the same thing in the eyes of that little boy.

Samson was there when the Territorial Army burned Manhattan—the only way the UA had to contain the infestation. They didn't even bother to evacuate anyone before closing the bridges and setting it ablaze. Anyone left they assumed to be either dead, sick, or an Awoken. Samson had to swim across the Hudson River and hide from patrols to save himself from the flames.

This was going to be the first time he had returned since.

Unable to hear any more horror stories of the past, I went to pack. There, lying on the ground in a heap, was everything in the world that I could call my own. I had a feeling I'd never come back to Detroit, so I took anything I'd ever want to see again. It wasn't much.

I wore the knee-length coat that I liked so much and threw on some jeans, wool socks, and a red turtleneck shirt I'd found in my pile of clothes. My white sneakers were still damp from trudging through the snow, so Diana helped me find a new pair. These were made of a tougher canvas and even had a warm suede lining. I threw the rest of the items that I wanted, including Minchin's card, in the backpack and slung it around my shoulders. I tucked the phone and charger from Minnie in a deep pocket safe inside.

After eating some bacon Samson cooked for us (that I still

maintain is the best I've ever had), I went off in search of Avon. My regret from the night before had turned to shame in the early-morning light. There was so much I hadn't said to him. I wanted to explain myself before we left for New York so that he'd forgive me both for the vote and the awkwardness in the club.

The main room in the station was already bustling by the time I made my way down. Seeing the train cars reminded me that I'd never gone to see Damien. I wanted to talk to him about everything that had happened the previous day in One. I assumed he'd already heard rumors of it. As I'd discovered, secrets didn't keep long in Awoken camps.

It had to wait. I couldn't be sucked into Damien's bubble again. Into the peace and security that I found in his company. As much as I wanted it, I couldn't go back to that sense of complacency. Speaking to Avon had to be my priority, and then maybe I'd reward myself with the ease of a conversation with Damien.

A few steps away from the train, someone tapped my shoulder. I turned around, hoping to see Avon, but instead found Chris. My face must've fallen with disappointment because she asked, "Not who you were hoping for?"

"No." The bite in my voice was a misstep but not a mistake.

Not only was I upset with Chris for the summit yesterday, I also just didn't trust her. Every time I saw her, I pictured her eyes darting to the door just before Wade's death. A part of me believed she was the leak that Minchin had spoken of, the person responsible for the raid in Chicago.

"I'm looking for Avon. Have you seen him?" I asked.

"He went out with the hunting party. He'll be back soon."

I nodded. Then my anger got the better of me. "I couldn't find you after the meeting yesterday. What were you doing all evening?" Accusation shaded my words.

She laughed like I was kidding. Then she realized I wasn't. "I was communicating with our allies in Canada to arrange the supply drop in New York. Medicine. Dreno. *Your* medicine. Or do you not want me to keep your ass alive?"

"Not if it's like how you kept Wade alive."

Chris stepped toward me aggressively. "Do you have a problem with me?"

"Should I?" Centuries can go by, and the world can still feel like high school.

Chris threw up her hands in futility. "You know what, I'll see you when we leave for New York. Try not to fuck anything up before then, like you did at my mom's."

I deflated, utterly speechless. My guilt choked me, and I dropped my eyes to the ground. As bad as I felt, I still couldn't bring myself to apologize, not to her. Caught in this silent standoff, I wondered who would break first.

"Forget it," Chris finally said with a shrug. For the first time, she embodied her young age and seemed no more than a girl, homesick and worried, desperate to put on a brave face. She wiped her eyes before tears could form.

"Have you spoken with Damien yet?" she asked, pointedly changing the subject.

I shook my head. "No, why?"

"About his request to transfer to another camp."

"What?" I asked, blindsided. "Damien's being transferred?"

"Avon told him he has to run it by you first. You're our leader, right?" With that, she turned and left me. Alone in the middle of the busy platform.

I didn't think I'd heard her right. Or if I did, I thought she must've been trying to mess with my head. The problem was that it was working. As people passed by, bumping into me and jolting me from side to side, the station seemed to close in around me. I felt hot. I felt sick.

Suddenly, I turned around and ran straight for Damien's train car. Hoping beyond hope that Chris was lying. I tore through the sliding doors, swept up in a whirlwind of adrenaline and emotions. Then, as if I slammed against an invisible barrier, I stopped in my tracks with a gasp. Damien was there, and he was packing. Actually, he was almost done packing, tucking some final things into a small leather messenger bag that he then slung over his shoulder.

Damien didn't even turn around to see who'd come in. He knew it was me. And he knew why I was there. Even without seeing his face, I felt a coldness in him that seemed so foreign to the man I'd come to know.

There were a million things I wanted to say, wanted to shout, but I couldn't decide what to start with. I was paralyzed, staring at his neatly made cot that no longer bore any evidence that he'd ever been there. It hit me. Chris was telling the truth. Damien *wanted* to leave. The brashness I had storming in morphed into a quiet realization that my only friend might not be with me tomorrow.

"You heard," Damien said casually with his back to me still. He folded his blanket and laid it on the bed.

"Chris told me." I inhaled sharply. "I don't understand." There was a pleading in my voice that revealed, to both of us, the desperation I felt.

Damien turned around. I studied his expression. I was relieved at first as there wasn't anything unkind in his face, but then again, there wasn't anything friendly there either. The man standing in front of me felt like a stranger.

"Avon said I needed your permission." He said *permission* like it was a curse word, spitting with distaste. "Well? Can I go?"

"Go? Why do you want to go? Is this about Avon?" I asked, worried that the rumors of my betrayal had made their way to Damien and changed the way he thought of me.

"What's wrong with Avon?" he asked curiously.

"Nothing," I quickly replied, relieved. "You can't leave, Damien. Not now. This is it. We're going to wake up Max!" I took a few steps toward him. Damien instantly recoiled. I stopped, feeling unwanted for the first time in his company.

"I know," he said. "Avon told me that too after your meeting when you were supposed to come back here. Congratulations. It's everything you've wanted since you woke up."

He smiled, but there was no happiness behind it. He smiled at me the way you'd smile at a DMV agent so they'd process your paperwork a smidge faster. It was the smile of someone who didn't give a shit about anything but getting what they wanted.

I rubbed my face, trying to wake up from this bad dream, or else to figure out what the hell was going on.

"Look, I'm sorry I didn't come here after the meeting. I had a lot on my mind. That can't be what you're pissed at, but if it is, I'm really sorry."

"I'm not mad," Damien insisted.

"Then come with us to New York."

"You don't need me."

"Of course I do. *We* do!"

He bit his lip as he withheld his reaction. Optimism surged through me. There *was* some emotion inside of him after all. This realization emboldened me to step a few feet closer.

"You are barely healed, and you want to gallivant off to another camp? To do what?"

"Help them. Where I'm needed. What would I stay for?" It wasn't rhetorical. He was earnestly asking and then paused for my answer.

I racked my brain, trying to say something that sounded better than *You're the only adult in this world who is my friend and actually seems happy when they see me*. That was a bit more pathetic than I wanted. So finally, I parroted back the words he'd told me: "The movement. Changing the country. Doing the right thing in a beautiful broken world."

"I can't do that here anymore. I thought I could. But I can't. Not with you . . ." His voice trailed off until a silence that was as big as an elephant stood between us.

In that moment, I wanted nothing more than to hear the words he'd left unspoken. In their absence, I inferred his true meaning. The only thing that had changed since I saw him last was that I'd been elected the leader of the Resurrectionists. The truth behind him wanting to leave was that, like the others, he didn't see me as a leader he could follow.

Damien looked away as he composed his thoughts. "Let me go, Al. Please, just let me go."

Tears started to well in my eyes. I tried to summon the courage I'd seen from Avon, tried to imagine what he would do. I resigned myself to the pain of losing Damien, but I wanted to hear him say it. Unsaid words wouldn't do this time. I pulled my shoulders back and stood tall, ignoring but not hiding my tears and pulling the same coldness Damien so masterfully wielded into my own bones.

"Give me a reason," I commanded.

"I told you. I—" He shook his head. Stopping himself from letting the truth escape his lips.

"Say it." Rage began to fill my body, burning me from the inside out.

"Just let me leave, Alabine."

"You owe me a fucking reason!" I shouted at the top of my lungs.

"You want a reason?"

Damien reached forward and grabbed the back of my neck, pulling me in close to him. He kissed me deeply, passionately, hungrily. I tasted the sweetness on his lips as his fingers brushed against the nape of my neck. And for an instant, just an instant, I kissed him back.

Then I pushed him off with as much force as I could, channeling my shock and outrage into an elbow to his jaw.

Dazed, he backed away as far as he could until he sat on his cot. He rubbed his chin, unable to look at me. Whereas I couldn't tear my eyes away from him.

"Now can I go?" he asked sheepishly.

There were two explanations whirling through my head. He either kissed me to piss me off so I'd let him go, or he kissed me because he . . . wanted to kiss me. If I forced him to explain himself, it would change everything between us. Either way, I'd lose my friend. I couldn't lose Damien too.

"No." My tears receded. I firmly held my ground. "You're coming to New York as we planned."

Damien exhaled a sad laugh. He looked up at me with dewy eyes. "Whatever you say, Alabine Rivers." Slowly, he pushed himself to his feet, walked past me, and left.

Alone, I tried to catch my breath and understand what just happened. Then, absentmindedly, my trembling fingers reached up to feel my numb lips.

AFTER A FEW MINUTES, I stumbled my way out of the medical car. I don't think I took a single breath in the time between Damien's leaving and my feet touching the station ground. The cold air burned my throat as it passed into my lungs. A familiar feeling of not wanting the air, not wanting life, coursed through my body. It started with one short cough; then it quickly devolved into a full-on coughing fit. More than air pushed out of me. I wiped the blood from my mouth, my fingers grazing my lips once again.

He kissed me. I kissed someone who isn't Max. The thoughts consumed me. I tried suppressing them as hard as I could, pushing them down like my life depended on it.

It worked.

On the far side of the station, there was a crowd forming that caught my eye. I squinted to make out what the fuss was about and saw Avon on a parapet.

Finally. Avon.

Standing in front of a growing mass of people, Avon had his hands outstretched like he was calming a wild elephant about to charge, respecting the crowd's presence but entirely in command.

"I know this is exciting," he projected over the hundred or more people gathered around. "But please allow the appointed group to come to the front and collect their supplies." Around his feet were white packages—supply parcels for the group of us going to New York.

The crowd shuffled back as a few people agilely sliced their way through, forming an inner circle around Avon and the parcels. I stretched onto my tiptoes to try to see their faces but could only make out Chris.

For the moment, I kept toward the back. Seeing me for the first time since the club would be an unwanted distraction for Avon. As I watched from a distance, I marveled at the way he interacted with the energized, nervous crowd.

A voice called out, "It's true then? You're leaving us to wake Max Green?" The people erupted in a sea of whispers and conjecture. More shouts popped out of the din:

"Max Green is all the way down in Atlanta!"

"What about the raids?"

"You're abandoning us!"

"No, they're going to New York City!"

The shouting lulled into anxious whispers at the mention of New York. Avon found the man who first spoke out and locked eyes on him, answering him as if it were just the two of them there. "No one is being abandoned. We're leaving on a routine exploratory mission. As you all know, the locations of the other camps were compromised, so we are going out to find new homes for them. Securing safety and medicine for every Awoken and Resurrectionist is our number one priority."

The crowd responded to Avon with nods and shouts of approval. It was a good cover, but the truth of our upcoming adventure had clearly been spreading already.

Chris stalked at Avon's feet, pacing back and forth at the base of the platform like a guard dog. She kept her gun in a holster that spanned her chest under her coat. Her clothes bunched over the poorly hidden object.

"Come on, everyone, move along," she commanded. "If you're not with the traveling party, clear the area."

People mostly obeyed, lingering only for a moment to catch sight of the chosen few preparing for their mysterious voyage. Soon enough, though, people trickled away, and the intense energy dispersed. Then I heard a whisper.

"That's Alabine Rivers."

Behind me a young Awoken woman and her friend were pointing at me.

"I heard she was awake."

Not knowing what to do, and wanting to be polite, I waved. That was the wrong thing to do.

The two women, soon followed by many, many, many more of the dispersing crowd, focused their rapt attention on me and closed in. At first, the realization of my presence engendered a sense of wonderment. A teenage boy touched my arm. "Your story saved my life." A woman put one hand out, hovering just inches away from my chest, and put her other hand tight against her own heart. I let the positive energy fill my soul; closing my eyes, I rode high on the warmth and love emanating from the people around me.

Then someone bumped into me. I opened my eyes as I stumbled off balance. With the help of some good Samaritan behind me, I was able to find my footing. Then there was another shove. And another. All too soon, I was in the middle of a mosh pit, being pushed and pulled by people trying to touch my hands or face, or any part of me they could reach. My wig fell off and was lost in the writhing crowd. I tried to beg for space, but no one seemed to hear me. Those closest to me, in fact, were being just as trampled as I was. It was a tsunami, and I was entirely caught in its wake.

"Stop! Get off her!" Avon's shout could barely be heard over the cacophony.

"Avon!" Calling out, I hoped that he'd be able to find his way to me.

The pressure of bodies around me forced me to the ground. There were some people who tried to pull me back up to my feet, but others were still grabbing at me. It was hard to differentiate a helping set of hands from the threat.

Then an arm wrapped around my waist.

"Keep your head down!" It was Damien. Holding tightly on to me, he shielded my body with his. Finally, Avon pushed his way toward us. I reached out and grabbed his hand, hoping he'd be able to reel me to the surface. I couldn't see anything. I couldn't find a breath. Avon pulled on my arm, and Damien lifted my waist, but I wasn't budging from beneath the weight of bodies.

Suddenly, a loud gunshot rang out. Everyone ducked. Some people screamed. For a moment, I worried that another raid was happening, but the shot wasn't followed by any more.

"You're better than this, my friends!" Eliza shouted from the outskirts of the circle. She stood there, gun pointed at the ceiling. "Give Alabine some space." At this command, the crowd obliged and backed away from me.

Avon helped lift me from the ground and pulled me to safety.

"Thank you," I muttered to him, still dazed. He nodded. There was so much that needed to be said between us. So much I needed to say. But another thought quickly pushed into my mind:

Damien.

Expecting to see him just behind me, I quickly whipped around, but he was already gone. Through the crowd, I could see only the leather messenger bag slung around his back as he walked away.

I turned back to Avon just soon enough to see him too disappear into the crowd. In an instant, they both were gone. Eliza and Diana stood guard on either side of me.

"Come on, Alabine." Eliza thumped a white parcel into my chest. Then she slid a gun into my belt. It stabbed into my side. "We'll shelter in my office until we leave."

"I'll round up the others," Diana said before darting off with purpose.

Eliza wrapped her arm around my shoulders and ushered me away.

INSIDE ONE, ELIZA PLOPPED me down into the large plush chair. Papers and objects that already cluttered the wingback poked at my back. I inhaled long and slow in the relative quiet.

Since I had lost my blonde wig in the crowd, Eliza rummaged up a new wig for me with long brown hair, similar to my real hair. After running my finger through it for a moment, I gratefully put it on top of my head, happy to once again be a brunette.

Then a pissed-off Avon burst into the train car, demanding to speak with Eliza. Without acknowledging me, he pulled her around a set of bookcases at the far side of the room. They began arguing about Eliza's decision to load the parcels through the front in full sight of the camp. I could tell by Eliza's tone that she was defensive, and Avon was having none of it.

Meanwhile, Gina and Dr. Noah came in the already cramped train car. I watched Avon when Noah entered to see if he'd react at all. He didn't.

Gina stood next to me, her bag slung over her back. "Heard you caused a ruckus and got us all locked down in here until we leave for New York."

Too frazzled to jab back, I shrugged.

Moments later, Chris entered along with Samson, who squeezed my arm warmly as he passed by. Then Damien pushed in through the sliding door. We made eye contact for a moment, but it was fleeting, and I was unable to read anything into it. He was quick to busy him-self packing up the gear haphazardly piled in the corner.

"Need help, brother?" Samson asked Damien, heading over to assist.

I continued to catch my breath as the party filtered in. Now, separated from the rest of the camp, the New York contingent was clear to me: Avon, Eliza, Chris, Gina, Samson, Noah, myself, and Damien. Together we plus Diana made nine.

We were the raiding party.

George was there too, but he was to stay behind and run the camp in Eliza's absence. At first, Eliza assigned Diana to stay, but despite Eliza's insistence, she wouldn't agree to that plan, and thus George was appointed interim leader.

The door opened one final time, and Diana walked in with Minnie trailing behind her.

"No," I blurted out. Everyone looked at me. "Minnie, what are you doing here?"

Before she had a chance to respond, Eliza stepped forward. "She's coming with us to New York. I thought we told you."

"No. No, you didn't, and no, she's not coming. She's a child! And she's sick!"

"Hey! You're sick too. It's not your decision," Minnie snapped back defiantly.

"Maybe it is!"

"It's not," Damien coldly barked from the other side of the room. "This is why we woke her. The facility in New York hasn't been used in decades. We're going to need her to bring it back online and wake up your Max." He then emphasized, "If we're going, she's coming."

I didn't know this Damien. I wasn't a fan of this Damien.

"I'll be okay, Alabine," Minnie assured me. She held my hand. "I promise." I squeezed her hand, silently holding her to that promise. I still hated the idea of her coming, but clearly I was outnumbered.

I pulled Minnie into my lap and wrapped my arms around her as Eliza called the attention of the overpacked room. "I know some of you are justifiably nervous about going to New York. Being some of the first people to ever set foot there since the infestation, it's understandable that you would be on edge. Remember that they burned the city, completely sanitizing it. We'll be safe," Eliza reassured everyone.

"Sure we will," Chris sarcastically replied. Her rebellious edge masked her insecurity. I knew that, and yet it still annoyed me.

Eliza ignored her and continued, "The good news is that everyone is scared to go into the city, not just us, so this facility is completely unmonitored. We won't run into any Territorial Army goons once we're inside city limits. But before then, we're exposed and at risk. We'll take all precautions, travel by night, stay off patrolled roads. Everyone has to be on guard."

"The goons are a little busy right now hunting down the displaced camps," Chris snapped. "They'll give us the cover we need. Unarmed children are good decoys."

"You don't have to come with us," I growled. Chris held up her hands in a *whatever you say* gesture.

Avon cleared his throat and stepped forward, cutting through the tense air. "Because New York was completely shut off, more so than any other city, we need to restart the power. The cryo facility where Max is held has been in maintenance mode using its closed-loop solar panels and geothermal reservoir to keep the bodies preserved. We'll need much more power than that to wake someone up. So we need two volunteers to splinter off from us and turn on the wind and water-dam stations, south and north of the city respectively. It'll be a solo mission and, I won't lie, likely very dangerous."

Immediately, Damien raised his hand.

After a beat, Samson raised his hand too but looked less sure than Damien. "If it's in disrepair, I may be able to fix it. I used to work in engineering. Before." He meant in his first life, though he sounded uncomfortable admitting he had a before.

Avon nodded. "Very good, Samson. So Damien, you'll go north to the Hudson Valley and activate the hydropower at the dam up there. Samson, you'll go south and hit up the wind power station. Hopefully, at least, one of them can come online. We'll need that power flowing back into the city as soon as possible."

Avon rolled out a large map on the table. It was hard for everyone in the room to get a good view of it. We squeezed in close to lay eyes on what Avon pointed to, which wasn't a map at all; it was a blueprint.

Diana leaned in, her eyes focused intently. "Is this the facility?"

Avon nodded. "Eliza, me, Chris, and Gina will run cover. Once we're in—"

"I know what to do." Minnie's youthful voice commanded the room of adults. She ran her fingers over the blueprints, reading the utility lines with a clarity that was lost on me. "I'll need to get to this room." She pointed to a space in the basement. "And we need full power access by the time we get there," she stipulated with authority.

"You'll have it," Damien replied from the back corner. "Samson and I should go now. Travel separately from the group. We'll be faster, and we could use the half day's head start."

"Good," Eliza agreed.

I stepped forward, concerned. "Wait, you said we need to travel by night."

"Two men on the road shouldn't cause many questions. And Damien has clear papers. They'll be fine." Eliza turned to Damien. "There's an extra van outside. Take Highway 91. It's a direct shot."

Diana grabbed keys out of the desk drawer and tossed them to Samson. In one scoop, Damien collected his things, slung the messenger bag over his back, and left without a glance. Samson was still fumbling to shove everything into his pack, so I darted out after Damien. I wasn't going to let him go with so much unsaid.

"Damien!" I sprinted through the sliding doors back onto the platform, now eerily empty. He slowly turned back to me. I wanted to say so much, ask so much. *He kissed me.* Now, face-to-face, I chose not to. I said the most important thing: "Be careful."

Almost surprised, he smiled sweetly. "Don't worry about me. You just keep breathing." For the first time all day, I saw the Damien I knew.

Before either of us could say anything else, Samson limped out of One. He and Damien headed off toward the street exit. I watched them go, worried this would be the last I'd ever see of either of them. Once they were out of sight, I went back inside where the meeting was continuing.

"Good." Avon was hunched over the blueprints, thinking. "Chris and I will go with Minnie while Eliza and Gina will take Noah and Alabine to the resurrection bay. Diana will stay outside with the vans and keep lookout."

Chris nodded in agreement of the plan. "The kid will boot up the building, then it's all up to you, Al." She looked up from the blueprints and directly at me. Everyone else did too.

"Me?"

"You're going to wake up Max." Those were the first words Avon had said directly to me in what felt like a lifetime.

Noah put his hand on my shoulder, gently urging me out of my shock. "Don't worry. I'll step you through it. I've already put his file in your bag. It has all the information you need. His ID number, his trigger word—"

I laughed to myself. "I know that one already." The pieces of our remembered love nestled into my heart. I knew what his trigger word would be; it would be the same as mine.

As I thought about *Rosebud*, Max appeared behind Dr. Noah. My two lives bleeding together in front of my eyes. He reached out to me. Fighting my desire to run to him and throw my arms around him, I convinced myself he was just a memory.

Not for long, I thought. Hope gripped inside me, and my lips curled into a slight smile.

Chris stepped toward Avon. "Based on what I'm hearing from my contact in the Canadian government, our supply drop will be coming via an unmarked cargo ship into New York in the next few days. If they're not delayed."

"And that'll have medicine?" I asked excitedly. "For all of us? And Max too?"

Chris nodded.

Avon patted her on the back. "Well done."

I considered how different my new life would be once Max was here. Hungry for a moment's peace once we were reunited, I asked, "If Canada is so willing to help, why don't we just go there once we have Max?"

Eliza touched my shoulder. "Even though I'm sure Canada would make an exception to their Awoken refugee ban for you and Max, crossing the border is far too dangerous."

"And it won't help the rest of us who stay behind," Avon punctuated.

"Not sure if that matters to Alabine," Chris groaned. "She might just want to take Max and live happily ever after in Canada. Leave the rest of us to deal with all this shit."

"Easy, Chris," Avon urged.

"Of course that's not what I'm suggesting. I didn't know there was a refugee ban," I clarified. "The plan is great." It was. I was going to get Max and my cure. All the hardships in this life were finally going to be bearable, together.

With the details agreed upon, we only had to wait for cover of night. For the next ten painstakingly long hours, I memorized the blueprints, Max's file, and our plan to wake him up. Then the eight of us slipped out the back door without even a goodbye to the rest of the camp. I will always warmly remember Detroit as the place that healed me.

Three days later, the camp was raided by the Territorial Army. Somehow the long-guarded secret of the camp's location was divulged to the enemy. Thankfully, the Hideaway, Eliza's club, survived. It remained a home for those who needed it.

But the Detroit camp fell. An astonishing three hundred people escaped with their lives because of George, who died protecting them. It would've been an outright massacre if it wasn't for his bravery.

The night we left, I couldn't have known that any of that was going to happen. I had one objective: reuniting with Max. And I was so close.

THE RESURRECTIONIST GUIDE TO
AWOKEN REFUGEE STATUS

GREEN = CRYOGENICS FULLY LEGAL. POTENTIALLY ACCEPTING REFUGEES. PLEASE WRITE TO THE LOCAL EMBASSY FOR SPECIFIC APPLICATION RULES AND PROCEDURE.

YELLOW = SOME LEGAL RESTRICTIONS ON CRYOGENICS AND RESURRECTION. NOT ACCEPTING INTERNATIONAL REFUGEES.

RED = CRYOGENICS IN ANY FORM IS ILLEGAL. AWOKEN ARE ILLEGAL. VARIOUS DEGREES OF PENALTY FOR IDENTIFIED AWOKEN. AVOID AT ALL COSTS.

GREEN	YELLOW	RED
EAST CHINA	EU (EXCEPT FRANCE)	UNITED AMERICA
KOREA	CANADA	MEXICO
BRAZIL	CENTRAL AMERICAN UNION	UNITED ARAB STATES
TERRITORIAL RUSSIA	EGYPT	BRITANNIA
JAPAN	BANGLADESH	FRANCE
UNITED WESTERN STATES	INDIA	NIGERIA
SOUTH AFRICA	AUSTRALIA	INDONESIA

NOTE: THE ABOVE LISTED COUNTRIES REPRESENT ONLY THE LARGER COUNTRIES THAT HAVE CLEAR DOCTRINES CONCERNING CRYOGENICS. FOR A MORE COMPLETE LIST, PLEASE CONTACT YOUR CAMP LEADER.

14

THE JOURNEY WAS HARD. We moved quickly through the dark of night. From camp, we headed east to the docks, where we spent a grueling night on a small boat crossing Lake Erie. To avoid being spotted by patrols, all our lights were turned off, and the only sound was the low hum of the motor. I'd never been so cold before. Even death was warmer. My very bone marrow was frozen. The cancerous weight in my lungs threatened to crush me with every wave thrashing against the boat. I closed my eyes, gritted my teeth, and willed my weak and disease-ridden body to resist the relentless onslaught.

Once we finally got to the other side of the lake in what used to be Buffalo, Noah helped me stumble off the boat with Minnie tucked into my arms. On the shore, hidden among the trees, were two vans. According to Chris, the Canadians had dropped them there.

It was a relief to her that they came through with this small favor. It was an indication that they'd deliver on the larger supply shipment too. Chris told me that Wade's alliance with the Canadians was tenuous at best. They weren't particularly sympathetic toward Awoken and didn't believe in the Resurrectionist cause. Helping us was simply a way for them to goad the UA into a fight they'd been looking to pick since losing Toronto during the North American War almost half a century ago. But since then, with the UA's turn away from technological advancement, the UA military had fallen behind those of most other major countries. A war against Canada's formidable forces would surely mean a heavy defeat. It was a conflict the UA was desperate to avoid.

Until the Canadians had a justifiable reason to declare war, they were satisfied playing their little games. Diplomatically, they couldn't be the ones to fire the first shot. However, the tensions were coming to a boiling point, and everyone knew Canada was looking for any excuse. Being the rope in a game of tug-of-war between two world powers was a dangerous role for the Resurrectionists to play, but there wasn't much choice.

Regardless of their motivation, the Canadians seemed to come through when we really needed it so long as we didn't ask too much. Hidden vans were within the realm of acceptable aid. They had even stashed care packages in them: Dreno, food, and medicine. Sadly, no bottles of cancer-curing pills.

Piling into the vans, we divided into our separately tasked groups. Diana drove one van with Chris, Minnie, and Avon, and I was in the one driven by Gina with Eliza and Noah. During the few short hours of the winter daylight, we stayed off the main highways and slept in the vans camouflaged behind trees. At night, we drove as fast as we could through the winding back roads.

As much as I wanted to, there was never a time for me to speak with Avon during those two tense days. The vans traveled miles apart from each other so as not to draw attention. But even in the moments when we were all together, no one really spoke at all. Not even Minnie, our resident chatterbox. We were terrified of being found out, of this whole mission being thwarted by a patrol officer in the wrong place at the right time, so meals were spent in silence, and the hours driving through the night became a maddening chore of meditative isolation.

In the void, my two lifetimes blended together. I found myself riding the blurred border that spanned a century. Sometimes I'd look over to see Max or my best friend, Andy, sitting next to me in the Canadians' van. And even stranger, sometimes Eliza would be with me at Jessica DeWhitt's campaign rally, chanting "Black Lives Matter."

I tried hard to hold on to reality and then convinced myself that, in that moment, reality was unimportant. In reality, I was full of cancerous tumors, cold, alone, and scared. My brain was simply doing what it could to self-soothe.

The two vans met up at sunrise for a final rendezvous before entering the city, and I used every ounce of determination to drag my consciousness into the present. We pulled behind a dense part of the forest on the side of the road. Gina announced that we were an hour outside the city.

With only a short drive left, this was my last opportunity to speak with Avon. There was so much that was going to change after this, and I didn't want to drag our baggage any further. He could die. I could die. I had already died once with too many regrets. I wouldn't let it happen again.

He was discussing the final details with Chris and Eliza when I approached. In the way he looked at me, I could tell he knew exactly why I was there.

"Give us a minute, please," Avon said. Chris and Eliza walked off without a word, sensing the weight between us. We mutually allowed a beat to hang, neither speaking, simply acclimating ourselves to each other's company.

Finally, I decided to start. "Minnie reminded me that it was Christmas two days ago."

Avon smiled as a flood of happiness overtook him. "Every Christmas, after church, I'd get to eat the most delicious food you could imagine. My mom was the best cook." He looked as if he were tasting the meal on his lips in that very moment, caught in the isthmus between lives that I knew all too well. He opened his eyes. "It's a struggle, living multiple lives at once. It's hard to come back, you know?"

I nodded, knowing that if I looked past him into the woods, I'd see my own Max beckoning me to a happier time and memory.

"Have you thought about trying to find your family?" I wondered.

My question yanked Avon from the Christmas table and into the dark dewy forest an hour outside of New York City. He looked exhausted. And sick. "Maybe, but only when knowing me wouldn't put them in danger." A sad thought took over him. "Actually, my mother has probably passed on by now, but it would be nice to see my brother again. Someday."

I cleared my throat. "I've been trying to talk to you about the other night."

"I know. I've been avoiding you."

"I know." Wondering where to begin, I took a breath. "I'm really happy for you and Noah." Avon's eyes darted around, worried that we'd be overheard.

"Thank you," he responded quietly, clearly relieved. "I should've told you. I've just learned to be careful in choosing my friends."

"I'm sorry. That must be horrible to carry."

Avon looked at me in a way he had never before. Like he was actually seeing me as a real person.

"That night in the Hideaway was not entirely why I was avoiding you." Now was his turn to take a breath as he racked his brain trying to come up with the least offensive way to say what he had to say. "At that meeting in One—"

"I'm sorry," I interrupted, not needing him to recount the way in which I failed him. "I promised you I would have your back in there, and I didn't. That was shitty of me, and I feel bad, but your plan assumed that I'm someone I'm not. It wouldn't've worked, and too many of us would've died. I had the opportunity to stop it, so I did." Avon looked away. I reached forward and touched his arm, eager for him to understand. "Because of Max, you might think I'm used to people caring about what I have to say. What happened in that meeting has never happened to me before. I've always had to fight to be heard and even then . . ." I struggled to find the words. Somehow the apology that I had been thinking about for days was coming out as a self-pitying rant.

"Have you considered that you're fighting for the wrong thing?" Avon asked. "Being heard is never as important as hearing." Then, with promise in his eyes, he looked out over our group, broken and tired as they were. "Wade's plan was to save that facility in Atlanta because it was the right thing to do, despite the risks. Wade's plan was to unite the Awoken camps so we'd stand a chance. Not just a chance to keep from losing, but a chance to win."

"It's a nice thought," I admitted. "But it's hard enough trying to stay alive. How can you have such hope? When all that's around us is death and hate?"

"Faith," he responded. His hand floated to his necklace tucked under his shirt. "Faith and trust. You may not have faith, but I'm asking you to trust me that you are more capable than you think you are."

"I'm just a girl," I said with a trembling voice. "As much as you or I may want it, maybe Gina and Chris are right . . . I'm just not a leader. That's why I *need* Max. I can't do this alone."

"That's not true." Avon leaned in, energized. "You're Alabine Rivers."

I rolled my eyes. Sure, I intellectually understood that it meant something to him, but to me it was just a name.

Avon read my mind once again. "Even if you weren't, you aren't just some girl. We need *you*. You make bold and unconventional choices. Lord, you froze yourself before it was a thing to do and before you even knew if you'd come back. Not many other people would've done that in your place."

I laughed. Avon did too. Then a beat of comfortable silence passed between us.

He reached out and squeezed my shoulder. "Look around . . ." I did. I looked at the dark lonely forest that surrounded us. "We're here, Alabine. You led." There was a somber quality to his voice. "What I'm asking is when the time comes to make another decision, you listen. To what I have to say. What Chris and Gina have to say. Max would have."

Attempting to hold back tears, I looked around to see where Chris was. I spotted her by the fire talking to Gina, well out of earshot. Just before I turned back to Avon, Chris's prying and concerned eyes caught mine.

"I don't trust Chris," I finally admitted. It felt good to say it out loud. The weight of a secret lifted. "Wade didn't either. Or he was concerned about her loyalties, at the very least. Minchin told me there was a leak. I think it's her."

For quite a long time, Avon was deep in thought. His eyes subtly darted back and forth like a computer processing vast amounts of data. I thought he, like me, would steal a glance of Chris. But he didn't. He didn't need to. He trusted her. Implicitly.

"Maybe the time has already come for you to make a decision," Avon said pointedly but kindly. "If you trust me, trust her. She's one of the good ones, and those are few and far between." I heard him, but honestly, I still believed he was wrong. I had more information than he did. Before I could respond, Avon implored, in as serious a tone as he could employ while remaining friendly, "Alabine, if you want to wake up Max, you're going to need to trust her."

We kept our eyes locked, unblinking. This was the last thing between us that kept us apart.

I exhaled. "Okay." I didn't mean it. He didn't think I did. But we both accepted it as a promise for me to try and trust her. To trust him. I always felt like I was on Avon's team, and for the first time, I knew he was on mine too.

Feeling exhausted, and with a growing weight on my chest, I wanted to excuse myself to go back to the vans to sleep, but before I did, I had one more thing to divulge.

"Damien kissed me." I blushed.

Avon burst into laughter. "Oh no. Poor guy."

"Right?" It occurred to me then that I hadn't thought of it from Damien's perspective. If he did have feelings for me, it must've been hard for him. He knew that I was the most spoken-for person in the world then, the everlasting love with Max and all.

"A lot of what he said to me makes sense now," Avon muttered, recollecting their conversation when Damien asked for a transfer to another camp.

"I've been dying to tell you since it happened," I said, relieved I finally had someone to confide in. To connect with.

"What did you do?"

"Elbowed him in the jaw."

Avon laughed again. "Yeah, seems about right." He then looked at me, and his expression changed, I suppose because I wasn't laughing. I wasn't even smiling.

"Do you think he'll be okay turning on those power plants?" I asked. "You said it was dangerous." My heart caught in my throat, and I coughed.

"I think so." He wisely wouldn't promise more than that. Instead he watched me, studied my expression. "You shouldn't feel guilty about that kiss, you know."

"I don't," I said quickly. Lying.

"Max isn't here." Once again, Avon adeptly responded to what I was only thinking.

I sighed. "I know. And I miss him. So much." All kinds of emotions clung on to my words. "It's just . . ." I couldn't bring myself to say it.

So Avon did for me. "Anything that's good, that's not death and pain, you get to hold on to." He looked over toward Noah, who was laughing with Minnie near the vans.

"Are you?" I asked. "Holding on to the good?"

Avon smiled a sweet and pure smile. Then he nodded yes. I'm not even sure if it was conscious. We were both incredibly lonely and just now realizing we could have each other's friendship if we chose it, and in that moment, we both did.

I said good night, then retreated to the vans.

As the sun rose and began to cast a golden haze through the tall pines, I tucked into the bench in the back of the van and tried to sleep. But it didn't come easily. I couldn't calm my mind long enough to doze off. And, even more distracting, I couldn't stop coughing. Cold air always made it worse. It hurt to breathe. It hurt to move. My dying had truly caught up with me.

If Damien were there, he'd have been right by my side with a Dreno shot in hand and a charming story to distract me until I felt better. But he wasn't there. And any Dreno we had left I was saving for Minnie. I lay there in pain, exhausted but not ready to sleep. So I caught respite in another place. I wanted Max.

Rosebud.

I'm in my large pleather chemo chair. I have a particular chair I always use. The nurses know to keep it aside for me on days I am scheduled to come in.

And I'm coughing.

"Sorry. Sorry about that," I say as I look up. The treatment room is beige with a few framed paintings on the wall. All in all, it is very nondescript. Except not today. Today, it's different.

Rosebuds are all around me. They're on the floor and on the tables next to the IV bags. Battery-powered candle lights line the windowsills. This normally sterile and unimpressive room that I know annoyingly well, down to the peeling paint, is made up to be something special.

"Go on then." It's Max. He sits across from me, watching me with bated anticipation. There are tears in his eyes.

"What was I saying?" I ask.

"Your life," he prompts.

I love him. I miss him. How can I miss him? He's two feet from me.

"My life? Right. Yes. Thank you."

I can't think of where I've been or where I'm going. I notice my own tears but feel quite detached from them. I decide to continue where I left off:

"My life. It is already yours. It has been since you did that stupid dance in my living room. I'm asking you to make your life mine. I want it. I want it for every second I have left. Which isn't that many seconds."

Outside the room, I notice smiling faces peering in through open doors. They're familiar faces. They're my nurses. I've seen them every two weeks for what seems like a lifetime. And yet I can't think of their names. One is Barbara. Or is it Brooke? The women giggle to themselves as they bashfully watch us.

Stay focused, Alabine. "Sorry. Like I said. It isn't that many seconds."

Max's tears fall down his cheeks. "It's enough," he says. "Whatever time we have, I'll take it. It's always been enough, Alabine."

"It'll never be enough, Max."

"Please. Before I explode. Just ask me."

I do have a question for him. My heart flutters at the thought. It's a big something to ask him. Something I planned for weeks with the giggling nurses. The reason rosebuds are strewn about the otherwise unimpressive room. But I'm not ready. If I ask him, all of this will be over. I know that for a fact somehow. And I don't want it to be over.

Completely unmoved by my wants, blood fills up in my lungs. I'm going to drown if I don't get it out. I cough. And cough. And cough.

"I'm sorry. I can't," I mutter through the violent and incessant coughing. I died. I'm dying. I will die. It doesn't much matter, does it? The time will never be enough.

Max falls to his knee in front of me and clasps my hands in his. He's about to speak, but I put my finger over his mouth. I want to do this. I gather my breath, and my courage.

"Max Green. Will you marry me?"

I cry. He is already crying. He opens his mouth to say something, presumably *Yes*, by his expression, but he stops.

Then, completely outside of my own will, I slump down over the large pleather chair. I can't move my arm. Or my head. I watch helplessly as Max reaches for me.

"Alabine? Al?!" He shakes me, then turns to the blushing nurses standing just outside the room. "Help! Someone please help!"

Brooke comes rushing into my view. (Or maybe it's Barbara.) I don't know what's happening. Everyone around me looks worried. Very worried. The nurses push Max out of the way as they lift my lifeless body onto a gurney.

"What's going on? Stop!" I call out, but no one responds. They don't hear me. Did I even hear me? They cut my shirt open as we fly down the hallway. Fluorescent lights stream by overhead.

One. Two. Three.

"Clear!"

My body convulses as electricity pounds through every single nerve. I shout "Max!" My plea goes unanswered by the collection of white coats around me.

I reach out for something, anyone, and finally, my hand finds his. Max. My Max. I gasp for air. Max holds my hand. Then I know.

This is the day that I die. This is the day that I . . .

I'm in my large pleather chemo chair. The particular chair I always use.

I'm coughing.

"Sorry. Sorry about that," I say as I look up. Something feels wrong.

"Go on then." It's Max. He's sitting across from me. There are tears in his eyes.

"Where was I?" I wonder.

"Your life," he responds.

"Right." My life. That's where I was. I've lived my life. "I'm sorry. I guess I'm a little confused. Haven't we done this before?" I ask Max.

He just looks at me and smiles. "Yes. Many times. Too many times."

I can't remember the details, and he offers nothing more to ease my confusion. Until I figure it out, I decide to continue where I left off: "My life is already yours. It has been since you did that stupid dance in my living room. I'm asking you to make your life mine. I want it for every second I have left. Which isn't that many seconds."

Max's tears fall down his cheeks. "It's enough. Whatever time we have, I'll take it. It has always been enough, Alabine."

"It'll never be enough, Max." Sadness envelops my body as I feel the darkness creeping in. I look out the door, where I expect to see giggling nurses, but instead I see the darkness. Like the lights are off. Like every light in the entire world is off except in this bright, oh so very bright, room. And the darkness is coming closer. Just on the other side of the open door. Ready to invade.

"Please. Before I burst. Just ask it." Max sounds impatient. Almost angry. Like the darkness is inside of him too.

"I don't want to. If I ask it, this will be over."

"You don't have a choice, my love. You need to ask me."

I don't want to be here. This isn't where I want to be. This is the end. There's no more after this.

Trembling, I bring myself back to the question. "Max Green. Will you marry me?"

He opens his mouth to respond and the world freezes.

One. Two. Three.

"Clear!"

This is the day that I die. This is the day that I . . .

⋮

I'm in my large pleather chemo chair. I'm coughing. "Sorry. Sorry about that," I say as I look up. "What was I saying?"

Then I scream.

The room is in darkness. The light from battery-operated candles fights to pierce through the darkness. It's just enough for me to see

Max. He's inches from my face, hanging in a bag. Dead. Terrified, I desperately try to get away but am trapped in the enormity of the pleather chair.

Suddenly, inside the bag, Max's eyes open. He tries to breathe but can't. He opens his mouth, and a rush of amniotic fluid pours inside him. Drowning him. He's dying. Summoning my bravery, I try to pry the bag open. I scrape and tear at the thick plastic with all of my strength, but it doesn't budge.

"Help! Someone, please help!" Help doesn't come. Max is dying. The darkness in the room growls. It roars as I watch Max drown to death.

"No! Please!"

One. Two. Three.

"Clear!"

This is the day that I die. This is the day that I . . .

I'm in my large pleather chemo chair.

"Sorry. Sorry about that." I look up and see Max across the beige nondescript room. Far away from me. He's at his desk.

"I want to kill them all," he mutters.

A woman walks over to Max holding a pizza box. She runs her hand lovingly across his back. She turns toward me, and I gasp. She has no face. Just darkness.

I reach out my arm toward Max and am surprised to see that it's covered in white lace. Reaching down to my body, I feel more lace and tulle. A smile spreads across my face.

He said yes.

I don't want to die. I want to marry him. I need to stay alive to marry him.

You need to remember when you married him.

Except the voice inside my head isn't me. It is assertive and calming. It's Wade's voice. I'm eager to listen. I look up and see Max standing in front of me. He's wearing a tuxedo. We're outside.

"You'll remember in time," Max says as he smiles.

One. Two. Three.

Clear.

.
.
.
.
.

It wasn't the restful and replenishing memory I'd hoped to fall into. I felt sore, aching from my skull to my toes. My Lucid Memory was different this time. My lives were bleeding together in a confused jumble like they hadn't before. I wondered if this was all normal, but something told me it was not. None of this was normal.

I couldn't shake the feeling that the darkness was coming for me. As I tried to process what I'd just experienced, I could only conclude that it was the last memory I had before I died. The Lucid Memory looped over and over as if my brain didn't want me to see the end of it, to see what came next. I was so confused, and yet I was smiling. I remembered; we were engaged. Max wasn't just my boyfriend. He was my fiancé, if even for only a minute. I let that part of the memory warm me in the otherwise bitter cold.

It took me a while to come back to the present and remember where I was. Time was fleeting, or my perception of it at least, and I'd been in so many goddamn vans over the past few days.

Eliza put a hand on my shoulder. "You're okay. We're almost there."

Bringing my mind into the present, I looked out the window. It was dark, but I could just barely make out the apocalyptic New York City, lying dormant all around us. Not Chicago or Indianapolis or even Detroit looked anywhere near as dead and abandoned. Unlike Detroit, where nature was taking claim over the land, here was nothing. Animals had left. Weeds didn't even dare grow. Corpses of dead trees spotted the desolate landscape. This was an alien planet—a charred corpse of the once vibrant city.

Everything was covered in black ash. Most buildings still stood tall among the wasteland around them but brandished the scars of burn marks on their facades. The city was haunted with memories, ghosts, and terror. I could feel it. I could see it in the faces of those around me. The lore of New York City preceded our arrival and made even Gina shudder under its shadow. We crossed the river Styx, praying to come out alive.

As we took Houston across the city, I silently watched the vacant streets pass by, mouth agape. We crossed the Williamsburg Bridge. It swayed with our unwanted presence. Manhattan had borne the brunt of the damage from the fallout of the infestation. The island was quarantined then incinerated to a char of its former self. In the surrounding boroughs, I saw that there was still scars of the blaze, but not quite as devastating.

Eventually we made our way to a massive skyscraper in Brooklyn. It was so tall that the top disappeared into a low-hanging cloud. The black iron bones that made up the building's foundation poked through the crumbling facade. Many of the windows on the bottom floor were shattered, while any remnants had blown away long ago. What might have been a colorful exterior was now hidden beneath layers of ash.

The van that held Avon, Minnie, and Chris was parked in front. Diana waited in the driver's seat. The others had already begun their expedition inside the ominous facility.

Without a word, my party collected our things to lug down to hell and disembarked the van. Eliza took a moment to kiss Diana goodbye. Their love reminded me of Max. Of why we were there.

Entering the building, I swear I heard its very foundation moan. We organized ourselves into the planned defensive formation. Gina took the front; Eliza took the rear. Both had guns at the ready.

Our plan was in action. Avon, Chris, and Minnie were headed toward the utility room a few floors below the ground. They were going to jump-start the building and get it back online so that we could call Max's preservation bag to the resurrection bay and wake him up.

I had run through the plan so many times, I stopped seeing the ways it could go wrong, could only see how it was impossible to screw up.

We made our way to the elevator shafts. Gina pressed the call button. Nothing happened.

"No power yet," she declared.

There was that small detail. Damien and Samson. They had gone to two separate power plants to try and bring power back to the city, which had been shut off a decade ago.

"They still have time," Eliza qualified.

"Come on," Gina ordered. "Let's take the stairs, it's a ways to go."

Twenty-three floors down, to be exact. These cryo facilities used the subterrane to efficiently maintain the freezing temperatures. The most advanced facilities, like this one in New York, used geothermal and off-grid solar power to be completely self-sustaining in keeping the bodies on ice, but anything beyond keeping the dead preserved required more power. Hence the importance of Damien and Samson's mission.

The monotony of our descent through the dark stairwell exacerbated the bone-chilling feeling that we were entering some sort of underworld. The only light to guide our way came from the headlamps and flashlights we carried. No one in the party spoke unless entirely necessary. At first, the sound of our feet scraping against the ground seemed soft and muted, but in the absence of any other noise, it became grating.

Max appeared just on the edge of where the light from our flashlight dissipated into the black below. I couldn't see his face, only his back, as he silently led us down into the depths.

It was a disquieting repetition of stair after stair. Landing after landing. My awareness slipped from my body. I felt neither pain nor exhaustion anymore. And no matter how fast or slow I walked, Max was always there, the same distance from me, just out of reach. I wanted to warn him that the darkness was there waiting for us in the lower levels of this building and that it would finally take us if we weren't careful, but I reminded myself that we were headed to our salvation, to his rebirth, and not our collective death. Despite my feeling otherwise.

I had to stay present. I pushed Max out of my mind and focused on reality as hard as I could. But without my wanting it, in the vacuum Max left behind, the unmistakable taste of sweetness touched my lips. I felt a tingle on the nape of my neck. At first it was Max, but now it was Damien whom I couldn't keep from haunting me.

He kissed me.

Terrified, I wondered if Damien had died during his mission. I wondered if now the darkness knew the sweetness of his lips and was taunting me with it.

Finally, we arrived at subfloor twenty-three. Gina held up a hand. We stopped. Slowly, she approached the door, ready for anything. It seemed too easy, but she simply turned the handle, and the door opened. Without power, the security locks were disengaged. We poured out of the stairwell into the somehow-even-darker resurrection wing.

I had obsessively studied the map of the building. I knew the path to get to the resurrection bay. I could walk there with my eyes closed. Which was a good thing because the darkness was claustrophobic, and our flashlights did little to stave off the confusion of where we were.

As we walked down the hallway, I ran my hands along the wall to feel for every corner. We had to take a right at the third hallway, then go through the double doors and make a quick left. Then enter the third door on the left.

Twice, Gina led us in the wrong direction, and twice, I had to whisper to her to stop and turn back until she reluctantly relinquished the lead to me. I guided us the rest of the way.

We finally arrived at the resurrection bay. Through the door's narrow window, I saw a light. I stepped closer, confused why there would be this single, solitary light in the sea of darkness. And then it moved. It was a flashlight.

There was something inside.

At Gina's silent command, we crouched to the ground. She readied her pistol, and then, inside the room, the flashlight went out.

Gina flung me aside and tore open the door, gun drawn. "Hands up!" she commanded.

Eliza rushed in behind Gina, shining her flashlight at the intruder. Peering out from behind his raised hands, shielding his eyes from the light as well as the threat of Gina's bullets, was—

"Damien!" I rushed forward and threw my arms around him. I didn't care if he was mad at me. I didn't care if he didn't want to hug me back. I was so happy that he was alive.

Hold on to the good.

Damien slowly wrapped his arms around me. He then pressed his lips to my ear. "Al, you have to get out of here," he whispered.

"Grey!" Gina lowered her gun. "What the hell are you doing here? Where's the power?"

Damien let me go and stepped forward. He opened up his lanterned flashlight so that it lit the room enough for us all to see one another. "The dam was completely destroyed."

"Shit!" Eliza grunted in frustration. "It's up to Samson then."

"We don't have time to wait," Damien said urgently. "I saw a UA patrol crossing the bridge as I was making my way back here. They must not have completely abandoned the city like we thought." He turned to me and grabbed my hand. I saw deep concern in his eyes. "We have to get out, now."

Just then, a red light on the wall started flashing. Everyone froze.

"What's going on?" I nervously asked.

"Aha!" Gina slapped her hands together. The sound reverberated through a decade of silence shivering with the disruption. "He's done it!"

Looking back up to the red flashing light, I realized what Gina had already figured out. This meant that Samson had turned on the power. This meant that we could wake up Max.

"Al, please." Damien tugged at my hand.

Before the light, I was going to agree with Damien. We could come back at another time once we plotted the UA patrols. We could be more prepared with this new information. But that little red light changed everything.

"We have to do this, Damien. We can do this!" I let go of his hand and turned away. "Minnie said it would only take her a few minutes to get the room online. Let's be ready."

Eliza grabbed me by the elbow. It was gentle, but clearly there was distress in her interruption. "I need to go to Diana. If there is a patrol coming, she's a sitting duck up there."

"Of course."

Eliza nodded in gratitude and took off toward the now powered elevator shaft. I felt Damien's eyes burning in the back of my head as Noah and I took our places in the control room.

Through the large glass window, I took in the space. It looked just like the lab where I woke up. There was a glass box in the middle of the room. Just above it, on the towering ceiling, was a mechanical slot door. This was where the bags would come through, ready for resurrection.

When I had awoken, I was much too out of sorts to fully recognize or appreciate the awesomeness that was the resurrection machine. Seeing it again, I was astonished by its terrifying beauty.

It was twenty feet tall with a highway of braided tubing running the full length of the beast. When a bag entered the room, the machine would power into action, delivering the fluids required to bring a corpse back to life. It arched over the glass coffin that caught the body as it dropped from the bag. Then, like a scanner, the machine moved back and forth over the newly living creature, regulating temperature and blood pressure, until the specimen did what I eventually did: chose to live.

I pulled out Max's file and found the number I would need to input to call Max's bag from storage and into this room. I didn't need to look, not really. On the journey here, I'd memorized most of Max's file, including his storage number.

22615

Much like myself, Max was now defined by a string of numbers. The numbers that were a part of me, under my skin, in my body. Max would soon trace them with his own fingers.

I found the unlit keypad on the large desk in front of me as we continued to wait for Minnie to boot up the room. I briefly wondered if she was in danger, or if she was going to fail. But I pushed the thought out of my mind. It hadn't been a few minutes yet. I needed to give her a few minutes.

The system was mostly automated, and Noah had done this before. My mind tried to focus on the series of steps I needed to take, but all I could think was, *I'm about to hold Max. This isn't a memory. This is real.*

As promised, within minutes of getting power, Minnie booted up the room. From somewhere else in this hellhole of a decaying building, the thirteen-year-old genius delivered my future with Max to me.

All of the lights in the room turned on. The knobs and bulbs scattered across the control room table lit up, and most important, the resurrection machine yawned to life.

"You ready, Alabine?" Noah asked me. I nodded. My hands shook as I typed the numbers into the keypad:

22615

I hit enter, and the room shook. The whole building felt as if it could fall down. Loud mechanical noises rustled from the deep and echoed into the silence.

I watched the row of lights on the control panel charting the loading process of the requested bag. First, it was just one light. Slowly, each light in the line illuminated, indicating that Max's bag had arrived. I gasped when the door in the ceiling pried itself open.

This was it.

Someone held my hand. My rational mind assumed it was Noah. He was, in fact, the only one in the control room with me, but in truth, I knew it to be Max. His touch was tender and loving. We fused together and blended until we were one.

Then I looked over and saw him there, serene and calm. We looked deeply into each other's eyes. He ran his hand over my cheek, and I leaned into the embrace. I felt him; as much as I felt my heart, I felt him there. I knew it wasn't real, but in a moment he would be.

There was so much I didn't know, but I was the most certain of one thing in the entire world: Max was the absolute fucking love of my life.

"Alabine . . ." Noah said, his voice trailing off.

In a blink, Max disappeared, and behind where he had stood, Noah leaned across the control panel as he gaped out the large window. There was dread in his eyes. No, it was horror.

My heart stopped beating as I turned and saw for myself. The bag descending from the ceiling—Max's bag—was cut open. Fresh blood dripped from its gash.

The bag was empty.

PART
FOUR

15

MAX SAID "I LOVE you" to me for the first time 809 feet above the ground. We'd been dating only for a few months. It was New Year's Eve, a few days after my first chemo treatment. I was completely wrecked and yet stubbornly insistent that Max and I ring in 2019 in as big a fashion as we could. We took the day-long train ride from Chicago to New York to meet his friends at a party on top of a building in Times Square that one of his friends worked at. From where we stood over the thousands of people on the street below, waiting to watch the ball drop, the view of the city was astonishing. I already knew it was a night I would never forget.

As I counted down the last minute of 2018 with a champagne glass in my hand and healing poison running through me, Max slipped his hand under my shirt and began tracing his finger along my back. My skin prickled in recognition of the intimate touch. Soon I realized he was spelling something. Through the celebrations and noise, I focused on his movement, trying to figure out its meaning. Then I realized: he was writing "I love you," tracing the letters with his fingertip.

I turned around to him with a coy smile. "Are you writing something?" I already knew the answer, but I was going to make him say it.

"Hey. I'm just rubbing your back here," he said with a large grin. "You're gonna miss it." He pointed at the ball that was starting to drop behind me.

"Tell me what you were writing, Max Green!"

He laughed and pulled his hands away. But I was too quick for him and recaptured them, pinning them behind his back. We pressed our bodies together. I leaned in, our lips tantalizingly close.

I whispered, "Tell me."

He paused a beat. This was it. My heart fluttered. I wondered what I was going to say back. *Do I love him too? Of course I do. How can I love him after only a few months? Am I crazy?* The thoughts flitted through my head like the images of a silent movie. People around us began moving in slow motion.

But instead of confessing his love for me, he whispered, "Never."

Infuriated, I playfully pushed him away, but this time he was too quick for me and pulled me back into him. I wriggled and writhed, feigning pain, and we fell to the ground like children on the playground.

Around us, our friends began counting down from ten. Below us, the whole city was doing the same. As one year was coming to an end and a new one about to start, Max and I stared at each other. When the ten seconds passed and every voice erupted with "Happy New Year," Max kissed me.

He pulled back, and I saw his expression change. "I love you," he said.

After that, in the many times he told me he loved me, it always felt like he was saying it for the first time. He wore this look of profound revelation, like he was rediscovering over and over again, in the little and big moments of our life, that he loved me.

"Same," I said back. Afterward, I was self-conscious that *same* was the word I chose to tell the love of my life that I loved him for the very first time. Not the most romantic story. But in the moment, it was perfect.

So, while perhaps strange, it was not entirely unwarranted nor unwanted that all I could feel while that thick plastic bag descended from the resurrection machine was the comforting feeling of Max's finger tracing "I love you" on my back. Burning the words into my skin. I was his, and he was mine. Forever.

And yet the bag was empty.

He's dead, I thought. The mutilated bag continued its slow descent as bright red blood dripped from the gash down to the floor below. I couldn't take my eyes off of it. No one could. We all stood there in a stupor.

There wasn't a scream loud enough inside me to carry my pain. There was nothing inside of me. Nothing except a belief that this wasn't truly the end of Max. It couldn't be. This wasn't the way our story would end.

I desperately scanned the scene for clues as to what had happened. The blood was freshly dripping, so this didn't happen decades, or even days ago. The Territorial Army had found out he was here and beat us to him by mere hours. The how or why didn't matter. In truth, nothing mattered. He wasn't there. Max was gone.

I wish I could say that I don't remember much about the moments after I saw that empty bag descend from the rafters. I wish I could say that I blacked out and came to days or years later, when the pain wasn't so near. But unfortunately, I remember every damn minute in perfectly stunning detail. I remember Damien rushing into the control room, scooping me into his arms before I collapsed to the ground. I remember him carrying me out of that godforsaken building. I remember lying with my head in someone's lap as Diana drove us as fast as she could through the streets of Brooklyn.

I remember pleading with Avon. Maybe Max was already awoken. Or perhaps that horrible bloody bag was never actually his. I proposed these scenarios to Avon plus countless more in my devastation.

Avon never offered me more than "I hope so." Even in my despair, I could tell that he didn't believe it. He was never a great liar, especially not to me. Any hope he claimed to have was only to placate me. He believed Max was dead. They all did. I knew it from the way they wouldn't look at me.

And then I remember crying. Sobbing uncontrollably.

Eventually we stopped at a random brownstone on a random street. The building had no significance to anyone, which was exactly why it was the perfect hideout. UA patrols would have to search every building in Brooklyn to find us.

The brownstone, like the rest of the city, was long forgotten. Dust and cobwebs that hadn't even seen a spider in years covered every surface. Some of the windows were shattered, and the paint curled away from the blackened walls. While superficial elements had crumbled in the purifying flames a decade before, the bones of the house remained intact and strong, and even some furniture had survived with only cosmetic damage.

I was catatonic when Damien deposited me onto a mattress with scorch marks in one of the bedrooms. Any strength I had withered under the pressure of my grief. I didn't want to live. Not without Max. So I just lay there until my vision tunneled into nothing.

Hours passed. Floating in the limbo between wake and sleep, I dreamed of nothing. I don't mean that I didn't dream. My dreams were vividly of nothingness. The long, haunting, empty vacuum that is nothingness.

The sun hadn't yet risen when I woke. The night that would never end continued to rage outside the brownstone window. It was only after a moment of stillness that I realized it wasn't my grief that had woken me; it was something else.

The phone in my pocket was vibrating.

The familiar vibration happened three times before I pulled the phone out and stared at it in stunned disbelief. I tried to determine in which life this phone was ringing. The lines between my two lives had been blurring more and more; maybe Max's death was the final straw to catapult me into full insanity.

The screen was alight with an incoming call—"Private Number." The corner, where for the last two weeks it had said "No Service," now showed a full four bars next to the letters "UAN." United America Network, I surmised.

It seemed impossible. There were no longer cell phones in this country. They weren't necessarily illegal. It was just that they had fallen so out of favor that companies stopped making them, much like the VHS tape from my time, and discontinued the cell service that supported them.

The vibration stopped, and a bubble popped up onto the screen: "Missed Call." I felt lightheaded, so I took a deep inhale and moved to unlock the phone when the vibration started again. "Private Number." My thumb hovered over the answer button. Before I consciously decided, I pressed the digital green button and heard a *click*.

"Hello, Alabine." It was a man's voice. Smooth and friendly. I instantly recognized it. It was the almighty secretary of science himself, Gene Minchin. "Sorry to call you so early. Hope I didn't wake you."

Of course the government continued to use cell phones with their own protected, private cell service. They had already kept all the other technology for their advantage; cell phones were only a natural extension. Allowing me to keep my phone wasn't some moment of altruism. Instead it was a crucial move of the chess game that day that I didn't even see happen. A direct line to me when they needed it most. When I was at my most vulnerable.

"Alabine? Are you there? Sometimes the connection on these things is tricky. Can you hear me?"

A moment passed, and I didn't say anything. Then another. And another. Every second that passed, I almost spoke. Maybe it was the shock. Maybe the grief. Who knows. The result was I stayed silent. Minchin's shallow breathing was all that passed between us.

Then he spoke. "It appears you don't want to respond to me, which is your right, so I'll start. You jump in whenever you decide you want to." He chuckled to himself. "I called to see if you had reconsidered the offer I gave you in Montrose. Have you thought more about coming to help the president stop all this violence? I still have those little pills waiting for you." He rattled the bottle so I would hear the clinking of the pills against the glass. He waited a moment to give me a chance to speak. I didn't. "Now, I know there's a lot on your plate. Goodness, we're all very busy these days, but I'm worried for your safety if you keep choosing to stay with those . . . those terrorists."

It was unclear if he was insinuating that my safety was in peril because of the people I was with, or because the UA was going to attack us soon. Regardless, it was a threat. A thinly veiled one at that.

"They are a horrendous group of people, these radicals. I can guarantee that they don't care about you. And they certainly don't care about your Max Green."

Rage exploded out of me. "Don't you say his name! You murdered him!" It was the first sound I'd uttered, and it fell with the weight of a meteorite crashing to the earth.

He laughed at the accusation. Or maybe just at me. "Well, hello, Ms. Rivers. You are there indeed."

"I will make sure you pay for that with your life." I meant every word, and Gene knew it. He didn't respond right away. He didn't laugh. There was nothing, only silence.

He cleared his throat. "I'm not sure what you've been told, but neither I nor anyone I know killed Max Green. He's still under ice as peaceful as can be. I'm looking at his bag right now."

My heart leapt into my throat. "You took him. You ripped his body out of that bag."

"Well, yes, there was a troop of very skilled soldiers that went to New York. And yes, they found Max Green, but they didn't harm him."

"There was blood on his bag," I muttered, trying to make sense of it all. "It was cut open."

"A charade, I believe. That wasn't Max's blood, or even his real bag, if I understand the details of the operation correctly. I thought you might need those so-called friends of yours to believe without a doubt that Max was dead so you can leave them. Without Max to hold over your head, they can't control you anymore. If the bag were simply missing, they'd try to lie to you or tell you they'll find him. I gave you a gift of freedom, Alabine."

"You're lying." Max was dead. I wasn't going to let this spineless man convince me otherwise and give me doomed hope.

Minchin laughed. "Why would we kill Max Green when we need both of you to put an end to this conflict for good?"

I'd had enough of his lies. "I'm done." I was pulling the phone from my ear to hang up when it dinged. An incoming text message popped up on the screen. Trembling, I clicked on it. It was a photo.

The photo was dark, but it clearly showed a hanging cryo bag with a man inside. It looked exactly like Max. *It's not possible*, I thought. I wouldn't allow myself to believe Minchin, and yet tears started to cloud my vision. I was about to spit back that it would take more than a blurry photo to convince me until I saw the series of numbers printed on the bottom of the bag.

22615

Minchin was telling the truth. They had Max. Max was still out there. The room spun around me. I should've been happy. Ecstatic, really. But I knew there would be a steep price for this happiness.

Slowly, trembling, I put the phone back to my ear.

"Now that that's no longer weighing on your mind," Minchin said with smug satisfaction in his voice, "I have an invitation for you. I'm not sure if you're aware, but we're having a big parade in a few days for Patriots' Day in Atlanta. President Billy Redden is making a fantastic speech. You should come and join us. After the president's speech, you can get on stage and make a statement announcing to all of United America your condemnation of the Resurrectionist terrorists."

Another proposition. I knew what he was going to offer me. And still, I asked, voice shaking: "Why would I do that?"

"Because if you do, we'll wake Max up for you. I think the celebrations would be a perfect time for you and Max Green to be publicly reunited. Then you ride off into the sunset. Live happily ever after. A fairy tale come true. We'll never even have to speak again if you don't want. This country wants to see you two with your happy ending. Then we can finally put an end to all this turmoil in an otherwise peaceful country."

He paused for a moment, then said, "And before you just say no again, I really want you to think hard. You're a good person, Alabine. Respectable person. So, I'll let you in on a secret." His voice lost some of the pompous tone it often carried, and he spoke kindly. "You were dropped into a war that has nothing to do with you or any other Awoken person. No one in the leadership of the Resurrectionists cares a lick about the Awoken. They care about one thing: power. This is about usurping control. Lovett wanted power. Thank God, at least, that he was killed."

I had to bite my tongue to prevent an outburst. Maybe he was trying to goad me into a reaction, but it didn't sound like it. He honestly thought of Wade as the bad guy. Minchin continued: "Now whoever replaces him will want the same power, and this war will never end. The Awoken are only an excuse. Mere pawns in this game to decide who gets to be king. You're the victim here. You didn't deserve to be woken up like this, but you're here now, so why don't you finally live your life."

His apparent earnestness caught me off guard. Minchin was offering me more than a life. He was offering me a peaceful one. No more being hunted. No more feeling like half a person without Max. I'd be lying if I didn't say I considered taking him up on it for a split second, but I knew that was only a fantasy. I knew I couldn't accept his terms and undermine the Resurrectionists. Still, I'd been through so much in the last day that I allowed myself a moment to consider what would happen if I did accept. And then I let the dream fade away.

Max was still in cryo somewhere. We would find him. Figure out a way to get him out. Another break-in. Another undercover plant. The specifics didn't matter. I was certain that we could concoct yet another plan to rescue Max, even it if took a few months. Max had been frozen for almost a century. The point was that he was still alive. That knowledge gave me the strength I needed.

"I won't turn on my friends. We'll find Max and take him back. That's a promise."

Minchin sighed. "No need to find him." Any undertone of kindness was gone. Disdain punctuated his words once again. "I'll tell you exactly where he is." He took a breath. "Max's body is in the Atlanta facility."

The walls of the small bedroom closed in around me. "But it's being decommissioned."

"That's right. You better hurry and try your daring rescue soon, then. Max doesn't have much time left."

"No. You wouldn't kill Max. You just told me that."

"Let me be clear, Alabine." His voice changed, deepened, like I was finally seeing the inner demon that lay in wait behind his wide grins. "We've been exceedingly gracious up until now, but you're trying our patience. The president and I would prefer a peaceful way out of this. You and Max bringing this to an end without a single shot fired. Or not. We could always benefit from another Eavesman Square tragedy. This is your last chance. If you don't come to Atlanta by the morning of Patriots' Day, we no longer have a use for Max. Or you." His berating tone shocked me into silence. "The facility is scheduled to be decommissioned to make room for the Redden National Park, and the bodies still inside will be incinerated in the blast. Including your Max."

A weak breath pushed out of my lungs. Every inch of me withered with exhaustion. "How can you hate Awoken so much?" I asked, honestly needing to know.

"You misunderstand, Alabine. I like you, I really do. I might not like who you are right now, but I like you. It just doesn't matter what I feel. All that matters is that the people hate the Awoken. And they do."

There it was. Wade was right. He said that in our first meeting: the only way to win was with the support of the people. The everyday Joe Schmoes of this country. Nothing was going to change until they did. And I had no idea how to change the minds of millions of people. Especially in the few days before the Atlanta facility was decommissioned. We didn't have time. I'd never had time.

I couldn't help but think if I had just agreed with Avon, gone with his plan to march to Atlanta, none of this would be happening. Max would be safe.

"If you attack us, we win. If you don't come, Max is gone forever, we still win. If you come to Atlanta and wake Max, we both win." He paused. "You owe those people you're with nothing. Get out while you still can, Alabine." Minchin's tone was somewhere between friendly and threatening. "The facility is being decommissioned in four days. As Max Green's next of kin, you let us know if you'd like to claim his body. We'd be glad to have you."

Click. The call ended.

The room stilled. The world stilled. I was crushed and crippled. Unable to cry or even feel the floor beneath me. While the sun peeked into the sky outside the window, I was acutely aware that each moment that passed without my doing anything was one less moment for me to do something. I ran through the options in my head.

One: Join the enemy and be reunited with Max. Join Minchin and Redden. Make a public statement condemning the Resurrectionists. It would be the end of the movement for good. Tens of thousands would die, and millions more would be decommissioned. Who was to say they wouldn't still kill me and Max at the end of it anyway.

Two: Figure out some magical way to get to Atlanta in time. Storm the facility and try to break him out. Especially risky as it was heavily guarded. Eavesman Square had proved how difficult that would be. It'd be trading so many lives for only the possibility of rescuing Max.

Three: Do nothing. Max dies forever.

My hand curled, gently at first, around my new brunette wig. It was trying so hard to be like my real hair and yet desperately failing. My hand then tightened into a fist, and I tore the wig off my head. I screamed as I threw it across the room with all my might. My weak body collapsed from this simple exertion, and I shrank into a pile of tears.

Max and I had been parted by death before, but this time was different. This time, I would be his executioner. My choice to stay would mean that Max and I would never be together ever again. On top of that, my choice would also be taking Max from all Awoken. And Resurrectionists. And the world. He was their true long-awaited leader. Who was I to take him from them?

Eventually I decided what to do.

My eyes were so swollen, I could barely see the room brighten as morning took over the night sky. I peeled myself off the ground and kicked my discarded wig to the side, swearing to never wear it again. Then, with only two weeks of stubble covering my scalp, I made my way downstairs.

Everyone was already awake, standing in the darkened living room. They were huddled around Samson, who had just returned from the wind power plant. He should've been met with cheers for his success. Instead he found us broken.

I watched them from the stairs for a moment. They were embracing each other, having just told Samson about Max. Someone described to him the empty bag that was cut open with blood dripping from it. A decoy to give me an alibi so I could take my leave from this group and join their enemy in Atlanta, but none of them knew this truth. Eliza had her arm around Diana's back. Minnie was wrapped into Gina's arms. Noah and Avon stood together, arms touching. Damien had his hand on Samson's back.

Chris wasn't there, and I wondered where she was. Max's capture just moments before our rescue was not a coincidence. There was still a traitor in our midst.

Damien was the first to see me, followed soon by everyone else. I saw in each of their faces how much the idea of Max meant to them, in a Christlike way. They had been awaiting his return for generations. They were the chosen few to fulfill the destiny, and they had failed. We failed. That was the story splashed across their forlorn faces. We had chosen to not march to Atlanta so that we could get him. And that choice was now for nothing. No, *I* had chosen. Because of me, it was all for nothing. I chose wrong. I failed.

"Avon . . ." My voice cracked. "Can we talk?" He nodded and followed me up the stairs.

"Al." Damien stepped forward out of the group. He looked at me, and I immediately wanted him to take me away from here. Away from everything. Shelter me from this terrible life. We stared at each other for a moment, him trying to find the words to say before resigning himself to "I'm sorry." His voice carried so much more than an offer of condolences for Max. I tasted sweetness on my lips, then turned away and led Avon to my room.

Once inside, I closed the door behind us and slid to the ground. Exhaustion. Grief. Cancer. It all weighed me down to the point where I could no longer stand. Avon said nothing, simply sat on the floor next to me.

I told him about everything. About the Minchin phone call. I showed him the photo of Max's bag, then outlined the deal Minchin offered. I listed the three choices as I saw them. Avon listened intently. Offering a loving hand squeeze when I had trouble speaking.

After I was done, he racked his brain for a solution. "Assuming you wouldn't have told me any of this if you had decided to join Redden, we can contact the nearest camp and get them to break into the facility and try to save him. We'd never make it ourselves in time, but maybe the Atlanta camp is still nearby. Given their current weakened state, it's even more likely they'd fail, or not even be able to respond. But I think it's the only chance at saving Max."

I bit my lip, holding back my emotion.

Avon softened and quietly asked, "What do you want to do, Alabine?"

"I want to wake Max up," I responded earnestly. "I want to ride off into the sunset like Minchin promised. I want a life that has always been just out of my grasp. I want time." Avon nodded along, concern creeping up behind his gaze. I hung my head and pushed the dream out of my body. "No. I'm not going to join Redden."

Avon flushed with relief.

This next bit was too hard to say while also keeping myself from crying, so I let the tears fall. "I know Max wouldn't want us to risk more lives to save him." My voice hiccupped as I tried to keep speaking. My voice failed me, but my thoughts couldn't have been clearer. Avon gently rubbed my back as I sobbed for a moment before collecting myself enough to speak. "It's just . . . what to do next is not up to me. I can't make this decision."

"You're asking me to make it for you?" Avon asked, surprised.

I shook my head. "I'm telling you that it's not my decision to make." I was drained. Dried. A shrivel of a person. In that vacuum, the right path to walk was unmistakable. "I want to make a difference in the world, I always have, and now I see that the biggest mark I can make is to ensure that you're the one leading this movement."

"What are you saying?" Avon asked somberly.

"Minchin told me that the Resurrectionists don't really care about us, that it's just about power. I don't believe him, but it made me see how important it is we're led by one of us. And while I technically am 'one of us,' you understand who we are and what we need way more than I do yet." I took a deep breath. "You're our leader. It should've always been you."

Avon looked at me skeptically. "Even if that means I won't try to save Max?"

I lifted my head and looked him in the eye. "Whatever you decide, I'll follow. This time, I promise I'll support you in every way."

Avon pulled me into a hug. I buried my face in his chest. He held me with his unwavering strength. I can't say it was at all easy for me to step aside and give up my position like that. I can say that it was one of the braver things I would ever do. I'm not the heroine of this story. It took losing Max for me to finally realize that. It took losing everything to see everything I had.

"Come on." Avon stood up and offered me his hand. The weight of it all was still crushing, but with his help, I found my feet.

Before leaving, I took one last look at the photo Minchin had sent me of Max's bag. I zoomed in as far as I could on his face. That image of him will haunt me forever. Dead. Frozen. Alone in the darkness. I took a deep breath and deleted the photo, preserving the memory of the Max I love. *My Max.*

We wouldn't tell anyone downstairs. If they knew Max was in Atlanta and we were choosing not to go to him, it would have been as if he died all over again. Only Avon and I could know.

We made our way back down to the dining table where the group sat in silence. Chris was now back from wherever she'd gone off to. The radio played music softly. DJ Raheem's voice curated the tracks that seemed to perfectly score the tragic moment. Their eyes fell on us as we entered the room.

Eliza stood. "I know everyone's tired, but we shouldn't stay here long. We should get on the road back to Detroit. We'll be safe there, Alabine."

The idea of retreating to the Detroit camp was appealing, but I reminded myself it wasn't up to me. I cleared my throat. "Avon's agreed to take over as leader."

"What?" Eliza shouted. "No! How dare you, Avon. She's grieving!"

Avon opened his mouth to respond, but I touched his arm, stopping him.

"No," I said, confidently. "This has nothing to do with Max." My voice caught with emotion when I said his name. I swallowed. "I expect everyone to listen to Avon from now on."

Without letting the moment stale, Avon stepped forward. We locked eyes briefly before he turned his attention to the room. "The death of Max Green is earth-shattering to everyone here. Wade is no longer with us. Max is no longer with us. We're on our own. We must honor their legacies by fighting for the world they believed in."

"Hell yeah!" Minnie shouted and pumped her fist in the air. The room lightened for a moment, moved by her pure excitement.

Avon took a deep, weighted breath. "The movement is on the brink of collapse. It's too late to do anything about the decommissioning in Atlanta, but our camps are still out there roving. They're fighting for their lives, and we have to help them. Everyone's future depends on it." Avon paused and looked around the room, then to me. I nodded, fully behind him, whatever he decided. "I have a plan. One that doesn't just beg for the scraps to survive but gives us a real future." He took a breath. "I'm going to call all the camps to New York. Here. All fifty thousand Awoken."

The room stilled in a collective gasp.

Completely stunned, I couldn't look away from Avon. It seemed dangerous. It seemed crazy. I felt my lips curl into a proud smile, assured in my decision and in awe of the man beside me. He was going to save us all.

"Why the hell would we do that?" Eliza scoffed.

"Wade used to talk about taking a city and making a safe home for Awoken," Chris muttered in remembrance. "He didn't think it could actually be done."

"It can," Avon said with strength growing in his voice. "And we will do it. It means no more hiding. No more camps. It means all Awoken coming together as one where we'll be stronger and can actually demand to be heard!"

"You can't do that," Eliza protested with an eye roll, like the plan was so insane it didn't even deserve the energy of her anger. "We can't just take New York City."

"Why not?" Gina snorted. "Haven't we already? I don't see anyone here. The UA abandoned it years ago."

Eliza studied Avon, trying to determine how serious he was. Her face fell when she realized that he meant every word. "We'll be sitting ducks if we bring everyone here. They'll wipe us out in one fell swoop. Staying apart. Staying hidden. That's always been our way! Max himself believed that was the safest strategy to keep the movement alive."

"Sit down, Eliza," I barked with a tone that surprised even myself. Wide-eyed, Eliza obeyed. Avon looked at me with gratitude in his eyes before turning back to the room.

"That might be the way of the Resurrectionists, but that's not the way for the Awoken. A Resurrectionist can always go home. But an Awoken has nothing to call home. We can't keep fighting for status quo. Begging for our lives. To run until we have nowhere else to run. Hide until we have nowhere else to hide. That's not surviving, that's them winning. That's confirmation that our lives are worth less than theirs. We can't wait for someone else to validate us. We have to validate ourselves. We've been playing by their rules for too long. It's time we make our own."

Gina pounded her fist on the table in agreement.

Chris stood up. "The Canadian ship should be here any day. There will be more than enough supplies to go around. We were going to distribute them among the camps, but if everyone comes here . . ." Her words faded into a thought. Then a smile spread across her face. "This could work."

Avon continued, further emboldened. "We're going to bring all of the Awoken camps here as soon as possible. We're going to make this our home. And you better believe we're going to fight for it."

Gina pounded her fist on the table again, louder. This time Damien joined in with her. Then others joined in too. Eliza remained silent, but seeing that even Diana was banging her fist, she realized she was outnumbered. The emphatic percussive rhythm took over and filled the brownstone. It was the heralding of our future. Of hope.

Avon allowed himself a small smile. "Come on, there's a lot of work to do."

They sprang into action and set in motion Avon's dream for a new future. There were many logistics that needed to be figured out to bring tens of thousands of people to New York. There was no more trying to play by their rules. No one said the word, but we all knew what we were doing.

We were seceding from the UA.

It was all I could do not to collapse. So, with Avon's approval, I settled into an overstuffed armchair in front of the fire while the world spun around me. In these people, I saw what my future could be without Max. These people were my friends, quickly becoming my only family, in a world in which Max Green would never exist.

It was a world that I had refused to live in when I was first awoken, before Wade handed me Max's phone and told me that we were going to be reunited. When I put Gina's gun to my head and begged her to pull the trigger. When all I wanted was the darkness to consume me again.

A lot had happened since the day I saw that billboard, and yet there was still that part of me that didn't want to keep living like this. It was too hard. So, in front of that fire on that cold night in late December, I decided to keep on living just for that day. I didn't have to choose to live for years, months, or even weeks without Max. Just that day. Then the next day I would see if I made the same decision.

Before long, it would no longer be up to me. I wouldn't need to hold Gina's gun to my head this time because the cancer was going to take me soon anyhow. I swore I'd use the little time I had left to help Avon; then maybe I'd just allow myself to fade away. Back into the darkness, where I'd be neither loved nor hated. I wouldn't be anything. And that thought soothed me.

Soon enough, Max was there, sitting with me in the overstuffed armchair. I couldn't see him, but I felt him. Felt his arms wrapped around me, holding me in close to his chest like he had so many times in our life together. I mindlessly stroked the hairs on his arm and tried not to think of him frozen and dead in a bag thousands of miles away.

I told him that I'd never leave him if he never left me as I fell asleep in his arms. In order to survive until tomorrow, I needed this good feeling and held on to him as hard as I could, but for the first time, he was slipping away. We didn't have much more time.

I didn't have time.

AN ORDER FROM THE 64ᵀᴴ UNITED AMERICAN CONGRESS
ESTABLISHING THE REDDEN NATIONAL PARK

Whereas it is of the utmost importance in this country that land preservation is pursued and achieved at the highest standards:

By virtue of the authority granted to this body of government by the Constitution and the lawful citizens of this land, it is heretofore decreed as follows—

1. There shall be created a National Park of 900,000 acres in the southwest area of what is currently known as Atlanta in the territory of Georgia. This land will have the protections and considerations of all National Parks. There will be no presence of any manmade structures or development, and any current such development must be cleared to allow for the Park's formation.

2. There shall be allowed on these lands no hunting without a permit issued from the National Park Service whose mission and duty it is to maintain a sustainable preservation of native species.

3. Deforestation or any removal of native plants for commercial uses or otherwise is strictly prohibited on these protected lands and shall not be allowed under any circumstances.

4. In requirement of the aforementioned clearance of protected land, on the first of January 2122, the buildings at 1-30 Darwin Lane known as the South Atlanta Cryogenics Preservation Campus will be demolished by detonation. All property and remains still occupying National Lands as of 12:01 p.m. on the first of January 2122 is forfeit, becoming sole property of the Federal Government to be destroyed.

It is so decreed. It is so lawful.

P.R. Williams

House Majority Leader

16

THE CALL WENT OUT:

Come to New York City.

Avon's plan was set in motion. Through the scrambled radio channels that were Wade's remaining legacy, it quickly became clear that the call was being answered. More than a hundred roving camps were so fragile and desperate for a home that they asked few questions before altering their perilous journeys. They headed toward us, toward this long-forsaken city in which we had committed to building a home. We had to be ready.

We needed supplies. Food, weapons, and, above all, medicine. Supplies that we didn't have. If Chris was to be believed, an unmarked supply ship was en route from Canada carrying, among everything else, my cure. We just had to wait. At Avon's insistence, I had formed an uneasy trust in Chris, but my gut was screaming that something was still wrong and more bad things were going to happen. Soon.

The day the call went out was filled with the hustle and bustle of plans being made and followed. Of arguments and shouts. Of celebrations and love. I was surrounded by it all and not a part of any of it. People whirled around me like a hurricane with me as its eye. Hopelessly alone in the chaos.

Late that night, after everyone had retired to bed, I sat in front of the dwindling fire, staring off into eternity. Hopelessly missing Max. The pain was so deep, so complete, that it consumed my every thought and movement. You see, it didn't matter to me that Max's body was technically preserved for another three and a half days. I had to push out any thought that he was still out there, or else I would've gone mad. It was as if, with the decision to not go to Atlanta, the facility was already blown to smithereens. He was already gone. I had no hope left.

In my grief, I found myself wishing beyond anything that my life had been different. It was something I had done many times before, each time as futile as the last. You'd think at some point I'd learn my lesson, but I never did. So I sat there wishing that smoke bomb had never hit me in the neck. I wished I had never felt my skin melt into his, fusing us together as one. I wished I could feel complete without him. Most of all, I wished I had never died.

Then, amid all this hapless wishing and drowning in the thick goopy swamp that was my despair, I found myself no longer beside the fireplace of soot and embers but instead outside the door to the attic stairs. Though I didn't remember passing through the dark and empty hallways, I knew why I was there. I did find some surprise, however, that my feet actually took me. They were more courageous than my heart.

For you see, behind that door, up the stairs in the attic, was Damien's room.

I knocked softly. There was shuffling inside, followed by the squeaks of rickety wooden stairs under the pressure of the feet descending them. Damien opened the door. His look of surprise was quickly replaced with a smile. That smile was one of the first things I saw when I woke in this life. If *Rosebud* was my trigger and connection to my old life, his smile was my connection to this one.

"Are you okay?" he asked. His hair was half pulled back. A few curls rebelled against such confinement and fell loose, framing his face.

"I didn't wake you, did I?" I asked, very intentionally not answering his question.

"No. Not at all. Come in."

We made our way up the old staircase. The attic room was simply laid out, a mattress on the floor with the items from Damien's pack messily unfurled around it. There was a lamp in the far corner that cast a dim, warm light across the room, only softly fending off the shadows that had remained undisturbed for a decade.

He stepped into the room, muttering something about the mess. Before he could wander too far ahead, and before I lost my nerve, I grabbed his hand. He stopped. My finger brushed against his palm. He didn't turn back to me. He didn't say anything and neither did I. We just stood there, a few feet apart, not looking at each other, me holding onto him.

He realized why I was there.

"Please. Don't," Damien said finally. He peeked over his shoulder, and I saw a quiet fear in his eyes. The same fear was in me too. I was terrified. But touching him felt good, and I needed to feel good. To feel something.

The overwhelming sadness fell from my throat, down deep into the pit in my stomach. It was still there, I could still feel it, but in that moment, at least, I wasn't drowning in it. I could finally breathe.

With a deep inhale, I stepped closer to him, my fingertips grazing up his arm until they reached his shoulder. He remained frozen in place, not daring to move a muscle, perhaps worried if he did he would lose all semblance of restraint.

"Alabine, I can't . . ." Damien tried, pleading with me again. I was trembling. His skin prickled under my touch. "You're just missing Max."

Yes.

"No," I whispered before leaning into him. Our lips almost touched, he didn't back away, but also I couldn't bring myself to kiss him. Max flooded into my mind. Our first kiss. Our last kiss. Our life that would've been. I saw it all in front of me. In that split second, I fell into Max's embrace. I felt his lips on mine, his arms wrapped around me. His love for me pulsed through every vein and every heartbeat.

In my hesitation, Damien clasped his hands around my shoulders and firmly pressed me away.

"Leave, Al." He walked across the room and leaned heavily over an ash-covered half-broken desk in the corner. Without Damien's touch, all the emptiness and pain returned.

It was then that I realized I did love him too, in a way, and I didn't want to hurt him. It was unfair of me; I know that it was unfair for me to ask this of him. But I needed to feel something other than pain. Other than loss. Other than fear. I needed to breathe, and Damien was fresh air.

"I need you, Damien." My knees buckled. "It hurts too much right now," I gasped between my tears.

Damien finally turned around to me, but I didn't see him. I saw Max. I couldn't hold myself together anymore, and I fell apart on the floor. Trying to breathe. Inhale. Exhale. It didn't matter. I was suffocating. His hands wrapped around my arms, then moved to my face. I wasn't sure if it was Max or Damien. It felt like both and neither. It felt like the darkness. Like nothing.

His hand gently guided my chin up, and I looked into Max's eyes.

He is right here, holding me. We are in our apartment, and I am dying, and he is holding me. We kiss. It's long and deep. The most perfect kiss. We have a million of these perfect kisses, each one better than the last. I melt into him.

"I don't want to live without you," I say.

"You have to," he whispers.

I remember this. I am remembering this, but the words are reversed. He's saying what I said to him the night after my doctor told us the diagnosis was terminal. There is no more fighting medical science can do. Only prayer. That doesn't work either.

I fold a strand of his curly hair behind his ear. Except Max doesn't have curly hair. Damien has curly hair.

"It hurts too much right now," I breathlessly repeat as I press my cheek to his arm.

"It's okay. I'm here." Max twirls my hair in his fingers. I don't have hair. And yet he still twirls it. Salty tears trickle down my cheek and onto my lips.

"But soon you won't be," I say.

"Everything dies, Alabine." He smiles warmly. "We'll say goodbye before the end."

"We'll say goodbye?" I innocently ask. Hope sneaks into my voice.

"We said goodbye," Max confidently confirms.

I nuzzle back into him. Burying my nose deeply into his chest. "Yes, I remember. We said goodbye." Max pulls me up to his gaze. I love the way he holds me. It hurts for me to miss him this much when he's right here. "Will you kiss me?" I ask.

Max smiles. "You never have to ask." And then he kisses me. I see a flash of us at ninety years old together. Kissing still. Madly in love. He must've seen it too as he presses his lips harder into mine. It feels like if we never stop this kiss, we'll make it to ninety and still be in each other's arms.

Alas, the kiss ends, and the vision fades. Here we are, in the prime of our youth. And somehow we're both dying. I run my hand along his face, memorizing every line and curve, but I don't dare look him in the eye. I'm too scared.

Max starts to say, "Goodb—"

"Wait." I stop him. I'm not ready. We didn't have enough time. There will never be enough time. He allows me these few more seconds as he holds me. Silently I promise him that I will never forget him. That I will honor his life. Our life together. Finally, I say, "Okay. I'm ready."

Max gently hugs me. "Goodbye, Alabine."

I fight it: the urge to cry, the urge to die, the urge to melt into him. I breathe. Inhale. Exhale. Then, finally, I meet his teary eyes.

"Goodbye. Max."

Damien's eyes stared lovingly down at me. There was no century separating my two lives anymore. I was living both simultaneously, standing in both times at once. Except I had no footing. I had to save myself. There was no choice if I wanted to live. I had to commit to this life, to this reality. I reached out for Max.

No. Not Max.

I reached out for Damien. With all the strength I could gather, I pulled him into me. We kissed. It was a perfect kiss. It filled the hole in my heart. It pushed warmth through me. And yet my old life refused to release me. It tugged and clawed at me, trying to rip me out of this attic and back to my apartment. To Max. My Max.

He's gone. Let me go. He's gone.

I kept thinking it over and over again, rejecting the overwhelming urge to fall back into Max's arms.

He's gone!

Then it stopped. I only felt Damien's lips. His hands wrapped around my waist. My hands pressed into his back, urging him closer. I couldn't let him pull away from me. Not now. He was my only tether to this room. To this life. I was clinging onto him for my very survival.

And he let me. Thank God.

My hands were already unbuttoning his jeans when I realized what they were doing. He pulled my shirt over my head, then wrapped his warm arms around me before the cold air dared touch my skin. He picked me up off the ground where I had fallen in complete despair only moments before. That collapsed woman was an entirely different Alabine than this one now in Damien's arms.

His teeth scraped along my shoulder. My fingers twisted into his hair. He smelled like sweat and honey. There was a fire growing inside of me. A heat that rumbled through my bones, warmth as I hadn't yet felt in this life. It wasn't just a need to survive anymore. Suddenly, it was a desire for more. I wanted Damien. Urgently, passionately wanted him. I hooked my legs around his waist as he carried me over to the unmade mattress on the floor and laid me down.

He took a moment, a breath, and stared into my eyes. There was still fear there. He was holding back, worried that I was seeing Max perhaps. I wasn't. I saw him. I was with him, fully and completely. He smiled—*that smile*—and kissed me.

Wrapped in each other, all the pain faded away. Max faded away. That night, Damien was everything I wanted. He was real. And he loved me. We loved each other.

THE NEXT MORNING, I woke up just as the early light started to peek through the shuttered window. The attic was still, laden with the late December chill. Tucked deeply into the mothball-smelling blanket, I slowly roused out of my sleep to a comforting warmth. It was a particular kind of warmth that I recognized. It drew from not just one but two bodies.

My sleep had been so restful that not even a dream could break through. As my consciousness pulled further into wakefulness, I felt the weight of the body next to me and worried that I had once again slipped into another time. When I looked down, however, I was relieved to see Damien's curly black hair. He was nestled into me, sound asleep, his arm draped heavily across my body. I felt him wanting to melt into me. I wanted to melt into him, more than I could admit.

As quietly and gracefully as I could, I slipped my naked body out from under Damien's arm and braved the cold on the other side of the blanket. Collecting my clothes and wriggling my way into them, I was reminded of the many times I'd snuck out of bed, leaving an unknowing one-night stand asleep under the covers.

It didn't matter how much I wanted to feel that same nothingness. Damien was inarguably different. He was Damien. In another life where I had never known Max Green, I knew that we would be two parts of the same whole. But not now. The bright morning light assaulted me with the unavoidable truth: in this life, I would always belong to Max.

As I dressed, regret twisted in my stomach. Partly because I had slept with someone so soon after learning I'd never see Max again. Partly because of what I did to Damien, that I took advantage of his feelings for me. And partly because of the flutter in my stomach that made it impossible to ignore my own deeply passionate feelings for him too.

The giddiness, the guilt, the cold, the grief, and, of course, the cancer—they were all inside me at the same time. They filled me. Choking me. It was not something that I was up for discussing with Damien once he woke up, so I continued my stealthy exit and tiptoed across the room toward the staircase that led down to the main house. My hope was to sneak back into my room unseen. The last thing I wanted to do was explain to Avon or Gina or, worst of all, Minnie why I was sneaking out of Damien's room wearing my same clothes from the day before.

After only a few steps across the attic floor, the silence that masked my escape was interrupted by a series of strange digital blips. My heart raced, worried the noise would wake Damien and give me away. I stole a quick look behind me. Damien hadn't stirred.

If not for being the only sound in the room, these quiet tonal blips would've gone unnoticed. But in the stillness, their fast rhythm reminded me of how the old fax machine in Jessica DeWhitt's office used to sound: tinny, digitized, and certainly out of place in this luddite world. They were so out of place that, at first, I thought that I must've been hallucinating them. Until I remembered: it wasn't that this world was rid of technology; it was that only select people had access to it. And those people wanted to destroy us. If those blips came from the enemy, they meant the beginning of the end.

I had to find them.

I took a few more steps forward, and the blips slowed, then stopped. I took a few steps backward, and they resumed. Listening intently, I finally realized they were coming from me, specifically from my pocket. Feeling it like a hot coal in my jeans, I slid out Max's phone and looked at the network bars, still full, with "UAN" next to them.

How could I be so stupid?

I'd seen enough spy movies to know that the bad guys can always track the good guys through a cell phone. I was too grief-stricken, too much in shock from choosing to abandon Max, to have thought to turn off the phone.

"Damien!" I whisper-shouted, trying to wake him and help me devise a plan. He didn't move. Helpless, and with the impression we were under imminent attack, I summoned the courage to take a few rushed steps toward him so I could shake him awake. Again the blipping stopped.

A pattern was emerging. I stared at my phone. Nothing had changed except where I was in the room. I stepped backward, and the blips resumed. Then I walked forward again, and they stopped. Slowly, foot over foot, I walked around the room tracing the boundaries of where the sounds started and stopped. Eventually a semicircle began to form out of my careful and slow steps.

In the center, there was a small dresser. Nothing special, it was clearly put up there for storage long before the residents abandoned the place during the infestation. Perhaps it was a child's dresser, as it looked like it had baby blue paint under the charred shell.

In a trancelike state, I opened the drawers, not knowing what I was searching for. Each drawer was empty until I opened the bottom one and found a simple brown leather bag.

It was Damien's bag. I remembered it from the Detroit camp. The image of him slinging it over his shoulder when he packed up in the hospital car flashed into my mind. At first, my fears were assuaged. What I found was not a bomb or a symbol of an attack; it was Damien's bag. What could be evil about Damien's bag? And yet the blipping continued. And the trembling in my stomach did not cease.

I looked over my shoulder to the mattress on the floor. Damien slept on it peacefully, completely undisturbed by my movements. I watched his chest rise and fall slowly, half covered by the blanket that was haphazardly thrown atop the otherwise bare bed.

I opened his bag. Worry that I would be caught in this personal intrusion was drowned out by my overriding need to know what was inside. Something in there was causing the interference with Max's phone.

A knife. A compass. A notepad. Gloves. A wool knit hat he had worn the day before. Nothing out of the ordinary.

Relieved, I started to remove my hand from his bag when I felt a small slit in the lining. Without hesitating, or thinking, I reached my hand through it. Immediately, I felt the cold sharp edges of something metal. My fingers clasped around the rectangular object as I racked my brain for what it could possibly be. I pulled it out, back through the tight slit, and stared at the object for a long while, trying to understand. Trying to see that it was something other than what it appeared to be. Meanwhile, Max's phone continued its explosion of incessant digital blips.

The object was simple enough. Black metal with silver accents wrapped around a slim rectangle. A blue light blinked on and off with predictable regularity. My fingers trembled over the outline of a *U* and an *A* inscribed on the front.

Suddenly, I felt a hand on my shoulder. I whipped around, ready for attack, for a raid, to see children dying in their own blood. Instead I saw Damien. He looked at me with this object in my hand. He was still, calm, entirely unemotional.

Trying to formulate words or a question, I continued to turn the object in my palm. *This could mean nothing*, I thought to myself. There was so much about this world I didn't know—why make assumptions? Or he could be the victim; this object could have been hidden in his bag without his knowledge. But with each passing millisecond that I stared at the unfeeling determination on his face, it was hard for me to continue to doubt.

"Go on," Damien said. "Ask me. I won't lie to you anymore."

Lie? Anymore? This seemed to be some sort of nightmarish hallucination. Something my brain was doing to process the guilt I felt from sleeping with him.

Pinned against the dresser, I wanted to escape. To be anywhere else in the world but there in that attic. I started to shake. Realization set in that I was scared of Damien, and that very thought terrified me even more. I had to get help.

From the ground, I tried scrambling to my feet and darting away, but Damien was too quick. He grabbed my wrist and pulled me back into him.

"Don't," he said while I tried to twist free. There was a restrained strength in his grip that was almost violent. Then he softly whispered, "Please." I stopped struggling. He wasn't angry, not even surprised or defensive. It was as if he had already resigned himself to how this scene would play out. "Ask me what you want to know."

I wrenched my wrist from his grasp and held out the object. "What is this?"

Damien nodded. "It's a tracking device."

"Did you know it was in there?"

"Yes." The world stopped turning.

"How did you get it?" I asked.

"It was given to me."

"When?!"

Damien rubbed the back of his neck anxiously. "When you all thought I was going to the water dam to turn on the power. I never went there."

His admission rattled around in my head as I still clung to disbelief, slowly backing away from him until I bumped into that dresser. He stepped toward me, and I held up my hand signaling for him to stop. He obeyed.

"Why do you have a tracking device, Damien?"

"You know why, Al."

I clenched my eyes shut, refusing to let his words be true. "Minchin said there was a leak. It's how they found the Chicago camp."

He nodded.

Tears blurred my vision as I fought to keep from breaking down. Images of that horrible scene in Chicago ran through my head. "The raid?" I finally stammered.

"I was the one who told them you were there."

"All those children?" I could barely push out the words.

Damien heaved a heavy exhale. "It wasn't supposed to go like this."

"Oh, they weren't supposed to be slaughtered and burned alive?"

He paused, studying me, before he answered, "They were. The incineration was part of the order." He spoke like a true soldier: calm, blunt, and brutal. Totally disassociated from the horrors done at his hand.

"Why?" I asked, breathlessly.

"It's not my job to question orders."

"No," I gasped, trying to put my true meaning into words. I couldn't. So I asked again: *"Why?"*

This time, Damien understood. He shifted his weight and ran his hand through his black curls while his eyes searched mine. He shrugged. "It's who I am."

"What about last night? Was that who you are, or was that also just an order?"

"Last night . . ." He swallowed the words as his eyes darted around the room. "That wasn't . . . Alabine, I—"

"Stop." I interrupted, realizing I couldn't bear any more of his lies. As I struggled to see through my disbelief, I had a glancing thought that this was all a big joke. That he was having a good laugh at my expense.

Chris was the leak, not Damien. I was sure of it. It couldn't be Damien. Kind Damien. He never could've turned on the movement.

"Did Minchin offer you something? Does he have something on you?"

"No." Damien replied simply. "It's not like that. I didn't take a deal. I'm a soldier. It was my mission to infiltrate the resistance."

I burst into laughter through my tears. Hoping beyond hope that he'd start laughing too and we'd fall into each other's arms. I'd playfully chastise him for playing such a mean joke on me; then we'd snuggle back under that mothball-smelling blanket and forget this ever happened.

But he didn't laugh.

After taking a deep breath, I asked, "What now?"

"I don't know." He hung his head. A long moment passed during which neither of us said anything. My feet were glued to the ground, glued to him. He then looked back up at me. "The secretary told you about Atlanta. Go there with me." He said it like it was a fantastic idea. "It's the right place for you, the safest place. These people don't stand a chance against the Territorial Army, Al. They're all going to die, and so are you if you don't leave with me. I can protect you." He reached out his hand for me to take. "Let me keep you alive like I promised."

The lump in my stomach grew heavier as I began to see the full picture. "Wait." I held up my hand like I was conjuring an invisible force field, keeping him at a distance. "*You* know about Atlanta?"

Damien's eyes flashed with fear realizing that he had given too much away. He knew what I would next surmise.

"You're the reason they knew Max was actually in New York."

He didn't confirm it. He didn't need to; I knew it was true. Max was going to die in that Atlanta facility because of Damien. It was then that he changed. His eyes shifted. He became a lion stalking its lame prey. He was ready to pounce, and I, the lame prey, had to try and escape.

I made the first move, lurching toward the door; Damien jumped after me. I only made it a few steps before he wrapped his arms around my waist and restrained me in a tight hold. I couldn't breathe and fell into a deep coughing fit.

As life marches on, you might forget about the cancer, but the cancer never forgets about you.

My lips went numb, and my legs could no longer hold my weight as my body starved for oxygen. Slowly, Damien eased us both onto the floor.

"Breathe," Damien urged. "Alabine, it's okay, just breathe."

I didn't understand why Damien was trying to comfort me but didn't have the time to try and understand it. I focused only on having the strength to somehow escape. I had to tell someone about Damien. About Max. About everything.

Then Damien let go of me. Suddenly free, I dug my elbows into the rough and worn wood of the floor as I writhed and wriggled my way, inch by inch, toward the attic door. I had to get out. I knew very little in that moment except that I had to get out. I was dying, yes. But first I had to get to Avon and warn him.

I felt a sharp pinch on my thigh. Crisp dry air rushed into my lungs. After a quick moment of confusion, I realized that Damien had injected me with Dreno. Saving my life. Again.

He crawled up next to me and held my face in his hands, treating me so tenderly, and yet I was his hostage. "There. Breathe. Just breathe."

"What are you doing?" I asked in a hoarse whisper. If he was truly the enemy, I didn't understand why he was saving me.

A look of true sorrow overcame him. "I don't know." He let go of my face and sat back onto the floor. I pushed myself up. Neither of us looked at the other. I was too scared to see his face.

"So, what now?" I asked again.

Damien didn't respond. He looked at the floor, trying to come up with an answer to our unanswerable situation.

"Fine," I said. "I'll tell you what's going to happen. I'm going to call for Avon. He's going to come up here, and you're going to confess everything."

Damien shook his head. His black curls bounced against his cheek. "They'll kill me, Al." He looked me in the eye. "Avon will kill me."

He was probably right.

Damien's eyes looked to the window above the mattress. The blanket, still warm from our bodies, was crumpled on top. I had a momentary flash of the night before. Being in each other's arms. Feeling real touch for the first time in a century. And realizing it was all a lie.

"Give me two minutes," he said.

I scoffed. "Why would I do that?"

"Because I know you hate me right now, but I also know that under all of that hate you do care for me. In spite of Max. In spite of this." He sighed. "In spite of me."

I thought for a moment. "You're right." I admitted through clenched teeth. Damien's brow lifted hopefully. "I do hate you."

Disappointment cut through him like a knife. I could feel it in his change of breath.

Without a word, he stood and walked calmly toward the window. Watching him, I wondered if I should just let him go. This was Damien, after all.

"Damien," I said. He stopped. "Don't." It was a threat.

He didn't turn around to look at me. Instead he resumed his slow steady pace toward the window. He reached forward and opened it.

I closed my eyes. Preparing myself for the next few minutes. Then I screamed, "Avon!"

As I darted out the attic door, in the corner of my eye, I saw Damien push through the window, abandoning his confidently slow pace for an all-out chase.

He fell his way down the three stories to the street below while I stumbled down the old staircase. I was still weak. My knees wobbled as I willed myself to keep my balance. I bounced off the walls of the narrow hallway, making my way downstairs.

All the while, I was shouting, "Avon! Gina! He's going out the front! Stop Damien!"

It was still early. When I passed each room, the various doors flung open in alarm. I saw a sleepy and confused Minnie. Samson was farther down the hallway, dressed only in his underwear, running as fast as he could. He jumped down the entire flight of stairs to the ground level.

When I reached the front door, it was already wide open. Outside, I saw Avon sprinting down the street, calling out to Damien, "Stop!" Damien kept running, not looking back once. But his speed was no match for Avon's, and before the end of the block, Avon had tackled him to the ground.

When Samson caught up to them, he dove into the ensuing struggle and helped wrestle the thrashing Damien into submission. "Easy, brother!"

I stood on the stoop next to Gina, who was watching the action with a vindication in her gaze. Like she had been waiting for this. Like she finally understood. While for me, it seemed nothing in this world made sense anymore.

The street was entirely empty save for us. Perfectly white snow covered every inch of the ground except for a few footprints and the chaotic mess where a shirtless Damien was pinned to the pavement.

The chaos simmered, and everyone looked to me for an explanation. Eliza and Diana came out of the door. One of them put her hand on my shoulder.

I looked directly at Avon, meeting his eye. "He's it," I said, out of breath. "Damien's the leak."

VERBATIM TRANSCRIPT OF
SUSPECTED COMBATANT INTERVIEW

DECEMBER 29, 2121

(ROBERT SAMSON and CHRIS SMITH, interrogators)

ROBERT SAMSON: We're recording now.

DAMIEN GREY: (moans)

SAMSON: Let's get him a drink of water. There's a lot of blood on his face. Can you wipe that up too? Great. Thanks, Chris.

GREY: I want to speak to Alabine.

SAMSON: She's not here. It's you and me, brother. So, this is how it's going to go. I'm going to ask you questions, and you're going to give me truthful answers, if you can even discern truth anymore. You will answer out loud so it can be recorded. If you do not answer or do not answer truthfully, I will ask Chris here to flip that small switch, which will send a varying degree of electricity through your body. I have a knob that determines the degree. Is that understood?

I see that you nodded, and normally I'd now ask Chris to flip her switch because you didn't answer aloud, but I'll let it slide this one time in case there was an issue with my

clarity. So let me ask one more
time, and I request you answer
verbally. Is what I've said here
understood?

GREY: Yes.

SAMSON: If you think that beating you took
           before hurt, you're in for a real
           treat. Now, let's start with who you
           are and where you come from.

GREY: I was born and raised in Virginia.
           I'm a second lieutenant in the
           Territorial Army for the United
           America.

SAMSON: That's pretty high-ranking for
           someone so young. How did you
           advance so quickly?

GREY: I'm good at my job. Clearly.

SAMSON: Chris. Do it.

GREY: (groans)

SAMSON: Doesn't feel good, does it?

GREY: I want to speak with Alabine.

SAMSON: Chris, again.

GREY: (groans louder)

SAMSON: I asked if the electricity surging
           through your nerves does or does
           not feel good. Answer me.

GREY: It does not. I need to speak with
           Al.

```
SAMSON:   What was your mission here?

GREY:     Infiltrate the terrorist organization
          known as the Resurrectionists to
          gather intel. Use my influence in
          the movement to sway decisions for
          the benefit of the UA counter-
          resistance.

SAMSON:   Who do you report to?

GREY:     (laughs) I've proven that I'll play
          your little game. You can shock me
          all you want. I won't answer
          anything more unless Al asks.

SAMSON:   The issue is, she doesn't want to
          see you. And I don't think you'll
          tell her the truth. I think you'll
          only tell the truth as a last
          resort. So, I'll just turn up the
          dial then. Chris, if you please.

GREY:     (pants and whines)

SAMSON:   You're doing this to yourself.

GREY:     I know she's behind that door.

SAMSON:   Chris.

GREY:     (wails) Come in, Alabine! Ask me
          yourself!

SAMSON:   Chris!

GREY:     (screams)

SAMSON:   I can do this all day, Damien. I
          think you're underestimating how
          pissed I am at you, brother.
```

GREY: Please. Just let me speak to her. Alabine. Alabine, I—

SAMSON: Let's try this. Is your name even Damien Grey?

GREY: Damien (unintelligible)

SAMSON: What was that? You'll have to speak louder.

GREY: Damien Standard.

CHRIS SMITH: That isn't a relation to Tom Standard, is it?

SAMSON: Answer her, Damien. Damien? Chris, pull it.

GREY: (screams and pants) I'm his son. (cries)

SAMSON: You're the son of the general of the Territorial Army. Hmm. I guess that helped with your quick ascension in rank. Not as good at your job as you thought.

GREY: At least get her out of here. It's not safe.

SAMSON: Why's that, brother? What is the plan for the UA counter-resistance force? When are they planning to attack?

GREY: You can turn your little knob up as much as you'd like, brother. I won't answer to anyone except Alabine.

```
        SAMSON:    I'm asking you. Why isn't she safe
                   here? What is the plan for the
                   UA counter-resistance force?
                   Chris.

         GREY:     (moans)

        SAMSON:    Answer the question. Again!

         GREY:     (screams)

        SAMSON:    Did he black out?

         SMITH:    (checks Grey) Yes.

(ALABINE RIVERS enters room)

        SAMSON:    You shouldn't be in here.

ALABINE RIVERS:    He didn't tell us when they'd attack
                   again.

        SAMSON:    Maybe I pushed him too hard.

        RIVERS:    No. Next time, go harder. He'll
                   cave.

         SMITH:    He said he'll talk to you.

        RIVERS:    He'll lie to me. This is the only
                   way to know we will get the truth,
                   right?

         SMITH:    I don't know, Al. Torture can be
                   very unreliable in getting at the
                   truth.

        SAMSON:    You sure you want us to do it
                   again?

        RIVERS:    Yes. As soon as he wakes up.
```

(AVON WILLIAMS enters room)

AVON WILLIAMS: This has gone far enough. You're
                       done. Everyone out. Are we still
                       recording?

(END OF TAPE)

17

THE CAMPS STARTED TO arrive in New York City.

It began on a freezing morning before dawn. The day after we found out about Damien, before the sun had even begun to rise, Avon received a radio transmission on one of the scrambled radio frequencies announcing the arrival of a nearby camp. They were coming from the coast of Rhode Island. Or what I knew to be Rhode Island. Now it was part of a larger unified New England territory.

The people in this camp were hardened. Even before the diaspora caused by the information leak in Montrose, they'd had the reputation of being a gritty, no-nonsense kind of people. They lived off what they could fish and sheltered in caves, one of the few camps that wasn't in an abandoned city. Beaches and coastlines were still populated by regular citizens, so they had to be careful. Before the Montrose leak, authorities generally knew of their presence, but turned a blind eye in exchange for a generous piece of their fishing escapades.

After Montrose, the pressure to finally cleanse the area of illegals was too much. So the camp fled their home and had been roving around ever since, hopping from one temporary shelter to another, trying to avoid detection. They were the first to answer the call to come to New York, traveling by crowded rickety boats to Brighton Beach.

On that freezing morning, I stood in the middle of the street outside our brownstone and saw them emerge from the night's darkness shrouding the city. Snow fell gently to the ground. At first, the faces of those at the very front were all I could see. The soft light from the moon and stars, still desperately clinging to their place in the morning sky, reflected off the travelers' cold cheeks. Soon enough, as they continued the final steps of their very long and tiring journey, the full contingent emerged into the light. Seeking shelter. Seeking kindness.

We were worried about the massive losses sustained by these displaced camps over the past week, but this one had stayed mostly intact. They were a couple hundred people strong, Awoken and Resurrectionists alike.

Other camps weren't as lucky.

In their faces, partially obscured by falling snow as they marched toward us, Avon told me he saw the future of our people. I saw it too. A city for Awoken, made by Awoken. A home where we could live undeterred by the swaying opinion of political regimes. Where we wouldn't be hunted. Where we wouldn't be illegal. United, we believed, we could finally take a stand.

After Avon's decision to call the camps to us, Gina led a massive effort to identify buildings nearby that were still functional enough to house the droves of people hopefully headed our way. Homes that had withstood the sanitizing flames.

There were enough.

Diana led the Rhode Island Coasters to a stretch of intact brownstones about a half mile away from ours. It was near the water, where they could restart their fishing, which would prove to be a vital source of food.

As the day went on, more and more camps funneled their way into the city. I learned as much as I could about each group—where they came from, what they were like, how we could best integrate them into our growing community. Before he died, Wade had done an extraordinary job of accounting for the various groups and their leaders using the scrambled radio channels. And still, there was so much that remained unknown. Avon took Wade's baton and was not only running with it, but putting it on a fucking sonic-speed rocket. He had a dream in his head that neither I nor anyone else had dared dream. With each additional camp trudging their way over the bridges into Brooklyn, we were all that much closer to a new reality.

Our brownstone was the center of activity. We began to refer to it as Lovett, a tribute to Wade. Samson found expired paint in the basement that he used to write over the street sign on the corner. The avenue became the first in the city that we renamed: Lovetts Way.

We were no longer a part of United America. Only they didn't know it yet.

With our dream came many logistical concerns. The elusive Canadian supply ship was nowhere to be seen, and Chris hadn't heard back from her contact for days. We had the power we would need, for now, thanks to Samson. But food was scarce and clean water was running low. The camps brought some supplies with them, so they could be self-sustaining for a little while. And although all camps came armed with a few pistols and hunting rifles, no one had anything that could defend against a raid. That was troubling enough. However, the main concern was that we did not have the medicine the more recently Awoken required—including me, Avon, and Minnie. We were sick, dying, and only had a few remaining Dreno shots. If the Canadian supply ship didn't come through, this entire dream would collapse.

Noah naturally stepped into the position overseeing medical care. As camps arrived, he collected the medical supplies and filled the dining room at Lovett with them. He had a plan to set up a hospital in the nearby cryo facility as soon as possible.

Although we felt unprepared, the arriving camps did bring with

them a sliver of hope for our little group from Detroit. A shining beacon of light to clutch on to in the wake of all the shit. In the wake of
Damien's betrayal.

Damien was locked away out of sight. We didn't talk about Damien
being a traitor. Or that he was the leak that had led to the Chicago raid
and the capture of Max. That basically everything that had happened,
the reason why these camps were roaming around without a home to
begin with, was because of Damien. We didn't talk about any of it
openly, even though it consumed our thoughts. It was too painful. He
was locked away, and Samson was tasked with getting answers.

Tens of thousands of refugees were making their way to us. It
would take weeks, maybe more, for every camp to arrive. We needed
every able-bodied Awoken and Resurrectionist to fight together to
defend ourselves against the Territorial Army. Until they all arrived,
we were vulnerable. We worked under the idea that there was an impending attack. We knew it was coming, but we didn't know how or
when.

That's where Damien came in.

After greeting the Rhode Island Coasters and seeing them off with
Diana to find their homes, I walked toward the white brick townhouse
three doors down from Lovett. It was an ugly drab building with broken shutters and peeling paint. It had been burned too badly in the
fires to be habitable or used for anything besides Damien's prison.
Samson chose it for the out-of-date and generally unsafe wiring running through its walls, allowing him to create the electrical system he
used on Damien.

It was two days until Patriots' Day and the decommissioning of the
Atlanta facility. The sun was creeping its way above the buildings
when I unlocked and opened the squeaky front door.

Damien was down the hallway on the other side of the white paneled bathroom door. I stared at the brass handle, wanting to burst in.
I wanted to tear his head off, stab him with a knife, choke him until

he met the darkness to which he had sent Max so easily. A thousand scenarios of torture and murder gleefully ran through my head.

Between these thoughts of killing Damien were the jumbled memories of sleeping with him. The comfort I'd found in his arms was impossible to deny, and I hated myself for it.

Everyone knew about our tryst. While it too was never discussed, it was obvious why I was in Damien's room so early in the morning. Everyone correctly assumed the reason. The looks of confusion and disillusion that brushed across their faces when they saw me were nothing compared to how I felt looking in the mirror. Still, their disappointment was gut-wrenching.

Samson touched my shoulder. I hadn't heard him approach, but I knew it was him. I squeezed his hand, grateful for this small sign of commiseration. Damien and Samson had become close during our time in Detroit and even more so on their travels to New York. He too felt deeply betrayed by the man on the other side of that paneled door.

"Eliza is calling a summit at Lovett." Samson's voice was soft and reverential. Although he hadn't said anything, I assumed Samson was an avid supporter of Max and me. He had been Awoken for more than a decade and spent a good chunk of his time in this second life fighting for his very existence. Max was godlike to people like him.

"Are you going in there to interrogate him more?" I didn't want to discuss politics with Eliza. I wanted to leave all that for Avon to handle. I just wanted to sit on the other side of this door and listen to Damien's screams. For each one that Samson tore out of him, I had fifty louder and more painful screams inside of me.

Pity darkened Samson's eyes. "I'm just bringing him water. Avon said we had to stop."

"I don't care!" The rage in my voice made me sound so unlike myself. Unlike who I used to be. Now I felt like an entirely different person. I couldn't tell if I was more me, or less me. Regardless, I wanted pain as penance.

"I know," Samson said, placating me. "You should go to Eliza's meeting. She asked me to fetch you." I didn't budge. "If you don't, they'll just send someone else."

The idea of Avon or Gina coming over and chastising me was enough motivation. I pushed myself off the ground. My body ached. The gunshot wound in my arm. My cancer-heavy lungs. It all hurt. The Dreno Damien had given me had long since worn off.

Stepping outside, I turned around to look down the hallway as Samson entered the bathroom. With the door open, I caught a glimpse of Damien for only the briefest of moments. He was slumped over in his chair. The only thing keeping him upright was how tightly his arms were tied to the wooden slats behind him. He was beaten, but unfortunately not yet broken. The bathroom door swung closed.

I left the old brownstone and made my way to Lovett, where Eliza and the rest of them were waiting.

THE OLD HEATER THAT ran through Lovett's thick walls did little to fend off the chill. It was in desperate need of repair, which was not high on the list of our priorities. I kept on my knee-length coat as I entered the kitchen where people were gathered.

The room was simple, white tile and black appliances. A stove and refrigerator that looked like they were from the 1950s. No microwave. Nothing more than the bare necessities. And yet, similar to Helen's house, it exuded a simple charm. Or it would've before the fire, but now the peeling wallpaper and cracked ceiling gave more of a chilling vibe despite Eliza's thorough job cleaning up the debris.

Avon was hunched over a pile of maps on the breakfast bar while Eliza and Chris were heatedly debating if we'd ever see the promised supply ship. Noah was in the adjacent dining room, busy with the cluttered table of medical supplies. I wasn't sure where Diana and Gina were. I was particularly disappointed not to find Gina there.

Despite wearing her disdain for me on her sleeve, I felt safer in her company.

Although I still hadn't seen Minnie that morning, I was glad she wasn't there. I assumed she was either still asleep or tucked into her bed fiddling with wires. Avon agreed with me that, while brilliant, she should stay away from these types of meetings to somewhat preserve her innocence.

Also, Minnie was getting sicker and sicker by the day. I barely had time to address it, as so much had been going on, but there was no denying the dimming in her eyes. Her heart was failing, the final phase of her illness. She didn't have much longer.

There was a toaster-sized radio in the middle of the kitchen counter. A low static rumbled from its single speaker. When Eliza and Chris finally stopped bickering, with Eliza having the final word, the room fell silent for just a moment, long enough for me to hear DJ Raheem's all-too-familiar smooth voice behind the static. Distant and yet unmistakably there.

"Hello, good morning, and good day. As the year comes to an end, we're left to reflect on what we've accomplished and how the next year will be even better."

I stood in the corner, quietly watching the scene unfold. Fuming about Damien. Missing Max. Terrified of what was to come.

Eventually Eliza noticed my presence. "Oh, good. Alabine, you're here." Avon and Chris looked over toward me. I couldn't read the expressions on their faces. We all looked so tired. "Just waiting on Diana now."

The room returned to silence while we waited. I wanted to talk to Avon and convince him to keep trying Samson's interrogation methods to get Damien to give up the UA's plans, but my gaze fell on Chris, and I knew there was something that I had to do that I'd been putting off. I gestured to the other room, asking Chris to step aside with me so we could speak. She nodded and followed me into the back bedroom. Eliza's eyes tracked us curiously.

With the door latched behind us, we had the privacy I needed. "I want to apologize for how I've been treating you." It was something I'd been meaning to say ever since I learned the truth about Damien.

Chris looked genuinely shocked at my admission. "What's with the change of heart?"

I shrugged. I'd hoped we could leave it at the apology and simply start over, but I wasn't going to get off that easily. "I knew there was a leak. Minchin told me. And Wade, before he died, he said he was worried you flipped while undercover in Montrose."

Chris's eyebrows arched as a wave of understanding crossed her face. "Ah. Wade always did have a healthy suspicion that served him more often than not."

"I thought I saw you look at the door just before the guards came through to kill Wade. Obviously now I know you aren't the leak." Guilt built up inside me. "It's just that . . . I guess I just wanted to believe that somehow you orchestrated Wade's death. Because then it wouldn't be my fault. But it was. Like whatever has happened to your mom is also my fault."

At the mention of Helen, Chris's lip quivered. She looked away, out the window, so I wouldn't see her tears. I had wanted to apologize, and instead I was rubbing salt in an open wound.

"Is there anything I can do?" I asked.

Chris shook her head. "I'm not even sure if she's still alive." After a moment of silence, she sniffled loudly, wiped the tears from her eyes, and turned back to me, a new look of determination on her face. "If we get through this, then we can take stock of all of our regrets and mistakes. But it's no use living in the past. My mom made her own choices for her own reasons. If anyone put her in danger, it's me, not you." Chris inhaled sharply. "And Wade's death was not your fault or my fault. It's what we all risk every day. Remember that all those people escaped because you took action and slipped me that note when it would've been easier to keep your head down. That's the Albine Rivers we need right now if we're gonna survive."

I nodded, understanding and grateful. Chris opened the door, and we walked back into the kitchen. She slid in next to Avon at the counter. I followed a few steps behind and stood on the other side of him. He reached over and squeezed my shoulder.

We sat quietly, no one looking at the other. All exhausted. All scared. Words weren't required between us in that moment. The radio filled the silence, a moment of calm before the storm we all knew was coming. We listened to DJ Raheem's voice while we waited.

Eventually, with the *click* of the front door, Diana appeared. She was accompanied by a handsome Resurrectionist man in a wheelchair.

"This is Brian," Diana said. "He's the leader of the camp that arrived this morning."

It had been a while since I had met anyone new, so I was filled with a mix of excitement and fear. Brian bowed his head slightly and removed his knit hat, revealing his face still caked with dirt from the long journey. At first it seemed odd to see a wheelchair in a world that had treatments for most chronic medical conditions, but then I remembered Wade telling me about people who become Resurrectionists because they don't fit into the United America identity. Because even though they aren't born into that specific ideal, they don't see their differences as something to cure or fix.

I wished I had that same idea of myself. That same acceptance. The truth was, if there were suddenly a way to cure being an Awoken, to cure what made me different, I still wasn't sure I'd be strong enough to refuse.

"Thank you for welcoming my camp here," Brian said. "The roads are not safe. I'm not sure how much longer we would've lasted."

Avon shook his hand. "We're glad you made it here, Brian, and we're happy to join with you."

Brian stared at us, clearly so many questions running through his mind. "So, this is it? This is all that is left of Wade's people?"

"No." I said defensively. "Gina Han is around here somewhere. And there are a few dozen more of us at Eliza's camp. I'm sure they'll be here soon."

We hadn't learned about the raid of the Detroit camp yet, but I noticed a glimmer of worry in Avon's eyes. There was a lack of radio communication from George, so suspicions had already taken root.

Brian nodded, then said, "I look forward to meeting them when they arrive. You are all quite the legends around our camp. Our very own Mount Olympians that we tell stories of to the children as news comes through the radio." He looked at Chris in a way that told me they'd met before. "We all mourned his death with you."

The fact that he didn't name Wade paid all the more tribute to him. It was "His" with a capital *H*. There was only one person he could mean. We all collectively, intuitively, held our breath for a moment of remembrance.

Then Brian looked at me. "And this particular story from the Mount is proven true. It's an honor to meet you, Alabine Rivers." Like every time it happened, I was shocked that a stranger knew my name. I stood awkwardly and offered my hand, not really knowing what else to do.

He laughed, then shook it.

Avon sat back down on the kitchen stool. "We expect more camps to pour into the city as the hours and days wear on. Gina's patrol this morning spotted two more large groups of people coming in from the south and the west."

"That's great news," Brian said with relief.

"Yes. Except our patrols have also shown increased UA activity to the northwest. We're diverting all camps south to enter the city. It seems when we uncovered their spy and threw his tracker in the river, we stirred the beast."

"There are growing patrols all along the Hudson River too. We had trouble avoiding them as we made our way here."

"As you know then, we don't have much time," Avon said.

"What are they waiting for?" Brian asked.

Avon shook his head. "We're not sure. We're working on finding out." He didn't say it, but he meant Damien.

"What do you need?"

"Manpower. And lots of it. We need patrols, scouts . . ." Avon hesitated before saying, "Soldiers."

"We're only fishermen, but you'll have whatever you can find in us that's useful."

"Good," Avon said. "We'll send Diana back with you to organize the people we need." Diana stepped forward in acknowledgment.

Eliza leaned in, perhaps less than comfortable that Avon was running the show. Or maybe just uncomfortable that he was so good at it. "The big concern right now is the supplies," she said with an air of confrontation.

"My people will handle food," Brian responded confidently. "No need to worry on that account as long as you can stomach fish for every meal." We all chuckled. In truth, they would come through with more than just fish. Various algae prepared into delicious salads, and mollusks cooked so tenderly it seemed as though they were drenched in butter.

"That's very appreciated," Eliza said. "Noah, where are we on medical supplies?"

Before he could respond, the front door flew open. Chris, Avon, and Eliza instinctively reached for the guns in their holsters. Gina came bounding through the door, a cloud of falling snow surrounding her like a cape. Everyone stood down, but the grave expression on her face kept the room ill at ease.

Gina immediately looked over at Brian. It was clear she had something urgent to say but was uncomfortable speaking in front of this new presence. Avon took the hint and put a hand on Brian's shoulder.

"You and Diana should go back and gather the people we'll need.

We want to mobilize as soon as possible." Avon quickly escorted Brian and Diana out the door.

As soon as it closed, Gina bound into action.

"Come with me." She unloosed the pair of binoculars from around her neck and skipped up the stairs, taking three at a time. All of us in the kitchen scurried after her.

Once on the top floor, she led us out the window at the end of the hall onto the snowy fire escape and then up to the roof. The building was only a few stories high, but there was a decent view of Manhattan across the water.

The cityscape was drastically different from what I remembered. Skyscrapers had tumbled. Any color that once gleamed from across the bay was buried under a decade of black ash. A fog of decay surrounded the once iconic vista.

Towering a few blocks behind us was the cryogenics facility. Massive, imposing. I was magnetically drawn toward it. The place where Max was held for decades. Where a million Awoken still lay in suspended animation, waiting for new life.

Gina pointed out toward the Atlantic Ocean that lay a mile or so from us to the east. "Look there." She handed Avon the binoculars.

"What? What is it?" Eliza asked, impatient and cold.

A smile crept across Avon's face. "Looks like a supply ship."

Chris hastily ripped the binoculars from his hand and looked out toward the horizon. "They're here! They came through!" Chris jumped and cheered.

I couldn't believe it. Avon scooped me up in his arms, squeezing tight. It hurt—both of us, I'm sure—but it was worth every second. I took the binoculars from Chris and looked out where Gina directed.

There it was, little more than a blur off the horizon, a small, rusted, unmarked cargo ship carrying the hope that we would all live another day.

"What's wrong?" Avon asked Gina. I pulled the binoculars from my face. Gina wore a grim expression—even more so than usual.

She took the binoculars from me and gave them back to Avon. "Now look there. And there." Gina guided Avon toward the rising sun at various points along the horizon.

Avon's smile immediately faded. He lowered the binoculars. "UA warships." Despair hung in his voice. He had a look of defeat that I'd never seen on him before.

He passed the binoculars to me. Silhouetted by the bright morning light were two massive naval ships with UA insignia plastered across the hulls and massive guns affixed to their decks. They'd established a blockade between us and the supplies that we so badly needed to survive. The ships were in a standoff, unmoving.

"Are they going to sink the supply ship?" I asked.

"I assume they can't as long as it stays in international waters," Avon responded, deep in thought. "Not without breaking international laws. But it can't come closer or they'll definitely attack."

"So, it's just stuck?" Chris asked angrily. Avon nodded. Chris gestured out toward the horizon. "It's all right there! They came through like they said they would. It's fucking right there!" She kicked the ground in frustration.

Avon thought for a moment, then turned to Gina. "What about the other UA movements?"

"There are troops amassing deep in the Hudson Valley toward Albany. Nothing too close into the city except the ships."

"Good," Avon said with a slight relief in his tone. "Keep the camps coming from the south."

"Don't you see?" Eliza shouted, partly due to the increasing wind and partly for emphasis. "That's exactly what the UA wants. They're not trying to keep them out, they're keeping us in. They want to funnel every Awoken and Resurrectionist into this city. We're building our own prison. They've blocked us from our weapons and are going to wipe us all out with a single strike!" There was true fear in her voice. She looked out to the horizon, defeat in her gaze. "We're trapped. And on our own." I felt the hearts of everyone sink. The dream of a city safe for Awoken was evaporating.

"We will never be able to do this on our own," I muttered to myself, remembering Wade's words to me. Something inside of me began to stir. I was slipping away, slipping into a memory.

No.

I fought it, but the pull was too strong. Suddenly, standing between me and my view of the UA blockade, was Max. I knew he wasn't really there, and still, it felt so good to be near him again. He held out his hand and beckoned for me to go with him. I remained firm, still, unmoving.

Slowly, he walked toward me, his face alight with a glowing smile. He wore a stunning embroidered gold tunic and looked damn good in it. I still saw Avon as he continued to debate with Eliza, but I could no longer hear him clearly. It was as if he were underwater.

I didn't think the word. In fact, I actively stopped myself from thinking it. But it didn't matter. Max leaned in and whispered in my ear:

"*Rosebud.*"

.
.
.

Hello, good morning, and good day, my fellow citizens. It's Raheem here as always. Broadcasting from the be-a-utiful Montrose Center in Minnesota. Bringing you something very special today. A surprise you've all been waiting for, even if you don't know it yet.

My hands run along the white lace. Every detail, every stitch under examination by my intruding fingers.

I'm cold. Too cold for the large, bright commercial bathroom in which I find myself alone. I look in the mirror and see in my reflection a girl who doesn't yet know death. A girl who still wears joy and excitement on her face with ease. My long brown hair is curled up in a half-do. I'm wearing a lace wedding dress.

The air chills my breath into puffs of steam. The wind makes the cold all the more harsh. Except there isn't any wind in here. The wind is on the roof by the doomsday ships. Not here. Thank God they're not here. This place is not scary. This is a place of good.

And still, I cannot look away from the wedding dress. My hands shake as I realize what is happening.

I am about to get married.

It's the day Alabine Rivers forever ties herself to the love of her life, Max Green, on top of the towering skyscraper, and you'll hear it live right here on UA52.

I remember proposing to Max. The darkness looming outside the clinic door. And then dying. We never got married. I died before we could. Or so I had thought.

But that wasn't the end.

Those nurses brought me back to life. With paddles and a defibrillator. I lived. And now Max and I are about to get married. I struggle to catch my breath as I come to this realization. I will still die—I know that in some far part of my mind—but not today.

Alabine is wearing a clearance-rack dress from a bridal store in New York that she bought only an hour ago. And doesn't she look stunning?

While I look at myself in the mirror of the sterile bathroom on the fifty-second floor, I wonder if Max is nervous. Whether he too is staring at himself in the mirror, playing out the rest of our lives in his head. Listening to the radio.

Except there is no radio. Despite my hearing his broadcast, I know that Raheem doesn't yet exist. As reality slowly forms in my mind, the bathroom begins to fade into memory. Doubt creeps in. I feel the snow on my lips, on my tongue. I hear Gina's voice, but I can't see her or quite make out what she's saying.

And then I notice at the end of the impossibly long bathroom a single flickering light. It's the only imperfection in the otherwise spotless and modern restroom. This small distraction anchors me in this reality. The snow stops falling. The wind stops blowing. I'm just a girl alone in her wedding dress, staring at a flickering light on the ceiling. Curious, I slowly walk toward it and peer around the corner down a row of bathroom stalls.

He's there. Damien. At the end of the long hallway, he's slumped over in a chair, bleeding. The darkness surrounds him, waiting to pounce. I hold my breath, terrified. Quickly, I duck back behind the bathroom stall.

Out of sight, out of mind. The light stops flickering. My heartbeat resumes its normal rhythm.

Oh boy. That was a close one. Hang in there, folks. We're only moments away from the big event. Broadcasting to all of you lovely people out there.

Then I start to hear music. A single violin. The melody echoes against the white porcelain walls. Soon it overpowers DJ Raheem's voice. The music isn't coming from a radio but instead from outside the bathroom door. A glowing white light shines through the cracks around the large door. I wonder if this is heaven. If I have finally found something other than darkness in death.

I'm not dead. Not yet.

Slowly, I walk toward the door. Behind me, the light flickers. I sense Damien there, bloody and staring at me. It doesn't matter. He doesn't matter. I leave the bathroom and step out onto the roof.

It's not snowing. It's warm. The sun beams life and love onto my skin. The violinist plays from the corner by the edge of the building. Looking out over the city, I see just how high we are. Fifty-two stories high. And it's familiar—I've been on this specific roof before.

Isn't it beautiful? Like in a fairy tale. Their story will continue to inspire generations to come.

The roof is decorated with white rosebuds peppered over the ground. I see a silk carpet leading away from the door from which I emerged. My eyes follow it until I see Max. My Max.

He's standing at the base of a massive tower. An antenna that reaches so far up into the clouds, I cannot see its apex. Max looks up at the antenna too. And then back to me. He smiles.

Finally, I take in the full scene. Standing in the aisle that leads to Max, I'm holding a bouquet. This is our wedding. The aisle is lined by our friends. Andy. Max's parents. Jessica DeWhitt and Peter are there too. Peter even sheds a tear. Everyone's eyes are on me.

I see all of this, and yet I come back to Max—as I always do. And the antenna tower behind him. I'm drawn to it. Or to him. I'm not sure. I can't tear my eyes from it.

As I walk toward him down the silk carpet, I feel a warm light radiate from my core. Our eyes are locked. We are one person. Time stops for everything except my feet gliding toward him. He reaches out for me, and I take his hand. Our hearts beat together.

This country made them. As it made all of you. She will stand by you and protect you. Love you. Always love you. That I can promise, this country will love you.

My father is the officiant. He's dressed in his best teaching suit, complete with suede elbow patches. He smiles as he begins to marry us. In my heart, I know my dad is dead. In truth, I think it is a friend of Max's who agreed to perform the ceremony. But I'm so glad that now, in this moment, my dad is here, marrying us. I miss him. He's all the best parts of me.

"We're gathered here together in this strange and perfect place to witness the union of Alabine Rivers and Max Green." My dad turns to me. "Lovebug?" I remember how he always called me that. "Why are we here?"

"To marry the love of my life," I respond confidently. Everyone laughs a gentle and cordial laugh.

"No. I mean why *here*?" My father lifts his arms and gestures up to the antenna hovering above us. I stare at it, transfixed by it.

Racking my brain, I can't come up with the answer, so I look in Max's eyes, hoping he'll know. He doesn't respond, simply looks at me with an encouraging gaze. So, I decide to start talking and see if the truth comes out. "It's where Max told me he loved me for the first time. On New Year's Eve." Max nods. So far, so good.

Suddenly, we're no longer on the roof. We're standing on the stoop of a brownstone. He's no longer in his gold tunic, and I'm no longer in my lace. My eyes are glued on Max. He's giddy, smiling, practically bouncing up and down.

Just a quick interlude here. Please stay tuned as we get back to the main event.

I turn around this way and that, looking for DJ Raheem. Then a young man opens the door.

"We're getting married. Today!" Max says, about to explode.

"Finally! Congratulations, man! So happy for you both," Max's friend says as he hugs him, then me.

Max is beaming. "I know you got ordained on the internet to marry your sister last year. Can you officiate us?"

"I'd be offended if you asked anyone else! Where do you want to do it?"

"You remember the New Year's Eve party last year? On the roof of your work building. Can you get us up there again?"

We're waiting here.

Desperate, I look around again for the radio with Raheem's broadcast that I'm hearing. But there's nothing around us.

Max's friend snaps his fingers. "Yes, of course. It's beautiful up there. The antenna—"

Before he can finish, we're back on the roof. I feel sick with whiplash.

"Do you take this woman to be your lawfully wedded wife?" my dad asks Max. It's not my dad anymore. It's now Wade standing in as the officiant. I melt. It's Wade. I reach out and touch his hand. He smiles at me.

It starts to snow, even though there isn't a cloud in the sky and it's eighty degrees outside. I collect myself as I feel my brain being torn in a million directions. I look Max in the eyes, those lovely deep amber eyes that I've lost myself in so many times, and ready myself for the most important words I'll ever hear:

"I do."

There it is, ladies. Max Green is no longer a bachelor. You heard it first here on UA52.

Wade then turns to me. "Do you take Max Green to be your lawfully wedded husband?"

I want to say yes. I want to say I do. But I feel the darkness creeping up the side of the skyscraper. "Until death parts us?" I ask Max.

"Death cannot stop true love," Max says sweetly to me. "All it can do is delay it for a while." He didn't say that. Someone else did. None of this is exactly how it happened. But it doesn't matter. The point is that it happened. I married Max. I'm Max's wife.

Only if I say, *I do.* It's on the tip of my tongue. About to come out. But instead I turn my gaze to the antenna hovering over us. I let go of Max's hands and walk a few steps closer. It looks larger than life. The overpowering presence draws me in like a moth to a flame. Wade walks up to me and looks up at the antenna too.

"What is it about this antenna?" I ask him.

"It's the most powerful broadcast antenna in the world. Right here in New York City."

"Huh," I say before turning back to Max. "I'm ready now." Max holds my hand. We stare at each other. We breathe together. Then, finally, I say: "I do." He smiles.

"You won't ever have to be on your own," we vow to each other.

"We will never be able to do this on our own," Wade says. He's said this to me before. And finally, I understand what he means.

Finally, I understood what I needed to do.

18

THEIR EYES WERE ON us. From across the ocean, I felt them, like nails in the back of my skull, as the Lucid Memory of my skyscraper wedding faded away to the small snow-covered roof in Brooklyn.

Avon and Eliza were at each other, passionately debating our future. Our survival. Avon's voice deepened. "We've come too far. Lost too much. We won't just leave."

Within Avon was a fire. I saw it in him like I saw it in Max.

"Then all is truly lost," Eliza said, defeated. A heavy moment fell over all of us on that frozen rooftop as Eliza's despairing words hung in the air. Her negativity was an additional burden that we shouldn't have had to carry.

I don't mean to paint Eliza as the enemy. Those UA ships were the enemy. Eliza honestly cared for the future of the movement and simply didn't want to assume such risk. What she didn't understand, what I myself was only finally starting to grasp, was that we Awoken live without the assumption of life. So almost every risk is worth it. Max's life was worth the sacrifice. I knew that now with certainty.

Avon looked out over the ships on the horizon with a commander's determination. In that moment, he came to terms with what his decisions meant for everyone around him. He saw the sacrifices that would be made, and he accepted them. Because on the other side was a future worth fighting for. On the other side were lives worth living.

Not wanting to interrupt the sacred moment but also desperate to convey my recent revelation, I cleared my throat. Everyone's eyes turned toward me.

"I think I know how I can help. Why I was brought back." I looked to Avon. "I know how I can speak to them."

"The ships?" Chris asked.

"No. Everyone. Wade and Avon were right. We can't do this on our own. Minchin told me what mattered most was that the people of this country hate us. We need people, the normal everyday people of this country. If I can convince them, even just some of them, that our lives are worth something, then we can turn the tide. We can win."

"I'm glad you finally agree," Avon said with exasperation and a hint of bitterness. "But we lost that opportunity when we didn't go to Atlanta."

"That's where you're wrong," I said with a knowing glance. I turned back to Eliza, the resident Max Green historian, hoping to make a point. "Where did Max and I get married?"

Eliza didn't even need to think. "A skyscraper in Manhattan. It was declared a historical landmark, actually. Four Times Square." Then it clicked for her. She looked at me and grinned softly. "You can recognize the building by the towering radio antenna on its roof."

I nodded. Remembering my wedding was key. In a time when people no longer had phones, television, or the internet, mass communication was near impossible. A policy that kept the powers that be in charge. But there was one thing everyone did have: a radio.

DJ Raheem's radio show was so omnipresent that it had scored my entire second life. His voice constantly in the background. Inspired by

Wade's legacy, I was going to use the radio to communicate with the people of this country.

"We're going to hack into the radio signal and do our own broadcast," I declared.

Avon's eyebrows rose, impressed. "And what will you say to convince them?"

"The truth." I parroted back Wade's words from the day I met him. I finally understood them. "Give me the chance, and I'll convince them to help us. I'll put out a plea to the people to board that supply ship or to come in their own boats and ride alongside it through the blockade. The UA can't shoot at their own citizens. If we can get enough—a few hundred maybe—they'll be safe. The UA won't risk another massacre. Not if people hear the truth about who the real terrorists are."

"Eavesman Square," Gina said with a tone that told me she understood. If I publicly told the truth about who really set off that bomb, it could make people just suspicious enough of Redden to want to help us.

"They'll come. They'll be our shields, and they'll get the boat through. Then we'll have weapons and medicine. We'll be able to stand a fighting chance. They just need some inspiration. Some people are like Chris and just have good inscribed on their hearts. But most people are like me, they need a good story." I looked Avon straight in the eyes. "I can do this."

After a heavy beat, a smile brushed across Avon's face.

THE FIRE ESCAPE RATTLED when I jumped on it with the excitement of a child at Christmas. I scurried down the metal frame as fast as I could and flung open the first window on the third floor. I knew nothing about how to hack a radio signal, so this whole plan hinged on one tiny little person: Minnie.

She bolted upright in bed. Even in my haste, the first thing I noticed were the large, dark circles around her eyes. As much as I hated to disturb her rest, my plan was the only way she'd get the help she so desperately needed in time. I dove onto her bed, shooing away the darkness, at least for a moment.

"If I could get you to a broadcast tower, can you hack into the radio signal?" I asked out of breath, trying desperately to fend off a coughing fit. I felt the blood pool in my airways.

"What radio signal?" Minnie asked.

"*The* radio signal." I flipped on the radio that sat on the bedside table, and Raheem's smooth voice blasted through the speakers:

Like everyone listening here, I consider Patriots' Day my favorite holiday all year.

Minnie reached over and turned down the volume, annoyed. "You'd need something crazy powerful to overcome what they're blasting."

"That I can do."

Minnie grinned wide, excited for the adventure ahead. "And we'd need to know what frequency they're on. None of the radios here show what they're receiving. My guess is it's pretty top secret."

She was right. From Helen's house, I remembered that none of the radios had frequency dials. It wasn't like when I was first alive where there was a plethora of radio channels you could tune between, finding the one you wanted. There was one channel that everyone listened to, whether they wanted to or not: UA52. But I had no idea what frequency it transmitted on.

Minnie winced as she tried to push herself out of bed. I was resolved in what I had to do. If we were going to get Minnie, and me, and Avon, and everyone who needed it the medicine (and vitally important weapons) that awaited us on the unmarked Canadian boat, Damien had to talk.

I squeezed her tight, then held her face in my hands and looked her deep in her eyes. "You're going to save us all, Minnie Morales! Now do whatever you have to do, I'm going to get us that frequency."

Minnie giggled and jumped into action as I swooped out of the room.

On my way to the decaying brownstone that imprisoned Damien, I couldn't get the photo of Max's preserved body out of my head. Just hanging there in the doomed Atlanta facility, waiting for the end. Two days. He had two days left before the decommissioning would claim him. If it weren't for Damien's betrayal, Max would have been safe. I then considered that it wasn't betrayal that Damien was guilty of. He *was* loyal, only it wasn't us, or me, to whom he was loyal.

Regardless, it couldn't have been plainer: I blamed Damien for Max's imminent death. For the raid in Chicago. For Wade. For it all, really. In that short walk from one brownstone to another, I convinced myself that confronting Damien would bring me the closure I thought I so desperately needed.

There was a guard posted outside of the door who must've been from the Rhode Islanders. He was big, bearded, and had dirt over most of his exposed skin. He stood up as I approached. There was a look on his face of complete shock when he recognized me. I smiled politely, trying to hide my nerves, then entered the haunted house. Haunted by ghosts not of the past but of the present.

The bathroom that held Damien was at the back of the dark and cold building. After a slow walk down the long hallway, only a thin paneled door stood between us. Here it was, my revenge coming to fruition, and yet I couldn't bring myself to open the door. My hand trembled over the brass knob.

In my hesitation, I heard, "Hello?"

Damien's voice carried a hoarseness that I was unfamiliar with. It carried a pain and exhaustion that sent shivers down my spine.

"Alabine?" The sound of my name trembled as he breathlessly called out for me. There was a tinge of hope deeply embedded within his plea.

Although I wish I could say I summoned the courage to open the door and confront Damien, the enemy, on behalf of the future of the movement, that would be a lie. My opening the door came from some-place more instinctual. In his voice, I heard Damien's need for me. And so I answered.

Then I gasped.

His bloody and beaten body was tied to a chair in the bathtub. His feet dangled in a few inches of water pooled at the bottom of the claw-foot tub. The water around his feet was stained a dull red from his blood. His head wound, which I had worked so diligently to keep clean and on the path to healing, was open once again, flushed with infection.

The air smelled of burnt bacon. Electric wires were taped to his bare chest. Scorch marks radiated from these points, defined enough that I could see the path the currents had taken through his singed skin. His breath was labored as he arched his neck and strained to look at me. One of his eyes was bloodshot from a burst vessel. Every inch of him that I saw made it harder for me to keep my knees from buckling.

How easy it was to order Samson to torture Damien. An act be-hind closed doors is an easy one to justify, but standing in the blood-stained bathroom, I regretted ever even suggesting we use such harsh interrogation methods. This was stooping to *their* level. I wasn't this person. I swore to never be that person again.

"You came," Damien said with relief in his quavering voice.

Without a word, I leaned down and untied his hands from around the back of the chair. The ropes had dug into his skin like it was no more than wet clay. Horrified, I reached out toward the wounds. De-spite my gentle touch, Damien winced, so I drew back.

I took a seat on the chair just in front of him and found his gaze beneath his matted and tangled hair. In his eyes, he still held the sweet caring that I had come to know so well. Except now, it pissed me off. Now I knew he was a spy. I couldn't yet hold both truths, that he could be the enemy and yet still be a person who cared for me.

"You look sick," he said with concern.

"You don't look so great yourself," I snapped back. His face dropped, hearing the disdain in my voice, and so he reluctantly let go of any pretense that we were still friendly.

"What do you want to know?" he dryly asked. Suddenly, I felt like I was across the table from Minchin. *Finally,* I thought, *this is the real Damien.* I sat back in my chair, getting ready for our chess game. The back-and-forth where I had to determine what was real and what was deceit.

"Does it matter what I ask you? You would only lie to me."

He smiled. *That fucking smile.* "I told you, whatever you ask me, I'll tell you the truth. I owe you that much." The softness that crept through his words rattled me. "Did the supply ship from Canada ever show up?"

I nodded, wondering what opening move this was.

"That's great, Al," he said, unable to look at me.

"It would be. Except there's an entire armada blocking it from coming ashore."

"Yeah." He sighed. "I know. That was the plan."

I laughed, masking the pain I felt every time he confirmed just how involved he had been in the efforts to destroy us. "Okay. So, how long do we have before they bomb the city?"

"They're not going to."

"I don't believe you."

"They are only there to keep the supply ship out of UA waters." His response was so quick and succinct that I was left speechless. He didn't even take a moment to think. "The president would never order a bombing of his own city. Especially not with UA citizens here."

"The Resurrectionists," I said, realizing that the concept of a human shield was already successfully in action. "Redden is scared of looking like the bad guy."

Damien shook his head. "Maybe to an extent, but don't underestimate him. The president is a proud man. The only thing that really scares him is Canada. The smartest thing Wade ever did was form an alliance with them. The president would do anything to prevent a war he knows we'll lose." It helped me to know that Redden feared something. Then Damien's face darkened. "The warships won't bomb here, but they are carrying five teams of infantrymen that will raid the city for illegals. For Awoken. You can't stay here, Al. It's not safe for you."

Memories of Chicago swirled in my mind. The sounds of the raid in Nashville flooded my ears. Terror overcame me. I pushed it down.

"What are they waiting for?"

"More camps to arrive so they can do more damage with a single blow." This I believed. Eliza had surmised as much. "The plan, as I last heard it, was to wait until after the president's Patriots' Day speech. They don't want the celebrations in Atlanta to be upstaged."

The blood in my veins began to boil. "The celebrations in two days when Max's body will be incinerated?"

"Yes."

"How dare you?" I accused in a biting breathy whisper.

"You could still save him. He's there, perfectly preserved, waiting for you. Or have your feelings for him waned?"

"Fuck you."

"Anytime."

I punched him in the face. It burst out of me like a demon. I had never punched anyone before. My knuckles burned. Slowly, I sat back down.

Damien dropped his head. "I'm sorry. I didn't mean . . . If you do still love him as much as I think, why didn't you go?" He chuckled to himself. "You made me look like an ass. I swore that if they gave you the option, you'd run to him."

"You obviously don't know me."

"I guess I don't." There was a sadness in his voice that pierced through my armor.

I decided to respond truthfully. "We have a future here in this city. Avon has given us this gift . . . this dream. We can stand together as one people and have someplace to call home." I laughed weakly. "The old Alabine would've gone to Max, tried to broker peace, not made too many waves, but I'm not that person anymore. No amount of peace is worth sacrificing the world Avon can build. I don't have the right to throw it all away to save one man. No matter how much I love him. I know that I am finally doing the right thing in this beautiful broken world."

Damien's lips curled, recognizing the words he'd once said to me. "Do they know about Max?"

I shook my head. "Avon does. No one else. They might try some kind of suicidal rescue. Eavesman Square but worse. It was better to leave it as is."

"What about you?"

"I see a life here now. Maybe not the life I expected or wanted, but a life where I can make a difference for as long as I have left." Then I realized that I was crying. I looked deeply into Damien's soulful brown eyes. This all felt too familiar. He was comforting me in the way he always did. I laughed, pissed at myself for losing this round. "Man. You're good." I stood up.

"What? No, Alabine, I wasn't—"

I hated him. I wanted to hurt him at least a fraction as much as he hurt me. Since I couldn't bring myself to do so physically, I looked for other tactics. "I met your father in Montrose, you know. He seemed so cool and collected. Like he didn't give one flying fuck that his son was dying in the cells of that very building."

"I know he didn't care. He never has, why start now?"

"Is that why you do this? For Daddy's approval?"

"I do this because I love my country, and I was asked to serve her. I didn't have a choice."

"No choice? Is it that simple for you?" I shouted. "To kill all those children because you were told to. Did you ask any questions?"

"It wasn't my place."

"You're smarter than that, Damien."

"Fine. I did it because I believed people like you don't deserve to be here." He paused, then said, "I was wrong." His voice barely rose above a whisper, and yet I could tell that he was upset. He took a few deep breaths as he collected himself. "I love my country. I still do. I'm proud to be a soldier, to give my life for her. I love my country." He repeated it as if he were convincing himself. Then he lifted his head and looked me square in the eyes. "That doesn't mean I don't also love you."

The breath caught in my throat. My heart stopped, or raced—I couldn't tell. He was lying. Of course he was lying. I hated the part of me that hoped he was finally telling the truth.

Damien reached out and held my hand. I should've backed away. I should've considered that it was the start of an attack, but his touch was too intimate to be perceived as a threat. He traced the lines on my palm with his thumb. "It's why I wanted you to transfer me to another camp. So I couldn't keep doing things that would hurt you."

"Stop," I pleaded. "Haven't we both had enough? I'm tired. I'm so tired, Damien. What game is this?"

"It's no game, Al." He didn't drop his gaze. Didn't break eye contact. Didn't let go of my hand. He was daring me. To do what, I wasn't entirely sure. Love him, maybe. I wasn't going to call his bluff.

"Why me?" I asked.

He let out a sad laugh. "Trust me, I didn't plan this."

I shook my head. "No. Not that." Not *"Why did you fall in love with me,"* I thought but didn't say aloud. "Why did you convince Wade to bring me back over Max? I still don't understand that."

Damien hesitated. He let go of my hand and sat back in his chair. For the first time in the conversation, there was something he didn't want to tell me, making me want to know it all the more.

"Why, Damien?" I insisted.

He sighed and nodded, preparing himself. "When we learned that Wade was going to wake Max, we wanted to use it against him, knowing that if Max publicly spoke against the Resurrectionists, it would completely dismantle the movement for good. But we didn't think we could convince Max to switch sides." He paused, then finally said, "We needed you first. We'd convince you, and you would convince him."

All the strength left my body. Not that there was all that much in me to begin with. This was an absolute punch to the gut. The room fragmented behind a pool of tears.

"That's why you fought to wake me up? You wanted me because you thought I was weaker?" I asked.

Damien nodded, clearly hating the pain this was causing me.

"Great," I said with a sarcastic laugh. "Well, I always said I wanted to change the world. Guess I should've clarified that I wanted to make it better."

"But you surprised everyone. You surprised me." Damien exhaled. "Just look at what's happening. Look at everything you've accomplished." A small smile crept onto his face, like he couldn't hold it back. "Waking you up was the worst thing we could've done."

I released a stuttered breath. There was nothing more I could say. Nothing more I wanted to say. I leaned over him and gently retied his hands, trying to ignore his soft breath on my cheek. It was only after I had turned to leave that I remembered what had actually brought me there. I hated myself for being so forgetful, so distracted.

"What frequency do they broadcast UA52 radio on?" I asked.

Damien remained still, not saying anything, not moving. His head dropped to his chest, and his hair fell across his face. After almost a minute of silence, I was about to give up and leave when he cleared his throat. "444.725. Sorry. It took me a minute to remember."

And then I left.

WE MOVED SWIFTLY, KNOWING our futures depended on it. Soon enough, I found myself in Manhattan face-to-face with my past. The building at 4 Times Square was just how I had remembered it, save for the large plaque on the front declaring it a historical landmark: "The wedding place of Alabine Rivers and Max Green." Certainly an odd thing to see in the middle of Times Square. But the structure was the same. The same massive glass windows and formidable iron supports. As I stood at its base, I looked up to the top and tried to imagine how they ever built that massive antenna that protruded well into the sky. At the time of its construction, I doubt any one of the workers could've imagined that it would one day serve as the Hail Mary for a civil rights movement a century and a half in the future.

Minnie's body arched stiffly in Avon's arms as he carried her through the broken glass door. Despite the sanitizing flames unleashed on the city in the fight against the fungus, most of the buildings in Times Square were still erect. Scars of singed concrete peppered the landscape, but other than that, it sat peacefully in its decay. The streets appeared clean under the pure white blanket of snow that I assumed masked a multitude of sins.

I followed behind Avon, stepping into the long-abandoned building. Though the power was back on, the reintroduction of electricity had not jump-started the elevator system. Despite a moment of worry, Minnie assured us that there was still enough power flowing through the building to get the antenna to work.

On Chris's back, she had brought everything we would need to get the signal out. Samson had pillaged multiple brownstones for wires, electronics, and other instruments that could be deconstructed to give Minnie the raw supplies she'd require.

It was painful to watch her struggle. Dreno didn't do much anymore. It seemed like even if we got her medicine that very day, it might still be too late. Her bubbly personality, however, withstood all the pain she was feeling. I knew she was close to the end when I felt the coldness in the pit of my stomach every time I looked at her. We all wanted her to live, but that was out of our hands. The only comfort I took was knowing that the best we could do was to try and get the supply ship to land as quickly as possible.

Eventually we made our way up the fifty-two flights to the roof. As strong and stoic as he was, Avon became too tired by the end, having carried Minnie up the whole way, and had to pass her off to Samson to finish the ascent. Avon was unmatched in hiding his pain, so it was easy to forget that he too needed the medicine on that ship in order to survive.

There was only a small group of us there. In addition to me and Minnie, there were Avon, Chris, and Samson. Gina had stayed back to organize the incoming Awoken and Resurrectionists into fighting brigades. Noah was busy serving as the camp's doctor while Eliza and Diana were overseeing a million things, not the least of which were managing politics between the camps as they arrived and seeing groups safely to their new homes. Homes that we hoped could be permanent if our mission here succeeded.

Finally at the roof of the building, I stepped out. As vividly as I saw Avon and Minnie next to me, I also saw the white rosebuds on the ground and my friends standing in a line that led toward Max at the foot of the antenna tower.

I saw my wedding.

It felt different from my Lucid Memory, though. There was no question that this was a just a memory. The mirages blurred as I neared them. There was no touch or smell. This was just an echo, the way a memory should be. Time was starting to feel linear again as I became clearer on the future I had in this world.

Minnie pointed to the room at the very base of the tower. It was small, not much bigger than a shed. Chris broke the lock on the door with a heavy and swift kick. Inside was a nondescript metal desk surrounded by wire-covered walls.

With help from Samson, it took Minnie under an hour to construct her masterpiece. While they worked, I sketched out my major talking points using a pencil I'd found in the empty lobby and a sheet of paper from a safety manual in the small control room. In my first life, I had studied all of the best political speeches, and now I tried to channel what I'd learned into what would be the most important moment of either of my lives.

As I wrote down notes for my broadcast, I looked out over the desolate and deserted city, trying to remember how I had gotten here and why. Damien's confession mere hours before weighed heavily on me, distracting me from my purpose. So I thought of Max. My Max. Slipping Max's phone from my pocket had become a matter of mindless habit now. I comfortably played with it in my hand for a brief moment before powering it on. Minnie had turned off the cell service and made sure there wasn't any tracker in it. It was safe again. Purely a time capsule of Max's life.

Then—I can't really tell you why—I finally decided that I was ready to fill in the gaps of my first life.

I scrolled back through the photos and videos. Back through Max's life, back to the date of my death, and then I kept going. Hundreds of thumbnails of me and Max together flooded the screen. The life I had that I only still partially remembered: our wedding, our dates, our breakup. There it all was. The truth behind the warped narrative I was living in my Lucid Memories. These pictures both confirmed and clarified the moments that I was starved to remember. I saw the Alabine that I was, but more important, for the first time, I saw the Alabine that Max loved.

With the confidence I needed to go on, I looked back toward the small metal room, which began to hum with life and power as Minnie and Samson neared the end of their build. Chris turned on the radio we had brought with us from Brighton Beach. Raheem's voice droned through the speakers as it always did. Then Chris ran the radio to the other side of the roof and gave a thumbs-up to an anticipating Minnie.

"Here." Minnie held out a cable to me. "Plug it into your phone. You'll speak through the microphone." My hand trembled as I took it and did as she instructed. "Ready?" she innocently asked me.

I nodded.

Like a wizard, Minnie wrapped a final wire to another and pinched them into one being. Just then, everything and everyone went quiet. Raheem's voice was no longer broadcasting through the radio. In this heart-stopping moment, all I heard was the cold winter wind beating mercilessly against the towering metal structure.

"You're on!" Chris shouted in a half whisper from across the roof, trying to keep her voice from being picked up on the microphone. We found out later that it was. Her quiet and distant cry was the first thing that the normal, everyday people who lived up and down the country heard.

Minnie's nod indicated to me that it had worked. I was live to the nation.

Hello. Hi. My name is Alabine Rivers. I was born in Chicago, Illinois, in 1997. I died on January 30th of 2020. I was illegally brought back to life sixteen days ago in the dilapidated basement of a long-abandoned facility in the middle of nowhere. Since then, my life has been rife with fear and tragedy, more than I ever could have imagined.

Most of you already know of me, much to my surprise, because my husband, Max Green, told our story. I am not surprised that Max told our story and inspired so many people. It's a good story—trust me, I know; I lived it. And I always knew he had it in him, even if he didn't always see it. What surprises me is how you can all know me, know Max, know our story of love, and yet sit to the side while those like us are brutally murdered by the very people to whom you pledge your allegiance.

I am tired of the fighting. I am tired of the lying. So, let me correct two lies here and now:

First, Eavesman Square was a tragedy, but the bomb that took all those lives was set off by the Territorial Army. Your president ordered the attack. Not the Resurrectionists.

Second, and most important, we—the Awoken—do not carry the Devil's Touch. We did not cause the infestation. This is a lie to set you against us. Your secretary of science himself eagerly shook my hand when he welcomed me into his office. He knows without a doubt that I am not contaminated. None of us are. This is a lie perpetuated in the name of maintaining power by propagating fear.

Whether you continue to believe the lies of the past or the professions of the present, this country's standard practice to murder innocent people is revolting. And as its people, you are condoning the continuation of this practice far into the future, well after every Awoken is long vanquished. For after we are all killed, who will be next? Who will they have to make the enemy then? You see, this isn't about us, and it never has been. You believe their lies in order to make it seem like we're the enemy, when in fact the enemy is deep within you.

You hate us because you think we're different. We're not. We're all human, and humanity is united in its ability to love. And we do love—passionately, completely, entirely. It drives us to insanity and brings us back from despair. We love each other with our hearts and our minds. From our eyes to our toes. We love. With this love also comes hate—it's the balance that the universe demands, I understand that. But here, now, for me, for Max, I'm asking you to choose love.

I know that I am broadcasting to everyone, a wide swath of society. But I am not speaking to the people who take up arms against us. Nor the people who run in fear when they see us. I'm not so blind and arrogant as to believe I can sway their kind in one plea for help. No. I'm speaking to you: the people who choose not to look us in the eye for fear of engendering empathy. Those of you who have a voice in the back of your mind that says you would rather us not be murdered but don't want to rock the boat and be considered different.

To those whom I am speaking to, I'm asking you . . . No, I'm begging you to change the world.

We are in New York City. The city you all have left behind. We will make this our home. There's a supply ship twelve miles off the coast of Long Island that carries vitally important supplies: medicine, food, clean water. We need it to dock in Brighton Beach. To do so, it must sail past the blockade set up by your government. We need those supplies to have a chance at surviving.

We need you.

It is perfectly legal for any one of you to sail that boat to Brighton Beach. Legally, they can do nothing to stop you. Unlike us, you would not be arrested. Unlike us, you would not be shot. Unlike us, you would not have the breath torn from your lungs.

We need you to be our shield.

I know that so many people will listen to this and never move from the comfort of their homes. So don't rely on other people to do the courageous thing. You be that hero. One person can make a difference. Max was one person, and he changed humanity forever. Even one person choosing to show up to escort this boat to our shores will save tens of thousands of us.

Take arms, not for the defense of your flag, but for the defense of your fellow humans. I know some of you possess the courage to take a stand, even if, much like Max, you don't see it in yourselves yet. Join in our fight. Stand with us. A nation is not truly united unless we are all deemed worthy of life.

There is nothing else I can say. It comes down to this: you must decide. In two days, the ship will make its move toward land, and only with your action will it be successful.

If you choose not to act, you choose a path in which you will live and I will die. I know all too well the pain of death. I have seen the darkness on the other side, and it is something I want to deny until I'm wrinkled and old and can name myself a citizen of a free nation. The choices you make in life are all you have. So choose love.

In two days, I know exactly where I will be. I will be looking to the horizon in hopes that my love and faith in humanity will be confirmed. I will cling on to this hope with every ounce of my being, as I have a hell of a lot to live for.

19

PATRIOTS' DAY IS A celebration of when the United States of America was officially renamed United America. The bill passed with an overwhelming majority on January 1, 2055, to the cheers of millions. A new country committed to the promise of equality—so long as you ascribe to the same ideals. In the years after, Patriots' Day became a massive celebration across the country. Communing with one's neighbors in the outdoors, where the country's beauty could be appreciated, was upheld as sacrosanct. Picnics and dances became a popular way to spend the day. And a speech from the president was always expected. These speeches were so important, so widely heard, that they had the power to define entire administrations.

This year's celebrations were to be broadcast to the whole nation from Atlanta. From the steps of the cryogenics facility where Max's body was stored. This was President Billy Redden's first Patriots' Day speech. Redden proved in his first year of office that he was different from the former president, who had grown increasingly unpopular before he stepped down. Redden declared himself a leader of action, and Patriots' Day was going to be the crowning moment of his administration. Establishing a national park and decommissioning the largest cryo facility to date in one fell swoop. After his scheduled speech at two p.m., Redden would push the detonator and a square mile of buildings would be cleared away.

All eyes were focused on Atlanta, especially after the embarrassing and unprecedented hack of the national radio broadcast that was heard by millions. Of course it wasn't mentioned in any newspaper. There wasn't a whisper of response from any UA media or the administration itself, and yet still, the government was on thin ice. People were nervous. Worst of all, people were asking questions.

As the grand Patriots' Day plans were being crafted in Atlanta, Awoken camps poured onto our island. They were broken, fragmented, and weary for a safe home. They came in vans, on foot, and some even by horse-drawn wagons. They too heard my broadcast, which lifted their spirits. Throughout all the camps, in fact, morale was high. I had spread hope, which in return gave me a sense of purpose that I never found in my first life. I told myself that even if my broadcast did nothing, if no one came to our aid, giving hope to the hopeless made it worth it.

That said, we wanted my plea to work. We needed my call to be answered. The massive warships on the horizon that stood between us and the supplies we so desperately needed were a constant reminder.

Mere hours following the broadcast, the Rhode Islanders' patrols spotted a few citizen boats arrive. We were initially elated until we realized they were there to join the UA blockade. They were not coming to *our* aid but rather coming to the aid of the Territorial Army. This news devastated us and squashed the morale boost we briefly enjoyed.

However, the chessboard continued gaining pieces. On the morning after the broadcast, we were thrilled to see two Canadian battleships anchored in international waters close to the unmarked supply ship. Although everyone knew the supply ship was from Canada, it wasn't flying its flag and identified itself as a private trading vessel. So the battleships showing up represented the first time Canada outwardly declared its alliance with us.

Chris learned through her sources that *publicly* the battleships were there to make sure the UA didn't break any international laws. Privately, however, they were hoping this skirmish would give them the justification they needed to threaten war on the UA. Of course we would have preferred that they officially joined our fight, but this was the next best thing. They wouldn't pull the first trigger, but they damn well were going to keep the fight fair. My speech was replayed across the world, and now the world was watching. It was still David and Goliath, but at least Goliath wouldn't be able to cheat.

This relationship was quickly put to the test when one of the UA warships crossed into international waters and threatened the supply ship. The Canadians were quick to send their battleships in, forcing the UA vessel to return to its own waters.

Chris was delighted to see just how strongly the Canadians were holding the line. This was a fight they'd been wanting to pick for a long while. Although Canada took a more complex stand on the issue of cryogenics, the Canadian prime minister personally abhorred the way Awoken people were treated in the UA. But mainly, she was pissed about the occupation of Toronto. This was a win-win situation for them. They garnered diplomatic points with their allies for upholding international laws while finally showing their own citizens that they would stand up to their bullish neighbor. They weren't backing down, and the UA clearly wasn't willing to push them too far and risk all-out war. Seeing Canada's massive battleships next to the UA's warships was proof of how much Canada's military had surpassed the UA's in the recent decades. Redden was justifiably scared.

On the first day of the new year, the sun rose like a guillotine blade. It was the day Max was going to die forever. It was a day I knew as New Year's Day, but everyone else knew as Patriots' Day. Normally,

I would've been nursing a champagne hangover. Perhaps snuggled into Max's arms, our only plan for the day to eat greasy food and watch TV.

In this life, however, I found myself standing on the sidewalk outside of Lovett, handing a kitchen knife to a terrified fourteen-year-old blond boy. The steel of the knife froze my fingers as I picked it up. It had been tossed into a large cardboard box with dozens of others. The day before, I'd gone with Gina, Diana, and Eliza to scavenge for weapons. Kitchen knives were the most reliable finds along with saws and hammers.

These items were to be used as protection against the impending raid we expected promptly after Redden's speech. After the destruction of the Atlanta cryo facility—that's when they were going to strike.

We anticipated close combat, like when the UA forces raided the Chicago camp. Though the warships put on quite the show, Avon trusted the intel I got from Damien that they weren't planning on bombing us. The Resurrectionists who walked side by side with us provided a certain shield. Bombing legal citizens would be internationally condemned. So we readied for an invasion. A raid. The difference between New York and Chicago was that here, at least, we wouldn't be taken by surprise.

All we needed was for the supply ship to safely cross through UA waters. We knew we didn't stand much of a chance if the supply ship couldn't make it to our shores. These knives wouldn't last long against the Territorial Army's guns and flamethrowers. Everything depended on that ship, but like Max, we were running out of time.

The theory we held was that the UA would not attack if the ship was behind a shield of legal citizens, and with the Canadian muscle keeping the UA warships in line, it seemed our plan might just work. All was looking good except for the small fact that, as of the morning of Patriots' Day, not a single civilian boat had joined in rank with the supply ship.

My plea for help failed. No one came to our aid.

So without any better options, we did what we could to prepare with kitchen knives and hacksaws. A line formed down the block as people awaited to receive their poor excuse for a weapon. Everyone was so young. And scared. The hopeful energy that had filled these streets in the days before was all but gone. There was a silence that held the fear of death in it. The cold had relaxed a bit after a foot of snow fell the night before. The relief in weather, however, didn't keep a general gloom from descending over the camp as the realization set in that not a single regular civilian wanted to help us in our fight for our lives.

The fourteen-year-old boy was on the brink of tears when I handed him the knife. He was skinny, no more than a hundred pounds, and frail. The months-old stubble of blond hair on his head just barely poked through. I couldn't, and didn't want to, imagine him going toe-to-toe with the UA forces. There was no other choice. So I smiled and handed him the frozen knife.

"Good luck." It was a pathetic comfort to the scared child, but it was all I had to give. The boy walked away as another stepped up to replace him.

Early morning passed quickly as I attempted to encourage the Awoken who were lined up, readying for battle. In their eyes, I saw fear and uncertainty; I saw death and darkness; but also, most important, I saw a glint of resolve to fight for their new home.

During my work, I found myself regularly glancing down the street toward the dilapidated white building that held Damien. I hadn't gone back, too scared to see him like that again and too scared of what I might say to him. Samson reported any updates to me, although there weren't many. Damien had offered no more information to help us. He'd stopped talking entirely, in fact, not even to ask for me. Samson had a look of despair when he confessed that Damien was different after our conversation. Broken. A shell of the man he was. I had no idea what the future held for Damien, but he wasn't my priority.

By nine o'clock, we had made it through most of the line. I fought every instinct to sit down. To take a break. Thankfully, before I embarrassingly collapsed, Avon pulled me aside. We walked down the sidewalk, out of earshot of anyone else. From there we had our privacy, but I could still keep an eye on the line of people and jump in if they needed me.

Avon offered me a mug, from which I took a thankful sip, relishing the burnt tongue I was sure to receive. Apple cider, by the smell of it. I coughed as the surprising sting of alcohol singed my throat. It was more than just cider. Avon laughed at my displeasure.

"Gina found some rum. Thought you could use it to warm up."

"Yeah. Thanks." I tried to swallow. This was a comforting inch closer to a normal New Year's Day. After such a trying few hours, I allowed myself to sink into the ease I felt when I was with Avon, who had become the older brother I never had.

From his red cheeks, I assumed he had been up on the roof looking out at the ships. I hadn't dared go up there again, so it buoyed me that he seemed calm. I stared at his face in hopes of gleaning some of his courage for myself.

"Well? What news?" I asked.

Avon sighed. "The supply ship's captain radioed. If no one shows up in a few hours, he's turning back."

"What? He can't just leave us to die!"

"He can't make it through on his own. We've run out of time." I saw resolution in Avon's face. It was powerfully calming, despite the horrible news. With a tone of authority, he continued, "I'm leaving now to take a group of us to the beach. Diana is going to take the others north to ward off an attack from the troops stationed by the Brooklyn Bridge. When they invade after the speech, if the ship hasn't made it to shore by then, we'll have to fight with what weapons we have."

"The weapons we have are knives."

"Gina and I have found almost fifty guns among the camps. We will give them a good fight."

"But—" I tried protesting. Avon raised his hand, silencing me.

"They won't take prisoners this time. They'll just kill us. We have to take our chances . . . and pray."

I looked out over the line of people receiving their weapons. They all knew the pain of being nothing, and here they were facing death yet again. I was too. My stomach catapulted into my throat.

"Do you want me to go with you or Diana?" I asked.

Avon looked me in the eye. "You're not coming." He put his hand on my shoulder. "You'll be a witness to what happens from the abandoned airport near the beach, and then you will broadcast another message telling people about the atrocities you see."

"What? Witness? No, I'm going to fight like you and Diana!"

He grabbed me by the elbow and pulled me around the corner. I was speaking too loudly, and people were watching. Out of sight, he let go of me.

"You're no good to us dead. If we have a chance of surviving, it's up to you to change people's minds. You had the right idea with the broadcast, but once wasn't enough. It'll take time. If you stay alive long enough, I'm certain you can do it. Make this, today, mean something."

"There must be another choice," I pleaded.

"We're out of choices," Avon said with an infectious calm. "They've never given us any choices."

I wiped the tears off my cheek that were starting to freeze. "What about you?"

"You know your place, and I know mine. We're dying one way or another. I'd prefer it was on my terms. My first death was not one I chose. This life was not one I chose, but God put me here; I'm certain of it." Avon exhaled. "It's in this life that I finally found love. Found a good man who cares for me with all his heart. If I die, I die knowing love. And you know that's a powerful thing." He sniffled back tears and stood up straight. "It's been an honor to know you, Alabine Rivers. And it will be my honor to lead these people to fight for a just cause. There isn't much more I could hope for in death."

Pale and weak, Avon was ready to spend every ounce of strength he had left defending this refugee city that he built and loved. He had the vision for our future that no one else dared to dream. He truly was our leader and our hero.

"Is there . . ." I tried collecting myself enough to speak. "Is there anything you'd like me to say for you? Or anything you'd like me to tell your family?"

Avon smiled and shook his head. "I recently saw my brother, Joshua, in my Lucid Memories. I told him everything I never dared to when I was alive. They're not really memories anymore, I guess."

"Yeah." I sniffled back tears. "Mine have been changing too. I'll never see Max again except in them. So at least we have that." Redden's Patriots' Day speech was going to start soon. Max only had hours left, at most.

"Oh, cheer up, Alabine Rivers," Avon said encouragingly, though he was unable to bring himself to smile. "You and Max are destined to be together, in this life or the next."

"You know as well as I do that there is no next life," I said bitterly.

Avon rubbed his cross necklace between his fingers. "You don't know that. I believe that when you die, really die, there could still be more. Maybe there was only nothing because we were on ice. But in true death, that's when we see the light. Have hope; I know I do."

Avon pulled me into him and hugged me. I felt his tears against my face. Then he looked down to me. "I've told Gina she's going with you too, though don't expect a willing companion in her."

"I bet she was pissed." I chuckled through my tears.

Avon nodded. He wore a gravely serious expression as he contemplated what was ahead of us. "Hide. Stay safe, you understand? Survive. It's up to you. Use your voice to make our deaths mean something. Convince people that they mean something."

"I will," I said solemnly. "What about Noah? Shouldn't he come with us?"

A tear fell down Avon's cheek. "I tried. But he told me that he wasn't a soldier and didn't take orders." A sad laugh trickled to the surface. "He said he's needed here. With me."

I nodded, understanding, and with my heart breaking. He turned toward the crowd that was amassing on the street and started walking away.

"Wait!" I shouted, not able to let him go. He looked back to me. "You don't have to do this, Avon." It wasn't going to make a difference, but someone needed to say it.

He smiled. "I do. This world is a good place when people stand up for what's right. These people deserve to live in that world." He looked up at the buildings around us that were filled with his people. Our people. Then he looked back to me. "Goodbye, Al."

It was a goodbye that needed to last a lifetime.

"Bye, Avon."

I watched as he led hundreds of terrified but inspired people to the beach where the future of our world would be decided. My suffocating emotions had to be stuffed deep inside me. I had work to do.

After the militia departed, I helped Gina load our van with the supplies we would need to survive. As we were packing out to leave, the remaining people who were too sick or young or frail to fight moved their few possessions into a basement on Lovetts Way that had been selected as the safety bunker. They were being sent there to hide out and hope Avon's militia could hold back the raid.

They could still run, I thought. But there was nowhere for them to go. And, more important, the point was to stop running. To make a stand, even if it meant the greatest sacrifice. With a somber determination, teenagers barely out of puberty boarded windows and sheltered themselves in with children half their age. At least they stood a better chance than the people in the Chicago camp. The streets around us that had been filling up hour by hour with incoming refugees eventually cleared. The world was eerily quiet once again.

My body did not take well to the ascending and descending of stairs needed to bring our minimal supplies into the vans. Soon I felt my muscles give under the stress. Starved for oxygen by my failing lungs, I had to sit on the stoop in the cold, unable to move or think or do anything but focus on inhaling and exhaling.

The Dreno had run out. It had been days since the shot Damien gave me. More than two weeks since the pill from Minchin. And almost three since I was awoken. I was living on borrowed time. After a few moments, I felt Gina's hand on my shoulder and looked up at her through glassy eyes.

"It's started," Gina said.

Looking down the block, I saw a small crowd gathering around a radio that was balanced atop a wide concrete railing on the stoop of a neighboring house. I tried to stand, but my elbow buckled under my weight. Gina's small but surprisingly strong arms caught me before I face-planted into the sidewalk. She lifted me and wrapped my arm around her shoulders so I could lean my weight into her. We hobbled over toward the radio together.

"My fellow Americans." President Billy Redden's voice boomed out of the small speaker with the sweet, friendly tone he was renowned for. Sadness washed over me. This was the beginning of the end. Max's end. "I stand here on this auspicious day with a full heart. Behind me is a vestige of a violent and chaotic time in our history. A time when we challenged God himself. And, well, we lost."

The crowd around him erupted in cheers.

"But we have righted the ship. And now we give these lands back to God as we decommission this relic and christen the Redden National Park."

Gina squeezed my arm. "Come on. We gotta go."

With great effort, she hoisted me into the van. Minnie was already lying down in the backseat. She gazed out the window with the distant look that I knew meant she was in a Lucid Memory. I hoped she was around her kitchen with her mother, cooking their favorite meal together. I hoped she was a million miles away from this cold van.

We needed a bit more time. Avon needed me as witness to the attack and then report it to the world from 4 Times Square. I needed to stay alive long enough to do that. Minnie needed to stay alive long enough to help me.

Those were our orders.

Soon Minnie came out of her trance, and our eyes met. She stared at me with a determination that told me she would not let us down. If a thirteen-year-old girl could do that, I must be able to as well. For Max. For Avon. For everyone.

As we pulled away and drove down Lovetts Way, I took a last look at Damien's brownstone, certain that I would never see it, or him, ever again. My life was seismically changing once more, and this time I knew Damien wouldn't be there on the other side to wake me up. I tried to remember the sweetness on his lips when he kissed me, but I couldn't recall it. There was no good there to hold on to.

We headed to an old airfield where we could watch the events unfold. It was right off the highway, so we'd have a quick and easy escape out to Times Square. We had to just hope that we wouldn't be chased.

On the drive to the airfield, we listened to Redden's speech on the radio.

"There has not been a day before and there will not be a day again that we can so confidently declare a widespread victory against the terrorism that has been plaguing this great country."

As I listened to his voice drone on, I clung on to what little life I had left. The fabric of time and reality slipped through my fingers. I turned and saw Max sitting next to me in the van.

.
.
.

Soon we're not in the van at all. We're in my hospital room. Redden's speech from the steps of the cryo facility plays on the TV in the corner.

I'm not in the bed. Instead I'm standing behind Max, looking down on him as he sits just at the bedside. I can't see his face, but I hear him crying softly to himself. I know then that this is the actual moment I died. There is a monitor slowly beeping, tracking the last moments of my heart.

Or perhaps his. For he is about to die too, though he doesn't know it.

"This will once again place United America as the moral leader of the world!" Billy shouts from the screen in the corner of the room.

The TV hovers over us, demanding its due attention. I look up to it. The feed cuts back and forth between a massive wide shot that shows thousands of people in attendance, screaming, yowling, and crying like they are at a Beatles concert, and an impossibly tight close-up of Redden's face. His pores and growing wrinkles are plastered across the screen. His pupils retract as he looks up into the sunlight and smiles.

"Life is not what we decide it is, my friends. Life is what God decrees." The crowd cheers. They're filled with elation and anger.

I briefly remember that I am in a van. I look over and see Gina driving next to me. But I'm not ready to go back. Not yet. I want to be with Max until the very end. The heart monitor continues its unwavering beeping. A countdown clock.

Slowly, I gather the courage to turn back to Max. I peer around his body, expecting to see myself lying in the bed in my last moments of life, but instead of seeing a sickly and dying body, I only see the darkness. The gluttonous and thriving darkness in all its glory. The bed is filled with a stark nothingness where my body should be.

Gasping, I turn my head away, and without realizing it, I lean against Max's shoulder. He doesn't turn around, I still don't see his face, but he reaches up and gently touches my hand. I look down to our interlocking fingers, wondering if he knows that I'm there. I'm no longer in that bed—it's only darkness there—but I'm here. Here for him.

He doesn't know. He continues to face the bed and pour love into it. I want him to hold me, comfort me, not because I'm dying but because he is.

As Max and I share this intimately unspoken moment together, the annoyingly bright TV screen radiates images of the final moments of Max's life. Billy's smile orchestrates the whole event. His teeth are so white, the pixels in the screen seem to burst from overwork.

"Alabine?" Max mutters.

I'm astonished to hear his voice. He doesn't know if I can hear him. I can. I want to throw my arms around him and tell him, but I don't. Instead I hold his trembling hand. The heart monitor's beeping speeds up, ever so slightly, giving Max the encouragement he needs to continue.

"It's okay, Al. You can let go. I'll be okay. You don't have to worry about me anymore. Just let go." Tears drop from his face onto the starched bedsheets.

I fall to my knees behind him, still gripping onto him. "How can I let you go? I love you, Max. My Max."

Then, finally hearing me, Max turns around. He sees me and smiles through the tears. He holds my face in his warm hands. The beeping monitor distorts and flattens into a continuous high-pitched sound.

On the TV, Redden spreads his arms wide and looks up to the sky as the building behind him erupts into a brilliant golden cloud of fire and destruction. Redden is consumed by it. The television screen is consumed by it until it can no longer be contained. It erupts into the hospital room, engulfing me and Max. The darkness in the hospital bed cannot even withstand the radiating light from the explosion.

My ears ring with the high-pitched screech as I squeeze Max's hand. Even as my sight goes in the bright light and my hearing is broken by the detonation's deafening shriek, I can feel him. I clutch on to that sensation with every fiber of my being.

Let go, Al.

It's not that I hear him. It's that I feel him. I feel our bodies as one. We are one. At last, my feeling goes along with the rest, and I release his hand. But still, we are one inside the light.

In every life.

In every time.

In every world.

Max Green was now dead.

As the bright light cleared and my ears stopped ringing, my consciousness clawed itself out of my past and into my present. Redden's speech was over, and the Atlanta facility was a pile of ash and rubble.

Back in the van, behind the radio's chaotic broadcast of jubilant cheering intermixed with the remittent rumble caused by the explosion, I heard a tugboat horn.

"Alabine! Look!" Gina leaned over the steering wheel. I grabbed the binoculars next to me and looked through them to the vast ocean in front of us.

And on the horizon, I saw the most wondrous and spectacular sight.

We heard her plea. <u>I'm writing this now to tell you that I</u> believe her. There is a young patrol officer with whom <u>I</u> have spoken who also believes her. He was there when Secretary Winchin shook her hand. With his own eyes, he saw the deception.

They have lied to us. About so many things.

Stand with me, a Christian, a baker, a concerned citizen, and most importantly, a mother. We must help these people.

We will sail from Snug Harbor at noon on January first.

Let freedom Ring,

Helen Smith

P.S.-

Please enjoy the strawberry oat cupcake enclosed.

20

THOUSANDS OF PINK BOXES filled with baked goods were found in organized piles at every train station from Indianapolis to the Atlantic on the morning after my broadcasted plea for help. Authorities confiscated the boxes as they found them, but that wasn't before most had been snatched up by the crowds of commuters. Inside each pretty pink box was a note that convinced hundreds of people to set sail for Coney Island from Snug Harbor, eighty miles south.

Moments after I listened to the destruction of the cryogenics facility in Atlanta, moments after Max's death, I witnessed Helen Smith riding toward the UA blockade at the helm of the supply ship. From the abandoned airstrip across from the sandy Brighton Beach shore, I watched her push in toward the enemy through my dim binoculars.

As Wade said, we'd never be able to do this on our own. We needed one person to declare our worth and turn the tide into a tsunami. And we found that one person in Helen Smith.

Her entire life, Helen felt as if she were a slip of seaweed at the bottom of a vast ocean, being tossed side to side by the whims of forces that she couldn't see. She spent her life clinging on to anything she could so as not to be swept away.

Helen was never a radical. She loved her country and was grateful for the prosperity it granted her. And yet there was something festering in the pit of Helen's stomach that told her she was different from what was desired. She did all she could to assimilate. She worked long hours at the local bakery so she could buy the most fashionable clothes. She married a successful man when she was only twenty years old and then used some of his modest funds to start her own bakery.

The perfect glass globe that she built around her life began to crack when her husband died from the Devil's Touch, leaving her and her young daughter alone. His family tried to claim what was left of his money, including parts of her bakery. She fended them off as best she could, but they took enough.

To maintain the facade of normalcy, even after her husband's death, she sacrificed so much—the price of acceptance in a world where rejection could be fatal. She maintained the picturesque home in the perfect town. The business was thriving. Most important, her neighbors accepted her and looked to her for advice.

So when her thirteen-year-old daughter chose to join a renegade group of political extremists led by a charismatic man, her glass globe finally shattered, and once again, she was tossed about by the erratic ocean currents. People began whispering. She wasn't invited to neighborhood meetings. Worst of all, she lost her daughter.

A few years after Chris left home, Helen received a letter from her daughter, begging her to join the fight for Awoken rights by opening up her home to refugees. She agreed, only for the chance to reconnect with her daughter. Helen lived for her daughter's quick visits every few months.

Year after year, she was terrified every time a group of dirty, infested Awoken showed up on her doorstep. Afraid that they might rob her or hurt her or make her sick. Afraid that she might be discovered and labeled a sympathizer. Soon, though, she suspected that the

Awoken posed no health threat to her. She spent so much time with them and never got so much as a rash. Nonetheless, not once in all those years of providing a safe house did she believe in the cause.

After our night at her home and the ensuing police raid, it was easy enough for her to convince the authorities that she had been held hostage by the terrorists and they had stolen her permits. She had planned for this inevitable scenario and, thankfully, it worked; she avoided arrest. Once the dust settled, she began to realize that the handsome young man who'd promised her daughter was still alive was probably lying. She had nothing left.

Until one cold afternoon, sitting around the fire listening to the radio, she heard Chris's distant voice. Her daughter calling out from beyond the grave: *"You're on."* It was so faint, Helen didn't for a moment consider it was anything more than a waking dream. An angel sent to guide her. Chris's ethereal voice whispered a message that it was her time to act. Helen listened intently during my subsequent broadcast.

Suddenly, it clicked. She understood that her daughter became an activist because Helen unknowingly raised her to be one. Helen's fear of not being accepted radiated through every aspect of her life. And while that fear motivated Helen to hide, Chris chose to fight so she wouldn't have to hide in the first place.

In her daughter's memory, Helen decided to change the world. She and her only two remaining friends took the train from Indianapolis to Atlantic City. At every stop along the way, they snuck off and deposited bakery boxes on the platform with individually handwritten notes organizing the resistance.

By dawn on Patriots' Day, there were already far more people at Snug Harbor than she had expected. By the time they needed to set sail, there were more than a hundred boats ready to cast off at her order. Like Helen, these brave people were compelled by my broadcast to right the wrongs of this country. History has always been built on the backs of brave people.

Twelve miles off New York's coast, they convened with the supply ship. Helen and dozens of others boarded, providing the shield I had asked for. The shield we needed. Standing at the helm of the ship, as they sailed into UA waters, Helen felt Chris's spirit beside her. For the first time in her life, she wasn't afraid.

And then, suddenly and terrifyingly, I saw with my own eyes a UA warship fire on the supply vessel. On Helen.

I screamed when the torpedo hit the lower left hull. From my distance, I couldn't tell what damage had been done, but it was clear that the ship had been fatally wounded. There was no warning shot, no signal to turn back. It was an unwarranted attack on a civilian vessel. I expected that the Canadian battleships would retaliate like they had before when the UA warships crossed into international waters, but this time they just sat there.

"What are they doing? Canada should fire back!" I screamed.

"The supply ship crossed into UA waters and isn't flying a Canadian flag," Gina responded. "They're probably pissed, but they don't have any grounds to launch a counterattack."

It may have been unwarranted, but it wasn't illegal for the UA to shoot an unmarked ship within their own borders. The Canadians had nothing legitimate to retaliate against.

"Innocent people are on that boat!" I screamed with tears in my eyes.

"Apparently it doesn't matter, Alabine," Gina said sadly. That was the answer. The human shield meant nothing. I'd sent all those people, including Helen, to their deaths because once again I'd believed that goodness would prevail.

Then, in the chaos of the attack, a smaller UA assault ship carrying infantrymen peeled away from the warships and turned toward the beach. Toward Avon and our people.

"Damn it!" Gina grunted from the driver's seat of the van. "The raid is starting!"

On the two-way radio, we heard Diana shouting, "They're moving across the bridge!"

This was it. We were surrounded. Terrified, I looked across the channel and past the sandy beach toward the red brick tenements where Avon and our people were entrenched. The raiding forces were on their way, and the supply boat was sinking. It was going to be a massacre.

Not knowing what else to do, I flung open the van door, ready to hurl myself between the oncoming invaders and my people.

Gina grabbed my arm. "No. Avon gave us an order. Abandon your post, and I'll shoot you right here." She was dead serious. I stopped my ill-conceived attempt to save the day and stood by, preparing to watch my friends die.

Stuck in a van, miles away, I was helpless. I always felt so helpless in my life. Against my parents. Against my boss. Against my cancer. Helpless.

Not in this life, I promised myself.

Trying to think of what Max would do, I had an idea. Frantically, I searched the pockets of my coat. Maybe I'd lost it. Maybe I'd thrown it away. All of these regretful thoughts poured into my mind as I couldn't find what I wanted. What I needed.

Finally, I winced as my finger was cut along a paper's edge. I grabbed the offending object and pulled it out of my pocket. Minchin's business card.

The phone that I'd turned to so often in these last few weeks to save me was now going to save all of us. I booted it up. After a moment, the picture of Max and me appeared on the lock screen.

For a brief second, I allowed myself to stare at it, at our love. Drawing strength from the picture, I unlocked the phone, turned the cell service back on, and waited for the icon in the top right corner to show a signal.

"What are you doing?" Gina asked.

"Negotiating," I responded.

Nothing in this life came easily to me. Never knowing what to do or how to act, I was crippled in fear of doing anything. At that meeting in One, I thought I wasn't strong enough on my own. Not anymore. Now I knew the power I wielded in this world. More important, I knew exactly what to do with that privilege.

The signal appeared, and I dialed Minchin's number. It rang only once before the familiar click of an answer.

"I'm glad you called," Minchin's voice oozed and crackled through the phone. "But I'm afraid you're too late. I told you that you had one chance to save Max. Now we're handling your friends our way."

My palms started to sweat. I couldn't think of Max. It would break me. So I refocused on the assault ship that was getting closer and closer, filled with soldiers ready to raid the shore. There was no time for his games, and I knew Minchin could never give me what I needed. Though he would shudder to admit it, it wasn't within his power. But there was one person who could.

"I want to speak to the president," I demanded.

Minchin laughed. "I'm afraid that's not possible. President Redden is celebrating the opening of his national park."

"Will he still be celebrating when the Canadians declare war?" I spat back, remembering the one thing Redden feared.

There was a long pause. I hoped, in that pause, he realized he was speaking to a very different Alabine from the one he had met before. I was stronger. Without Max, I was alone. But strong.

"What do you want, Alabine?"

"I'll only speak with President Redden. I assume you're there with him. His ships are on the brink of starting a war with Canada. I'm the only one who can end this. Put him on now, or I hang up."

Another pause.

Soon enough, there was shuffling and muffled voices. Then, much to my surprise, I heard: "Hello? Gene, is this on?"

His voice caught me off guard. It was the voice I had just listened to over the radio. It was the voice that ushered in Max's death. My throat tightened, my mouth dried, and the world spun around me.

"Ms. Rivers, can you hear me? This is President Billy Redden," he said with a touch more authority. "I don't use telephones much, you see. I try to leave that to the scientists and diplomats. Just never trusted them all that much." He spoke uncomfortably fast, as if he would never be able to speak again if he stopped talking. It wasn't what I thought the president would be like.

"I want you to call a cease-fire." My voice sounded calm, but I felt like a balloon about to pop. I had no idea if this was going to work.

Billy laughed.

"Call your ships off, now," I demanded louder.

"Ms. Rivers, you must be mistaken. We're there to keep the peace." The saccharine tone in his voice grated like nails on a chalkboard.

"Then keep it!" I shouted while stifling a blood-filled cough. "Your forces fired at a civilian ship. The world is watching what happens here today. Clearly we have powerful friends. Walk away, Mr. President, before this gets worse for you."

There was a pause. I assumed he was conferring with someone, probably Minchin—maybe General Tom Standard, Damien's father. Then he came back on. "You must be mistaken. We were merely protecting our own territory. The ship was unmarked and trespassing in UA waters. But I am glad you are watching. Are you in those lovely brick buildings with the rest of your friends, Ms. Rivers? I believe my men will be there soon. Will your 'powerful friends' save you in time?"

I looked out toward the beach, toward the brick buildings lining the beach that Avon and the other Awoken were barricaded inside of. I imagined the massacre that would take place if I failed. All the doubts I'd held my entire life were screaming so loud in my head I couldn't remember what leverage I had or what my plan was or how in hell I was going to convince a world leader to surrender.

"The Canadians are desperate to start a war with you." I wiped the sweat off my forehead, hoping the president couldn't hear my terror.

"If you don't retreat, I'll tell them to attack." It was a bluff and he immediately knew it.

He laughed again. "Now, there, there. Why don't you calm down?" I wanted to reach through the phone and tear out his throat. "The people might listen to you because of who you are, but I know you don't hold that kind of sway over a foreign nation. We have ambassadors and diplomats who handle these kinds of things. You're just a little girl." His words filled me with embarrassment, believing that I could actually make a difference. I kept trying to hold onto Avon's faith in me as Billy continued. "Looky here. I can tell you're sweet. You're not meant for a life like this. One where you have to fight and run and get your hands dirty. Now we've looked into it and talked to the scientists and found out a way to put you back in a body bag. Put you on ice. Bring you back after all this is sorted. To live the life you want."

My stomach dropped. He was offering all that I had wanted since Damien woke me up, before reuniting with Max was even an option, and now Max was gone again. I looked at Gina beside me. Although she couldn't hear the conversation, she stared at me like the future of the world was being decided.

It was.

I was glad the president offered me this chance at an easier life. Thrilled even. Because in that moment, it was so easy for me to turn it down. I chose life. I chose this life. A life without Max, yes, but as hard and fraught and painful as it was, it was mine, and I was going to live it.

Confidence surged through me in a way it never had before. I didn't care in the slightest about playing any games or listening to his bullshit for a moment longer. I remembered my leverage and found my voice. "Mr. President, although you might think you are the most powerful man in the world, you are no more than an insignificant speck. Better men than you have come and gone in the blink of my eye. You've lived one life and are only fifty-something. I am more than a century old. I have experienced true love and true hate. I know loss and death and sickness. While you only know platitudes and charades, I know the darkness. I was nothing, and through that I was connected to everything. Hell, you barely know how to work a telephone. I am the bigger and better person. There's no way you win this."

He was silent for a long time, until:

"What are you doing all this for anymore? Gene gave you an out. We offered you the future you wanted. And now Max Green is dead."

"I know. I chose this over him, and I'd do it all over again." No tears came flooding to my eyes. No Max from my past appeared to soften the blow. It was just me and Billy. When he cleared his throat nervously, I took the opportunity to continue: "Declare the truce. Or I'll tell the world what happened here today. I'll tell them exactly what I saw."

"And what is that, Alabine? Like I said, we've done nothing wrong."

"You must be mistaken. I saw UA warships attack a vessel flying a Canadian flag in protected international waters. Not UA waters. I saw you commit an unlawful act of war."

It was a lie, yes, but it was no bluff.

"That's not what happened," Billy quietly responded.

"Like you said, people listen to me, I've proven that with my radio broadcast. And even more will listen to my second one. I will tell them exactly what I need to so the Canadians have what they need to declare war. You might hurt us today, but you will lose everything in the process."

Billy's silence told me he understood exactly what I was threatening.

"You know, I really should thank you for all of this," I said with a laugh.

"Why is that?" He was angry. The playful condescension that smothered his words was gone. He sounded like a child not getting their way.

"With Eavesman Square, and the Devil's Touch, and even the pervasive hatred of all Awoken, you have shown me that the truth doesn't matter. What matters is the story that is told. What matters is what people believe. That's the power I have. I'm living proof of the power of a great story."

He said nothing at first. That was it; that was the final card I had to play. It had to work. My heart was racing. With every second that passed, the supply ship sank farther into the ocean and the UA assault ship drew closer. Those infantrymen would be ashore in only a matter of minutes.

His silence seemed to last forever. In the space between us, I could hear my failure. This wasn't going to work—I was now certain of it. Changing the world is impossible if it doesn't want to be changed.

Finally Redden spoke. "You have one of our men. We want him returned."

It wasn't the response I'd expected. He was referring to Damien. A million different emotions flew through me before I landed on a response. "Fine." I wasn't sure if that was the right call, but I knew I'd give him anything to make the violence stop. Then I realized this was Redden's counter-negotiation. Which meant he was considering. Which meant it was working.

"Call off your ships," I restated, enunciating every syllable.

There was another long pause and another throat clearing. "You know, this won't stop us forever, young lady. We just won't let go of an entire city."

"You'd be surprised what you have to sacrifice for peace," I replied. Redden was giving in. He was threatening me, yes, but I could feel this was leading to him backing down. So I asked, "Do we have a deal?"

He hesitated. There was a long beat in which I'm sure he conferred with Minchin. Eventually Billy came back on the line. "In light of the current circumstances, I'll authorize a temporary truce." He moved away from the phone, and in the muffled distance, I heard him ask, "Gene, how do I do this again?"

Then he hung up.

MINUTES LATER, AFTER A frantic drive from the airfield to Brighton Beach, I hobbled my way across the sand as fast as I could with my arm slung around Gina's shoulders. Behind me, a half-crumbling Ferris wheel squeaked and swayed in the relentless winter wind. A few hundred yards in front of me, still out of earshot, Avon ambled down the beach toward the water, utterly stupefied by what he was seeing. Around him, hundreds of our people were doing the same. Not a soul on that beach could believe their eyes.

The assault ship had turned around. Every single one of the UA's ships was leaving, and the rowdy civilian boats were following suit too. The raid was called off. The way was open.

As fast as I could, I ran to Avon. I found myself unconsciously repeating, "They're leaving," over and over again. It started as a breathless whisper, then grew louder and louder until I screamed, "They're leaving!"

Hearing my cry, Avon turned toward me. The sun shone gloriously behind him. The moment he saw me, he smiled as wide as his cheeks would allow. He ran toward me, and when we finally met, we fell into a deep embrace.

Gina, not one for an outward show of affection, peeled away from us and toward the tide to watch what was happening. The Canadian supply ship was almost sunk, but the people on the ship's deck had been busy throwing containers off the side to a crowd of smaller civilian boats waiting below. Offloading our precious supplies. As they filled up, these completely ordinary and wondrously brave people pushed past the invisible twelve-mile barrier delineating international waters to bring our lifesaving supplies to land. To us.

Chris ran up to me and Avon. "What did you do, Al?"

"Me? Turns out not much." I sighed in relief. The three of us stood there, taking in the beautiful sight of the small army of boats filled with supplies, coming toward us. I rested my head on Avon's shoulder.

When the first boat made landfall, Gina rushed up to help them unload. We sprang into action as other boats surfed into the shore.

Then we heard, "Chris?" The voice was distant, buried in the beating wind. Chris turned toward the cresting tide, and there, standing ankle deep in the waves, was Helen.

"Mama?" Tears filled Chris's eyes. A few slow, unbelieving steps by both women brought them together. Trembling, Helen held Chris's face in her hands. Chris wrapped her arms around her mother. They were so at home in each other's arms, they melted into each other. It didn't matter what I'd done. Helen Smith saved our lives. She saved the movement. She was our heroine.

I was so filled with emotion, and cancer, I couldn't even take a breath. All I could do was smile. Then I saw Patrol Officer Ralph wading up through the waves. My jaw dropped.

"The last two days, all I've thought about was the look on your face when you saw me." He was beaming.

"What the hell are you doing here?" I asked.

"After I left Montrose, I decided to try and find out more about you, and from the permits we confiscated, I decided to go to Mrs. Smith." He gestured toward Helen, who was still staring in disbelief at Chris, caressing her daughter's cheek, entirely unaware of our presence. "I told her what happened," Ralph continued. "About the secretary touching you, and you saving my life. I told her everything."

"Seems we owe you a big thanks," Avon said, striding over. I recalled Avon wrestling Ralph to the ground and holding him at gunpoint. Ralph must have remembered the same moment as he tensed up in Avon's presence. His gaze fell to the ground, and he shifted uncomfortably.

"Not really," Ralph said. "I wasn't planning on doing any of this. It was Helen's idea. I just came along for the ride." He looked at me. "But I'm glad I was able to pay you back in some small way for saving my life."

Then Ralph hugged me. In all that we had been through together, it was the first time that he had touched me, and in that touch, he acknowledged me.

Behind him, a young woman trudged through the wet sand up to us. It took a moment; then I remembered who she was.

"Block A7. Pretty girl."

"Rebecca," she corrected. Ralph laughed.

"Of course. I know," I said, remembering when Ralph told me her name, back when I was so desperate to find some humanity in him. And now here it was. Then I saw a ring on Rebecca's finger. "You said yes."

The young woman cleared her throat and smiled bashfully. "Yeah." She fiddled with her simple engagement ring, radiating love.

Behind us, Gina and a team of very strong people dragged the supplies from the small boats. She was steadfast in loading as many bins marked "Medicine" as she could into our van before speeding off with Minnie in the backseat toward Lovetts Way. There, Noah was waiting to parse through the incoming supplies.

It would take countless infusions and surgeries, but Minnie Morales was yet another notch in the ever-growing list of people's lives Noah would save. She got the medicine that she so desperately needed, and she lived.

Minnie lived.

Hours later, I walked into Noah's makeshift office in Lovett and received the small bottle of red pills that for so long had eluded me. One pill twice a day for two weeks. No more cancer. It seemed like fireworks would go off in the sky and trumpets would blare, but it was only a simple moment with no fanfare at all. And that's just the point. It was the gesture, by Helen and Ralph and all those people who simply showed up, that declared my life worth saving. To the present day, I can name myself cancer-free.

But before all that, the hundreds of us found ourselves enwrapped in celebrations on the beach. Among the hugging and general merriment, the jubilant and sporadic cheers soon turned into a unified group singing:

> *My country, 'tis of thee, Sweet land of liberty, Of*
> *thee I sing;*
> *Let every tongue awake; Let bond and free partake;*
> *Pray rocks their silence break, Let freedom ring.*
> *Our fathers' God to thee, Author of Liberty, to thee*
> *we sing;*
> *Soon may our land be bright, With holy freedom's*
> *right,*
> *Protect us by thy might, Let freedom ring!* ·

This song started on the sandy shores. It continued all through our march down the streets of Brighton Beach, past the towering cryogenics building, as we made our way home. It was a song that for so long heralded a land that hunted us and anyone who was hated. And now we were claiming it back for ourselves.

Lovetts Way was bursting at the seams with people cheering and waving colorful rags in the air as impromptu flags. Children beat on plastic tubs as the parade marched through the row of brownstones previously left and forgotten by time, now reclaimed as our home.

Through the crowd, I spotted Samson standing outside the white brick brownstone that held Damien prisoner. The desire to celebrate with him overcame me. But it was a desire to celebrate with the Damien that I'd known and loved. That was no longer the man in that building. As a part of the terms of the cease-fire, Samson drove Damien the next day to a train station in Pennsylvania. When he was escorted to the van to leave, our eyes met from across the street. We didn't say anything. There was nothing to say. He simply smiled, and I did too. Then he left.

Damien wasn't my future. Neither was Max. And yet that's the thing. I *had* a future. I had time.

Avon hadn't left my side once since we'd embraced on that cold windy shore. Then, after our triumphant march from the beach, we saw Noah standing on the stoop of Lovett. Avon ran full speed toward him. Not many were paying attention; however, it is important to note that in broad daylight, in the middle of a crowd, Noah and Avon kissed. And it was a really good kiss. Their love seeped through me and warmed my soul.

Gina passed by, and without a word or a look, she patted me on the back. It knocked some of the air out of my lungs, but I laughed. It was the closest I'd ever get to Gina's approval.

I looked out over the street and surveyed our victory. I saw Minnie, weak but alive. I saw Chris, wrapped in her mother's arms as if she were still a little girl. I saw Avon and Noah, desperately in love. Eliza and Diana leaned out a window waving a flag and kissing. Even Ralph, ever the patriot, was singing with Rebecca.

I knew things weren't over. The future would hold more fighting. There'd be more attacks and more hate. Over the next five years we fought a war that brought more loss and pain than I ever could have imagined. But I can sit here today and tell you that it was worth it. What we were fighting for made everything worth it. I found the home and family in these people that I was always so desperate for.

Eventually, after the years of fighting, we were arrested by the Territorial Army and forced to stand trial. And we lost that trial, but we appealed. And we appealed again. Finally, we've found ourselves back in front of the Supreme Court almost a century after Max Green won his original case. This trial, at which you will decide whether Awoken lives are worthy and legal.

But on that sunny day in New York City, we celebrated our victory. That day, it was enough.

Looking back on it, I wish I could say that on top of everything else, I also defeated the darkness. That with medicine and Dreno in full supply, I forgot about the coldness in the pit of my stomach. The missing chunk of myself that I am also incomplete without. However, it stays with me even today as we sit here now. Like the love I have for Max Green, there are some things that can never die.

I told you before that this is a story about love. Now you know it is a story about all kinds of love. The love between parents and children. The love shared by two halves of the same soul. The love of one's country. But most important, it's about the love for each other. With this story, I urge you to see that life, no matter what form it takes, is worthy. For it is either this or the darkness.

Unless, like Avon, you're one to believe in hope.

EPILOGUE

THE COURT: Thank you, Mrs. Rivers, for your
               account of the events in question.
               Your testimony will prove to be
               invaluable in this Court's decision
               on the legality of resurrected
               lives. You have clarified many
               incidents that have merely existed
               in speculation to this point. The
               State's well-argued case will have
               many things to rebut in their
               closing, of which I have no doubt
               in their tenacity to do so. Mr.
               Gibson is chomping at the bit over
               there.

(Some laughter)

MRS. RIVERS: I'm sure he is. For a week, Mr.
               Gibson filled this room with the
               words of those who would see every

one of us exterminated. While I hope
I've done enough, remember that what
I've said here is only my story, my
perspective on what happened and
why. Everyone who was with me back
then has their own story: Avon,
Gina, Chris, Minnie, Samson, and
countless others. Each story just as
important as my own. I hope you'll
listen to as many of us as you
can. Or as many of us who are
left.

THE COURT: Indeed, Mrs. Rivers. Are there any
further statements you would like to
make before you're asked to step
down?

MRS. RIVERS: What more can I do to urge you and
the other judges to decide that our
lives are legitimate? That inherent
in our existence, in each breath we
take, our lives are worth no greater
or lesser than your own, Your Honor.
I hope that is what my testimony
showed. I came into this world
scared, alone, afraid of who I was.
Now I have made a life for myself
here. A life to be proud of. It's
the American dream. As much as one
can claim, I have found my happily
ever after.

THE COURT: A seemingly strange sentiment
coming from someone on trial for
their life. Although, I can't deny
that even I am aware of what you are
referring to. You are married and
are in the family way, no?

MRS. RIVERS: Your Honor is well informed.

THE COURT: Indeed. I try to stay away from personal matters, but in this instance, your situation is a relevant factor.

MRS. RIVERS: I don't understand.

THE COURT: Has your counsel, Mr. Reynolds, told you whom he intends to call as the next witness? Are you aware of who this next witness is?

MRS. RIVERS: Yes. He's sitting right there.

THE COURT: Given your history with this individual, it will undoubtedly be difficult for you to hear his testimony and questioning. Considering your fragile condition, Mr. Gibson has requested that the Court remove you from chambers.

MR. REYNOLDS: That is absurd, Your Honor!

THE COURT: Sit down, Mr. Reynolds. Think of what's best for your client's well-being.

MR. REYNOLDS: I'm certain that Mr. Gibson's request isn't motivated by my client's well-being.

THE COURT: Be that as it may . . . Mrs. Rivers, I'll allow you to stay, only if you so wish.

MRS. RIVERS: Thank you, Your Honor. But I do wish to stay. After all this time and everything that has happened, I want to hear what he has to say. I

want to watch you all listen to his
story.

THE COURT: Very well. Mrs. Rivers, you may take
a seat. Mr. Reynolds, proceed.

MR. REYNOLDS: With the Court's permission, I ask
our next witness to come to the
lectern and submit his testimony to
the Court.

(Inaudible mutterings)

THE COURT: Sir, will you please introduce
yourself.

WITNESS: My name is Omar Zare. I died in
twenty—

MR. GIBSON: Objection, Your Honor. The witness
has already perjured himself.

THE COURT: Sustained. Sir, you will honestly
identify yourself to this Court or
you will be dismissed.

MR. REYNOLDS: Pardon me, Your Honor, but the
witness gave his legal name. He was
resurrected in June 2122 from bag
22925, registered under the name
Omar Zare. Under United America law
Statute—

THE COURT: This Court does not need you to
quote statutes, Mr. Reynolds. Your
witness will tell this Court who he
is. Who the world knows him to be.

(Witness and Mr. Reynolds speak privately. Inaudible.)

MR. REYNOLDS: Very well. Submitted under
objection.

THE COURT: Let the record show. Your witness will continue as instructed.

WITNESS: If it pleases Your Honor, I have quite a few identities and am known for a number of things. First, perhaps, is that I am the current elected leader of the Awoken. However, I imagine you don't want me to stop there. To be certain, I am the man whom the president of this country thought he killed, as well as the man whom he has tried to kill countless times since. But most important, I am Alabine Rivers's husband. My name is Max Green.

(END OF TRANSCRIPT)

Max. My Max.

ACKNOWLEDGMENTS

They say authoring a book is a solitary endeavor. While there were indeed solitary hours spent just me and Alabine, this endeavor was anything but my own. At the very least, I always had the voices of my favorite writers in my head and fingers. Without their work, I would be a shell of myself.

Aside from those geniuses, the top billing of this acknowledgment must go to another genius, Talton Long Wingate III Esq., the absolute fucking love of my life. He took every step with me and held my hand when I didn't believe I could write another word. He is mine and I am his and we are parts of the same whole. I can say without a doubt that this story would not be what it is without him. My Max.

My son was always present with me as I wrote this story about love, whether in my thoughts or literally squished between my body and the desk. A big thank-you to him for sharing his first two years of life with this book as my second baby. He's grown from a newborn into a toddler while I grew into an author and a mother, and I loved every minute of our transformation together.

ACKNOWLEDGMENTS

I must certainly thank the Zhuzh for, as always, welcoming all of my letters and fostering a safe place for me to grow this story. Then a special thanks to Elizabeth and Lisa for your eyes, minds, and hearts. Immense gratitude to Melissa for all of our adventures in the real world that allow me to imagine these other worlds. To my mother and my sister, for helping me find the truth in my story. To Sunny, for guiding me and always being there with an answer to my question. To Dominic, for lending me your perspective and grace.

This novel came to be through the help and love of Issa and Deniese. There are so many amazing writers who don't find a champion who will fight for their words. I was lucky enough to find mine in these two extraordinary women.

Mammoth shoutout to Jen Ray, manager extraordinaire, who has seen this story through all of its various forms and passionately supported it in every state of being. Thanks to Albert Lee, for your undying enthusiasm and optimism, and Meredith Miller, for your thoughtful and caring advice. To Maya, for being such an inspiring and supportive editor. I couldn't have imagined a better or kinder process for bringing Alabine's story to life.

Most especially I'd like to acknowledge ProjectQ and Madin Lopez and all of the work they do. Thank you for making the world a better place, which my son, and all our children, will have the privilege of growing up in. I am your sworn shield, now and forever.

ABOUT THE AUTHOR

This is the debut novel from **KATELYN MONROE HOWES**, an LA-based, award-winning writer and Emmy-nominated documentarian. An Atlanta native and alum of NYU, Katelyn cofounded 1/27 Pictures, a documentary production company. Her work often tackles systemic inequities and combats uninformed bias as she strives to tell stories that upend the status quo.